"SUCH SOFT LIPS . . . ARE YOU AFRAID TO KISS ME?"

His thumb slid up and down her throat lightly, his eyes darkening. "Soft, soft skin," he murmured, as though to himself. Then, meeting her eyes, he said, "I know you're not accustomed to a man touching you. You bristle like a porcupine when I get too close to you. Don't be afraid."

Rebecca angrily slapped away his hand. "Of you? Never."

"Touch me," he urged softly, huskily. "Take off your gloves and touch me with your hands."

"No," she managed, fighting the desire to touch him.

"A small kiss, then, Becky. Just a taste and I'll let you go." He smiled gently.

She peered at him from beneath her lashes. "Then you'll let me go?"

Taking a deep breath, Rebecca closed her eyes and pursed her lips. Matthew held perfectly still as their lips met. She moved her mouth softly across his, discovering the texture of his mouth. He tasted of smoke and an intriguing scent all of his own. Rebecca heard herself moan softly, her lips parting. His free hand roamed her back, his broad palm warming her as it caressed.

Then, teasing her with small kisses, Matthew slowly released her. Rebecca breathed heavily, staring up at him. She tried to stiffen her weakened legs and quiet her racing heart. She cleared her throat, fighting the urge to wrap her arms around him again.

His smoldering gaze warmed her, making her feel womanly and . . . desired . . . and aching for his touch.

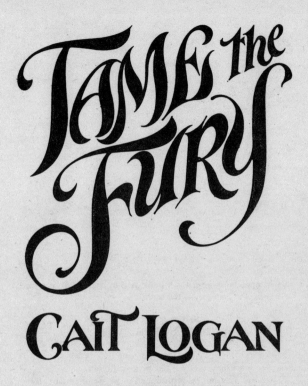

TAME the FURY

CAIT LOGAN

CHARTER/DIAMOND BOOKS, NEW YORK

TAME THE FURY

A Charter/Diamond Book / published by arrangement with
the author

PRINTING HISTORY
Charter/Diamond edition / August 1990

ISBN: 1-55773-372-4

Charter/Diamond Books are published by The Berkley Publishing
Group, 200 Madison Avenue, New York, New York 10016.
The name "CHARTER/DIAMOND" and its logo are trademarks
belonging to Charter Communications, Inc.

PRINTED IN THE UNITED STATES OF AMERICA

10 9 8 7 6 5 4 3 2 1

Inland Washington State has a wind that carries the scents of sand, sagebrush, and pine. This wind is the song of the land. Filled with stories of Indians, fur traders, cattle drives, prospectors, and settlers, the song remains forever. It drifts across the high mountains, sweeps across the wheat fields, and settles in the fruit orchards bordering the Columbia River.

Though my particular setting is fictional, I extend my thanks to all who have helped me to portray romance set in a new, rugged country. Especially to the people of Bridgeport and Brewster; my family; Diane Vancil; and editor, Joan Marlow; and the late agent, Ray Peekner, who did so much between them to start my career. A special thank-you to my editor, Hillary Cige, for her encouragement and confidence in me.

I hope you enjoy the melody. . . .

—C.L.

MY HIGHLAND HEART

Wi' night-black hair and emerald eyes,
The bonnie maid did so beguile.
Wi' thorny ways and dewy lips,
O'er highlands she ran free and wild.

Yet 'round my empty heart she curled;
I lured her to my fern veiled lair.
Wi' whispers soft and tender kiss,
I wooed fair lass of raven hair.

Bewitching lass, my heart's true luve,
'Til stars do fall; and sun burns cold.
Our kindling fire shall rise in flame,
Consuming all our hearts could hold.

Through rivers rage and cold snows deep,
I come to her, my luve, my own.
My midnight rose, my highland heart,
Wi' emerald eyes she calls me home.

—C.L.

Wi' night-black hair and emerald eyes,
The bonnie maid did so beguile.
Wi' thorny ways and dewy lips,
O'er highlands she ran free and wild . . .

Chapter One

Central Washington State, July 1902

"It's past the turn of the century, Papa. You can't parcel me off like dry goods. I will not welcome Matthew McKay as my husband tonight," Rebecca Klein stated shakily. She turned from the window overlooking the Columbia River to face her father.

When his steady gray eyes met her green ones, she knew Peter Klein meant to have his way—stirring her marriage by proxy into a flesh-and-blood reality.

Rebecca had been wounded once, and she didn't intend to let another man come close to her heart. Swallowing the dry lump of fear in her throat, Rebecca braced herself to fight. She licked her full lips nervously, gauging her father's set expression.

Rebecca had every ounce of his pride, and she wouldn't let him see the raw, shimmering fear rising within her. She'd been promised to a man before and still bore the wounds; Rudy had been her first love. Entranced, she'd been blind to his greed.

And when Rudy's greed was not met, he went mad.

This McKay was a mercenary, a fortune seeker, just as apt to bear that same cruel tendency. She lifted her head defiantly, crushing a letter in her gloved fist. She tossed the crumpled paper to her father's desk.

He settled back in his chair, waiting for Rebecca to begin.

"McKay's letter came in on this morning's stagecoach, Papa. It seems he is ready to begin our . . . marriage. No wonder you've been keeping me busy running errands. That was much easier for you to keep your little surprise quiet a bit longer."

A flush rose up her lightly tanned throat to stain her smooth cheeks. "It appears you've been playing Cupid, writing him about me; while you've been telling me that he was near death from an infected knife wound. 'He couldn't stand the shock of an annulment now,' you said. And so you put me off. I actually answered those letters he dictated to his nurse. And now he's circling like a vulture."

His gray eyes flickered, warning her to tread lightly. "He *was* grievously ill, near death. It would have been a cruelty for you to cut him then. Besides, you need a man, Rebecca. I thought it time—"

"Time!" Rebecca hesitated, trying to reason with her fear. "Papa, have you forgotten why I'm not properly married? And all this time we've managed—I've managed—alone."

Rebecca breathed heavily, thrusting a wayward, jet black tendril behind her ear. "I only agreed to *marry* McKay because Rudy left me at the altar and you were on your death-bed, Papa." Her eyes narrowed, remembering the past. "I wanted only to please you, then . . . so I was married, if only by proxy." Her left hand sliced the air, then rested on the butt of her holstered Colt. *"Kopet!"* she snapped.

"It *isn't* finished, Rebecca, and stop using that damned Indian talk," Klein ordered gently. He settled his large frame into the desk chair comfortably, preparing to wait out his daughter's tirade. Rebecca would not concede easily, especially after Rudy's treatment. He felt a dark curl of hatred for the man.

"Why not use the Chinook jargon, Papa? It's been the trade language of the Northwest for years, and I'm as good as being traded off—I am certainly not willing!"

Another man touching her, wounding her . . . a ripple of fear shot through her. She wrapped her arms around herself protectively. For two years she'd hidden her nightmares from her family. Now the frustration caused by Rudy's betrayal simmered near the surface. She had loved him madly, obsessively, drawn to him by sweet words and tender kisses. She felt her emotions wrap about her painfully, like an Indian horsehair lariat. Experienced with women, Rudy had easily twined his magic on her. At twenty-one she'd been a novice to his games and fell easily before his charms.

Clinging to his enticing words, she yearned for kisses and promises.

But in the end Rudy had wanted something other than her love; he'd wanted the Klein kingdom.

"At one time," she added wistfully, "I wanted to be a wife and mother."

Rebecca shuddered once, then felt the keen edge of terror slice through her. McKay was coming tonight, expecting a willing bride.

He could "expect" until the Columbia River ran dry in its basin. Rebecca stalked to the window and glared at the countryside. "McKay must be charmed. I thought he'd be killed when President McKinley sent him to the Boxer Rebellion, but he survived. Then later, in San Francisco, when he was stabbed and the infection set in, I though death would annul his grasp on me."

As Klein waited for her to continue, a meadowlark trilled sweetly in the July morning. Cows lowed to their calves in the grass pasture bordered by stately pine trees. The scent of Peter Klein's new apple orchard was as winsome as the Okanogan country opening to settlers.

While Rebecca stared moodily at the gray waters of the Columbia River, Klein sat quietly, waiting for her next outburst. He had not long to wait. He knew his daughter's wild temper protected her wounded heart.

Rebecca drew her broad-brimmed hat from her head, then slapped it against her trouser-clad thigh. Sawdust from the family mill flew into the beam of sunshine coming through the window. When she passed through that light, her hand riding the Colt's pearl handle, her ebony hair caught the sun in a blue-black sheen.

Placing her long legs apart, Rebecca glared down at her father. She breathed heavily, her thick braid crossing her chest to sway at her leather-belted waist, her full mouth tight and pale with anger.

" 'Marry McKay,' you pleaded from your deathbed,'' she repeated. "Thank God you didn't die from the pneumonia, but I thought you would two years ago, when I did as you asked.'' She held her breath, glaring at Klein, then continued hotly. "He was just leaving for China and the Boxer Rebellion to shovel out Americans on McKinley's orders.''

Rebecca stamped the floor with her boot, determined to break Klein's patient silence. He'd meet her with his own anger and agree to stop McKay's claim. "Then, I could see the sense of marriage by proxy. Two years ago I was vulnerable, raw from Rudy's handling of me. Beaten and left at the altar by my future husband wasn't sweet to swallow, Papa . . . something inside me died then. Later, when you were ill, it seemed to soothe you so, to know that I'd have a husband in McKay.''

Trembling, she tossed her head and the thick braid danced, gleaming down her back. "I knew how it cost you to have an unmarried daughter—a shame on the Klein name. 'No spinsters in the Klein family,' you said. At the time I couldn't see that San Francisco dandy settling down to the rustic life even if he survived the Boxers. But in this letter to me he says he wants to live on his father's homestead. Life up on the high country of the Chiliwist is hard, Papa. Matthew McKay isn't likely to be hardening his soft hands on the ax. He's more the kind to make others do the work.''

"You don't know him at all. I like the cut of young Mc-Kay.''

"And I'm not going to know him. The man is a carpetbagger and a mercenary.''

"He's been making his way, building for a time to return to his land.''

"He won't stay. He left once and he'd do it again.''

Rebecca waited, scowling down at Klein's thoughtful expression. "Oh, I know the Abraham McKay story—he was a

Scots mountain man who drifted up from Wyoming country following the beaver trade. He pulled an Okanogan chief off you just as the Indian's knife fell, missing your heart and slicing off your thumb instead. Abraham kindly tapped the chief on the jaw, and when he awakened, McKay made peace by giving the Indian a choice Appaloosa pony.'' She paused from her sarcastic recital, then demanded, ''Because the father saved your life doesn't mean I should have to worship at the son's feet, does it? Am I your gift to settle an old debt?''

Klein dug his jowls into his homespun collar, his heavy brows bristling together in a straight line. His daughter knew how to wound a man, he thought. Once she'd been a tender bud, waiting for a man's touch. Now she fought with fear and anger. He ached for her but remained determined to place McKay at her side. After that it was in God's hands.

His work-callused fingers traced the smooth surface of the massive oak desk. ''Maybe I have let you run too free. When your mother died—God rest my sweet Sophy—your brother Daniel was just a baby. You tended him while your brother Bruno and I worked the land.''

Remembering the past, he rubbed his chin thoughtfully.

While his sons, Bruno and Daniel, worked the lumber mill, Rebecca had chosen to tend the livestock and the land. She had worked as hard as any of the hired hands, laying out apple orchards and irrigation ditches, fed by the mountain creek.

Peter Klein leaned back in his chair. The tender, soft young woman would return, he decided . . . once she became a real wife. ''Maybe working our homestead so hard has taken the sweetness of the woman out of you, Rebecca. At twenty-nine it's time you knew the comfort of marriage.''

''The devil can take Mr. Matthew McKay, Papa. Because I will not. He can find another woman. Have the marriage annulled!'' Rebecca ordered curtly.

Klein caught the slight edge of panic fluttering in her harsh tone.

''Good Lord, that sham of a wedding was two long years ago, Papa! The only thing that kept me from annulling it myself was the fact that McKay wasn't likely to survive any of his adventures. . . . And he shouldn't have," she added darkly. "And clinging to that hope, I waited—saving your honor, by the way."

Klein, his own temper rising, strove for patience. He loved his daughter, but she could be as determined as a wagon freighter's mule. "Women are intended by the Lord to be the partners of men—"

Rebecca sprawled into a chair opposite him, her nails clawing at the dark varnish on the arms. "You come from the Old World, Papa. Germany is years away," she interrupted, her voice trembling.

Klein's eyes darkened with distaste as he stared at her legs. "German women don't wear trousers, Rebecca. And they marry—"

"This is America, Papa. Women's suffrage passed in Wyoming in 1869. Utah and Idaho passed it in 1896, and this is Washington State in the year 1902. These are new times, Papa. You can't just auction me off like a cow for old Bully Boy to breed!"

The leash on his anger snapped; Klein wanted the best for his daughter, and she only fought him with cutting words.

"Mein Gott!" He slammed his fist against the desk, rattling the ink beaker sitting upon it. "Haven't we just finished the Indian Scare of '91? And before that, the Nez Percé War. Chief Joseph is barely settled in at Nespelem, a few miles from here. Women need to be married—with a husband protecting them, giving them children." Klein thumped his chest with his thumb. "My grandchildren, girl . . . it's long past time."

"No. I will not play the role of McKay's loving wife," Rebecca said firmly—and finally. "I will take the matter up with him when he arrives." Rebecca's low voice trembled as Klein rose to his towering height, placing his knuckles down on the desk and leaning toward her.

Glaring at her from beneath bushy brows, he drew a deep breath, his face reddening around his thick mustache. The waxed and twisted curls stuck out like a Texas steer's longhorns. "This is a serious matter, Rebecca. As a woman you have certain obligations."

"So you have told me, Papa. Our family honor," Rebecca stated coolly, fighting the urge to plead with him. Hiding the unwavering panic gripping her, she dusted a piece of straw from her sweat-stained shirt. Framed by thick, black lashes, her emerald eyes flashed at him. "For the last time, Papa, I won't be the one to bear his brats." Rebecca stood, replacing her dust-covered hat on her head. Her knees almost buckled as she faced her father. She glanced at his clenched hands. "Are we quite finished, Papa?"

Klein took a deep, controlled breath. "You will be courteous to Matthew. You will wear that nice Sears, Roebuck dress in your closet. Do you understand me, Rebecca?"

Moving with feline grace, Rebecca strode to the door. The sound of her boots was muffled by the braided rug covering the floor planks. At the doorway she turned, tapping her finger thoughtfully against the smoothness of her cheek. "Bruno almost killed Rudy for hurting me, Papa. He's protected me since I can remember. I just wonder what would happen if McKay and I had a spat—like all newlyweds do, you know. Then what, Papa? Or in your plan have you enlisted Bruno's help?"

"Gott in Himmel!" Klein swore. "Now I know it is time for another man to take care of you."

"McKay won't saddle himself with a reluctant wife when it comes down to it, Papa. . . . If he's got any pride at all, he won't. I'll have my annulment."

"The man will hold," Klein stated firmly. "From the reports I've had about McKay, he sticks to a task once he's begun."

Rebecca felt her throat tighten with frustration. Her father could lose his patience, but she stood to lose far more. She'd cowered from a man once; in a rage he'd beaten her without mercy.

She remembered too well trying to run from the pain, only to have Rudy drag her back by her hair. Trying to protect her face, she'd felt his nails rip into her skin as he tore her cloth-

ing. She'd begged for mercy, crying out against his cruelty.
Never again would she beg. Rudy had cost her a measure of
pride that she could not afford to forget.

"McKay is like the salmon, Papa. Coming upriver to
spawn. I know he is. I remember him and Bruno talking
behind the barn, making bets on Matthew taking some poor
girl into the hay field. He was a rake then, and I have no
reason to believe he's changed where women are concerned."

Klein's face reddened and he shifted uncomfortably. Within
a few hours he could see for himself if the match was blessed.
If not, he'd gladly support the annulment. But until those
hours passed, Rebecca needed to be handled firmly. "It's a
man's responsibility to take care of his own. You're my blood,
and I acted in your best interests. McKay is a good man.
He's sowed his wild oats and he's ready to settle down. He
wants a family," Klein stated earnestly.

Rebecca's eyes narrowed, her gloved fingers clenching the
brass doorknob. "So, while I worried about saving the Klein
honor, you and McKay joined forces. It seems I have been
played for a fool. Congratulations, Papa."

Silence filled the small, book-filled room as father and
daughter stared at each other. Wills and pride clashed silently
for a long moment. The brass pendulum of the grandfather
clock swayed slowly, its steady tick beating against the drama.

"It is my duty to see you married. A year, Rebecca,"
Klein offered slowly, reluctantly. "If I didn't think him suitable as a husband, I wouldn't— Give the marriage a year,
and if it doesn't work, I'll back your decision to remain alone.
Until I go to my grave you'll never hear a word about marriage from me again. I'll swear it on our family Bible. It's a
fair bargain."

Rebecca faced him for a full, taut moment, weighing his
offer. "Agreed, Papa." Then, with one last meaningful stare,
she closed the door.

For a moment Klein scowled at the door's oak planks, then
he turned to stare at the mighty Columbia, beyond the window. Gray and sluggish on the surface, the currents beneath

were deadly. He remembered suddenly the "cow-killer" winter of 1890, and the resulting flood of '94. The countryside had needed men to recover from the hardships.

Thoughts of Rudy Johnson caused the bile to rise in Klein's throat. The blond drifter had intrigued Rebecca from the moment he'd been hired. For the first time she donned skirts with her father's approval, and soon Rudy sat at every evening meal.

In the parlor he had recounted his adventures with an easy laugh. But his gaze always strayed to Rebecca. Twenty-one at the time, she had shyly returned his smile.

But drifting was in his blood, and Rudy had left them repeatedly, to find his fortune.

Klein waited; a young man needed to get the wanderlust out of him before he became a family man; it was as natural as the Columbia winding down its basin. Rebecca had the dreamy look of a woman finding her young love. Certain that the drifter would settle, Klein decided to keep quiet as Rebecca waited for Rudy's return each year.

For five years Rudy had encouraged Rebecca until she glowed. Klein began to think of the day he'd be holding her children on his knee. As her dowry, he measured a parcel of land at the northeast corner of his new plat. He waited as the softness in his daughter's eyes grew, her blushes and her laughter increasing. Finally Rudy had asked for Rebecca's hand in marriage.

The night before the wedding Klein had announced his bridal gift in a toast.

"What?" Rudy had scoffed incredulously that night. "No more than that? A man could work himself to death in that timber trying to make something of it. Why not the wheat fields? Or the sawmill or the orchards here? What about the salmon cannery downriver?"

That night Rudy had taken his drunken temper out on Rebecca, beating her. She had worn the Colt pistol on her hip ever since, now the fastest "draw" in the basin. At settlers' gatherings Rebecca was asked to exhibit by shooting cans off a log. To the Indians she became Woman-Who-Holds-the-Lightning.

His daughter became a woman with a broken heart and shattered dreams. She was deadly quiet, her laughter gone. She drifted around the house like a pale shadow for three months. When he fell sick, she was his nurse, tending him as his cough grew worse.

Even from his sickbed, Klein sensed the new hardness festering within his daughter, and he hated it. Driven by her demons, she worked even harder, disdaining all that was feminine, anything that might draw a man to her.

Then young McKay's offer had arrived by stagecoach mail from Wenatchee: He wanted a woman of the land, ready for the hardships of the settler's life. Could Klein recommend a marriageable woman?

By then tales of McKay's whaling and lumber business had spread back to the basin. He'd served in Cuba and Manila and was headed for the Boxer Rebellion in China. Then he headed home to close out his business in San Francisco and return to his father's land. According to local rumor, Jake Baroque had deeded his land to Matthew, providing he was married by the age of thirty-five. Jake, a settler and a trapper friend of old McKay, had owned an adjoining homestead and was childless. The matter of inheritance was a practical one that Klein understood well; he would have acted the same way himself.

Klein kept an ear out for any stories that concerned McKay. He'd heard only good ones. On his sickbed he'd begged Rebecca to marry McKay, and since then he'd done a matchmaking dance with her.

He allowed himself a tight smile, thinking of how he'd posed Rebecca to McKay: an eager bride ready for marriage.

Then turning to Rebecca, he assured her that McKay's letters and gifts were merely the efforts of a sick man who would probably never leave San Francisco.

As the time neared, he'd snatched McKay's last two letters from the clerk himself. After all, matchmaking for his reluctant daughter was a skill he'd practiced for two years.

Rebecca had the wild country in her blood, and so did McKay. They both would hold through the storms: people bred to the land, loving it. It was enough to start a marriage and wash away the past.

Rebecca tramped across the polished planks, and headed for the large family kitchen. She didn't doubt her father's good intentions, but she did not intend to become McKay's blushing bride. She felt as wild and as angry as the wind sweeping the fire across the very tops of the pines. She'd been handed—lock, stock, and barrel—over to a "man the country needed." Were all men in cahoots?

He'd sent a few baubles from China and Cuba and San Francisco, but they meant nothing. Tucked away in a drawer were a high Spanish comb and carved jade bracelets. Well, she certainly couldn't be bought with trinkets.

The flat of her hand thrust open the door as she entered the kitchen.

Placing her hands at her waist, she glared at her two brothers. Seated at the long plank table, eating breakfast, they looked up. Her sister-in-law, Stella, was with them.

Bruno, tall and heavily padded with muscle, leaned back in his chair. He met Rebecca's hard stare with steady gray eyes. His smile died slowly, his face unreadable.

Bruno's massive hand stroked his wife's back gently. Stella leaned closer to him, shifting her body heavily to accommodate the new life within her. A gentle, plain woman, her expression was concerned. "Rebecca, what's wrong?"

"Ask these two, they know, no doubt," Rebecca snapped. "Try the name McKay."

"Whew!" Daniel shifted uneasily, unable to return Rebecca's accusing stare. At nineteen her younger brother knew how to measure her thunderous expression. In a dander, Rebecca could raise the ranch-house roof. His flush preceded his hurried interest in the stacked plate of food before him. He dived into the safety of his griddle cakes, eating quickly as he flicked a wary glance at Bruno's set face.

"Tell Stella, Bruno. Tell her about McKay arriving to claim his bride." Rebecca's boot heel began to tap the floorboards.

Maria, a house servant, stopped turning pancakes on the cast-iron grill. "Aeii . . ." Her smile died before she turned to tend the massive black wood stove.

"You knew, didn't you, Bruno?" Rebecca accused, facing her elder brother. "You knew that McKay wasn't an invalid. That he'd come slithering out of San Francisco . . ."

"I knew," Bruno admitted, meeting her gaze steadily. He rubbed the small of Stella's back. "I approve of the match, Rebecca," he added after a tense moment.

He'd known of his father's plot and had understood. After reading McKay's letters to Klein, Bruno had caught the scent of pines, the loneliness a man feels for the country that spawned him. Rebecca had the same love, and their match should be a good one.

"Traitor." She scowled, flushed by anger. "Am I living with a bunch of dry gulchers? Back shooters?" she demanded. "Oh, I've already admitted that the timely offer of Mr. McKay saved our family from ruination. And no doubt it helped Papa to recover . . . and then *McKay* is sick and Papa played me there too. *My husband* writes that he is well warmed and ready to take up our marriage."

She grimaced, as though the word soured her tongue. "McKay is arriving tonight. Judging from the postmark I think the letter was delayed along the way. Even if I wished to greet him as a wife, a day is not long enough to prepare."

Daniel chuckled. "Not long enough for Woman-Who-Holds-the-Lightning to take to the high country, you mean, Rebecca. . . ." His words died as his sister's eyes narrowed in warning.

"Don't ever think that I'd run from that dandy, Daniel," Rebecca snapped. "I'll wager that his hands are as soft as a baby's bottom." She turned to Bruno, her eyes tracing his face, reading his firm expression, so like her father's.

He said, "I doubt if he's a dandy. McKay once held off a flood of Boxers while his men prepared the ship to sail."

"Oh, please. I've already heard it all from Papa. Anyway,

he could have changed,'' Rebecca began hotly, then gauged the firm set of her brother's jaw.

She put her hands to her face, feeling the blood drain from it. She lowered herself into a wooden chair, her body as jolted as her mind by the reality of her proxy husband. This had to be a bad dream. She crossed her forearms on the red-checkered oilcloth covering the table and rested her head upon them. ''Don't you see, Bruno? I can't give myself to a man I don't know. Don't love.''

A quick glance at Bruno said he hadn't softened.

Maria's sandals slapped against the lye-whitened boards as she placed a coffee mug before Rebecca. The Mexican woman stroked her shoulders as Stella gently murmured, ''It will be all right, Rebecca. You'll see. I'm sure McKay intends to treat you sweetly. He's written you letters about how he wants to build up that wild country. When a man sends presents to his betrothed—''

Rebecca's head moved slowly side to side. Her voice, muffled by her arms, was a tremulous lament. ''I just can't—''

''You can,'' Bruno said finally, his deep voice quiet with conviction. ''You were born to this country, Rebecca. You're just the cut of woman McKay wants to begin—''

Her head raised, eyes flashing. ''*He* wants. *He* needs,'' she repeated hotly. ''What say do I have in this? And who would ever think that McKay would be serious about leaving his worldy pursuits for life in the Chiliwist? He can't fight battles there, or run his whaling business.''

Bruno smiled knowingly. ''But there's the land. It'll bind you. You may like McKay better than you think—''

''Hell and damnation! I will not, Bruno!''

Her brother chuckled, leaning back on two legs of his chair. ''Since you're so keenly interested, I might tell you a few things about Matt that you may have missed: Old McKay was a rustic, but fine, man.'' Bruno's voice rumbled slowly, his eyes narrowing as he remembered. ''Eric, his stepson, was mean as a snake, a human sidewinder. But Matthew was decent.''

''Was?'' Rebecca's head lifted, her glare accusing. ''What

do you know about him past that? Good Lord, Bruno. You
married someone you know and love. You grew up with
Stella. But this . . .'' A shudder racked her shoulders. ''Am
I to have no say in my life?''

''He won't hurt you, Rebecca, no more than I would,'' her
brother said, understanding her fears.

Rebecca's flush ran high. ''I was a child when he left the
countryside. But I remember him sashaying up to anything
that wore skirts with that silly grin on his face.''

''I like the cut of McKay.'' Bruno met his sister's glare
evenly. ''He's waited to return to the land, stored it in him
just like I would have done in his place. We've always known
he'd come back.''

Stella sighed and stood heavily. She patted her husband's
sturdy shoulder and padded from the room with a last tender
look at Rebecca. ''Everything will be all right, Rebecca.
You'll see.''

''Ah hum.'' Daniel interrupted as he stood, plopping his
hat over his blond curls. ''I've got to get the cattle moved to
the new pasture this morning. That mountain cat took another
calf last night. But Papa said he wouldn't range outside his
territory.'' He glanced uneasily at Rebecca. ''Good-bye.''

Daniel was big-boned, leggy, and lean, and his expressions
were as mercurial as his moods. Rebecca scowled at his
gawky stance. Daniel's wistful grins at females reminded her
of Matthew McKay's at the same age, she decided. Her
younger brother forgot the English language when a pretty
skirt drifted by. They are truly all alike, she thought disgust-
edly.

Daniel shifted his long legs uneasily. He frowned askance
at her. ''Rebecca?'' His voice was hesitant.

''Oh, go rope a cow or something!'' Rebecca instantly
regretted her waspish tone and softened it. ''I can manage,
Daniel.''

His worried expression immediately cleared. He grinned.
''Are you sure?''

When she nodded, Daniel danced out the door. Maria

grabbed a milking pail and, with a wary glance at Rebecca, followed him quietly.

Bruno frowned. "I know you, Rebecca. You're scared. If you plan to fight McKay's dream—and I think you will—do it toe-to-toe. Face-to-face with the man."

"I fight my own battles, Bruno. You know that. Except for the time you pulled Rudy off me." She watched her brother's expression harden.

Placing her palm flat on the table, she let the pain settle over her once more, like a dark, bleeding cloak. How exposed she'd been to him, how she had dreamed and loved. The now familiar fear crept inside her, clawing at her stomach, knotting it. She would not allow another man to hurt her.

She'd fought to salvage her shredded pride, scraped it into a meager pile and defended it as though it were gold. *McKay would not be the second man to tear her apart.*

Bruno drew a deep breath, expanding his barrel chest. "You haven't listened. Papa said that as rough a mountain man as old McKay was, he floundered about his Irish wife, Nancy, like a pup in love. She had . . . odd ways about her, yet she was a good woman. Some whites said that she was a witch woman, but the Indians believed in her magic. McKay worshiped her every breath and put up with her devil of a son. The way Eric tormented him, it's a wonder Matthew survived. But when Matthew was grown, Eric had met his match."

Bruno sighed. "Drink your coffee, Rebecca, and I'll tell you what I know about Matthew." When she obeyed, he continued. "I remember spending time hunting up in the high country with Matthew. Older than I am by a few years, he taught me how to track up the Methow River and down the Chiliwist Creek. We got snowed in at Three Devils Mountains overnight. Papa was mad as the blazes."

Rebecca's lips tightened. She met his eyes steadily. "Fine. Since then he's been to sea and to war."

The web of laughter lines bordering Bruno's eyes deepened. "For sure he's had some wear on him. He's got the know-how we need here; Washington needs men like him to get crops out to the world and get a fair price for them.''

He dismissed Rebecca's grimace and continued. ''The Mc-Kay location is ideal for trade from Canada and has the lumber the new settlers need. The earth is good for fruit.''

Bruno sighed. ''They had a bee field up there that made the sweetest clover honey. . . .''

''I've heard of the ranch. Supposedly it was deserted years ago, they say, when old McKay crawled into an empty log to die. His big white dog stayed until he, too, died,'' Rebecca added, intrigued by the stories of old McKay's death.

But Matthew McKay—coming to collect his bride—was another matter. ''He can weave his dreams without me.'' She stalked to the black stove to pour another mug of coffee. A drop skidded across the polished surface, its hiss matching Rebecca's seething emotions. She watched the coffee sizzle and dry into a white spot before returning to the table and her brother.

''I got caught in the crossfire, Bruno. Papa guards our family name like a dog over a bone. But I understand, and I know what having a spinster daughter means to him—that somehow he's failed. Left before the altar once was a disaster to our name, but if a new husband sights me and turns tail, the gossip will last for years. If I didn't understand how deeply he feels, I'd be on my horse now. I have no wish to be hurt again.''

''You are his pride. This marriage means everything to him,'' Bruno agreed. ''But he wouldn't have settled for Mc-Kay without knowing some good could come of it. He knows he's doing what's best for you.''

Raising his arms behind his head, Bruno continued his story. ''From the stiff-legged way Matthew walked sometimes, old McKay must have had a temper. The old man got surly as a caged timber wolf when his wife died. Their battles were the talk of the hills. Matthew ran away to sea at sixteen, and all the females in the countryside went into mourning. From what I know, he hasn't been back since.''

''I know all that; you're not tantalizing me a bit. I wish to

God I'd never heard of the man," Rebecca muttered. "I've agreed to a year. But I didn't agree to make him happy."

Impatiently she raked back a curl that was clinging to her cheek. "I'm cutting my hair down to the roots. It tangles, and McKay won't want a bald-headed wife," she threatened darkly.

Bruno chuckled, tugging her long braid affectionately. "You'll live, Sister. But I worry about McKay. . . ."

His hand remained, heavy and secure upon her hunched shoulder. His chair creaked as he leaned toward her, his expression serious. "Give the man a chance, Becky," he urged roughly. "You've always jumped into life. Do it now—build your own home, raise your own children. Don't live on the crumbs of others' lives."

"But I've managed." Rebecca waded through her emotions. Her older brother was deeply concerned. She read the truth in his clear gray eyes. Ever cautious, her brother had weighed the risk to her; he had decided on marriage to McKay.

"A year. If McKay turns tail, I'm free from Papa's marriage demands forever." She eased back into her chair, letting the coffee's warmth penetrate her cold hands. She wouldn't hand herself on a platter to him, not after Rudy. "Bruno, when I'm done with McKay, he'll wish he'd never heard of Rebecca Klein."

"McKay. Rebecca McKay." Bruno corrected, staring cautiously at her. "What are you planning to do?"

Her green eyes slanted up at him, her expression confident. "Wait and see, brother. Just wait and see."

At dusk that night a steamboat slid carefully into its landing on the Columbia River. A man threw a boarding plank onto the steamboat as Matthew McKay studied the mountains surrounding the mighty river. Lofty and dry, studded with pines and rocks, these mountains were the gateway to his home. There, the pines were lush, and the earth black and fertile. He'd grown up in that wild country, hunted in the ravines, and now he had returned.

The country was ripe for trading, for harvesting timber, and he intended to make his fortune.

In the bare light the sand and the granite rocks of the river territory portrayed the arid country he remembered. Drift-wood logs strewn across the huge round rocks marked the high waters of some past flood. A few miles upstream, Fort Oka-nogan had stood. Dismantled and used for firewood, she had been a sister of Fort Astoria at the mouth of the Columbia.

Pines dotted the countryside, but Matthew remembered the lush, red-barked forests of his high country. The scent of the burning pines came from the chimneys of the small com-munity, and Matthew breathed deeply. Gripping his carpet-bag, he mentally forced away the odors of San Francisco's crowded wharves.

The high country. It beckoned him as surely as it had his father.

He felt the old hunger rise in him. The wildness, the ex-citement, the utter peace. He had been gone too long making his fortunes, too long from the high country of his birth.

As he waited for the steamboat to be properly moored, he drew a small tintype picture of Becky from his vest pocket. Peter Klein had sent the picture upon Matthew's request.

Matthew held the picture to the light of the lamp bolted to the steamboat's outer walls. The tomboy he remembered had changed to a beautiful woman with a proud tilt to her head. Her thick ebony hair was primly confined in a crown of braids. He liked the slant of her jaw and wondered briefly why her letters were curt. She didn't exclaim over his gifts as would most women in his experience, but then they didn't have what he wanted. Rebecca held within her the strength to match the land and that was the important thing. Perhaps she had different tastes and he would come to know them later. More likely she was shy of her husband, as he had expected. He'd been told brides were difficult to understand. He hadn't taken time to deal with the matter, comfortable with Peter Klein's assurances that his bride waited eagerly.

He needed a strong woman for his plans, and Becky

Klein—McKay—suited his order perfectly. He wanted a woman accustomed to the hardships of the land. The marriage by proxy was timely. It served his needs to return to the high country and settle. The marriage would insure his legacy, the Jake Baroque homestead.

Matthew also needed the country to heal him. He'd seen enough sights of blood and terror to last a lifetime, unnecessary cruelty and selfish politics. Once he'd been a fresh-faced lad driven from his home by an ill father. Back then, his father and he would have killed each other eventually. He still bore the scars of his father's belt buckle. As a lad he'd had a choice for freedom, and he'd taken it. The world waited for him to explore, and he'd embraced the excitement like a hungry lover.

Now years and adventures later, he needed the peace of the land. He'd ached for it long nights and days, wishing palm trees were pine and foreign soils were his own mountains.

Matthew shrugged broad shoulders, restless to be free of the confinements of his dress jacket. He'd been successful in cities but they crowded him, just as the jacket had enveloped him. In the mountains a man could really breathe while building his life. When Peter Klein suggested marriage to Becky, Matthew suddenly saw his plans come to life. Now he had a woman of the land.

It had taken two years of shuttling Americans back from China, and finally the knife wound had laid him low. The knife had been sharp and deadly, its blade fouled to infect. He'd struggled for life, hot and feverish, placing the tintype of Becky next to his sickbed. From there he'd sold his business interests and healed, waiting for the time when he was strong enough to claim his bride.

The tintype reflected none of Becky's high spirits as a child, nor the way she jumped into help when needed. He chuckled, remembering the way she had almost knocked him over as he pulled a calf from her cow.

She would have changed, he thought, looking at the tintype. He traced the softness of her mouth and the line of her oval face. A beautiful woman waited for him and the beginning of their marriage.

Feeling more lighthearted than he had in years, Matthew stepped onto the gangplank of the steamboat. "Damn!" He grinned, feeling the call of the high country begin to seep into his blood.

Chapter Two

"McKay is bound straight for hell. I'll make one for him. He'll wish he'd never heard of me," Rebecca promised aloud that night as she sat in her second-story bedroom.

She ran her trembling fingers across her bottom lip, remembering her vow to remain alone after Rudy's deceit. She hated the shame of being played like a well-hooked trout. How funny she must have appeared to him—eager for the time when they would be in their own home.

What a fool she had been! Of course, in his rage, Rudy had said as much. He explained carefully how each year his other opportunities had failed and he was left with the unhappy pleasure of returning to her. She was his "last stone to choose."

Her window overlooked the moonlit ranch yard, and she could see clearly the light cast from the sitting room. In the distance, mountain coyotes howled. The night was clear, a contrast to her thunderous mood. The day had crawled by slowly as she remained isolated in her room, rocking in her mother's chair.

Once she'd opened up to a man, heard his soft words and courtly touches. And then the darker side: Rudy was her past, McKay not her future.

A soft, pine-scented breeze fluttered the curtains of her

window. The delicate French lace swept over the toes of Rebecca's dusty boots as they lay propped upon the sill.

She stretched, her body aching. She had perched for hours on the small rocker, watching the wagon road leading to the ranch. Bruno would drive McKay home from the landing; she wanted to study the man from a distance.

She pressed together her lips. Once marriage and children were her dream; now the bittersweet taste lingered on her tongue. The shattered dreams danced about her, and she could almost feel a lover's touch, hear a child's delighted laughter.

She shrugged, then unbuckled her gun belt. She unstrapped the Colt's holster from her thigh and eased the belt from her waist. "If I'm lucky, the boat will sink. Maybe it will hit the Brewster ferry cable again. He's probably forgotten how to swim, but the old-timers used to tell plenty of tales about his skinny-dipping with the Indian women," she muttered, plopping the gun belt on a starched lace doily. "Indian George said that all the Indian women liked McKay. Hah! They can have him."

The kerosene lantern glowed softly beside her four-poster bed as Rebecca stared darkly at the condemning document—her marriage certificate. Crumpled into a ball and tossed upon her mother's patchwork quilt, the paper had as much chance for life as a fish trapped on the dry rocks of the Columbia. Left on the banks of the river at low water, the carp flopped and gasped and died—as would McKay's heralded dreams.

Lost in thought, Rebecca gnawed at the corner of her bottom lip and toyed with her brain. *Husband.* Until now he was no more than a piece of paper tucked away, to be forgotten. But that tonight he would become a flesh-and-blood reality that would soon turn tail and run to his isolated ranch. Or turn back to the wharves of San Francisco.

Suddenly the coyotes' howls stilled and the crunch of wagon wheels on rocks began, then grew louder.

Rebecca turned down the lantern wick, then sank back against the darkness of the room. She used the fluttering curtains as a veil as she viewed the front yard. A wagon crept into the light coming from the house, then stopped. Bruno and another tall man leapt to the ground and moved toward the front porch. Chelan Sam, an Indian ranch hand, slid from the shadows to take the bridle of the lead horse. In a moment the horses snorted as they were led to the barn.

Male voices rumbled comfortably, and the heavy oak door to the drawing room clicked shut. Rebecca leaned back against the rocker, listening carefully to the blend of deep, masculine tones over the heavy thud of her heart.

She closed her eyes, feeling a wash of panic chill her body.

She recognized the various male voices—her father's, Bruno's, and Daniel's. It was the unfamiliar one that raised the hair on the back of her neck. The man's voice was huskier and sounded like the rumble of bull buffalo in heat, she decided moodily.

McKay. Her skin cooled despite the warm July night. McKay—a man coming to claim his woman.

Rebecca leaned back, adjusting more comfortably to the small rocker. She wore her work clothes, which smelled of horses and bore the grit of her day's work. She smiled coldly, pleased by the mud crust covering her boots. The dried manure represented the perfect picture she wanted to give McKay of his bride.

He'd expect lace and ruffles and curls, like any other man. How Rudy had liked her in skirts . . . But she intended to give McKay scow wallow.

She placed her hands across her flat stomach and interlaced her fingers, fighting the fine trembling of her hands. She waited, her heart thumping loudly beneath her camisole.

''Rebecca.'' Her father's booming voice carried up the stairway to her room. His tone was impatient and imperial, as though she were a child late for the evening meal.

It was time to meet the man she already feared and despised.

She feared him because he had the power to shame her family honor, a near death blow to her father. McKay, on a whim, could let the countryside know how he had been tricked into marriage with a woman who didn't appeal to him on sight. He had just enough contact with settlers to drive that stake in her father's heart.

He was a wanderer, just like Rudy. The cruel streak of greed was likely to be shared.

Rebecca closed her eyes, trying to still the icy fear slithering through her. She hated fear, recognizing it as a weakness, just as she recognized its cause: She'd been wounded physically and as a woman. McKay would be dead before he laid a hand on her.

Leisurely Rebecca rose and stretched her arms high above her head, then moved gracefully toward her bedroom door. With an effort she stilled the pleased curve of her mouth and turned the doorknob. Her boots echoed on the hallway boards and her palm caressed the smooth oak of the stair railing.

Her father and McKay watched her descent down the wide staircase. Both large men, they sat side by side on the delicate patterns of the cabbage-rose settee. Each man held a long-stemmed crystal glass. The finely tempered glass caught the light from the rose-painted lantern and the small flames of the fireplace.

Rebecca sensed her father's disapproval as she stalked across the braided rugs to the fireplace. But she stared boldly at McKay, a blatant male contrast to the delicate crocheted doilies on the backs and arms of the settee.

McKay's broad shoulders strained the cloth of his black dress jacket. The shadows shielded his face, but she felt his eyes follow her, raising the tiny hairs at the back of her neck. She'd been tracked by a mountain cat once, and now she tingled with the same instinct for survival.

When Rebecca reached the fireplace, she rested her hand on the wooden mantle and braced her foot against the stone hearth. She turned, facing the two men squarely as she hooked her thumb into her belt.

In the heavy silence her father's anger seemed to sear her as surely as the heat of the small fire burning at her backside. In the softness of the lamplight Klein's brows bristled, drawing together over his eyes. "Rebecca," he growled, frustrated.

"Yes, Papa?" she murmured sweetly. Through the room's shadows she boldly studied the younger man.

The floral print of the settee's tapestry emphasized his dark masculinity. Dressed in black, his white shirt was open at the neck, a dark string tie loosened to lay upon his broad chest. Noting his easy sprawl across the delicate furniture, Rebecca swallowed uneasily. McKay seemed to lounge like a mountain cougar comfortably sunning himself on a warm mountain boulder.

She watched the tie resting upon his chest lift and fall with each breath. He breathed easily while her heart thudded unaccountably in her chest. Sheltered within the vee of his open dress shirt, shadows of chest hair appeared. Her fingers curled about her brass belt buckle as she fought the knotting of her stomach.

She remembered his height, his dark hair, and his laughing eyes as he teased her. Now this new McKay made her nervous, her senses as aroused as a cottontail with a coyote in pursuit.

McKay had her nerves on edge, her fingers trembling—and she didn't understand, or like, the feeling.

McKay's left hand caressed the dainty stem of his glass, while his right rested easily upon the polished arm of the settee. The sight of the large, long-fingered hands sent a ripple of panic though her. He'd been ill and she had expected slender, soft hands but discovered dark, strong ones instead. Somehow she hadn't prepared for the strength of the man, for the aura of his absolute masculinity.

Had she really called him a San Francisco dandy? she wondered frantically, her skin tightening across her cheekbones. To someone living in the West this was a slur, and she'd used it recklessly in McKay's case. Meant to ridicule, the word was instantly tossed aside.

She boldly traced the length of his legs. Sheathed in dark trousers, a Western hat resting on the bend of his knee, McKay was lean and muscled straight down to his highly polished boots.

Sand from the river landing clung to his boots, reminding Rebecca of his ties to the land. Of her ties to him.

She couldn't belong to him—be his wife!

With a sudden chill she shivered, regretting her bargain.

Through the shadows Rebecca studied his face closely. Black hair waved across his brow, the ends curling at the wide collar. Beneath heavy dark brows—one was cut in two by an old scar—his eyes met hers. It was there still—just the faintest mockery, the black-eyed humor she remembered.

Rebecca straightened her shoulders, determined to get McKay's full measure before she started her war. Within her the fear rose. She couldn't allow herself to depend upon another man's smiles.

A day's growth of stubble darkened McKay's hard jaw. His nose was crooked, proof of his brawling days. But when her stare reached his mouth, Rebecca felt the dry lump of fear lodge in her throat. Long and firm and oddly fuller at his bottom lip, his mouth tantalized her. She could almost taste his brandy on her own mouth, almost feel the warmth of him. . . .

Again she trembled, strangely warm and uneasy. She gripped the brass buckle with suddenly damp fingers, feeling McKay's even stare beneath his thick black lashes. The weight of his gaze settled upon her almost possessively, and Rebecca shivered.

Her blood began to heat, to throb frantically within her veins as the steady, smoldering stare met her own.

In that moment she knew that McKay had come to claim his woman, to begin his destiny and their marriage.

A year . . . she thought in a wave of panic.

Rebecca pressed her lips together. She'd trusted one man but she wouldn't trust another. She sensed she'd have to jerk McKay up short and fast, getting things her way from the start. Or . . .

Matthew liked the look of his bride—a woman to share his life in the high country.

His thumb stroked the smooth glass in his hand, comparing it to the smoothness of her face. He liked the proud set of her chin, the defiant, flashing eyes.

Of course Becky would be as nervous as any new bride—he had expected that. But in a short time, after getting to know him, they could begin.

He felt his loins tighten. He'd kept to his marriage vows for two long years, and now, suddenly, Becky's full breasts and long legs sent him reeling with desire.

He forced his fingers to loosen their grip on the stem of the glass, fearing he would break it. He remembered Becky as a spitting tomboy tagging after Bruno, a flat-chested, chicken-legged child in tattered braids. But now, in the flesh, she was more beautiful than the miniature tintype.

He'd spent hours looking at that face, toned in tans and browns, but the living image was exciting, challenging.

Rebecca was a hell of a woman, he decided immediately, a fiery mixture of sun-touched, silky skin and green eyes. She bore the wild-eyed look of a Indian cayuse, a horse bred to suit the land—strong and agile. But she was as sleekly made as a Kentucky Thoroughbred. His gaze stroked the length of her long legs and slightly rounded hips, feeling desire tug sharply at his loins.

His fingertips tingled. He could almost feel her thick braid loosening in his hands, feel the lush, jet black strands cling to his body. He traced her slender neck and squared shoulders. She shifted slightly on those long legs, and Matt caught the full outline of her breasts in the light. He ache to cup their gentle weight in his palms.

He swallowed, forcing his gaze to rise to her face. Becky's oval face was mysterious and exciting, her flashing green eyes framed by black lashes.

Her full lips tightened beneath his perusal, reminding him that his sweet wife was likely to be untried in passion. He traced the enticing bow shape of her mouth, her sensual bottom lip. He'd been celibate for two long years, but he'd take the time to woo her gently into his bed.

She'd be worth it, he decided, uncomfortably aware of his

body heat. He'd give her a few days to adjust to him, to the reality of their marriage.

Matthew's thumb slid over the stem of the crystal brandy glass. He wanted her now, longed to cup and taste those full breasts.

Klein had assured him that Becky was untouched, a sweet, delicate-natured bride waiting for her husband. But he sensed a passionate woman lurking beneath that cool stare, a woman who would flow like hot silk beneath him. . . .

Her cheeks seemed pale, her eyes flashing at him from beneath her lashes. But then, brides were nervous, especially virginal ones. He noted her shiver, comparing her to an untried filly. Her slender fingers gripped her belt buckle tightly, and he could almost feel them clawing at his back as she sought release.

The shy bride, he reminded himself. But soon . . .

"Ah-hmm." Klein said, pretending to clear his throat. "Rebecca McKay," he growled, ignoring the accusing glare she sent his way. "This is your husband, Matthew."

There was no warmth in her eyes. Her chin rose fractionally. Her body went rigid as she watched McKay slowly rise to his feet. In the same motion he placed his hat to the settee's cushion and his brandy glass on the starched doily of a small table.

Rebecca took a deep breath, caught by his unexpected size and force. He was lean, moving like a mountain cat on the hunt, his eyes tracing her face.

In her lifetime no man had looked upon her as possessively, as purposefully as McKay did now. His mouth had a curve to it that she just didn't trust. Much too . . . enticing, she decided anxiously.

Rebecca's eyes widened as McKay straightened to his full height. Bruno stood six foot two, but McKay was at least two inches taller. His body was leaner and more honed than her brother's bulky one. The lines etched in his face were not kindly. Her mouth went dry; the room and her father slid into oblivion.

McKay closed the space between them, and Rebecca's fingers gripped the mantel tightly. His black eyes held hers, strangely bonding her to him. She shifted uncomfortably, reminding herself that rattlers used the same mesmerizing trick on their prey—and she didn't intend to be his prey!

Still . . . her senses reacted unpredictably to McKay. Her body heated up and her legs weakened as he moved, reminding her of a mountain hunter. But then he came from fur trader stock, she reasoned uncomfortably.

Flicking a glance down his lean body, Rebecca's breath caught in her throat. With an effort she dragged the air into her lungs, shocked for just an instant by the feminine softness aching within her.

She swallowed, forcing herself to remember Rudy. In that instant she knew that McKay was twice as dangerous as the drifter.

But then, she reasoned again, McKay had plenty of experience, running his black gaze up and down women, making their hearts race and their bones melt. The boards beneath her boots seemed to slant as Rebecca fought her body's reaction. Unaccustomed to this weakness, she shivered, wishing suddenly for the safety of her room.

A chill swept over Rebecca, soon replaced by the heat of McKay's tall body as he stood next to her. Fascinated by the length of his lashes, by his male scent, she felt her tongue moisten her suddenly dry lips. Instantly his eyes narrowed, following the movement.

The dark look caused her heart to race wildly. His gaze—hot and disturbing—lifted to her face. He frowned, his hand sliding down her left forearm. She shivered, feeling the rough heat of his skin pass over hers lightly. At her left wrist the large hand paused. A muscle beneath his dark skin tightened as slowly, carefully, each long finger wrapped around her fragile bones. He held her wrist lightly for a moment, a moment in which Rebecca's heart stopped. Then he steadily drew her toward him.

Holding her eyes, McKay slid a ring onto Rebecca's third finger.

''Hello, Mrs. McKay.'' His deep rasp swirled around Rebecca, taunting her as she tried to remember her promise.

Her heart thudded heavily as she forced her eyes down at her imprisoned wrist. Dark-skinned fingers gently shackled her paler skin, heating it. An antique wedding ring glowed against her skin. Three large rubies—blood red in the firelight—were intricately woven among golden threads. The heavy, ornate ring declared his possession as forcefully as the strong hand wrapped around her wrist.

Raw male ownership rode each muscle and sinew of his tall body. For a moment she allowed the old dreams of home and children to tantalize her. If she did not resist his claim . . .

Rudy's image came creeping back, the hot male rage and the slashing pain. He'd hated touching her even to hold her hand, he'd shouted. Hated her kisses . . . She breathed deeply, feeling her anger return. Mr. Matthew McKay could find some other fine cow to breed; he would not have her at his side.

She'd spent her time in hell and didn't intend to make another mistake.

Rebecca's eyes slowly rose to meet his black ones. Matthew saw a glimmer of fear riding in the green depths, soon replaced by anger. Her lips pressed against each other, her face paled, and her body tensed, resisting his claim as she tried to withdraw her wrist from his grip. She was strong, yet he held her easily, then moved closer, enchanted by the softness of her flesh, the emerald eyes slashing at him. She was a beauty and angry—no, just edgy with bridal nerves, he decided ruefully.

He smiled down at her, pleased with his bride. In time, man, he thought, cautioning himself. She's new to the game. Go gently now. . . .

Rebecca had the look of a high-strung filly and he felt himself warm to her. She had nothing to fear; she'd trust him soon enough.

Klein's pleased chuckle scraped along the length of his

daughter's backbone. "Well, Rebecca, don't you have something to say to your husband?"

Over the broad width of McKay's shoulder, Rebecca's eyes flashed at her father. His twinkling gaze met her own. Klein fought the urge to crow over his coup—the McKays were a good match. He raised his glass and drank the brandy down to the dregs.

Matthew's big hand slid away from her wrist and caressed Rebecca's palm with his smooth fingertips. "Hello, Becky McKay." The use of her childhood name startled Rebecca and she looked up at him. Scents of tobacco, bay rum, horse, and leather caused something deep within her to quiver. The subtle scent of dark musk blended with them, and she knew it was McKay's alone.

A year of scents and dark, hungry looks and that rumbling Scots-Irish burr—she couldn't possibly live with him! Her "Mr. McKay" was husky, sounding raw to her ears.

Matthew stared down at her thoughtfully. He leaned closer. His head tilted toward her as his body blocked her father's view. His voice lowered to a rasp, stalking her. "You are a beauty. I am well pleased."

A year, day after day . . . She fingered the heavy ring, twisting it on her finger. Taking a deep breath that drew Matthew's eyes to her breasts, Rebecca summoned her shaky courage. Before she saw the movement of her lips, she snapped, "I am *not* pleased with you! I want to talk to you about this . . . marriage. I want an annulment."

Shocked at the sound of her own voice, she realized she never could have stayed with him a full year.

His eyebrows raised, his tall body instantly grew taut, and his head went back arrogantly, as though she'd insulted him. "What?"

Rebecca took a deep breath, forcing herself to meet his dark, hawklike stare. "The sooner this marriage is annulled, the more quickly you can marry another woman. There's a lawyer in Cairo, about three miles from here. We can ride there in the morning—"

A year, she thought frantically, reminded of her father's offer. Impossible!

Matthew frowned, studying her thoughtfully for a long moment. Then he smiled slowly, knowingly. "You have a case of the bridal nerves," he murmured soothingly, his deep voice caressing her like warm velvet in the night. "I've waited two years for you, Becky—" he began gently.

"You can wait forever as far as I'm concerned, Mr. McKay!" she blazed, torn between panic and anger. How thick-headed could one man be? Surely he could see she had no intention of having a real marriage!

She'd spent her days dreaming of making a nest, only to have it kicked ruthlessly aside. McKay could sniff elsewhere for his wife. He had waited two years; he could wait longer.

It would be an eternity before she opened herself to a man's hurting hands again.

Hating the fear riding her, Rebecca fought to cover it with anger. Yet the fear danced on the edge, shaming her.

"Becky—"

Matthew's deep purr angered her. She sliced the air with her hand, interrupting him. "Don't Becky me. I grew up a long time ago."

For just a moment his head tilted arrogantly, his eyes narrowing on her upturned face. He breathed quietly. "It's been a long day." His eyes swept down her clothing. "You've probably worked hard—"

The man was sheathed in male arrogance, attributing her reluctance to bridal nerves! She spaced her words carefully, her temper in full bloom. "You really are slow-minded."

A muscle worked slowly beneath the dark skin of his cheek as though he were grinding his teeth. His big hand rose slowly to palm across his jaw. The sound of his stubble grated upon her nerves. "I've had a hard trip. And I've never liked nagging women," he warned softly.

Her eyebrows arched. "What? What did you say, McKay?"

His smile did not reach his eyes. "I said, we've both had a long day. You are nervous about me. I understand—"

"Bal-der-dash!" Rebecca stated carefully, forgetting her fears. The man's arrogance just begged for a cutting down to size.

She leaned back and eyed him down, then up. She shrugged. "I want out of the marriage, McKay. Now. I see nothing in you that I want." She inspected his crisp black waves. "In fact, I think I see a gray hair or two. Old," she stated finally.

She was fighting on another plane now, one of sheer, taunting anger.

"Too old, is it now?" Dangerously deep, McKay's tone crept softly across her like a cat, claws sheathed temporarily. When stroked wrong, McKay's voice settled into the soft burr of his Highland heritage. His eyes narrowed. "I don't think I'm quite over the hill yet."

After a moment in which she watched the muscles of his jaw move, he murmured, "Take your time, Becky. And don't be afraid—"

"Afraid?" Rebecca breathed hard, her anger shimmering within her. Her tawny brows lifted. "Why should I be? I can shoot the eyes out of a springing rattler. Which is what you remind me of," she added succinctly.

Matthew's expression hardened as he glared down at her. "As your husband I don't relish being compared to a snake."

Rebecca smiled sweetly. "And I do not intend to share your dreams, Mr. McKay."

"But you will, Mrs. McKay," Matthew returned evenly. Holding her furious stare with his dark one, Matthew raised his voice slightly. He spoke to Klein. "She's grown to be a beauty, Peter. I'll take good care of her."

Peter twirled his handlebar mustache. He'd just watched the McKays' first duel and liked the outcome. Matthew would treat his daughter with a gentle firmness. Tracing the younger man's face, Klein decided that McKay meant to keep his vows. But Matthew also had the look of a man on the hunt— excited by a woman.

Rebecca clearly wanted to throw herself at McKay, tearing off his flesh with her nails.

Peter's mustache twitched, betraying the grin he fought. At war, were they? Good, at least his daughter couldn't cool McKay's heels with her plans!

Matthew turned his broad back to her, sauntering back to the settee. He lifted the brandy glass in a toast to her. "To my bride and my marriage."

Klein finished the toast. "To you both. May your marriage grow with the new state. It's a grand start."

Numb, Rebecca stared at them both, twisting the ring on her finger. She sensed her father counting his future grand-children as he watched her over the rim of his glass.

She felt like a piece of driftwood, carried mercilessly down the great Columbia by the spring thaws. She'd seen a whirl-pool suck a huge log down into its depths and knew the feeling.

Without a glance at her McKay settled his long frame into the settee and began conversing with her father about grafting fruit trees and the price of seed. "I'll need some good stock, too, Peter. But the spring will be soon enough. Until then I'll tend the old place and plan our new house. There's much to do between setting up a lumber mill and setting up trade."

Seemingly forgotten, Rebecca eased to a small chair be-yond the light and studied the ring on her left hand. Gradually the rest of the family entered the room. She was aware of Bruno, Daniel, and Stella staring at her curiously as the con-versation rumbled on pleasantly. Stella picked up her em-broidery hoop and began pricking her needle through the baby gown.

Maria poked her head into the room. "Food now, yes?"

"In a moment, Maria," Klein said heartily. "Come meet Rebecca's husband."

Husband. Rebecca winced. Her father was proud of the marriage—they all were. But she would have him turning to more welcome pastures before the year was out. She frowned. She hadn't planned on McKay's smooth control, his deter-mination.

She hadn't planned on her reaction to him—his black, glowing eyes and his warm, light touch on her skin.

Nor the fear that still rode her, brought to life by McKay's possessive touch. She'd forgotten the shame of fearing, the deep wounding of her pride. And she hated McKay for making her remember that shame.

"Let me see, Rebecca." Stella lifted Rebecca's limp wrist and studied the ring. Her warm, brown eyes probed at Rebecca's dazed ones. "It's a fine wedding ring, Rebecca. Old and very expensive."

"It was my mother's ring, Stella. My father trapped one entire winter to buy it," McKay offered softly, watching his wife closely. "We can have the stones reset later if Rebecca has a mind to."

Rebecca stared at him blankly, then studied the ring. Old McKay had worshiped his wife, they said—loved her madly. The ring was proof of the elder McKay's love. Respectfully, Rebecca would not alter the design, despite the man who had possessively placed it on her finger.

Bruno patted her back, humor lurking in his eyes. "Matthew never was one to waste time." He admired McKay's smooth possession, his underlying gentleness. Matthew would be the wrong one to face when he had his sights set on a woman. Somehow, Bruno decided, Matthew would equal Rebecca's challenge.

A burst of laughter wafted over the room and Rebecca started, staring straight into Matthew's black eyes. Slowly, fractionally, his gaze wandered down the length of her throat and fastened on her breasts.

Shakily Rebecca stood. Her knees were as weak as a new foal's, her breasts thrusting at her lace camisole. She wouldn't stay in the same room with the man as his eyes stripped her clothing from her. One more hot, slaking look and she'd draw down on him!

"It's been a long day, Stella. Please excuse me," she murmured as she walked toward the stairway.

Matthew's hand tightened on his glass. Stiff-backed and angry, his wife moved as gracefully as a cat. Her long braid trailed sensuously down her long back to touch her swaying hips. She was slender-soft there, her buttocks firm against the coarse cloth. He'd once preferred a more fuller-bodied woman, but there was something primitive in Rebecca that lured him as surely as the wild country had called him home.

Matthew had the instincts of a gambler, and now his senses told him to play out his hand—claiming the stakes for his own. Rebecca was like no other woman he'd ever met: Her aura was of wind and flame; high country pines; and lush, fragrant roses. In those few moments she'd tantalized him, heated his blood.

Yet, beneath the tension in his body, Matthew knew his wife could fulfill his other, deeper needs. "Boyo," his mother's lilting voice whispered to him from the past. "You'll seek and find your prize. When you do, take it."

He shook his head, fighting the urge to smile. Every man had his destiny, and in Rebecca's flashing green eyes he had found his.

Her wish for an annulment had stunned him momentarily. But he had always like a good fight; it made the winning sweeter.

Then—at that moment—Matthew decided to win her heart as well as her body. She'd fight him. And she'd love him. He would see to it, he promised.

He'd never wanted a woman to love him, or wanted to love her back. But now he sensed that this strong woman's life and his would be intertwined; he'd found his prize and he meant to keep her.

He traced the length of her tall body. Her thighs were strong, her legs as long as a colt's. When she turned to meet his bold stare, her face paled.

Something passed between them—a hot, tight moment as each recognized the other as an opponent in a match that would not end easily.

Raising his glass to her, Matthew smiled slowly. "Sleep tight, Becky McKay."

Rebecca stiffened, turning to face him fully. Matthew met her furious green eyes evenly, waiting for the sound of her voice. He liked that sound, low and husky, defiant and beckoning. "Good night, *Mr.* McKay."

Her father cleared his throat uneasily. "It has been a long day. Good night, Rebecca."

In her bedroom Rebecca stared at the walls. Clad in her faded long johns, she snuggled beneath the patchwork quilt. She watched the shadows of the pine boughs beyond her window dance on the small varnished boards.

" 'Hello, Becky McKay,' indeed," she said, mimicking McKay in a syrupy tone. "The arrogant bastard thinks he can waltz in and claim me like a heifer he's purchased from a stockman. Well, he's got a surprise coming! He'll soon see things my way."

She punched the goosedown pillow. "I was just fine. . . ." She flopped onto her stomach and then onto her back. "I'll send him packing."

Maria had spent all afternoon preparing his room, which was next to hers. Her own father had passed her off like so much worm-infested meal. Her nails scored the fine muslin sheets. So Mr. Matthew McKay thought he could claim her when he finally decided to waltz back into the countryside, did he?

Her fingers stroked the wrist he had captured. She frowned, remembering the strength of his hands, the sliding caress as his flesh left hers. She closed her lids, and from behind them rose the image of his black, mocking eyes. Groaning, she thumped the pillow. "Well, sweet hell, who could have guessed the man was a giant? And dense in the head, to boot? Surely no man would want an unwilling wife."

She fought the softness within her, the feminine warmth she had long denied.

McKay wanted her as a woman. His eyes had been bold and possessive, promising. If she were to hold her freedom, it would be a fight.

Once she'd been a vulnerable girl, but no more. She couldn't bear the pain a second time. She'd lived with the shame of begging Rudy to stop hurting her. And McKay brought it all back in spades.

Rudy and McKay were both big men. She didn't have a

chance against the strength of either one of them, nor against their greed. She'd have to make sure she wounded McKay just enough to trim his sails and cause him to take his possessive black eyes elsewhere.

She couldn't let him see her fear. He'd use it against her.

Rudy had never angered her, even after the beating and the taunting. She'd hated him then, yet the anger was for her alone, her shame at loving him.

McKay had in one night raised her temper to wildfire, a rage that wanted to tear out at him.

She listened for footsteps as the house quieted. McKay's bedroom door creaked shut. His bed squeaked, and she heard boots drop heavily upon the floor. The quiet sounds screamed at her—dresser drawers sliding, stocking feet padding about the floor, muffled by the cured bear hide.

When McKay had angered her, she'd forgotten Rudy. Something about McKay caused her to want to throw herself at him, scraping and clawing. At the same time her knees went weak at his dark, exciting looks.

McKay would not be her future. She'd make his life hell until he freed her—it was just a matter of time.

Chapter Three

"Good morning, Bruno . . . Daniel . . . Papa. How are you feeling, Stella?" Her face averted, Rebecca took her place at the breakfast table the next morning.

McKay lounged in the chair next to hers, watching her profile intently. "Good morning," he drawled, the heat of his body tingling along her side. There was that rough-soft burr that reached inside her intimately, as though she were the only woman on earth.

She tensed, feeling so exposed to his prying gaze. He traced her profile with a lover's touch, and she could feel the raw edge of fear tingling around her.

"The baby is so strong, Rebecca," Stella answered softly, her eyes glowing. "He kept me awake all night."

"He?" Rebecca teased, placing her napkin on her lap.

McKay chuckled, leaning toward her. He was too big, Rebecca thought uneasily. Placing his arm on the back of her chair, McKay's breath brushed across her cheek. "I like babies," he whispered into her ear. "Do you?"

Rebecca inhaled sharply, edging away from his touch. "It *was* a good morning," she stated flatly, meaningfully.

He chuckled again, and she shot a hard stare at him. McKay's lean cheeks were freshly shaved, Maria's lye soap scenting his skin. Avoiding his mocking eyes, Rebecca noted the small scar on his hard jawline. Dressed in a shirt with full sleeves, McKay's complexion seemed darker against the light yellow muslin. A coarse black tuft rose out of the unbuttoned collar of his shirt.

A withered invalid with dreams that would never live, indeed! Her father had covered the Klein name well with his game. There would come a time when she'd let him have a taste of her revenge.

Just a taste. Because he'd acted with what he thought was best for her. And because she loved him.

But McKay, with his laughing eyes and husky Scots-Irish burr, needed a good taking-down at his knees. So he thought he had her, did he?

Rebecca's fingertips tingled. She had the odd impulse to touch that whorl of masculine hair escaping his shirt. She swallowed, gripping her fork tightly, aware that McKay continued to study her intently.

His gaze traced the violet patterns of her blouse and down the buff trousers tucked into her riding boots. His mouth curved slightly when he saw the Colt strapped to her thigh.

Mocking her, was he? Rebecca turned to face him squarely. "Have you seen enough, Mr. McKay?" she asked coldly.

Matthew smiled, cupping her stiff shoulder with his hand. His thumb caressed her collarbone lightly as she tried to shrug free. "Not nearly enough, Princess," he answered lazily. "I'm sure I'll see more."

"Princess?" she said scoffingly. But something within her shimmered and warmed. For just an instant Rebecca allowed herself to glare at him. "If you don't take your hand from me, McKay," she murmured, "I will remove it myself."

The scarred eyebrow shot up. "It appears you're not the pleasant bride this morning."

Rebecca took a deep, steadying breath that brought his gaze to her chest. The man definitely had other ways of touching her!

Taking care not to touch McKay, she carefully slid her chair back and stood. "Daniel, change places with me."

Maria placed filled platters on the long table: fried sowbelly or fresh side-pork sausage patties, fluffy biscuits, and a bowl of white milk gravy surrounded a huge mound of butter that had been imprinted in a tulip mold.

Bruno helped himself to half a plate of scrambled eggs as he watched his sister carefully. Rebecca usually ate a hearty breakfast, but this morning her stomach rebelled. "I'm not very hungry."

Daniel's blue eyes widened in disbelief. "You always eat like a horse in the morning," he managed around a mouthful of eggs.

"Daniel!" Rebecca snapped. "No one asked your opinion."

He scowled back at her. "No one ever does. She can be grumpy as a wounded grizzly in the morning, Matt. Remember that."

Matthew chuckled, a soft rumbling tone that caused the hairs on the nape of Rebecca's neck to rise. "She's just got bridal nerves. Women are like that. Soft and sweet as new lambs—"

"Hellfire," Rebecca muttered moodily. "That will be the day."

Matthew's heavy eyebrows rose. "Becky, I am truly shocked."

From the corner of her eye Rebecca saw his bare forearm—heavily muscled and darkly tanned—reach for a sourdough biscuit. Stirring her coffee, she dipped her head to hide her flushed cheeks. When she reached for the blue-willow sugar bowl, Matthew's large, dark hand wrapped around it. Taking off the small lid, he stated blandly, "Sweets to the sweet, my dear. Let me serve you. How many spoonfuls? One? Two?"

"I can serve myself, Mr. McKay," Rebecca whipped back at him, raising her head. Inches away from her, he smiled widely, and just for a moment her breath caught in her lungs. When he grinned, his right cheek dimpled. Matthew's black eyes sparkled behind long lashes, and staring at him, Rebecca thought her heart lost a beat before it began to race wildly.

His thumb stroked her upper sleeve slowly, and Rebecca sidled from his touch. Her senses urged her to move closer, to touch his dark skin, to slide her fingers across that dimple.

She felt oddly weak and warm, and she frowned, glaring hard at him. Damn the man's hide for making her feel this way! He probably had all sorts of little tricks to excite women. Well, he could throw them in the river!

"I'm leaving. I have work to do." She had to get away from those black, taunting eyes.

"Eat up, Becky. We've a long day ahead of us," Matthew murmured, his dimple deepening.

Rebecca frowned. "We? I have to check the new grapes and the irrigation ditches to the apple orchard." The projects had been given her to keep her busy, her father's matchmaking tactics at play. But now they would serve her purpose and keep her from McKay. She toyed with the scrambled eggs, avoiding his intense stare. She felt his breath on her neck.

"Why, Becky, surely you're anxious to spend the day with your husband. You're not afraid of me, are you?"

Rebecca felt the members of her family watch her curiously. Apparently McKay was not afraid to play his parlor games right beneath their noses.

"Not at all, Mr. McKay. Go play with a rattler," Rebecca returned evenly, meeting his taunting stare.

"Rebecca!" Peter said across the table. "Show some respect!"

Matthew's long legs stretched to imprison hers beneath the table. He exerted just enough pressure to hold her. "Nerves, Peter. I expected as much."

"Did you really?" She stared at him innocently, trying to loosen his grip. "Perhaps you bargained unwisely."

When she jarred the table, the dishes clattered. Her father gripped the edge, steadying it. "What in blazes is going on?"

"Ask *him*. He knows everything, don't you, Mr. McKay? All the little workings of a woman's silly brain."

He tensed, a muscle in his jaw working. Instantly pleasure bloomed within Rebecca.

"You're barely eating. We'll be gone all day, you know." Something dangerous moved in Matthew's black eyes, and Rebecca felt them lashing at her.

"All day?"

His fingers laced with hers possessively, refusing to loosen when she tugged sharply. "I want you to see the old ranch. We'll need to take stock and make lists—furniture, a stove, food, tools—for staying the winter up there." His gaze slid down to her mouth. He traced its full contours and his eyes suddenly lost their laughter, darkening. "It will be a long winter, I'm told."

Rebecca dusted her tan hat against her trousers. McKay's plans for the day offered her the perfect opportunity to make him change his mind about marriage. By the day's end he would see how ill-suited his unwilling bride was for his plans.

She breathed the fresh mountain air. In the early morning it was sweet with the scent of pine. Rolling her deerskin jacket, she tied it to the saddle skirt, then swung up into the saddle. Her stallion pranced, head up, wanting to race. "Easy, Wind Dancer. Easy, boy."

Her father had traded the Nez Percé for the Appaloosa. Fast and long-winded, Wind Dancer could easily leave McKay's chestnut gelding in the dust. She drew on the worn leather gloves with the Indian beading across the backs. Studying the design impatiently, she heard McKay's saddle creak, adjusting to his weight.

She glanced at him unwillingly. A tall man suited to a big horse, his legs curved easily to the horse's belly, his boots fitting the stirrups comfortably. Then he patted the animal's thick neck. A fancy, brass-decorated rifle in an ornately carved sheath was fitted against the gelding's ribs. Behind his saddle was the lunch Maria had packed, and another large bundle wrapped in yellow oilskin.

"We'll take the old horse trail by the Methow River. It's quicker than the wagon trail leading up from the river." Wind Dancer sidestepped as the gelding led the way from the ranch. Matthew's body settled comfortably into the saddle. Beneath his broad-brimmed black hat his features were tense, his leather jacket stretched tautly over his shoulders.

A meadowlark sang from a fence post as they wound through the purple clover blooms toward the pines bordering the ranch. He nodded toward a sandbar banking the Columbia. "A lot of gold was taken out of there during the mining rush, Becky," he remarked thoughtfully. "First the fur trappers and traders, then the gold rush and the Indian wars . . . this country hasn't had much rest, has it?"

Matthew half turned in his saddle, catching her eye and nodding to the grazing herd of mule deer. A porcupine, fat on clover, waddled into a stand of sumac brush. "It's been too long since I've seen that," he remarked softly.

The pine and spruce trees thickened, sumac and berry bushes covering the forest floor as Matthew carefully picked his way along the overgrown trail. Volcanic rocks bordered the trail, and chipmunks ran up and down the red-barked pines, disturbed by the intruders. Beaver, damming a rippling mountain creek, watched them pass. A bright-eyed hawk, perched high on an aspen limb, waited as they traveled through his domain.

After several hours they entered a small clearing, carpeted by small white flowers and high-meadow daisies. Matthew swung down from his gelding. Taking Wind Dancer's reins, he led the horses to the rippling creek.

Rebecca slid down, ignoring his outstretched hands. His eyes smoldered with just a hint of anger, but he said smoothly, "Very well, Princess. Suit yourself."

"Oh, I intend to have my way, Mr. McKay." She stretched, watching the horses drink the clear, cold water. They were peaceful animals—McKay was another matter.

Matthew talked to the horses gently, checking cinches and rubbing the animals' flanks.

Rebecca plucked a stalk of grass, sticking the sweet end into her mouth. She sprawled on a bed of buttercups, watching him lazily as he dusted his hands and unlashed the food bundle. Tucking it under his arm, he strolled through the sun-dappled clearing toward her.

"Shall we dine?" He grinned and the dimple crept out. "Such a sour face, Becky McKay. Surely no expression for a new bride," he said teasingly.

He settled against a tree trunk and spread the food before

him. "Good. Smoked sausage and freshly baked bread. Apple pie . . . my favorite." He wrapped a fat sausage in a thick slice of bread and handed it to her. "Eat."

She took the bread, meticulously avoiding the touch of his hands. "I intend to have the marriage annulled, Mr. McKay." She shrugged. "I only came with you to settle the matter. And it will be before we arrive home."

"Mmm." He munched on his sausage and bread, watching the horses graze. The sun cut through the pines to touch the rugged planes of his face and the grim set of his mouth.

"You're hardly the picture of the willing bride your father had painted, but there'll be no annulment, Becky. You'll be my wife. Together we'll plant orchards, and together we'll raise a score of children."

"Children!" Becky swallowed the sausage caught in her throat and threw the remainder of the bread to the bushes. "Not on your life, Matthew McKay! I'm only here today to settle the matter—"

"I'm growing a little weary of your delicate nerves."

"Did you think I'd welcome you with open arms?"

"I had that thought, yes." He nodded. "I knew that the wooing would take a little time. But we have our future at stake, and I'm willing to act the suitor for a time. In fact, I've seen couples still act like newlyweds after fifty years of marriage. I will court you, Becky. I can take the stiff-necked pride that causes you to fight me, but be warned, I will not let you go."

She stood shakily. "Never. I was forced into this marriage—trapped."

His voice was low and dangerous. "Forced into this marriage?" he repeated slowly as though chewing the words. "Now, that damages my pride, but make no mistake: You are mine now that I've seen you, and you are better than I expected. You'll be well worth my courting time, lass. And the loving will be sweeter for it. I intend to hold you firm."

Again the burr accented his deep voice, tingling along her neck. The intimate tone stirred something soft and feminine within her. Oh, he had his weapons. Distrusting him, her eyes narrowed. "I could never be fond of you, McKay."

He took a deep breath, his black gaze flowing over her and warming her from head to toe. "Fond? A lukewarm emotion for a favorite flower, not a man. I want more. I like the cut of my wife, Becky. Woman to man, I'd say you could keep me happy—once you're comfortable with me. It's just a matter of time."

"Damned if I will make you happy, sir! I'll shoot you straight in the trousers first," she promised evenly. She trembled as his hot gaze rode down her body, then back up to her flushed face. The man had a way of grinning that was indecent. "Oh, you'll see things my way soon enough. Shall we be going, Mr. McKay?"

Matthew rose to his feet with a long sigh. Then, grinning, he swept his hat before him and bowed from the waist in a courtly manner. "Your wish is my command, Princess."

Chapter Four

Rebecca glared at Matthew's broad back for the next hour. "Men," she muttered darkly, placing her hand on her thigh. "Court me, he says!"

She shifted easily in Wind Dancer's saddle, adjusting her boots in the stirrups. Princess . . . Rebecca mentally repeated Matthew's endearment. She watched a chipmunk forage through the fallen pinecones, stuffing his cheeks with seeds. "Who does that big oaf think he is, my Sir Lancelot? I managed quite well without him!"

Suddenly Matthew tensed, halting his horse quietly. Rebecca drew back on Wind Dancer's reins, guiding him to stand beside the gelding. As she listened, a high-pitched keening rose above the sounds of the forest.

"It's an Indian woman, Matthew," Rebecca whispered, listening to the pain of the song. "She's asking for help from the old gods. Her baby is sick, dying of sores and starvation; his eyes are matted closed." Slipping from her saddle, Rebecca followed the lament. Weaving through the dense underbrush, she heard Matthew following her. She turned to him, raising her finger across her lips in a sign of silence. He nodded, easing aside a chokecherry branch with his arm.

In a small clearing knelt a young Indian woman. Wrapped in a blanket, the girl swayed from side to side. Tears streamed down her round cheeks. She stroked a whimpering baby, swathed in skins and secured to a beaded cradle board.

Rebecca eased to the girl's side, then sat cross-legged, Indian fashion. She touched her shoulder and the girl's large brown eyes lifted. "My baby is sick. My heart is sad," she signed with her hands. "I ask Coyote for help. He is cunning. He will know."

Rebecca spoke quietly, and the girl replied with a sob. She leaned lightly against the white woman in a gesture of defeat. For a long moment Rebecca held the girl's shoulders, comforting her.

Then Rebecca picked up the baby, motioning for the girl to follow her to the horses. Intrigued by Rebecca's grim expression, Matthew stepped aside as the women passed. Dressed in a tattered doeskin dress, the girl turned to him. Her eyes traveled warily from his head to his toes. Suddenly her tearstained face became impassive.

Rebecca glanced at him. "Spread your shirt on the ground. It's cleaner than her blanket. Now," she ordered quietly. "This is Mary, from the Okanogan tribe."

Matthew obeyed, spreading his shirt upon the pine needles. Rebecca cradled the baby for a moment, staring at the garment. "You're a big man, McKay. That shirt is almost as big as a blanket. Here, hold the baby."

She thrust the cradle board into his arms, her glance daring him to object. Matthew tested the baby's swaddling gingerly. "This baby is wet clear through."

But Rebecca had turned and was untying her saddlebags. Frowning, the girl hurried to her. "Boston man bad," she hissed in a guttural accent, using the Indian *Boston* meaning "white man."

The girl needed reassurance, and Matthew watched as Rebecca chewed her bottom lip thoughtfully. Taking a deep, steadying breath, Rebecca strode over and glanced up at him. "No. He is my man," she murmured, avoiding his eyes. A dull flush rose from her neck to her cheeks as she dropped to her knees. She smoothed his shirt with quick, sure movements, then lifted her arms to him. Her eyes flickered, skimmed his chest for an instant, then looked steadily at his face. "I'll take the baby now, Matthew."

Matthew. The sound of his name on her lips startled him. For an instant Matthew forgot the soaking wet infant, forgot Rebecca's bold threats. With her cheeks gently flushed and her arms outstretched, he could almost feel the softness of her wrap around his empty life. His wife . . .

Once, in a wharfside brawl, he'd been hit hard between the eyes. He'd been dazed, barely able to stand. Rebecca's tender side had as much impact as the massive fist of that henchman. So all her brass covered a gentle heart, did it?

"That baby," she repeated slowly, as if he were dense. "Hand him to me."

The girl was wringing her hands and sobbing. *"Mema-loose.* Him *memaloose,"* she cried in the mixed language of English and Chinook.

Rebecca took the cradle board, laying it beside the shirt. "He won't die, Mary. I have good medicine," she said re-assuringly to the girl. Unwrapping the thongs binding the baby to the board, she peeled back the soaked doeskins.

Matthew crouched beside Rebecca, entranced by her graceful movements. In profile she was beautiful, confident as she lifted the frail baby onto his shirt. The black-eyed infant did not blink, though his eyes were matted.

Rebecca flicked an angry glance at Matthew. "Why are you looking at me like that? Stop staring, McKay, and go fetch some water from the creek. Take Mary's little bucket. I'll need your handkerchief to wash the baby."

She glared at him as though expecting an argument. But Matthew, determined to explore his wife's intricacies, simply obeyed. He handed her the linen handkerchief, mono-grammed with a large *M.* "Of course, Becky," he said, knowing she hated using anything of his.

"How gallant." Her eyes darkened before she turned to the baby lying on his shirt. When Matthew returned, Rebecca dipped his handkerchief into the small tin bucket and began to wash the baby, who whimpered, staring at Mary intently.

"Shh, little boy," Rebecca crooned softly. "Shh, little man." She began to hum softly, cleansing the baby tenderly.

Sitting beside her, Matthew had to touch his bride. She seemed unaware when he fitted his large hand to her back. All a mother's tenderness was there, he decided thoughtfully, as her slender hands passed gently over the baby.

Her muscles rippled beneath his palm as she worked. He liked the strong, supple feel of her moving beneath his hands.

The girl wrung her hands again. "Aieee." She began to glance uneasily at Rebecca, then down at her baby. Then, in a rush of Chinook and English and motioning hands, she spoke to the white woman.

Rebecca nodded, gently washing the baby's small feet, one toe at a time. "What is she saying, Becky?" Matthew whispered, noting the girl's anxious glances at him. "It's been too long . . . I've forgotten Chinook."

She continued to cleanse the baby, speaking softly. "She's been tossed out by her Indian husband. The baby is too light-skinned, he says. She's been surviving by trading *kinnik-kinnick*—leaves for the men's smoking pipes."

Rebecca patted the infant dry with the shirtsleeve. Taking a small jar from her saddlebag, she opened it to spread ointment over the baby's spindly body.

"I think we can make do. I'll send a note with her to the ranch—in case she gets there before us. The Indian footpath is more quickly traveled than the horse trail. We can always use another hand at the laundry or during canning."

Wrapping the baby in Matthew's shirt, Rebecca lifted him into her arms. "I'm afraid you've lost your shirt, McKay. This little fellow needs something clean on him for a time, until his sores heal." She rocked the baby, holding the small head close to her neck. As she cooed softly Matthew watched intently, fascinated. The black, shining hair of the Indian baby complimented Rebecca's skin, the sunlight catching in her own black strands.

For an instant he saw into the future, a black-haired son of his own wrapped in her arms. He wrapped his fingers around her slender neck, feeling the delicate bones and smooth flesh of his wife.

"Get your hands off me, McKay," she snapped, turning her head to face him. The image of the peaceful woman cradling a child—blissful motherhood—was shattered by a spitting wildcat with furious eyes.

"McKay?" the girl gasped, pressing her hands to her chest. "Woman-Who-Holds-Lightning has Boston man, McKay? Aiee!" She began to sob, twisting her hands. "Aieee . . ." she wailed.

"Oh, Mary, stop that," Rebecca ordered sharply. "Boston man McKay good."

The girl shook her head, her braids dancing. "No. No. Eric McKay. Him bad Boston man." She glanced warily at Matthew, then at Rebecca and the sleeping baby. "McKay bad," she whispered fearfully.

Rebecca slanted an oblique look up at him, tracing his broad shoulders and chest. "Do you have another shirt in your saddlebags?" she asked quietly. "You're hairy enough and big enough to scare a bear, let alone this poor little girl. She's been through enough."

"She's heard of Eric, that's for sure," Matthew muttered, getting to his feet. "I'll get another shirt."

Moments later he returned. Dressed in a red cotton shirt, he held a small tin of milk before Rebecca. He lifted a spoon. "I think this is a better idea."

Mary gestured frantically, signing to Rebecca. "She's afraid the tin holds Boston evil," his wife whispered, rising to her feet. She placed the baby in his mother's arms. "Stand back a few feet, McKay."

Solemnly Rebecca raised her arms to the skies. "Hold the tin away from you, Matthew. I'm going to shoot the Boston spirits out of it."

"Now, Becky," he began in earnest.

"Afraid?" she asked haughtily. "Don't worry. I am really quite good."

Matthew shook his head. "I like my fingers where they are, thank you."

Holding his eyes, Rebecca drew her Colt. She turned slowly, scanning the tall pines. "Do you see that pinecone on the highest branch, McKay?"

She aimed and fired; the pinecone fell. "Hit it at the stem. It's in perfect shape if you want to inspect it."

Rebecca's jawline was firm, her long-legged stance challenging him. "Remember it," she ordered grimly.

Shaking his head, Matthew stood back and lifted the small tin between his right forefinger and thumb. If she wanted to get rid of him quickly, now was her chance. Somehow he trusted Rebecca's tender side just now. "Blast away, Princess."

For just an instant he thought he saw her first small smile—a precious moment of lips and eyes. He shifted uneasily, looking away. That soft, shy movement of her lips fascinated him.

Then she spoke slowly to Mary, and the young girl held the baby closer, covering his ears. A shot rang out, the pungent scent of gunsmoke tainting the fresh air.

A drop of milk hit Matthew's cheek. The baby squawled.

Matthew swallowed, watched as his wife reholstered her Colt and sauntered up to him. "This is to ease poor Mary's worries about the bad Boston man—"

She tugged his head down to hers.

She kissed him lightly, a mere brush of her warm lips across his. Then, taking the tin from him, she walked back to the Indian mother and wailing baby.

Mary grinned impishly at him as she cradled her baby. Her head bobbed up and down. She giggled against the baby's thick black hair. "McKay good Boston man."

Her face darkened suddenly. "Eric McKay bad," she repeated firmly.

Rebecca sat and took the baby in her arms. Cradling the whimpering child, she looked at Matthew as he walked toward them. "Well?"

He grinned, dropping down beside her. "It worked, Princess. The evil is gone and Mary is happy. I'm proud of you."

Rebecca's lips tightened. "I really don't care if you are or not, McKay."

She poured the milk into the spoon, placing it against the baby's closed mouth. "Take it, little man," she urged, rubbing the back of the spoon back and forth across his lips. "This is good for you. Mmm."

Her softness had returned and Matthew breathed quietly. He watched her patiently rub the drops of milk across the baby's toothless gums. "Poor little fellow. Come on, dumpling," she said.

He wondered then about his vow to win Rebecca's heart, as well as her body. Perhaps it was she—an ebony-haired sorceress—who could capture his heart?

After a time the baby took a little milk and seemed at ease. She teased his chin with the unbound tip of her braid, cooing softly to him.

Mary, seated beside her, giggled.

"The girl is only fourteen or so, McKay," Rebecca murmured.

Mary giggled again, hiding her face behind her hands. "McKay kiss-kiss." She kissed the back of her hand and giggled again. "McKay big Boston man. Need big blankets. Big—"

Mary stooped suddenly as Rebecca's head pivoted toward her. "No more, Mary," she ordered between her teeth.

"She's right," Matthew teased. "I *am* a big man."

Her eyebrows arched, the vein at the base of her throat throbbing against the smooth skin. "Is it true that Irishmen kiss the Blarney stone, Mr. McKay? Don't get ideas to suit your size. Mary needed reassurance, and it seemed to be the right thing to do," she stated loftily.

He trailed a fingertip down her hot cheek. "Oh, I think we might kiss again."

He wanted her; desire throbbed within him almost painfully. But he could wait.

He would court her. Then she would come to him.

"I won't let you go," he promised in a rough whisper. "You'll be worth the wait."

"Never," she whispered raggedly. But Matthew saw the sliver of doubt—or was it fear?—before she lowered her lids.

"I am a patient man, Princess. And I've always liked challenges. Keep throwing down the gauntlet, will you?" he said, and left.

After leaving Mary, Rebecca followed Matthew. She hadn't liked his fierce promise, nor the warm lights dancing in his eyes. She had the odd premonition that McKay could be as smooth as satin or as hard as river flint.

Either way, he disturbed her. He touched something restless and empty within her, heating it and making her ache for more.

By early afternoon the trail ended at the crumbling edge of a canyon. Bright sunshine blinded Rebecca when they first emerged from the dense pines. Below them, nestled in the valley, were several outbuildings, a crumbling ranch house, and a barn. Overgrown fields and orchards spread around the buildings like a tattered patchwork quilt.

"See those rocks," Matthew said, nodding toward a small pyramid beneath a pine tree. "They mark the boundary of Pa's homestead. There's a Cayuse warrior and a white claim jumper buried beneath it. They killed each other on the spot. Died like two bucks locking horns in mortal combat."

He paused, straightening in the saddle and lifting his face to the wind. "It's still there," he murmured slowly. "The scent of my mother's roses." Matthew let the chestnut gelding carefully pick his way down the rocky slope.

As Rebecca urged Wind Dancer to follow, a cottontail rabbit bounded across the trail before her. The big horse reared slightly, then scrambled for footing as the rocks slid from beneath his hooves.

"Easy, boy!" Reacting instantly, Rebecca clamped her legs to his belly and held fast to the saddle horn. The stallion found safe footing and snorted almost arrogantly. She patted his muscled neck, speaking calmly, her glove wrapped in his dark brown mane. "Good boy, Wind Dancer."

When she looked up, she met Matthew's eyes. His expression caused her heart to pound. From beneath the shadows of his hat his eyes blazed fiercely at her. His jaw was hard, his mouth grim—Matthew looked every inch to be a seasoned Westerner. "Becky? Are you all right?" he demanded sharply.

She frowned and felt her hackles rise—she didn't need him taking care of her. He hadn't the right to any part of her. "I can outride you any day. Take care of yourself."

"You've a shrew's tongue, Princess. When a gentleman inquires about your health, you should be more pleasant." Matthew's face was dark, and for just a moment Rebecca felt a thread of uncertainty snake through her.

"And you're such a gentleman, I suppose," she shot back recklessly.

"I can be," he stated between his teeth.

"Oh, and where is all your fabled patience? You look as though you might have lost it," she taunted, feeling her anger rise.

He stared at her, the silence drifting between them. "It has an end, Becky." Turning in the saddle, Matthew shot a last scowl at her over the width of his shoulder. When he turned back to the trail, Rebecca stuck out her tongue.

At the bottom of the canyon Matthew dismounted. "We'll walk from here."

She hesitated. Matthew could throw out orders but she wouldn't jump to obey.

But *it* was there—the lure of a forgotten time, the dreams of a fur trader turned family man. The legendary McKay homestead, almost swallowed by the years, beckoned to her. Slowly, because she wanted to, she swung to the ground, holding Wind Dancer's reins.

"It's the same," he said softly, gazing over the homestead. "Beautiful and wild, even in its old age."

Matthew glanced at her as they walked, leading the horses through the thigh-high grass. He smiled, teasing her. "Beautiful and wild like my Becky—with the green eyes and the soft skin."

"Rebecca," she corrected instantly. "I'm damned tired of your use of my childhood name." But he was wrapped up in his own thoughts, walking slowly through the clumps of the bunchgrass.

He breathed heavily, as though absorbing the sweet aura of his childhood. He searched the overgrown fields and the wild mountains surrounding the homestead. "My God, I loved it here. I spent years yearning to come back, but something always got in the way."

"I've heard so much about this homestead," Rebecca murmured, looking around her. "It is so beautiful."

"That it is, Becky," Matthew agreed softly. "I remember when Pa's friends spent a month over there." He nodded to an aspen grove. "They were seasoned fur trappers, old Indian fighters, with a bluecoat or a Reb thrown in from the Civil War."

He smiled briefly. "They fairly drooled when Ma took her fresh-baked bread and pies to their camp—they called it a rendezvous. But they really just wanted some peace, a quiet place to rest their bones from the Indians. The Indians believe this is a special valley . . . Ma's healing powers had a lot to do with that. They thought she was a shaman."

He looked away, scanning the old homestead and plucking memories from time. "He bought her, an indentured Irish servant girl with a baby. She wouldn't have him without marriage. To get her into his bed—he stopped a gin-soaked traveling preacher and they were married. She was a small woman with flaming red hair who loved a rough, 'woodsy man.' Some said she had second sight; she healed with her herbs."

"I remember the story. Papa said McKay was like dough in her hands."

"Pa said he was daft over her. He was like a wounded bear when she died."

"And then you left?" she prompted, intrigued by Matthew's life. He had loved the mountains but had left. Why?

"I should have understood," he growled. "The man was in pain—"

"You were a boy," she interrupted gently.

"A boy who couldn't wait to get away from his father."

"Why didn't you come back sooner?" she asked, glancing

at the hard set of his jaw. Matthew's expressions raced across his face, his emotions spread out before her. The wind ruffled his hair, softening his rugged face. He smiled sadly. For a fleeting second she saw a boy in his teens, uncertain yet bold, challenging the world.

He shrugged. "At first it was pride. Then later, time just drifted away as I traveled across the world. When I heard of the Indian scare back in '91, I made plans to come back. Business interfered—logging and shipping around the Great Lakes got me a start in whaling. Then in '96, the Klondike fever broke and my passenger freight from San Francisco kept me running. Before that I was sent to Cuba and later to China. By then my business in San Francisco badly needed tending, and somehow I never got back. It happens. We run around, forgetting where we're running to. It seemed there was always another challenge—"

"I see." Rebecca sidestepped a chuckhole, tugging Wind Dancer's reins. The Appaloosa whinnied. "Oh, look! Over there by those rocks. A doe and her fawn."

Matthew glanced at the deer, then turned back to Rebecca. "They are lovely, Becky. Suited to the high country. You wouldn't be happy living in a city, would you?" he asked quietly.

Rebecca lifted her head, enjoying the warmth of the sun on her face. A bumblebee droned and the chirping of birds filled the air. "There is nothing like the high country. The water is sweet to drink and the smell of the pine is on the wind. It's much better than the sagebrush flats and the sand near the river. Though I love them, too."

"I feel the same, Becky," Matthew murmured, patting Wind Dancer's neck as he moved closer to her.

As she walked slowly beside him, Rebecca's senses began tingling. Her head reached his shoulder, his body much bigger and broader than her own. He had the look of a mountain hunter now, a lean Westerner walking his land.

The deep rasp of his voice moved something within her, something she didn't quite trust. Matthew did have a way about him, which made her feel soft and warm and vaguely wanting to be . . . cuddled by him.

She reached out to crush a dried stalk, suddenly remembering the sight of his bare chest. She had wanted to touch him, to push her fingers through the dark hair covering his chest and veeing down to his belt. Warily she inched away from him. Matthew's size and strength could overpower her easily, given the chance. She couldn't step too close to him. Not without her Colt.

Matthew patted her shoulder, his broad palm cupping it. "Don't look so fierce, Becky. You look like you're thinking of going on the warpath." He tugged her braid. "I'd like to see all this tucked up in a warbonnet."

She moved from beneath his hand. "When I do fight, you'll know it."

He chuckled, skimming a finger down her cheek. "No doubt. I wouldn't want to be on the business end of your gun. You handle it like a gunfighter. Why did you learn to shoot that particular way, Becky?" he asked quietly.

"Many of the women here wear guns, McKay."

"Over their skirts. Not low on their hips and tied to their thighs. Unless I miss my guess, your Peacemaker has had the hammer and the trigger doctored for a fast-draw shootout. Why?"

McKay was a tracker, prowling around the edges of a fear she'd fought for two long years. She had to protect herself against the weakness of her shame, keep him a safe distance from her wounds.

"That's my business," she returned, looking at him defiantly. She'd put Rudy into the past, and she didn't intend McKay to drag him out again.

Yet he had. A tiny sliver of fear went scooting through her, her stomach contracting, as though struck by Rudy's fists.

McKay was there by the grace of her father's honor and her love for her parent.

He studied her with one of those long, quiet looks that seemed to probe beneath her skin. "I see. In time, then, when you trust me enough to share your secrets.'' His statement was slow and firm and grated at her nerves.

"Your patience again, McKay?" she asked archly. "I could shoot holes all through it.''

He looked down at her, his eyes dark and brooding. "You just might be able to do that. But there will come a time—''

"You are surely thickheaded, McKay.''

"I am merely determined, Princess." Taking her left hand, he lifted it to his lips. He kissed the back of her glove, looking into her eyes. "And by the way, when you handled the baby, I noticed you weren't wearing my ring.''

There was that note of possession, of wearing his brand that brought back another time when she'd hungered for Rudy's simple gold band. Rebecca's knees went weak, her stomach knotted, and her breath caught in her lungs. She found herself returning his stare—drowning in it, her heartbeat quickening. "I . . . it didn't seem fitting . . . under the circumstances. I mean, it's much too pretty.''

"You're a lovely woman. You were made for lovely things. Made for a man. And I want you to wear my ring, Princess.''

Rebecca's heart skipped a beat. Part of her wanted to run. But a softer, warmer element wanted simply to place her bare palm against his rough cheek.

Within his black eyes, her reflection looked back at her. "I think we can manage, Becky," he whispered softly. The deep rasp of his voice slid over her like velvet. "We're two of a kind, you see.''

"No . . .'' Her heart raced frantically within her chest. Her body began that strange tingling as he lowered his cheek to hers, nuzzling her gently.

"Oh, I think so," he breathed against her ear. His jaw was hard, heating her flesh before he stepped back.

Rebecca trembled, feeling the scrape of his new beard still on her skin.

"Such big eyes, Becky.''

Matthew raised her hand slowly and sighed, nodding toward a small orchard. "Fruit trees. Pa must have planted them later. His first trees came from Okanogan Smith's orchard. Now there are several orchards started along the Columbia.''

Rebecca rubbed her hand against her cheek, dashing away his clinging warmth. She wanted no part of him touching her, hurting her. ''And on the Okanogan River. Some of the gold miners and trappers have made nice homesteads here,'' Rebecca added without thinking. ''There are settlers, post offices and towns . . .''

''We agree, then. This country is bursting with life, Becky. The railroads and the steamboats can take our harvests to the world. Wheat and fruit could make this young state famous. And we can be a part of it all.''

Rebecca shifted uneasily beneath his penetrating stare. ''We can do it, Becky,'' he whispered urgently. ''You and me.''

His fingertip raised her chin, his eyes narrowing. ''Smell the wind, Becky. Feel the dreams weaving around us. It's a new time and a new land.''

''I know,'' she agreed softly, caught by his excitement.

''I thought you would understand. You are high-spirited, Becky. There are secrets lurking around you that I want to uncover. But you're tender and steadfast—I saw that when you took care of Mary. You'd be a good one to have at a man's side. Or at his back in the bad times.''

Suddenly her throat felt dry. Matthew would want more than any other man, she decided instantly. When he spoke of his dreams, she could almost feel them move inside her.

She'd believed in dreams once. Believed in a man she'd given her heart to. . . .

''Give us time, Becky,'' he urged softly, running his thumb across her smooth cheek.

A coyote sprinted out of the house as they approached. The McKay home seemed to ramble endlessly in a nest of overgrown brush. The logs had settled, causing the house to slope at one corner. Wide, broken steps led to a large porch. The moss-covered roof had two large holes and was missing its wooden shingles.

McKay was silent as he walked slowly up the steps and through the open doorway.

Curious, Rebecca dropped Wind Dancer's reins to follow Matthew. The old planks creaked beneath her boots as she entered the house. Cupboards, with broken shelves, were empty. Doors leading into other rooms hung loosely on their brass hinges. Rotting aspen leaves littered a rusty black cook stove, and a black stovepipe slanted against a wall.

Matthew moved deeper into the house and she waited. The sunlight shot through the gaping hole in the roof. Pinecones had fallen into a mound on the rough-hewn floor. Passersby had discarded empty tins on the mound.

Time had tinted the windows blue, one smashed by a great limb lying upon the board floor. The smell of mold and decay spread through the large, deserted room, which had once served as a sitting room and a kitchen.

Matthew returned, his expression grim. For a moment she thought she saw pain, soon replaced by a hard look daring her to speak. "Not pretty, is it? The rest of the house is as bad," he growled, almost to himself. "I'm going outside."

Rebecca followed him, watched him move easily through the heavy brush toward the smokehouse. Matthew seemed to glide on his long legs, she decided. He moved gracefully, his broad back rippling beneath the red cotton shirt.

She crossed her arms across her chest and stood watching him. McKay had the kind of lean, muscled look—flat-bellied and trim-hipped—that wouldn't thicken with age. For a big man he moved lightly, stalking rather than walking, long legs quickly crossing the weed-encrusted grounds.

He took off his hat, wiping his forehead with his sleeve. Fascinated by the sunlight touching his rumpled waves of hair, Rebecca settled against an old hitch rail.

Matthew had a look about him that she liked, she admitted warily. Stripped of his city suit and dressed to ride, he could possibly make some poor woman's heart flutter. Black-haired and black-eyed, he had it in him to torment women. But she'd been burned badly by trusting another man and couldn't bear to open that door again.

Rebecca's mouth twisted and she could almost taste the bitterness rising within. She shifted her weight uneasily, glancing at a fat groundhog foraging at the back of an old chicken house.

Oh, he was the same breed of man as Rudy . . . a drifter, making his fortune and hungering for more.

But then Rudy had never really looked at her with that dark, smoldering look fraught with promise—and Rudy had never made her knees grow weak. . . .

Bending, she snatched a fallen twig from the earth, snapping it between her hands. To be used as a pawn for her father's honor was to be expected. But she had to stop McKay before he entered the dark domain of her fears, shaming her.

She clung to her pride, patched its tears, and now fought for her family name. McKay would not bring down that name.

She unsaddled the horses, swinging the heavy pack from the gelding to the old porch. She walked the horses to a small clearing near the house and tied their reins loosely to fallen limbs. They grazed on the tender green shoots of range grass as she tossed a horse blanket on the ground. Lying stomach down, she watched Matthew walk through the deserted orchards.

He did have a way about him. If ever a man had been beautiful simply to watch move, Matthew was that man.

She closed her eyes and remembered the stories of King Arthur and his Knights of the Round Table. She'd loved them as a child, dreaming of her own white knight. . . .

A bumblebee droned lazily over her head and the sun warmed her back—

She realized she had been sleeping when he shook her shoulder. "Wake up, Sleeping Beauty."

Matthew squatted on his haunches, shading her from the brilliant sun. She wiped her eyes, holding the blanket as she struggled to her feet. "Are you ready to leave?"

He stood, looking down at her intently. "We're here for the night, Becky. Everything we need is in the pack." The husky tone caught at Rebecca's raw nerves.

Fully awake now, Rebecca took a deep breath. What kind

of man would torment a half-awake woman? He was cruel, to boot—of the same blood as Rudy. "Not me, McKay. I'm leaving. You do what you want."

"I want my bride beside me. We need this time to know each other." He frowned, his finger tracing her cheek. "Don't tremble so, lass. You're wild-eyed and pale. I thought we were getting to know each other better. . . ."

Chapter Five

"We talked," she said, correcting him and twisting from his touch. "That's all. I made no promises. I will not make a home with you, McKay, let alone stay the night."

Matthew's frown deepened. Beneath his dark skin a muscle tightened in his lean cheek and slid down his muscular throat. "I thought you were beginning to see. Have I hurt you, Becky? What is this—"

Rebecca jammed her fists into her waist. Slip up on her like a rattlesnake, would he? McKay had the neat trick of lighting her temper like a match to a dried pinecone. So she was simply to comply with his plans, like a sheep led to slaughter? Surely the family honor didn't demand that sacrifice! "I will not spend the night up here . . . with you. The whole countryside will talk about us, you and me." Her cheeks heated and she tossed her head defiantly. The man had assumed his right of possession, his right to make decisions for *her* life.

McKay's eyes and mouth had a set to them she didn't like— much too stubborn. "I am going home now, Mr. McKay."

"You are staying, Mrs. McKay." His deep voice had a flat edge to it, as though he held the upper hand. She quickly traced the tense set of his shoulders. This McKay had a temper, barely leashed.

She'd seen a man's rage unleashed and cruel; bracing herself, Rebecca fought the fear sliding within. . . .

He stared at her from between narrowed lids, his head tilted to one side. He studied her until her heart raced and her flesh heated. She didn't like him trying to unravel her innermost secrets as though it were his right.

After a long moment he breathed deeply, then winked and grinned. "I haven't started to court you yet. You just might like—"

His dimple slipped into the darkness of his cheek and Rebecca glared at it. She blinked, cursing it. Her stomach fluttered and she clenched her fists to keep from launching into him. "You're arrogant. Out-and-out arrogant." She looked him up and down scathingly. "Court me? You?"

Rebecca's nails bit into her palms. Once she'd been courted and twisted and used. Perhaps all men played the same game. . . .

Before she could move, Matthew stretched out his arm. His long fingers wrapped around her neck. His thumb caressed the hollow at the base of her throat. "Who else would court you, Princess? I am your husband and you're a beautiful woman, my wife. See? Even now your heartbeat runs wild beneath my touch."

She couldn't move, held by the fear locking her limbs.

His thumb slid up and down her throat lightly, his eyes darkening. "Soft, soft skin," he murmured, as though to himself. Then, meeting her eyes, he said, "I know you're not accustomed to a man touching you. You bristle like a porcupine when I get too close to you. Don't be afraid."

Within her she repeated, "Afraid?" How dare he give a name to her tumbling emotions! She controlled the fear, concealing and protecting it. Yet McKay thought he had the right to enter her private arenas.

Rebecca angrily slapped away his hand. "Of you? Never."

He lifted his eyebrows, his black eyes dancing. "Of course you are. It's only natural for a virgin. Though after I've taught you to kiss, things between us will go more easily. Such soft lips. . . . Are you afraid to kiss me, Becky?"

Afraid? Why did he have to taunt her, challenging her control?

When his gaze brushed her mouth and lingered there, she trembled.

Rebecca danced back, looking up at him warily. She forced herself to swallow. "McKay, I warn you—"

He grinned, a masculine blend of twinkling eyes and white teeth. "And I warn you, Princess. I've probably got the best kiss you've ever tasted."

"Cocky devil, aren't you?" she managed huskily. She'd been kissed before too. But McKay's mouth seemed different . . . no, it couldn't be—

He took a step nearer and Rebecca immediately dropped her hand to her Colt. His grin widened. "I've been told that I do have a way about me. Shall we give it a try? Are those lips of yours really as soft as they appear?"

She couldn't breathe, her skin both hot and cold in the sweet mountain air. Her boots seemed to sink an inch deeper in the black, fertile dirt. She forced herself to swallow, her tongue darting out to moisten her bottom lip.

Matthew's gaze darkened, following the motion. "Come on, Becky. I'll teach you."

"I know how to kiss, McKay, thank you very much. But you take one step closer and I'll—"

Matthew caught her fingers and, with his free hand, lifted the Colt to toss it to the ground. "That's a nasty habit," he whispered, his eyes narrowing. "You could be dangerous in a high temper. I won't have you playing fast-draw every time I want to touch you."

He laced his fingers with hers. The warm strength of them caused her skin to tingle, her knees to weaken. The pad of his thumb smoothed the back of her hand, his eyes gleaming.

She wanted to draw away. Or to fight him tooth and nail. But somehow she couldn't move. Meeting his stare, Rebecca forced herself to breathe. Matthew had sighted down on her as though she were a doe before his rifle. She felt the air, still around them, felt her muscles tense.

"May I have that kiss now, Princess?" Bending over her,

lowering his head to hers, Matthew held her stare. His free hand soothingly stroked the fine hair at her temple. His voice held a rasp that made her tremble. "Your eyes are as big as saucers . . . as though a man could drop into green velvet if he looked long enough. Don't be afraid."

The heat of his body warmed her, filled her senses, and the word *afraid* echoed through the sunlight and shadows. From deep within, Rebecca found the strength to move . . . she had to survive.

"No!" She pivoted, holding Wind Dancer's blanket firmly, her heavy braid whipping against Matthew's chest. When she whistled, Wind Dancer pranced, lifting his head to free his reins from the light wrap on the fallen limb.

"Becky!" Matthew caught her arm but she slashed the blanket at his face. She was frightened of the fear rising within her, giving her strength.

He grunted, releasing her in his surprise. He caught the blanket and threw it to the ground. "What in sweet hell . . ."

Free now, she whistled for Wind Dancer once more and ran for the old house. Matthew's heavy stride sounded on the earth behind her. But he moved less quickly through the thick brush. Behind her, he yelled, "Damn it, Becky! Stop running like a frightened doe. I won't hurt you."

Did all men make promises they didn't keep? she wondered fleetingly.

McKay had jumped inside her fear and used it against her, controlling her. The knowledge sent a hot wave of sheer anger washing over her.

Who was this man to reach inside her?

"Get away from me!" Sensing him at her back, she turned, glaring at him. Placing her hands on her hips, she tossed her head. The thick braid slithered down across her breasts. "You're winded," she accused haughtily, looking him up and down boldly, as though he were a stallion up for sale. "Old. If you weren't the size of a moose, I could outrun you."

He stopped, head tilted, breathing hard. He scowled at her. "You're damned fast, woman. Though after a distance I would have caught you. I don't care for the idea of my wife

running from me at all. There's no reason to hurt yourself
over a little kiss. It happens all the time between husbands
and wives.''

"Hurt myself?'' she repeated, feeling like a cornered bobcat. McKay did need some rough edges trimmed off him if
he thought she would hurt herself. ''You're the one out of
breath!''

"I really don't like my wife running from me,'' Matthew
repeated carefully, his dark cheeks showing an angry spot of
color. His eyes glittered between his heavy lashes. The flat
of his hand rubbed his jaw. ''People will say that I beat you.''

"Oh, I suppose you'd do that too,'' she threw back angrily.
Right now she just didn't care what he liked or what people
said. But she did care about the way she flushed when he
looked down at her, as though he were the White Knight
claiming the hand of the Princess.

He'd called her Princess. Her eyes narrowed. A sweet talker
couldn't be trusted. She'd learned that with Rudy.

He breathed heavily, his lips pressed together so tightly
that they turned pale. ''I can think of much sweeter torment.''

For just an instant Rebecca wondered about his meaning.
Then her blood heated. Matthew could torment another
woman—Cuban señoritas and Chinese concubines—for all she
cared. She wanted out of his web. And she didn't like being
stalked. ''That will be the day, McKay.''

"Now, Becky, surely you can call me Matthew,'' he said
soothingly in that low drawl that made her want to . . . do
something.

She felt herself simmer in her anger, searching for the
words that would not cross her lips. McKay needed a taking-
down. His male arrogance sheared a little around the edges.

"Such a temper,'' Matthew taunted before he swooped,
wrapping his arms around her. Grinning, he lifted her from
the ground. Her boots dangled in midair.

He handled her as easily as a child, she thought dazedly.
For a big man he moved quickly.

His chuckle was rich with pleasure. ''A romp though the

pastures with you stirs a man's senses. But then, chasing you is a delight. You have such a nicely formed . . . backside. I'd hate to see your . . . mmm . . . softer parts covered with skirts and a bustle. Though when we socialize with the neighbors, I request that you at least wear skirts.''

Rebecca gasped, finding her hands helplessly trapped beneath his strong arms, her face near his. And the damning dimple.

"I've worn trousers for years," she protested, hating the catch in her voice. "You're lordly commands are useless."

"Time to change," he whispered huskily. "I won't have other men looking at those long legs of yours. I have the feeling that I'm going to be very possessive of you, Princess.'' From between heavy lids he intently studied the soft turn of her mouth. As though he wanted to taste her . . .

"You . . . are . . . fresh, Mr. McKay. A lecher for certain.'' Rebecca took a deep breath, then realized that her breasts were pressed against Matthew's chest. The solid muscle flattening her softness made her feel full and aching.

She remembered his darkly tanned chest, the rough covering of hair. She closed her eyes, and instantly the pale softness of her own breasts appeared behind her lids—pressed against the muscled planes of Matthew's chest.

Her lower stomach heated, her private feminine softness . . .

She forced her eyes open. Matthew McKay had all sorts of sneaky ways about him. A proper woman of the day didn't melt and think about . . . her naked body pressed against a man's! She squirmed within his careful grasp, realizing for the first time how gently he held her.

"A lecher," she accused shakily, aware that her cheeks were hot. "If it weren't for my father, I wouldn't come within ten miles of you."

"And you, Mrs. McKay, are quite a handful." Matthew chuckled and kissed her parted lips. His voice held a timbre that frightened her, darkly luring her. "Quite a stirring handful.''

Rebecca's fingers moved restlessly, wanting to trace that dimple sliding over his dark, rough skin.

He was too strong, too possessive and assured of his way with her. When would he turn on her? She swallowed the dryness in her throat, knowing that her pride could not stand a second lashing.

Running her tongue along her bottom lip, Rebecca tasted his light kiss. McKay played a taunting game, did he?

Why was she left with the hunger to taste?

His gaze darkened. "You have an untouched way about you. I'm pleased that you've saved yourself for me."

Closing her eyes, Rebecca frowned. Rudy had wanted to rake her virginity from her, his "prize" for courting her.

"I want down." His belt buckle tangled with her shirt, biting into the soft flesh of her abdomen. Matthew's body was too solid when pressed against hers. She felt him stir, hard and male, against her feminine softness.

Rebecca trembled, breathing hard. She fought the desire to push closer against him, to tangle her fingers in his wind-tossed hair, to feel the strands cling to her skin.

"I'll let you go for a kiss, lass," he said huskily, his eyes glittering as she nervously licked her bottom lip. "A small peck, right on my mouth."

Her eyes widened. McKay was shocking. "It's full daylight!"

He laughed outright. "Ah, Becky, are you going to make me court you, then? When it comes night?"

"Not at all. I don't want your kisses, your ring, your—" She closed her lips. Somehow her palm had come to rest on his bare chest. She felt the heavy thud of his heart beneath her glove. She lifted her hand carefully, easing back from him. The fire in her was too dangerous. . . .

"Touch me," he urged softly, huskily. "Take off your gloves and touch me with your hands."

"No," she managed, fighting the desire to skim the hair with her fingertips.

He breathed slowly, watching her intently. "A small kiss, then, Becky. Just a taste and I'll let you go." He smiled gently. "There's no help for it, lass. I am a determined man."

Men always bargained, she thought dully in some part of

her brain. Offering daughters and wanting wives, salving their pride. "Then you'll let me go?"

He nodded solemnly. "I promise. You have my word as a gentleman."

"A gentleman, he says," she muttered darkly. "I'm sure a gentleman would hold a lady against her wishes."

"Do it or I'll hold you like this until the morning," he ordered, grinning.

"If there's no help for it, then," she said with a tired sigh. Taking a deep breath, Rebecca closed her eyes and pursed her lips. She felt the easy rise and fall of his chest against her, the wide span of his hands smoothing her back.

"You kiss me, Princess," he urged roughly. "Put those sweet lips on mine."

"Oh, damnation," she whispered before pushing her mouth to his parted one.

Matthew held perfectly still as their lips met.

Rebecca felt the firm masculine contours heat her lips, felt his slight breath on her cheek.

It sprang back to life—the warm, melting need to touch him, to press herself deeper in his arms. To run her hands over the hard muscles and rough skin, exploring. . . .

She moved her mouth softly across his, discovering the texture of Matthew's mouth. He tasted of smoke and an intriguing scent all his own. She pressed her lips to the corners of his mouth, felt his lips stir, moving against hers.

She needed to move closer, intrigued by his taste.

Taking a deep breath, Rebecca heard herself moan softly, her lips parting.

The heat was there, throbbing between them, luring her to press tiny kisses along the line of his mouth.

After the moment when time stopped, Matthew groaned, lowering her feet to the ground. He raised his hand to cradle the back of her head, then eased his mouth down on hers.

Rebecca's fingers clenched, easing upward to grasp his belt. She clung to that leather strip as Matthew deepened the kiss, slanting his mouth across hers. His free hand roamed her back, his broad palm warming her as it caressed.

Then, teasing her with small kisses, Matthew slowly released her. "I like that . . . your lips all soft from my kiss."

Rebecca breathed heavily, staring up at him. She tried to stiffen her weakened legs and quiet her racing heart. She cleared her throat, fighting the urge to wrap her arms around him again.

His smoldering gaze warmed her, making her feel womanly, desired, and aching for his touch.

She took a deep breath, glancing away from him to see if the earth had melted since his kiss. She touched her mouth with her fingertips and for the moment allowed herself to return Matthew's tender stare.

"Don't worry so," he offered softly.

Smoothing back the tendrils dancing along her temple, he tugged her earlobe gently. "First things first, Becky. For tonight we'll do the best we can with the old homestead. There's sufficient food in the pack, and I can fix the stove with no trouble, while you clear out some of the dirt. Working together, we should be able to spend the night comfortably."

He bent, tearing wild grass from the roots while Rebecca stared at him.

Why had he stopped the kiss? she wondered in a daze, watching his almost graceful movements.

She had wanted more, wanted to wrap her arms around him, to cling to him.

She frowned. She felt like a salmon on land, left gasping for air while he calmly fashioned a broom from the grass.

She ran the back of her hand across her mouth, her lips sensitive to the touch.

Rudy had kissed her and had wanted her. He had complimented her and gazed at her like any proper beau. But, damnation, he had never made her tremble, made her ache. Was this Matthew's brand of courting? To prey upon her curiosity, her hunger?

She picked up her Colt, holstering it carefully. She watched Matthew from the corner of her eye as she folded the horse blanket. She held it against her, realizing the unfamiliar heaviness of her breasts. They ached uncomfortably. Why?

Him and his sneaky ways, she decided finally, glaring at him. Just who did he think he was, setting up rules for kissing and telling her that she was his woman? "Mr. Matthew McKay has quite a bit to learn about me," she muttered darkly. "I can't be shoved around with a few stolen kisses."

Matthew moved like a mountain cat, gathering the dried stalks into his hands. Moments later he presented her with a crude broom. She frowned at his wide grin. Looking like a pleased boy might weaken some feminine heart, but not hers.

She didn't have to play his game. Preserving her father's honor had nothing to do with McKay's lusty needs.

Threatening him with her stare, Rebecca grabbed the broom and strode to the wood steps. "If you come near me again, Mr. McKay," she threatened, lifting the broom to him, "I'll gore you with this."

She didn't trust the ebony eyes beneath the half-lowered lids. Rawboned, Matthew stood with his hands on his hips, his shirt open, revealing the black coarseness covering his chest. "Ah, you're a warmhearted lass, Becky. As sweet as taffy."

"Hmmpf!"

He grinned. With his hands on his hips and the wind ruffling his black hair, Matthew had the rakish look of a pirate. "I've always liked taffy."

Rebecca look at him down her nose. "Your sweet tooth is not my concern, Mr. McKay."

"Oh, it will be. I promise you that."

She raised her chin. "I'm only spending the night because of Wind Dancer. I don't want him lame."

"Of course, Princess," he agreed too easily.

"I don't trust you," she stated evenly. "You have sneaky ways about you."

His dark eyebrows lifted, his expression all innocence. "Me?"

Rebecca stalked into the house and began sweeping with a violence she wanted to use on Matthew. He made her feel limp and hot and angry, all at different times.

At this instant she knew the real meaning of the word *warpath*.

An hour later Rebecca stuffed the dry pinecones she had gathered into the round hole of the old stove. Striking a match, she lowered the flame, touching it to the cones. When they caught fire, she dropped small branches on top of the growing flames. The fire consumed the sticks and she thought of Matthew's kiss—how it had consumed her. . . .

A warm draft swirled around her face, filled with scents of crushed rose petals and dried lavender. The sweet scents bound her as a woman's lifting whisper asked, *"Rebecca?"*

Rebecca shook her head, clearing it, yet the draft continued to play on her face, luring her. The whisper was no more than the sighing of the wind in the tree boughs outside, she decided uneasily.

"Rebecca?"

Just then the door to the other room creaked, slowly opening. The draft stirred the musty scents, luring Rebecca to enter.

In the shadows a mirror caught the evening light passing through the old windows. The mirror shimmered, cobwebs swaying around it like old lace. Moving toward the wood-framed mirror, Rebecca felt the draft brush her face like a warm caress.

The dusty, silver square beckoned, strangely warm to her touch as she placed her palm flat upon it. The scents of crushed roses and lavender hovered near her, restlessly touching her senses.

Rebecca ran her fingers over the smooth surface and felt a warm wash of pleasure. She almost felt the woman who had owned the mirror smiling back at her.

Shaking her head, she walked from the room and firmly closed the door.

The front door creaked and Matthew hummed an Irish tune as he carried in chopped wood. "Good, I see you know how to start a fire. I like a useful woman."

"Of course I'm not helpless," she snapped. She didn't like the jaunty angle of his hat, nor the pleased look to his mouth. He'd gotten his way, had he? she fumed, glaring at him.

She plopped in a chair. Mr. McKay had better cherish his small victories because she was determined to win the war.

Night settled softly into the valley. The firelight flickered over the cleaned room, aiding the light of the candle on the table. Matthew carried in his pack, then opened it in a clean corner.

He glanced at her, lifting an iron skillet as easily as if it were a feather. "All the comforts of home."

Crouched by the open pack, Matthew selected his food-stuff. His back rippled beneath his shirt, his arms and legs muscular, stretching his clothing. He was strong, she decided darkly, remembering his arms holding her off the ground. And he moved quickly, though she could outrun him in a sprint.

Sleeves rolled up, boots off, his stocking feet padding between stove and table, Matthew was clearly home. He'd lost the look of the city and taken the look of the West. She didn't like that—not a bit. And she didn't like her future to be decided for her.

Rebecca protectively drew her jacket around her, barely checking her rising temper and sorting out the facts. Matthew had been prepared to spend the night at the cabin. In fact, her family must have known his plans.

"We could have ridden home today, Mr. McKay. I've ridden after nightfall before. But I didn't want to damage Wind Dancer," she snapped, prodding him. His confidence angered her every minute. She stood, feet apart, arms akimbo. "Just how the sweet hell did all the cooking gear and blankets get in that pack? I thought it was supplies for your ranch."

Matthew's dark gaze stroked the length of her taut body. "We needed time alone. We can't begin a marriage under the eyes of the whole family. Surely even you can see that."

He turned his back to her, tending to the skillet of sizzling potatoes. "By the way, I'm not cooking all our meals in the future. How do you like your steak, Becky? Bring them to me, will you?''

"You will find, Mr. McKay, that I don't like being ordered around.''

He raised an eyebrow. "But, Princess, I merely asked.''

Rebecca stalked to the pack. She snatched a likely-looking paper-wrapped parcel and threw it on the table. "There. Cook away. I want mine well done.''

That flicker of anger leapt in his dark eyes for only an instant, and Rebecca felt herself tensing for a brawl that did not come. "We're both tired, Princess. And my patience is wearing a trifle thin.'' Deftly he unwrapped the meat and plopped it into the heated skillet.

She glared at him as he prepared the meal with easy skill. He was the type of man to do everything with a certain grace, she decided darkly. But he'd have to find someone else for his marriage plans.

Placing the steaming plates on the table, Matthew stood to his full height. His hands spanned his lean waist, eyes narrowed on her.

He sighed, fitting his body onto a rickety chair. "You're spoiling for a fight tonight, and I'm not going to give it to you.''

"I really don't like you very much, Mr. McKay,'' Rebecca stated cautiously as she stalked back to the table. "In fact, I don't think I like you at all.''

She ate ravenously under Matthew's watchful eyes. "You've a hearty appetite for a woman.'' He sipped his coffee from a blue granite cup. "But the food was good, if I say so myself. There's nothing like the mountain air to build hunger.''

He took a small tin from his chest pocket. He flipped open the lid to reveal thin cheroots and offered them to her. "Smoke?''

Shoving her empty plate away, her fingers gripping the mug tightly, Rebecca leaned forward on her elbows, her eyes piercing the glittering of his. "I do as I damn well please, Mr. McKay. And I choose not to smoke.''

Matthew lit the cheroot and studied her through the blue-gray smoke. "Do you now? I've had a wearing day, or I wouldn't smoke, either. You tend to try a man."

He watched her fingers toy with a fork. "Why are you afraid of me?"

The slender fingers stilled, then curled tightly around the fork as he continued softly. "We're here to palaver. To lay our future out. I'm not insensitive to your fears."

Outside, a barn owl called, and above their heads, the attic mice scrambled into their holes. A mountain cat screamed, echoing Rebecca's fears, and she shivered.

"I've enough skill to take you wisely, lass. Trust me." He laced her fingers with his, his thumb stroking the callused mounds of her palm.

She jerked her hand free, slamming it palm down on the table.

"Ah, gently now," he cautioned after a tense heartbeat. "I'd hate to have to draw a splinter from your hand with my teeth. I'm still recovering from your kiss."

She met his gaze evenly. "Do not touch me, McKay. I cannot stand it."

"Oh, but I *am* going to touch you. I'm going to teach you how to make love." He brushed a fingertip across her lips and she jumped back, her hand covering her mouth.

McKay was stalking her, finding her weaknesses just as Rudy had done, she decided darkly.

"If it's any consolation," he drawled as he rose to his feet and stretched, "you've given me a bad moment or two. I had expected a bride eager to start our new life."

He collected the plates and stacked them in a washbasin, then poured boiling water over them. He tossed a cloth at her and began to wash the dishes. "Dry, will you?"

Rebecca wiped the first plate. "Well, then, you can see that I don't come up to your expectations. Surely another woman—"

Matthew looked at her over his shoulder. "I want a wife, not a slave, Becky. Remember that."

"Matthew," she said, trying the name on her tongue.

"Surely you can see that my father played us both in his game. The simplest thing would to be to dissolve—"

Running the tip of his finger across her lips, Matthew shook his head. "No. We can settle the matter between us."

"I don't like the sound of that." she began hotly, then stopped when his grin widened and she found herself simply staring at him.

When the dishes were done, Rebecca looked longingly at the crudely fashioned wooden cot. It was very large and wide, with thick ropes woven between the posts. Matthew had thrown the horse blankets over the ropes, then spread two large quilts over it all. The bedding looked so inviting; Rebecca yawned and sat to draw off her boots.

She eyed Matthew as he banked the coals for the night, then she padded toward the bed.

Rats rustled in the rafters above, disturbed that their home had been invaded. Exhausted, Rebecca settled heavily into the bed, the warmth of the blankets covering her soothingly. She sighed and Matthew turned toward her.

"Tired, Becky?" The hard day weighed down on her, and she turned away from him, drawing the blankets over her shoulder. Tomorrow would come soon enough—she'd ride out at first light, unhappy proxy husband or not.

A big hand was on her shoulder, turning her. When she opened her eyes, Matthew's dark face was just fractions of an inch from hers. Flattened to the ropes, bound by sleep, Rebecca stared back at his dark, intent gaze.

"Maria sent your nightdress. You'll be more comfortable wearing it. Shall I help you?" He stood, watching her as she flattened to the ropes in her surprise.

Clad only in loose drawers knotted around his waist, Matthew's body was outlined by the moonlight coming through the window. He held out the nightdress to her. His teeth flashed in the dark shadows. "Don't look so shocked. This . . . garment will hardly inflame my animal desires. But I prefer sleeping with it rather than your buckskins."

"You prefer?" she gasped. "You're not sleeping with me!"

"Of course I am. There isn't another bed," he reasoned,

looking at her closely. "Becky, I'm too tired to wrestle with you. Have mercy on me, please. Just put the gown on, or I will do it for you."

"You touch me and I'll—"

He held up a hand, staying her. "I know. I know. You'll shoot me in the kneecaps or in the trousers."

She frowned. "That's an interesting thought."

He tossed the nightdress onto her lap. "I had more pleasant plans for our wedding night. But right now just put on the gown while I turn around. The thing is as big as a sailing sheet. It's quite modest. You can draw it on and slip your clothing off beneath it."

"Hell and damnation! I will not, Mr. McKay! I'll sleep on the floor."

Matthew gritted his teeth, scowling down at her. He ran his fingers through his hair in a gesture of weariness. "You do try a man's patience, Princess. But if I have to wrestle you into that . . . thing, you're wearing it."

"Oh, I see," she snapped. "Where is the gentleman? All the fine promises of courting?"

"I want some sleep, woman," he growled. "Get on the gown."

Crossing his arms before his chest, he turned his back to her. "Now."

He was big, she thought, debating the moment. And seemingly in a bad temper.

The muscles of his back rippled beneath skin the color of burnished leather. White ridges crisscrossed its broad width. Rebecca had seen men without their shirts, but Matthew was leaner than her father or her brother. His waist was trim, his loose drawers cupping his taut rear.

"Keep your back turned, McKay," she ordered after a moment. "I'm not about to perform such a lascivious act for you."

She thought she heard him chuckle. "Becky, some women undress to entice their husbands."

"I doubt that," Rebecca returned staunchly. "Not unless they are loose women at heart."

"Another time we'll examine the matter thoroughly."

She swallowed, drawing the sprigged nightdress over her head. The tentlike gown settled around her. Slowly she unbuttoned her blouse, dropping it to the floor. Unsnapping her trousers, she wriggled out of them. "I'm finished."

When he turned, his slow grin widened, his perusal flowing over the voluminous, ruffled folds before she squirmed beneath the quilt. "Well, now, that's much better."

Rebecca tilted her head. "I don't like your tone, McKay. And I'm not seeking anything from you but an annulment."

"Undo your braid, Becky mine," he urged in a deep, rumbling tone. "You look like a wide-eyed child." Then his fingers caught the waist-long length, undoing the binding. In seconds her hair was draped around her shoulders, rippling in the moonlight. His hands smoothed her head and shoulders, arranging the heavy weight. He lazily fingered a silky strand, his gaze darkening.

She trembled. He was stalking her again, making her nervous. "I do not like your touch, McKay."

He shook his head, chuckling. Then he bent, lifting her easily and depositing her to one side of the cot. "Scoot over. The fit is a bit tight, but we'll manage." He shoved her gently, the ropes shifting with his weight. Her body rolled against his and Rebecca's hand shot out.

His chest was warm and steel-hard, her fingers wrapping in the coarse hair. Matthew slid his arm beneath her neck, gathering her to him with the other. His lips slid across her forehead.

She thrust against him, her fear rising. "You promised. . . ."

"Shh, love. Shh. I won't make love to you tonight. Lay here still in my arms," he said soothingly. "I want nothing more than to hold you next to me. Here, let me warm those cold toes of yours." His feet chafed the slenderness of hers.

"Somehow this is improper, I think." she stated, stiffening her traitorous body against his warmth. "You promised, McKay."

He sighed deeply and the warm flesh beneath her fingers

lifted. "So I did," he agreed heavily. "I'm beginning to regret promising you time."

"I hold you to your promise." Despite her will, her body seemed to flow into the hard contours of his. Matthew's toes toyed with hers, and she jerked back from the play.

"Aye, so I did. Holding you now, I realize it was a rash thing to do. You're a soft, soft creature, with dewy lips that taste like honey." His slow breath fluttered the tendrils at her forehead. "Listen . . . hear the night wind sigh through the pines? When I was a lad, I loved that sound. I've missed it."

His large hand slowly rubbed her back from shoulder to waist. The sound of his low voice soothed Rebecca, causing her to become drowsy.

He talked of owls, the creek beside the barn that had been diverted to feed the thirsty orchard. His mother working hard, laughing as she danced a jig with him. Feeding a growing family on fruits preserved in jars and dried on the shingles in the hot August sun. Eric, his half brother, wrestling him, taunting him. The death of his two small brothers and his mother, and his father's grief.

Rebecca's lids fluttered down. Matthew was a gifted story-teller and she fell beneath his rumbling spell. His fingers found her scalp and he rubbed it gently. "Rest on me," he coaxed softly. "You'll be sore in the morning from holding yourself so still. And we both need the sleep," he whispered in her ear.

"Tell me about the mirror in the other room."

"The mirror?" He hesitated. "Aye, it's still there. My mother's mirror."

"She loved it just as she loved lavender and roses," she murmured drowsily.

"How do you know, lass?" he asked, his deep accent returning.

"I just know. Tell me more," she demanded sleepily, soothed by the lazy stroke of his hand.

"Not tonight, lass." His fingers treaded her back, seeking all the aches and rubbing them. "Go to sleep now." He turned her gently and rested his arm over her waist. "Poor child. Wrested from her family into a life of servitude,'' he breathed into her hair. "Sleep now."

She fought the weight of her eyelids, fought the trust she had begun to feel for Matthew. Tomorrow she would set the matter straight.

At her back, Matthew's body curved to hers, spoonlike. She smiled drowsily, liking the cuddling and the soft feel of his breath touching her hair.

If she hadn't other plans, Matthew McKay was a comfortably padded bedfellow, she decided sleepily.

Just as she passed into sleep she felt a woman's warm caress brush her cheek, the scents of dried flowers wrapping around her . . .

Chapter Six

In the morning Matthew lay studying his wife, his hand supporting his head. The faint light of dawn slipped through the dirty windows to touch Rebecca's face. She lay curled to him like a kitten, her slender fingers resting upon his chest.

He felt his loins begin to stir, to harden. Rebecca McKay was a full-grown beauty, and she was his—despite her protests. He traced the tendrils playing around her face and the wide softness of her mouth—lips that could take a man to heaven.

Her cheekbones were high, slanting beneath the feathery length of her lashes. He smoothed her cheek with his thumb, the silky texture causing his mouth to go dry. Rebecca's breath tantalized his chest, flowing over his skin. She was his wife, the future mother of his children.

Matthew had never felt so protective of a woman, so possessive.

Rebecca was a woman of high emotions, in her fury reminding him of an equatorial storm at sea. But her tenderness with the Indian mother and child had exposed a softer side.

She snuggled nearer. The thrust of her full breasts and long thighs settled softly against him. Sighing, she lay back against his arm. Fascinated, he watched the pulse throb slowly at the base of her neck. The sweet tempo called to him, beckoning him past the two gaping buttons to the rising softness of her left breast.

Leaning closer, he caught the scent of vanilla and crushed wood violets. Beneath it all was the musky scent of a woman. The softness of her thigh felt like silk against his own. Torn between his promise and his desire, Matthew groaned softly. To sheath himself within her tight, moist body was his right. . . .

His heart thudded almost painfully against his ribs. She'd admitted to being wounded, and bolting at his touch had been instinctive. To deepen the wound would gain him nothing. Time, he thought, cautioning himself with determination.

He smiled grimly, half amused with himself. Rebecca had a high-nosed temper that made him want to tease her. He felt a tenderness for the vixen. She'd been mishandled, and now it was his lot to use patience to win her.

But that fool hadn't touched the hot-blooded side of her. Her surprise after their kiss was too real. Matthew ached to kiss her awake, to show her the sweet desire he felt.

Groaning, he eased himself from her side. "Damn fool," he muttered, drawing on his trousers. "This is a high-stakes game."

Matthew tossed a few pinecones onto the stove's coals, then fed the crackling flame with kindling. He watched the fire grow as surely as the ache within his trousers. He scowled. He intended to court the daylights out of her. From her kiss the previous day he knew that Becky McKay could match his passions once she got started.

"Becky McKay. Wake up, Princess." The deep male voice annoyed Rebecca and she swatted away the hand shaking her shoulder. Grumbling, she snuggled to the dark sanctuary of the blankets. "Let's have none of this, Becky McKay," the deep, raspy voice coaxed, tinged with gentle laughter. "Give your husband a smile and a kiss this fine morning."

His jovial, bantering tone stirred the mists of her sleepy brain. Husband? Matthew McKay. A black-eyed giant of a man, taunting her. Laying down silly male laws and ruining her life.

Drawing the quilt higher, Rebecca slowly opened her eyes. In the muted light Matthew's eyes sparkled with laughter, his new beard nearly covering his strong jaw. His head blotted out the view of the old cabin and she scowled up at him. "Oh, go away."

"Why, you nasty-tempered little owl." Laugh wrinkles deepened beside his eyes. "We slept together our first night, Becky. You snuggled against me, as sweet as any willing bride. Aye, it was a memorable night." His firm mouth held a wry smile. "A kiss to start the day . . ." He leaned closer.

Freshly awakened and vulnerable, the remembrance of pain and fear leapt in Rebecca, sending her into wide-eyed terror as she huddled away from him. She trembled, bound by the memory of Rudy hurting her with slashing fists and boots.

Matthew's frown was deep, forbidding. The hard angle of his jaw shifted as he gritted his teeth. "Whoa, now. What's this about?"

She felt the cold sweat of fear again. Her fists snatched the quilt to her protectively. He'd shamed her, knowing that he'd seen her fear.

He glanced down at her white knuckles. "Easy now," he said soothingly as he stood slowly. "Easy."

Beneath the layers of the nightclothes, Rebecca was cold. Matthew bore that same hateful look as Rudy—furious, frustrated. "Go away," she managed, trembling, sliding deeper into the shelter of the blanket.

She cowered for the second time in her life, knowing it . . . hating it.

A muscle contracted in his swarthy cheek as Matthew stared down at her. "I'll be getting to the bottom of this." His tone was threateningly soft. "Aye, you'll tell me the reason," he repeated, as if to himself. "You look like a doe caught in a trap. The fear in you turns my stomach."

He shakily threaded his fingers through his hair. "Sweet Jesus, I've never hurt a woman in my life. I thought you had grown to trust me a little. What's milling around in that tight little mind of yours?''

When she didn't answer, her tongue flicking across her trembling lips, Matthew sighed. ''I don't like the look of your fear,'' he murmured softly, running his hand lightly across her hair. ''It hit me in the belly like a bare-knuckled fist just now.'' With a dark scowl he turned and padded to the stove. ''Get dressed, Becky. I won't look. Surely you can trust me enough for that.''

Cautiously Rebecca slipped from the bed and grabbed her clothing. ''I'll dress on the porch.''

''Fine,'' he agreed curtly as he turned over the sizzling bacon in the skillet. The line of his broad back was taut and forbidding as she slipped out the door.

She dressed quickly, in fresh trousers and a soft blue calico shirt. Then she scanned the rustic beauty of the old homestead, inhaling the pine scent. The air was fresh and moist and welcome—unlike the man within the house, Rebecca decided.

The morning mists clung to the deserted fields, a feather-light sweep of blues and glistening dewdrops. It was a beautiful place, like a grand old lady fallen upon hard times and begging for care, she thought. A small herd of deer bounded off into the mist. A snowshoe rabbit dressed in his brown summer pelt hopped behind a fallen log. Beyond the shroud of the fog, a steam gurgled merrily.

In the distant swirling mists a dab of color caught her eye. Dropping her gown to the boards, she stepped carefully off the porch. A short way from the house, the red spot seemed to hover in the fog.

Drawn by the red color, she walked toward it. Her foot touched a flat rock, then another. Walking from stone to stone, she saw several red blooms. ''Roses,'' she whispered, entranced. She smiled, thinking of the big rough woodsman laying a rock path to his wife's flower garden.

Pine needles jabbed her bare feet and she stepped more cautiously. A ramshackle fence protected the overgrown ruins of an old garden. Large red roses caught moisture on their velvety petals. An ancient trellis supported the weight of pink blooms, the heavy vines tangling with the broken limbs of shrubs. Lilies of the valley nestled in another corner of the white picket fence.

The arch of a rose arbor stood in the center of the abandoned garden, heavy with vines. Small yellow roses studded the greenery, like sprigs of color on a cotton dress.

Easing her way through the thorny vines, Rebecca touched a heavy bloom. She swept the morning dew from the blood-red rose with the tip of her finger. "Poor pretty little thing. So alone and forgotten," she said soothingly, amazed at the beauty of the deserted garden. "Though someone has cared enough to water you."

She didn't notice Matthew following her. For a moment he studied his bride. The fog swirled around her, outlining her long legs and bosom. Her hair flowed down her shoulders in a satiny black sweep as she lifted her forefinger to a rose. She touched the petals reverently. Delicately tracing her fingertip over the rose, she half turned, exposing the tender length of her neck.

Matthew's stomach tightened almost painfully. She had tried his patience the day before, but now Becky was all bewitching female—as soft and delicate as the blooms she touched.

His mother's garden had survived, and he wondered briefly if a Nez Percé woman, Annie, still visited the old homestead. As a young girl Annie had dug camas roots in the far pasture. Then his mother had offered her sacks of flour and Annie had returned the favor by faithfully carrying water to the flower garden.

Rebecca smiled softly, like a child enchanted by a new toy. But Matthew remembered her earlier fear. When he had awakened her, he'd seen into the heart of her. Becky had her dark secret—what was it?

"Becky," Matthew called softly by the yawning gate. "If you like, we'll clean out Ma's garden and plant new flowers."

Surprised by the sound of his voice, she pivoted. Her wrist

caught on the sharp thorn of a rosebush and her bare heel bore down upon another spike. "Oooh!"

Holding her wrist, Rebecca hopped on one foot toward the fallen gate. "Damnation, McKay! Now look what you've done," she accused, scowling at him. Her unbound hair caught on the briars of the climbing yellow roses. Rebecca snatched furiously at the rippling strands, trying to work them free. Breathing hard, she swept her injured hand back through her hair, facing him. "You are a sneaky man, McKay. Just as I said."

"I am nothing of the kind." He grinned widely, moving through the growth toward her. "I've come to rescue the fair damsel in distress. Hold still, Becky."

"My name is Rebecca, sir. Kindly remember that. You and your 'lass' and your 'Princess' . . ." She sniffed, placing her injured wrist against her mouth. She sucked the blood from the scratch. When Matthew began to work her hair free of the thorns, Rebecca watched him warily.

"At times you *act* like a princess, Becky," he said teasingly, brushing the back of his hand against her flushed cheek. When her eyes flashed up at him, he kissed her mouth lightly. "I like to think of myself as your Sir Galahad, charging to the rescue."

"Hmmpf! I know a skunk when I see one. You are not a chivalrous knight, Matthew. And I can rescue myself . . . given time."

"Your compliments almost make me swoon." He caught the length of her freed hair in his hand, twisting it into a silken rope to draw her a step nearer. "I agree, it is hard to act gentlemanly around you. Most trying. At times you're as thorny as these bushes. But I will unravel your secrets as surely as I untangled your hair," he promised softly. His voice lowered. "I don't like you sidling away from me. Whatever ails you, it has not been of my doing."

"You startled me this morning, that's all. What woman wouldn't be frightened to find a man your size leaning over her? With that silly grin?"

His eyebrows rose. "Silly? Perhaps I enjoyed waking you. Perhaps I had just stolen a kiss."

"You frighten me, Matthew," Rebecca admitted slowly. "You . . . pounce. One of these days you may startle me at the wrong time."

He chuckled, lifting her easily up into his arms. "I like the thought of that. I just might get one of those sweet kisses—when you're not all worked up to hate me. Could it be, Princess, that behind all that fury you just might care a little?"

Her eyes widened. Open her heart again? "Hell and damnation, no!"

Holding herself back from his chest, Rebecca stared into his eyes. "You have that wicked look about you. Like just before you pounce."

She squirmed, and when he grinned, she decided to remain still.

"I do like you moving in my arms," he drawled in a tone that caused the hair on the back of her neck to rise.

"I'm not used to being handled like a weak child. Let me stand."

"But I like the feel of you against me," he persisted, gathering her closer as he strode toward the house. "You snuggled against me like a kitten last night. You almost purred."

"I did not," she stated hotly as he placed her gently to her feet on the porch.

He ran a fingertip down her nose. "You surely did, Princess. Ran your hands all over my chest and—"

"That is enough!" She glared at him. "You make me sound like a—a hussy, Matthew."

He sighed heavily and turned her toward the door. Placing his hand low on her back, Matthew guided her into the house. He patted her bottom gently. When she jumped—rubbing the same area with her palm, her eyes flashing—he lifted his eyebrows, all innocence. "Just a little love pat, Princess. But I can tell you that a husband is fortunate to have two women in one—a lady in public and a hussy in the bedroom."

"Mr. McKay!"

He grinned wickedly. "Shall we dine, Princess?"

"You are hopeless." Matthew's grin caused her own, though she fought the movement of her mouth for an instant. "If you're quite finished tormenting me, I am hungry."

As they ate, Rebecca stole glances at Matthew. His beard was thick now, covering the hard set of his jaw. His unruly hair curled around his head, as dark as the silky length of his lashes. His shirt was open, exposing the whorls of coarse hair—he did not resemble the city man who had arrived at her father's house. He looked like a man in his element as he stabbed the bacon and folded it in a thick slice of Maria's bread.

Tearing off a chunk of the food, he chewed, staring darkly at her. He wanted to know, she sensed suddenly, about her reaction to him when she awoke. Matthew had the look of a persistent man, one who sought out mysteries and uncovered secrets.

But not her secrets. Rudy had scarred her, the wounds unseen. She wanted all the doors closed on the past when she had so blithely trusted another man. Matthew would not badger it out of her.

Holding her eyes, he raised the granite cup of hot coffee to his lips. "Damn!" He wiped his mouth with the back of his hand.

Rebecca couldn't resist teasing him—just a slight scratch on his wonderous arrogance. "Did you scald yourself, my lord and master?"

"Brat!" he answered in a growl. He touched his lip gingerly with his finger. "You shouldn't make fun of a wounded man."

When she giggled, he stared at her curiously. Rebecca stared back, caught by his darkened gaze. Matthew kept trying to see inside her and she didn't like it. She didn't need the man to go strolling through the private moors of her heart.

For there lurked the painful shame, the weakness she had never admitted to anyone.

For a moment his dark eyes traced her flashing eyes and set mouth, then Matthew's big hand wrapped around her wrist. He tugged her around the table to sit on his lap. Hold-

ing her arms down, he thrust his face against hers, arching
her backward. His lids lowered as he watched her tight lips,
refusing to ask to be set free. "You're an enticing little witch,
you know, lass," he murmured huskily. "Shall I kiss you
until you beg?"

She'd begged once and wouldn't again. "Beg for what?
You've nothing I want, McKay!" Braced over his arm, Rebecca could feel his heartbeat against her breasts.

"Ahh, I don't know about that, woman," he growled, settling his warm face within the cove of her neck and shoulder.
He nuzzled her flesh with his parted lips, stroking his tongue
on the taut cords of her neck until she shivered. "I think I
will make you beg for a kiss."

His big hand slid up her blouse and cupped the fullness of
her breast. The soft kneading of his fingers startled her.
"Don't touch me there, McKay," she gasped, prying at his
wrist with two hands.

His thumb rubbed across her breast, and lightning bolted
through the length of·her body. She arched back from his
hand. "That's indecent!"

He chuckled, a raw sound of masculine pleasure as his
large hand firmly cupped the weight of her breast. "Indecent? I could show you indecent." He settled her more fully
upon his thighs, and Rebecca felt his hardness rise beneath
her hips.

"Good lord, McKay. What are you doing?" she gasped,
shocked by the answering warmth between her thighs.

"Pleasuring," he said against her ear, gently biting the
lobe. "The name of my game is pleasure."

The heavy sound of his breath tingled through Rebecca as
she began to melt. His hand kneaded her other breast, and
she felt a hot flush surge through her. "Well, hell and damnation," she whispered in amazement as her body arched to
his touch, flowing beneath it.

Matthew's lips curved against her neck. His head lowered
until his mouth touched the hollow at the base of her throat.

Rebecca's breath came in short gasps as his lips worked a
warm trail downward. "Ah, you are sweet as taffy to taste,

Becky McKay.'' His voice rumbled against her skin as she went taut. ''Aye, turn this way,'' he said with a groan.

Astounded by the heat growing in her, Rebecca squirmed, trying to free herself. ''McKay, you're taking liberties. . . .''

He kissed her then, rubbing his lips across hers, lifting, brushing, tasting until Rebecca melted against him.

Matthew liked his woman warm and pliant against him, her green eyes heavy-lidded. He barely breathed, feeling her body soften, the timid flutter of her fingertips touching his chest.

She sighed, moving beneath his hand, and the warm color rose from her neck to her cheeks. ''Matthew . . .'' Her tone was an aching invitation.

He trembled as he carefully unbuttoned her blouse. Very slowly he placed his lips to the pale flesh lying above her heartbeat, feeling her tremble, awakening to his desire. . . .

Her breasts were white and mauve-tipped, shimmering in the hazy light. The sight of them tore his breath from his lungs. Locked in his desire, he lowered his lips to the sweet, tantalizing taste of her left breast.

Rebecca gasped, her body tightening in his arms. He suckled gently, aware of her shifting beneath him, aware of the perfume of her skin ensnaring him.

She began to tremble violently, her fingers clutching his shirt. From within Matthew found the strength to resist his desires, to kiss a trail up to her mouth gently.

Against her lips he whispered, ''Aye, I feel it too. The earth moved. . . . Don't tremble so.''

''Matthew, I don't know—'' she began shakily, her eyes misting.

''I do, lass. Just rest against me. Here.'' He tucked her head under his chin and rocked her in his arms.

When she stopped trembling, he whispered against her temple, ''Don't be frightened. What you are feeling is part of being a woman.''

She took a deep breath and he sensed her pulling together her defenses. ''I think I would like to stand now. If you please.''

When she stood, he glanced at her breasts, color darkening his cheeks. His expression was stark desire and desperation. "Cover yourself, woman! Have you no heart?"

When Rebecca looked down, she blushed. The aching peaks of her breasts thrust impudently upward. "Oh, my goodness. Oh, my!"

Matthew stood slowly, placing his hands on his hips. He ran a finger down the valley of her breasts before she could swat it away. "You are a tempting woman, Mrs. McKay. Now I'll have a harder time courting you slowly to my bed. Your taste is sweeter than taffy."

Her foraging fingers had opened his shirt, the heat from his body burning hers. She sensed his need and his restraint. His big hand trembled as it rose to rub the back of his neck. "A bridegroom doesn't have an easy life," he grumbled. "But a little kiss would help to soothe."

"No more kissing." Dry-throated, she gazed into the heat of his eyes. Desire tightened the skin covering his cheekbones. She felt the tautness of his big body, still craving hers; a summer storm seemed to crackle around them.

He placed his hands on his lean hips, his eyes daring her. "Do it, Becky. Place that sweet mouth on me gently. Ease my aches."

She shivered, unable to move. Taking her hand, he placed the palm over his lean cheek.

The roughness of his cheek chafed her hand pleasantly. His skin was warm and slightly moist as Rebecca's fingers trailed over him. She felt him breathing, holding still, watching her carefully as she studied the scar cutting his eyebrow, the hardness of his jaw blending into the dark column of his throat. Drawn by the male textures, Rebecca trailed her forefinger across his brows. His lashes were long and soft, feathering his cheeks. "Aye," he coaxed softly when she stared into the velvety blackness of his eyes. "Aye."

The soft touch of her hand skimming his face raised his desire once more and he swallowed. He was as weak-kneed as a toddler. "That's enough."

The sunlight seeping from the door touched Rebecca's

flowing hair. It sheathed her in rippling ebony waves, veiling the creamy, mauve-tipped mounds and framing the pale oval of her face as she studied him curiously.

His laughter filled the small room. "Ah, you don't know what to think, do you?" He grabbed her wrist, rubbing her palm over his hair-covered chest. "Here, touch me again, lass. You liked it."

Rebecca jerked her hand away, holding it behind her back. She dug her nails into her palm to stop the pleasant warmth of his chest lingering there. When Matthew's gaze warmed, fastening to her breasts, she crossed her arms over her chest.

"Stop tormenting me, Matthew," she snapped, quickly buttoning her blouse. "If you've quite finished—"

He shook his head, laughing. "Oh, I think there might be more. But not now. You look thoroughly surprised with yourself. But then I suppose it's the nature of brides, passionate creatures."

Rebecca's dark eyebrows drew together. "I am not a 'passionate creature.' "

"I wager you are," Matthew answered quietly.

"And from your actions I'll wager you have had experience with several . . . tarts," she flung back hotly. "Men like tarts, don't they?" she asked, remembering Rudy's coarse remarks.

He trailed a finger down her hot cheek. "I have enough experience to know that we should not linger in a room with a bed. Would you like to see the old orchards?"

"Will you stop pouncing?" she countered, backing away. She trembled, torn by the urge to run and to stay, exploring him. "Goodness!"

Sunlight danced through the shadowed tree limbs as Matthew saddled their horses. He was home and glad of it, Rebecca thought, brooding as she watched his hands move surely over the task of bridling the horses. He whistled a Highland tune, patting the horses' flanks as he tightened the cinches.

Cramming her hat over her newly braided hair, Rebecca brushed past him to raise a boot to Wind Dancer's stirrup.

Suddenly big hands spanned her waist, lifting her easily into the saddle. He chuckled as she slapped at him. "Don't be so touchy, Mrs. McKay. It's quite the gentlemanly thing to do—for a husband to help seat his wife."

She stared down at him, forcing herself to abide his caress on her knee. "Somehow I don't like the sound of that."

His palm roamed down her thigh, squeezing it gently. "I thought you wouldn't, Becky."

Rebecca scowled down at him, drawing Wind Dancer's reins taut. The stallion back-stepped as Matthew swung lithely into the gelding's saddle. He held her gaze as he reined the horse sharply, leaving her to follow as he inspected the broken and overgrown orchards.

The mists left the valley and hovered over the pine-covered mountains. An eagle soared high, catching the wind currents in his wings and drifting over his domain.

Dismounting and walking the horses through overgrown fields of clover, Matthew and Rebecca were silent.

Fir and pine trees sprouted on the once cleared fields. A huge gnarled orchard stretched in ramshackle lines to the bordering pines. Irrigation ditches, filled with fallen debris of dead branches and weeds, coursed along the rows of broken fruit trees. An old barn stood gray and forbidding in a sweeping field, daylight cutting through the weathered planks.

Matthew dropped his reins, slid from the horse and walked to the barn. Arms akimbo and legs spread wide, he stood in the huge doorway, looking into the blackness.

Rebecca eased down from Wind Dancer, walking through the waist-high weeds to the shelter of an elm tree planted long ago. She wiped her forehead with the back of her hand and slapped her hat against her thigh. The mountain sun burned hot, cooled by the pine-scented breeze. She stretched, easing taut muscles. Leaning back against the trunk of the tree, she waited.

This was McKay's intended kingdom. She caught a handful of wild rye heads and tore them from their stems, settling into her thoughts. He wanted a wife, did he? She'd have to be careful now that she knew him—he moved with soft touches and softer words. Much more stealthily than Rudy. And he moved quickly. Oh, he knew how to kiss, how to stir a woman.

She had been so hungry for him. But she'd be a fool if she allowed him his way. She'd be asking to be spread upon the ground and walked over as he journeyed to his kingdom. She threw the rye to the earth, crushing it beneath her boot. McKay was a possessive man. She could tell when he talked about the land.

Yet she remembered his hands on her breasts, the husky timbre of his voice, his passion rising hard against her. She shook her head. It was a matter of experience: He knew how to play the game; she did not.

No doubt Matthew wanted his wife dressed in skirts while she liked to wear trousers. No doubt Matthew wanted frills and ribbons, while she liked to dress comfortably. Oh, he'd want it all, she decided finally. The cooking, the babies, and at night he'd want more. . . .

There was a temper running beneath his tormenting ways. She couldn't afford to be at the end of it. Rebecca met the startled brown eyes of a grazing doe. Matthew could be handled. But how?

He strode from the shadowy barn, breaking a trail through the weeds to her. His face was lined, cobwebs clinging to his shirt and flossing the unruly curls. He stared past her to the old orchards, his mouth grim. "We have a lot of work, lass."

His work, his land, she thought, watching his frown deepen. "Are you ready to leave now?" she asked, straightening from the tree. Matthew was silent as they mounted, walking the horses through the untended fields. She eased Wind Dancer nearer to the chestnut gelding. "McKay?"

He scanned the fields as they rode, letting his horse pick over the chuckholes, the reins loosely woven trough his fingers. She had seen him angry and laughing, but the quiet contemplation made him seem more vulnerable.

He scanned the skeletal orchard, the dangling, worm-infested apples starting to turn red before their proper time. "Home is here." Matthew's deep, quiet voice broke through the heavy sound of her heartbeat. He dismounted, carelessly hitching his horse to a fallen branch. "My father brought these trees as dead sticks to the valley when he was a young man. Before he met Ma."

He walked through the weathered trees, scraping a peel from each roughened trunk with his thumbnail. "I want to see how many are alive. I'll be laying another orchard. We might be able to use these for grafting, I think. The stock is sturdy but the fruit is not as sweet as the new strains. We'll have to prune them down to nubs come winter."

He nodded toward the pine-studded mountains. "There's good timber up there. We'll have our own mill and way station, and sell to the settlers."

She swung to the ground. Matthew's dream was none of her concern, but the excitement in his low voice reached out to her.

He turned, drawing her against his side, his hand cupping her shoulder. "It's still a new land, Becky. Clean and new as a babe. Smell the air." He drew a deep breath.

So he had his dreams and was trying to rope her into them.

Rebecca eased his fingers from her shoulder. "Don't paw me, Mr. McKay. I've had enough of your ways."

The scarred eyebrow lifted. "You have? You seemed to like me touching you earlier." He drew her to him, locking his arms around her. "Shall we wrestle? I like you squirming in my arms."

Of course he'd like to feel her weakness, his male arrogance demanding capture, submission. Her face flamed, bracing her palms against the muscled planes of his chest. "You are a crude man, Mr. McKay."

"And you are a delightful, desirable woman, Mrs. McKay. I'm going to make you want me." His eyes darkened, touching her lips. "You're mine, Becky—no matter how much you fight me."

His gaze caressed her lips. "Am I to look forward to a life of dry little pecks from you? Or are you going to open your mouth for me?"

"You? Never." Her eyes strolled down his broad shoulders and narrow hips to the strength of his thighs.

He tapped the tip of her nose with his finger. "You'll pay for that remark, Becky mine. I'll take my payment in your sweet kisses."

Rebecca took a step backward, lifting her chin. "I will not stay here with you."

He studied the solemn set of her jaw. "I don't think it is such a good idea myself now. You're a tempting morsel for a hungry man. Are you aware that I've honored my vows and remained celibate for two long years? Do you know what it cost me this morning, to stop making love to you?"

While Rebecca chewed her lip and wondered, he tugged her braid. "I see you're going to have to think that one over, Becky." He scratched his chest and stretched, reminding Rebecca of a grizzly on the hunt.

"There is just one more place I want to see," he murmured, gazing at a small knoll with a single pine tree.

Rebecca glanced at him, caught by his intensity. Then, instinctively, she knew. "Your parents?"

"Aye." He began walking toward the knoll, and Rebecca found herself following him. A breath of wind stirred the tendrils about her face like a caress. Rebecca stood absolutely still, feeling . . . It was there, the warm scent of a woman, lavender and roses . . .

For a moment she closed her eyes. The sunlight stroked her head and shoulders like a blessing freely given. Enchanted, Rebecca smiled softly and opened her eyes to see a huge, glorious butterfly flutter around her flat belly.

She opened her palm slowly and the butterfly perched upon it. In another moment it was gone.

Matthew moved through the dry weeds to the fallen boards and began righting them almost reverently. He worked slowly, fashioning four crosses. When he was done, he came to stand beside her, placing his arm around her shoulders and holding her to him.

It was a silent moment but one in which Rebecca knew that Matthew McKay's emotions ran deep. "They were good people," he said simply in the soft, rolling burr. "To the day I die, I'll wish I had come back sooner."

Chapter Seven

Frolicking in the meadow, surrounded by daisies and Indian children, Rebecca gave herself to the morning and the laughter. The gay melody echoed through the mountain air, reaching Matthew, who stood beneath a stand of aspens.

Stopping to rest, they'd come across a band of Indian women digging for roots. Within moments the children had drawn Rebecca into a scrambling chase with wild, happy shouts.

Shredding the long stalk of bunchgrass, Matthew followed Rebecca's path through the tall daisies and sunflowers. She had a wild, free look about her, an open happiness that Matthew knew he would seek later.

He tossed the stalk into a tiny, rippling creek. In her element, surrounded by children, Rebecca's giggling flight through the daisies was a picture to last a man forever. Wearing a coronet of white flowers, she snatched a toddler and tossed him lightly, making the child grin widely. Then a girl of five leapt at Rebecca, bringing her down to the ground. Another round of wild giggles shot through the meadow.

Few women could match his wife, Matthew decided slowly. Rebecca had a quality for enjoying life and laughter, though she had hidden it. He wanted her as at this moment: happy and free, loving the flowers and the sunlight.

In a flurry of flowers and dusky-skinned children, Rebecca

gently fought her way free. Running with the toddler on her hip, she hid behind the large trunk of a pine.

Smiling to himself, Matthew patted Wind Dancer's mottled flank. Rebecca, playful and laughing, hid herself well. But now he knew.

Hours later Matthew tugged the brim of his hat down, shielding him from the late-afternoon sun. Still watching her, he took a deep breath, inhaling the fragrant scent of the new orchards and the sprawling freedom of the wild new land. Rebecca loved the land and the people. But more than that, he knew she was what he had searched for in all the women he'd known—a strong woman with a tender side who could make his blood run hot.

He noted the way her fingers moved, as if missing the Colt that usually was lashed to her hip. He had asked her not to wear it, and surprisingly she had conceded. Rebecca had folded her gun belt and holster carefully and jammed it in her saddlebag. It was a small concession, like her smiles.

He'd seen a tender side of Rebecca with Okanogan Mary and her child, and later in his mother's flower garden. She'd given herself to the playful moment with the children.

Matthew frowned, remembering her wild fear earlier. Rebecca had been badly frightened. How?

She reined Wind Dancer to a halt and the stallion munched on the grass. "What will people think if you keep eyeing me like a hungry drover?" she asked tightly.

Matthew chuckled, enjoying the way the sun danced around Rebecca and caught the fire in her eyes. "They'll think, my love, that I'm responding to my impatient bride."

"Change your look, then," she ordered sharply. She reined Wind Dancer back from his outstretched hand, her look challenging him. "Do you want to see what you've trapped, McKay? Perhaps I had better demonstrate."

Setting Wind Dancer into a steady gallop, Rebecca began to stand upright on the horse's back. For a moment Matthew felt his heart lurch, his heels digging into his horse's belly to keep pace with the Appaloosa. "Becky!"

Standing on the Appaloosa's mottled rump, Rebecca laughed. "Race me, Matthew. It's not far to the ranch." Easing down into the saddle, she turned quickly, foot in stirrup to lie beside her galloping horse.

Matthew knew that grabbing the Appaloosa's reins would upset his stride and Rebecca could be in danger. He had little choice but to ride beside her and watch.

Grinning at him, Rebecca held the saddle horn and swung her feet to the ground, leaping back into the saddle to repeat the motion on the other side.

His horse worked to keep up with the powerful Appaloosa, and Matthew felt his palms grow slick with fear, his face chilled in the sunlight. She challenged him then, a beautiful symphony of sight and color and movement, a woman and her land. She was complete without him, he realized.

"That lass has a lot to learn," he muttered grimly as Rebecca raced toward the Klein ranch, leaving him in her dust.

From a sloping canyon wall another man watched her graceful ride. Dressed in fringed leather and a black, straightbrimmed hat, Jean Dupres traced the Appaloosa stallion and the woman. "She knows how to hide a horse, Apache style," he murmured to his Arabian mare.

He noted the strong movement of her legs controlling the stallion. "She has no fear," he decided aloud.

What was it about the woman that held him? he wondered, watching the tall, lean man follow her. He smiled, lifting the Arabian's reins. This woman knew her place—the rivers and the mountains and her white blood. Of mixed heritage, Jean still had to find his heart.

The mare's long, slender legs shifted on the rocky slope, accustomed to the flat tundra regions of Canada. Jean frowned, thinking of his purpose—to visit Chief Joseph, to seek his dreams. He took one last glance at the horsewoman. She had set her path, and he had yet to find his.

Righting herself in the saddle, Rebecca rode slowly into the ranch yard, leaving Matthew to follow.

Daniel was in the pen next to the barn grooming his horse when Wind Dancer pranced through the gate. Her younger brother eyed Rebecca's set face, as well as Matthew's dark one in the distance.

She leapt down from the saddle and tossed Wind Dancer's reins to him. "Take care of him, Daniel."

"What's wrong, Rebecca?" he asked just as the gelding drew to a halt near them.

"Bridal nerves, Daniel," Matthew stated in a low, dangerous voice as he neared them. "She'll get over them." He slid from the horse and tossed his reins to Daniel. "Don't look so worried, little brother."

Matthew and Rebecca stared at each other, the air crackling around them. Daniel cleared his throat.

Towering over his wife, Matthew bent down his head, forcing Rebecca to lift her face. These two looked like Mexican cocks eyeing each other before they fought, Daniel decided. Rebecca was taut with fury, and Matthew's jaw moved as though he were gritting his teeth.

"Tend the horses, Daniel. It's been a long trip," Matthew growled, wrapping his hand around Rebecca's upper arm, dismissing her effort to free herself. "My bride is tired. And I've learned she has a nasty little temper."

"Tired? Temper?" Rebecca shot back, raising her chin.

"That's right, Becky." Matthew's eyebrows drew together, his face savage. "We're not putting on a show for Daniel."

Rebecca glanced at her brother's blank expression. "What are you staring at? Don't you have anything better to do?"

Daniel took one hard look at her flushed, rigid face, then retreated into the barn, leading the horses. He shook his head, unsaddling the Appaloosa. "Women! She ought to be happy she's finally got a husband."

Bruno walked from the shadows, a pitchfork filled with hay in his hands. "You mean our sister, of course, Daniel."

Daniel began loosening the stallion's cinch. "I saw them coming down the mountain. Rebecca left him behind in a cloud of dust, then started those pony tricks. If Papa saw her . . ." He hefted her saddle to a sawhorse and flung the striped Mexican blanket over it. "Matthew isn't too happy, either."

Bruno tossed the pitchfork into the wooden barn walls and it twanged, sticking deeply. He grinned. "I can still do that trick. I'll help you rub the horses down. They've been ridden hard." He stroked the gelding with a towel. "There, boy. Easy now."

Daniel frowned and Bruno patted his shoulder. "Don't let it worry you, little brother. Marriage is for two people, not a crowd. They've just got a lot to learn about each other."

The younger Kléin rubbed down the stallion. "She's riled, Bruno. And she's not wearing her gun."

"She's not?" Bruno tried to cover his surprise. "Well, maybe she just decided not to wear it."

Daniel's hand skimmed the horse's mottled rump. "She *always* wears it."

Bruno shrugged. "Maybe Matthew didn't like it. He'll have a say in what she does from now on. Who knows?" he asked easily. "I expect Rebecca will have to make some changes, the same as he will. Leave them alone for now, Daniel. Believe me, they'll work it out."

"You ought to see them stare at each other. Rebecca looks like she'd like to draw down on him. And Matthew looks like he'd like to . . . Whew!" Daniel exclaimed. "I thought newlyweds couldn't get enough of each other."

"Leave them alone, Daniel. Matthew will be a good husband to her," Bruno cautioned. "Rebecca isn't too happy with the idea of their marriage by proxy becoming real just yet."

"I'm worried about him, not her," his brother returned with a wink. "He may be the one who needs the help."

"Then we'll have to give it to him. If he asks."

In the middle of the ranch yard Matthew turned to Rebecca. "You could have been hurt."

Between her teeth Rebecca hissed, "I learned to ride almost when I learned to walk. I'm sorry if that doesn't suit your qualifications for a wife, Mr. McKay. Go find another more likely candidate."

His fingers caressed her inner arm. "Oh, you are what I want, Becky," he growled. "And I intend to have you."

He bent, kissing her hard and quickly, cupping the back of her head with his palm. "I am a little angry with you now. You could have broken your neck on that wild ride. And I wouldn't like that at all. It would be a waste of all that silky skin and those long legs. I am a patient man, Becky. Just don't try me too much."

Her head jerked back. "Or what will you do?"

"Make this marriage real."

It was the supper hour, the sun lowering behind the high mountains. Matthew stood beside the millpond, watching his wife leap across floating logs, gaffing them viciously. His hand tightened on the blanket wrapped around a light meal and a bottle of wine.

Rebecca had hidden from him for two hours. The curious, sliding glances of her family made him uneasy. Okanogan Mary's oblique stare followed him as she plucked a chicken in the ranch yard.

Finally he had excused himself in search of Rebecca. He was not happy; a man had his pride, after all.

Rebecca leapt from log to log in the pond, gaffing the timbers that had formed a small jam at the mouth of the creek. She worked furiously, hooking the metal into the logs and racing back and forth across them. He frowned, laying down the blanket. The logjam was too small to prompt all her frantic efforts, yet she prodded and poked, leaping from log to log.

Matthew held his breath as a big timber rolled in the water. Rebecca quickly ran backward on the wet bark. She slowed, controlling the great log expertly beneath her logger boots. He smiled; it appeared his bride worked out her pique by playing lumberjack.

"Becky! Over here," he yelled above the sound of the rushing creek feeding the pond.

She turned, balancing her gaff against another log. Peering

into the shadows of the pines, she almost lost her footing and had to scramble as the log rolled in the water. Straightening, she ignored his call and leapt to another log, prodding it loose from two other timbers.

"Becky! Come here!" She smiled then, a slow, taunting movement of her lips in the half shadows.

Her beauty entranced Matthew. Wearing worn pants and red long johns rolled up at the sleeve, she moved gracefully from log to log. Her braid snaked around her shoulders as she danced on the bobbing timbers. "Come and get me, Matthew," she called, tossing her braid behind her back. "I dare you."

He grinned, feeling his anger ebb as her smile widened. Those few smiles were precious to him. "So you want to play games, do you?" Matthew called, bending to pull off his boots. "I've untangled a few logjams in my time."

Rebecca's bold smile died as Matthew stepped into the icy water. He paused to roll up his trousers, then waded deeper into the pond. He vaulted to a log, and it bobbed beneath his weight; the rough red bark pricked at the soles of his feet. The log turned, rolling beneath him as he found his balance. Carefully negotiating the logs, Matthew made his way to Rebecca.

She whipped the braid back over her shoulder with a toss of her head, her expression grim. "You're full of little tricks, McKay," she accused, raising the gaff and snaring at the log supporting him. She jerked hard, watching him balance precariously. "You are far too arrogant. I think I'll dunk you."

He grinned, hopping to the other end of her log. "Dunk me now, Mrs. McKay." He winced as a small branch dug into his tender insole. "Ouch!"

Rebecca set the spikes of her boots into the wood and walked backward quickly, testing him. The broken branch caught his insole again and he grunted. "Think how nice it would be to have a willing wife, McKay," she taunted, beginning to run forward, spinning the log. He caught the rhythm of the timber, running easily with her.

"But not half as spicy, Becky," he answered, grinning widely at her grim face. "Perhaps your spirit is why I want you so much. But then it could be your tender kisses. Or you snuggling to me in the night, fondling me . . ."

"Such confidence," she gritted, running faster. "A good cold wash might cool you."

His longer legs easily kept pace. Panting, Rebecca glared at him, her face flushed. For a big man he moved very gracefully. "What are you . . . grinning at, you . . ." Her temper rising, she swung the gaff at him.

Matthew caught it and jerked it lightly. "You don't really want to hurt me, Becky. In fact, I think you've come to enjoy our little skirmishes."

Pulled steadily toward him, Rebecca just had time to right herself when he hurled the gaff onto the bank. Caught off-balance, she felt herself lifted and carried over the logs until Matthew stood holding her on the bank.

Laughing, Matthew brought her down onto the grass, lying on top of her while she struggled for breath. Pinning her arms to her sides by his elbows, he framed her face with his hands. He shook his head, still chuckling. "It's been a while since I've walked the logs. But it was worth it to capture you."

As she fought to get her breath he pushed a wet strand from her cheek and locked his fingers in her hair. "You smell like sweat, Princess," he remarked with a wide grin. "But you're right where I want you."

"Let me go, McKay," Rebecca gritted out between her teeth. He was heavy and impossible to dislodge as his legs clamped hers still. She struggled harder when his grin widened.

"If you don't stop flopping around like a trout on the bank, I'll think you're trying to entice me."

"I wouldn't want to come near you," Rebecca snapped. "You're crushing me."

"No, I'm not. I'm being very careful not to hurt you." He lightly ran his thumb over the winged line of her brows, then settled to stroke the fine hair at her temple. "You do get hot around me, don't you? Why?"

He studied her furious expression, sliding his free hand down to touch her lips. He traced the firmly pressed contours gently, then followed the line of her jaw to her neck.

Matthew undid the buttons at her neck slowly, his eyes sparkling with laughter. "I think I'll torment you just a bit for that crazy ride on Wind Dancer."

Rebecca trembled, feeling his hard body heat hers. "Get off me, McKay," she warned.

He peeled back a corner of the red wool and studied her chest intently. "What are you looking at?" she snapped as his fingertip slowly stroked her collarbone.

He met her stare innocently. "Why, lumberjacks are usually men with hair on their chests. But you're smooth. . . ."

Rebecca found his hip with her fingers and pinched. "Ouch! So you still are in a temper," he whispered, his accent deepening. The pad of his thumb slid along her jaw to raise it.

"And you are an overbearing—" Rebecca's breath caught in her throat. Matthew stared at her like a hungry man, his body hardening above her.

"I want you, Princess. I doubt that I have wanted another woman as badly." His hand reached down, stroking the inside of her upper thigh. When she trembled, caught by the gentle caress, he eased his long legs between hers.

She had wanted this, she knew instinctively. To be held by him. He moved gently and lightly upon her, and she knew that he took care not to crush her. Matthew seemed to take great care when he touched her, as though she were small and delicate and very, very feminine.

He touched her as she had touched the roses, cherishing their velvet beauty. Her heart contracted. Did Matthew see her as a beautiful woman?

She studied his high cheekbones, the disheveled curls he had tried to tame with a comb. And the enticing line of his mouth. Firm and warm against hers, his lips always asked— provoking, enticing.

Despite his great size, Matthew had always treated her as if she were . . . a princess.

Her softness absorbed the fine shudder that whipped through the length of his body. A drop of sweat slid down his temple and into his collar. Passing over her body, his palms trembled slightly. Suddenly she realized how much the effort his restraint had cost him.

She raised her hand, her fingers lightly prowling through his rumpled waves. She had wanted to touch the black curls, to feel them cling to her fingers.

Her fingertip followed the line of his ear, then slipped into the crisp hair at the nape of his neck.

When he had kissed her breasts at the cabin, his hair had been as cool as silk, brushing her skin. Her fingers drifted over his cheek, warmed by the smooth surface.

She felt him against her intimately. He settled lower and her thighs began to quiver. "Gently now, lass," he said soothingly, caressing the gentle sweep of her hip with his palm. He stroked her easily, warming her upper legs. His eyes darkened, smoldering beneath the black fringe of his lashes.

"It's broad daylight, McKay," she whispered weakly. His gaze was fierce, possessive, as it roamed her upturned face.

"It's twilight. Just before night. You are so soft," he groaned, easing his broad chest against her unbound breasts. He turned from side to side, like a mountain panther rubbing himself luxuriously on a soft bough. His eyes closed, a darkening flush rising in his clean-shaved cheeks.

He adjusted his hips lower, until she felt him thrusting against the place where her thighs joined. "McKay . . ."

When his lids raised, his eyes were glowing like coals in the dim light. "Aye, lass?"

The low timbre of his voice lodged in her flesh, weakening it. The primitive need rising from him like the heat of a raging forest fire began a warmth low in her belly. He followed the movement of her tongue, tracing her bottom lip, dampening it. He moved against her. "Do you know what I want from you, Becky?"

Bending his head and brushing the corner of her mouth with his lips, he murmured, "A simple kiss."

Then his mouth was on hers, warm and persuasive.

Rebecca fought her response, fought her lips rising to meet his.

She was warm, fighting for breath as his mouth parted and gently nibbled at the closed contours of hers. His breath swirled around her, heating her skin. He trailed a row of kisses to her ear, following the delicate shape with his tongue.

When she gasped, her blood heated by the slow insistence of his mouth, Matthew nuzzled her jaw. "Aye, Becky. Yield . . ."

Obediently her lips parted, her eyes closing as his mouth tenderly took hers. Her fingers splayed open, trembling before they lay along his hips, trailing slowly upward. "Matthew," she whispered huskily when his kiss deepened, "leave me."

"Yield." His tongue played sweetly, enticing hers, and Rebecca felt her body grow soft. Matthew's teeth nipped lightly at her bottom lip, his hands moving down her sides, kneading, warming, caressing.

He lifted to one side, skimming his palm down her breasts and somehow unbuttoning her long johns and unsnapping her trousers. "Your boots have spikes. May I take them off?"

When she protested, groaning and moving hungrily against him, he moved quickly. Somehow his bare skin pressed against hers, the cords and muscles in his arms moving her, half lifting her. He eased her down on his shirt, spread over the pine needles.

He looked at her a moment, as though admiring her against the rich tints of earth and fallen leaves. "Aye, Becky McKay," he whispered raggedly, "you'll do. With your eyes dark and waiting and your cheeks flushed with my kisses, you are a lovely sight."

Gently, inch by slow inch, Matthew slid her arms from the long sleeves of the undergarment. When she lay drowsy and warm before him, his face darkened. "Do you want me,

Becky McKay?'' he asked, running his dark hand over her pale skin.

In response Rebecca caught his wrist with her fingers and urged the palm of his hand over her right breast. The firm, rough weight seemed a claiming, and she barely breathed beneath his possession, staring up at him.

''Are you going to kiss me, McKay?'' she managed huskily as her breast swelled to his touch.

He sighed, looking down at her, all harsh angles and broad shoulders and dark, gleaming eyes. ''Aye, that I am, Mrs. McKay.''

The rising moonlight shafted through the pine boughs, and the pond water lapped against the banks soothingly. He stroked her body with the flat of his hand. His touch was reverent, feather-light, leaving her aching and entranced.

''You are so lovely, lass, like the dewy petals of a rose,'' he whispered roughly. ''I will be very careful.'' His fingers trembled slightly as he traced the round perimeter of her breast. His hand urged the long johns and her trousers lower, finding the knot of her drawers, loosening it.

Rebecca's fingers ached to touch the dark triangle of hair covering his chest. Lightly she traced the contours of his broad shoulders, aware of his big hand opening, lying warm and possessive on her stomach. He trembled as her fingers trailed to his chest, circling his flat nipple delicately.

''My lass,'' he said with a gasp, taking her wrist. He urged her open palm across his chest and groaned again. ''Aye, like that.''

The heat of his body and the tickling of her palm drew Rebecca's mouth to his flesh. Matthew trembled, his hands unsteady as they smoothed her hips.

In that instant, apart from her desire, Rebecca felt a poignant tenderness for Matthew McKay. She smiled against his throat, flicking his skin with her tongue as he had plied her. ''My boots . . .''

He shuddered, his skin sliding enticingly beneath her fingertips. ''Ah, it seems my lot to rescue the damsel in distress today.''

Rebecca lay back as he turned to unlace her boots. Running her hands across Matthew's back, she felt each movement of his rippling muscles. Hard and smooth and beautiful, she decided. She tugged his shirt from his trousers and he stilled, waiting.

"Are you undressing me?" he asked carefully as he finished unlacing her boots. He drew them from her, running his hand over her ankles and higher. He turned, and the movement brought her hands flat on his lean belly.

Matthew inhaled sharply, holding her gaze. He undressed slowly as she watched, intrigued by his lean body, the moonlight stroking his dark skin. "Would it be too forward, Becky, to ask you to touch me again?" he asked softly as he lay down at full length beside her and gathered her to him.

Hard and soft, rough and smooth. Sheltered against him, Rebecca had the odd feeling of belonging to him. And he belonging to her. She felt very womanly, treasured and desired as he looked into her eyes. Rebecca slowly raised a fingertip to his lips. He sucked it gently. Her eyes widened as the caress caused her entire body to contract. "What are we doing, Matthew?"

"Sharing, making love," he said, soothing her. "Just what we're expected to do. You like me touching you, don't you?" He traced delicate patterns over her bare shoulders, down her breasts and belly. He tested the smooth skin of her inner thigh, trailing his fingers upward until she stiffened, catching his hand.

"Matthew!"

Gently caressing her musky softness, Matthew urged her to her back. He settled his chest fully upon her soft breasts. While she adjusted to the broad planes of his body, flattening her breasts against him, he stroked her deeply, intimately.

Within her a sweet wildness rose, a desperate need to touch, to feel.

Rebecca's hips moved restlessly, her arms going around his neck. Clinging to him, she urged huskily, "Kiss me, Matthew."

When he did, the gentleness rising into hot passion, she

clung to him. Her lips lifted to his, her hips beginning a slow, unfamiliar rhythm. "I'm so warm, Matthew," she whispered.

He chuckled, sliding his cheek along the damp silkiness of hers. "Aye, that's true. I am too." He touched his tongue to her left breast, plying the dusky rose tip until she drew his head against her. Gently drawing the sweetness into his mouth, he probed deeper into her moistness.

"Oh, my . . ." Rebecca groaned, rising to meet him. Her blood ran hot and fierce, tiny grasping movements beginning low in her body.

"Easy, now, my lady," Matthew coaxed hoarsely. "Slowly . . ."

Easing himself over her, Matthew settled within her thighs. Her legs quivered and she breathed in short gasps. "Matthew?"

He nuzzled her neck, tasting the delicate flesh with his tongue. "Soon, Becky . . ."

Gently, slowly, taking the greatest care not to frighten her, Matthew rubbed his hips against her, letting her grow accustomed to the hard length of him. She groaned, moving her legs restlessly.

Matthew caressed the smooth flesh of her thighs, then gently placed her legs around him. "Like that," he whispered against her lips.

For a moment he held her, letting her adjust to him. But Rebecca trembled, wanting more, urging her hips against him.

Matthew groaned as she found the tip of his desire and paused. "Becky . . ." he whispered raggedly against her ear.

He stroked her hair back from her face, lowering his mouth over hers. With the sweetest of kisses he urged her lips open, his tongue tantalizing hers.

Answering his teasing forays with her own, Rebecca felt his large hand slide beneath her hips. He caressed her, kneading gently. She felt herself opening and blooming, raising her hips as he slid barely inside her. "Oh, Matthew," she groaned, wanting to move inside him, wanting to . . .

Beneath her fingers he tensed, shuddering. "There's time."

And then, the sweet honey began to flow as she felt herself adjust, open to him.

His lips roamed her parted ones as she held still, letting him know her.

His breath was ragged, his heart thudding heavily against her as Rebecca clung tightly to him.

Matthew kissed her cheek, watching her intently as she accepted him fully.

For a fraction of time she lay beneath him, wondering as he held himself too quietly, his desire leashed . . .

With an almost helpless groan Matthew moved deeper, to touch the wildfire within her.

Rebecca dropped into the flames, sought them as she clung to his broad, safe shoulders. He was her anchor then, and they moved into the eye of the fire.

The throbbing began, the dark drumming steadily within and around her as she moved with him, against him.

It burst suddenly—the red heat of their desire—leaving the honey-sweet taste of total pleasure.

As the circling rings within her slowed, Matthew thrust deeply, his face hot against her neck. She heard him cry out, as though he were in sweet pain, his heart racing against her. And then he was still, breathing as though he had run a long race.

He rested upon her, soothing her, stroking her, murmuring. "My sweet Becky . . . relax now, lass."

Rebecca nuzzled his cheek, liking the damp, hot feel of his skin. He trembled, his muscles taut beneath her palms. For a moment she savored the tenderness, the mating of his body with hers.

Totally vulnerable to her now, Matthew breathed more slowly. "Becky," he whispered huskily. "Are you all right?"

She trembled, and he eased to one side, holding her closely in his arms. "Becky?"

When she opened her eyes, Matthew's expression was tender and filled with concern. He tilted her chin up to his gaze. Her cheeks heated beneath his careful scrutiny, and she tucked her face to the strength of his neck.

"I . . . burned," she managed shakily.

He rocked her against him and she felt his chuckle grow deep in his chest. He stroked his large hands down her bare back and then up. He hugged her, laughing. "Aye, that you did, lass. You nearly burned us both your first time."

She leaned back on his shoulder, curious about what had happened. "Did I hurt you, Matthew?"

His eyes widened in surprise. "How, lass?"

"I don't know, but you cried out." Rebecca avoided his tender gaze, laying her cheek against his solid shoulder. He felt so safe after the torrid storm, stroking her, holding her. She burrowed more closely against him.

What had happened? What had she given him?

"I cried out in pleasure, Becky." He wrapped his fingers around her neck, rubbing the tense muscles there. "I am worried about you. Have I hurt you? You were so tight. . . ."

She remembered the slight burning pain before he entered her fully. He had entered her body and made her his woman. And she had opened to him. Why?

"The next time will be better for you," he said soothingly, dropping a light kiss on her temple.

She trailed a timid fingertip over the harsh planes of his face. "Such a savage look, McKay. Dark and brooding."

His scarred eyebrow arched. "I'll show you brooding in a moment. For now you've just tossed me a neat surprise. I hadn't expected . . ." He grinned ruefully. "You winded me, so to speak."

Her finger explored his lips and he caught the tip between his teeth, sucking it. "We should stop this now," he warned gently. "You're too new to the game."

She studied his rumpled, boyish look. He seemed quite pleased with himself. She felt the need to ruffle his confidence—just a little.

"It was not as bad as I thought," Rebecca stated thoughtfully, offering her other fingers to his mouth, each in turn.

"But not as good, either. Actually the kissing was much more pleasant."

He chuckled. "Then I will have to study the matter."

"Matthew! Where are you?" roared a male voice. Heavy boots plowed a trail through the brush, headed directly toward them.

Matthew tensed. "Hell! I'd know that voice anywhere," he said, easing away from her. "Cover yourself. It's my brother, Eric." He shook the rolled blanket free and covered her tenderly, as though she were a child. He stared at her with longing in his eyes and Rebecca sensed his reluctance to leave her. "Stay here. I'll be back. Alone." He hopped on one foot as he slid one leg into his trousers, then the other. With a last hungry look over his shoulder he stalked toward the bushes and his brother.

Rebecca lay quietly, missing his body against hers. She listened for a moment, then stood and stretched lazily. She frowned, drawing up her tangled drawers and unknotting them. Why did she feel shaky and warm and so hungry all at the same time?

"So you've been rolling in the hay with your woman, have you, Matthew?" a male voice drawled in the night. "Is she good?"

Matthew spoke quietly. "Rebecca is my wife, Eric. Watch yourself."

Eric chuckled. "From the looks of you, boyo, she'd drain a man dry."

A sharp crack echoed through the night, the sound of a fist hitting a jaw, and Eric cursed. "You've had your first and last warning," Matthew said quietly.

Listening to Matthew's low voice, Rebecca's knees went weak. If his brother could tell that they had made love, surely her entire family would know. . . .

Snatching up her long johns, she buttoned them shakily, then tugged up her trousers, fastening them. She jammed on her boots and knotted the leather thongs. She could deal with the entire family, but for now she didn't like Eric and his damning remarks.

Weaving through the bushes to the two brothers, she came up behind Matthew and chanced a glance at his broad back. He was tensed, his fists clenched at his thighs.

Rubbing his jaw, Eric spotted her. "Ah, the Lady McKay comes to visit, brother." He was larger than Matthew, and his eyes shone like cold silver in the moonlight, stripping her of her clothing.

Rebecca's hand fluttered to her chest and she blushed. Matthew's sharply indrawn breath caused her to look at his grim features. He looked as if he were holding himself on a very thin leash.

After a tense moment Eric clapped Matthew on his shoulder. "I see now why you've claimed her, boyo."

Matthew shrugged free of his brother's hand. Rebecca saw his face, taut in the dappled light as he faced Eric squarely. "We meet again, Eric," he stated roughly. "Why, I wonder?"

Eric grinned, a flash of white teeth. "Why, brother, I came to meet your bride. Perhaps to renew our family love. Surely you're not going to send me away after so many years. It would cost you so little, considering the old man named you as his only heir."

Rebecca glanced at Matthew's face and found it grim. In his neck a taut cord stood out in relief. "He had his reasons."

"Did he, boyo? Or did Ma set her spells on him?" Ignoring his brother's fierce look, Eric took Rebecca's hand and kissed the back of it. His silvery eyes gazed steadily down into hers. "Congratulations, Mrs. McKay. Welcome to our family."

His voice was low and smoothly polished, unlike Matthew's deep rasp. Eric met his brother's hard stare. "She's a beauty, Brother. I'd have her myself, if she wasn't already taken. Interesting," he murmured, the silvery eyes drifting over her. "Your usual taste runs to more rounded stock wearing petticoats. I see she wears the long johns in the family."

"Go to the house, Rebecca," Matthew ordered in a cool tone, the flat of his hand pushing gently at the small of her back. "We'll discuss all this in the morning. Eric and I have a lot to say to each other tonight."

"Good night, sister dear," Eric rumbled inches over her head as she passed by him. "Sleep tight."

She glanced at Matthew's hard face, then walked on quivering legs to the path that would take her home.

Chapter Eight

Eric watched Rebecca's stiff back disappear into the darkness. He scratched his bruised jaw. "She may be wearing lumberjack gear, but I can see why you're touchy."

"That's enough." Matthew felt all the old anger come flooding back. Eric had a way of taunting him into a fight. "Rebecca is my wife now, Eric."

"They always favored you, didn't they? Even Ma." Eric leaned back against a red-barked pine tree, careless of his fine percale dress shirt. He placed his boot against the trunk comfortably, studying Matthew.

He blew smoke through his nostrils and flipped his cigarette onto the fallen pine needles. A small flame began instantly in the dry tinder and he ground his heel on it. His silvery eyes watched Matthew weave through the bushes to retrieve his shirt.

"Ma's little boy . . ." he taunted as Matthew returned and slowly drew on his shirt. "I heard you married Rebecca by proxy, Matthew."

"Did you?" Matthew buttoned his shirt carefully. Eric had the look of a hungry wolf, looking for an opening to hamstring his prey. Matthew knew it was wise to listen to Eric when he had that cunning look; as a child he'd missed listening to Eric's ramblings and it had cost him.

"A Klondike dog pusher brought the news up from Seattle

two years ago. He got it from a Basque sheepherder who passed through here that summer, at just about the same time old Chief Joseph started whining about being buried in the Wallowa Valley. Too bad they didn't bury him and the rest of the Nez Percé the minute they put on their warbonnets. The only good Indian is a dead one—unless it's a pretty young squaw—''

''You haven't changed in twenty some years, Eric. Why did you come back?''

Eric stared at him coldly and Matthew wondered how they could share the same mother. She had been a loving-natured woman, always excusing Eric's brutality. ''Rebecca.''

Matthew settled his shoulder against a tree, leaning his weight against it. If his wife were included in any of Eric's plans, the matter was a dangerous concern. Using patience it was possible to untangle Eric's twisted thinking, and Matthew settled back to explore the intricacies of his brother's plans. ''Go on.''

While Matthew continued to look at him steadily, Eric drawled, ''You're lucky to be alive, brother. I heard the story way up in the Klondike. Bruno nearly killed the last man who touched her. Rudy thought he had Rebecca and the Klein land in the palm of his hand. When he found the old man had parceled out the poorest piece of land for his only daughter, Rudy lost his temper. He slapped her around once or twice before Bruno stepped in.''

Now he knew the cause of her fear, Matthew thought quietly as he listened. The thought of a man's rough hand against Rebecca's smooth cheek caused him to clench his fists. He felt the rage within him rise but carefully tethered the dark temper that could rule him. A few slaps would not cause Rebecca's wild-eyed fear; she was too strong. Her fear had been caused by something much worse. There would come a time and he would have the whole story from her. ''Rudy,'' he repeated. ''What is his last name?''

''Doesn't matter. He's dead. Bruno left him half a man and he didn't care much about living.''

Forcing himself to remain quiet, waiting for Eric's plans, Matthew asked quietly, "Why are you here, Eric?"

Eric's silvery eyes moved beneath his lids. "Why, I just happened to stop at the Klein house and the old man invited me to stay awhile—until I get on my feet. He probably doesn't want to turn away your only living relative. I just happened to be taking a walk after supper when I came across this . . . little soiree." He chuckled, and Matthew stared at him, wondering again how they could share the same mother.

Eric glanced at the millpond, then at the full moon. "I really couldn't see you coming back to this godforsaken pile of sand."

"I am back. And Becky isn't up for grabs, Eric."

Eric laughed, a rough sound crossing the gentler ones of the night. "Or you'll pound me again, little brother? I gave you that shot but I won't again. I plan to stick around—just to see if you do have her under your thumb."

While aboard ship, Matthew had seen wounded sharks devour their own entrails when they scented blood. Eric's eyes had that same wild glitter. Unless he had changed, Eric lacked conscience. "Why go out of your way?"

Eric laughed, a sound without humor. "You're my only kin, Matthew. Maybe I just wanted to see you, my only brother."

"I doubt it. Too many years have passed."

"So you finally ran away from the old man. Just the way I did," Eric said with a sneer. "He was a bas—"

"The circumstances were different, Eric. You had just slit Jeremy Jackson's throat and killed the Cayuse warrior who shared his camp. Pa did you a favor by running you off. You'd have been hung. You shouldn't have kept Jeremy's saber. That old Reb was well liked."

"Hell! No one but Pa had any idea who did it. He could have shut his mouth."

Matthew shook his head. "He wasn't the kind of man to put up with murder, Eric. What did you do with the forty packhorses that were stolen?"

Eric shrugged and stretched. "Sold 'em. They brought

good money in the gold fields. Horse steak tastes good when you're hungry.''

He leaned forward, his eyes narrowing. ''Listen, Matthew, an old miner heard Rudy describe Rebecca's land for the dowry. He said there's a rich strike up there—plenty of color. When the gold rush hit here in the sixties, there was a hundred thousand dollars taken out. The old man said that land would outyield anything this country has ever seen.''

''This country has been mined for years. There are still miners up in the Nespelem hills—''

''Hell, boyo! The old man said the Chinese had a placer mine up there like none he'd ever seen. Said they had sacks of gold stacked in a cave. Then the Indians massacred most of them, and the rest piled rocks over the entrance and just walked away. They won't work the diggings of their dead—superstition or something.''

''What are you planning, Eric?'' Matthew asked quietly, knowing Eric's greed would lay low everything before it.

Eric leaned toward him, his face intent, eyes glittering. ''Get Rebecca to sign that property over to you. Then you sign it over to me. We'll go half on everything, and that way the Kleins won't be able to get their hands on it. We'll set up the biggest mining operation this country has ever seen. We'll make Sutter's Mill down in California look as poor as a Cayuse pony. What do you say?''

''No.'' Matthew shifted away from the tree. ''And if I hear of you meddling in my marriage, I'll come for you . . . blood or not.''

Eric's expression turned ugly. ''You're still the same after all these years, aren't you?'' He sneered. ''Wanting everything for yourself. And all the chips falling your way . . .''

Matthew fought to keep his temper. But beneath his stormy mood lurked the fear that Eric could destroy his tenuous relationship with Rebecca. ''You're welcome for a while, Eric. But be on your guard—one wrong move toward my wife and I'll call you out,'' he stated mildly.

Leering, Eric rubbed his trousers with the flat of his hand. ''I could keep her happy.''

Taking a deep breath, Matthew fought his anger, trying to remember that the blood of his mother ran through Eric's veins. He turned, walking toward the house. Beneath his leashed temper Matthew felt a soft, dying breath. How his mother had loved Eric! Sadness wrapped around him, burrowing deep inside. Eric hadn't changed; his sickness remained.

"Pah! You're soft, Matthew. You always were."

But Matthew strode toward the house and Rebecca. He knew now why she had been frightened.

Rebecca stood before her bedroom mirror, feeling the evening breeze rush through the windows to cool her hot face.

She slowly unbuttoned the woolen long johns to her waist. The insides of her breasts were pale against the red wool, sensitive and aching after Matthew's possession.

If Eric hadn't arrived . . . The thought caused her to tremble. Matthew had held her tenderly later, stroking her as if she were a tender rosebud. In her entire life she had never been looked at so intimately . . . so tenderly. He had made her feel as though she had given him the one thing in his life he desired.

Trimming the lamp low, she undressed until she stood naked before the full-length oval mirror. The moonlight slipped into the room, lighting her body against the shadows. Barely breathing, she slowly turned to the side, watching the reflection of smooth skin and long legs. She watched herself turn again, examining her body. Matthew's touch still lingered on her skin, and yet she looked the same.

She lifted the large porcelain pitcher and poured water into the basin. Using soap and washcloth, she began to bathe slowly, remembering Matthew's large hands claiming her, tutoring her gently. Rebecca passed the soapy cloth down the valley of her breasts and lower. She placed her palm flat against her lower stomach and thought of him resting there. The tender ache within her was not unpleasant. Yet he had entered her, joined their bodies with his magic. She closed her eyes, then inhaled, tasting him on her lips again. She passed the cloth lower, moving it slowly over her inner thighs. He had made love to her gently, with the greatest of care.

Now, preparing for bed, she felt alone and empty.

Why? How had he changed her?

Finished with her toilette, she turned again, standing to face her reflection.

She touched the slight marks on her throat. Matthew had shaved, but his few hours growth of beard had chafed her tender skin. Yet in her passion she had felt nothing but his lips, his hands passing over her. Strange, she thought, staring at her face. A softness and a glow lurked around her eyes, darkening them as though she knew all the magical secrets of the world.

Her skin burned now, and there was a lightness, an eagerness, within her that waited for more. Within her prowled a hunger, needing . . . She had burst through the stars with Matthew, and she trembled now, remembering the force of that journey. She touched her right breast with her fingertip and the sensitive cords within her tightened.

Behind her, there was the sound of a door opening and closing. She tensed, feeling the hunger and excitement rise as she sensed Matthew entering the room. Rebecca drew her towel before her, shielding her body from his dark perusal. It was as before—her senses knew exactly when Matthew entered the room. Her blood flowed through her veins like hot lava, and her skin felt hot. "I locked the door. You shouldn't be in here."

"Locks are meant to be opened between a man and a woman. Lord, you are a beautiful woman, Rebecca." In the shadows, Matthew's voice—a deep, sensual rasp—wrapped around her.

He walked into the moonlight that shone through her window, sharing the small silvery patch with her. She couldn't move, trapped by the dark glow of his eyes in the shadows above her. "I . . . was just getting ready for bed."

She licked her lips, her tongue finding them swollen and sensitive. Her fingers trembled, tightly holding her towel against her, and she fought to keep from walking toward him.

What was happening to her?

Holding her eyes, Matthew began to unbraid her hair. He worked slowly, intently, his large fingers stroking the length gently. "You are more than perfect," he whispered, easing the rippling strands around her bare shoulders. "What are you thinking now, I wonder? Are you sorry we made love?" The words were spoken slowly and thoughtfully as Matthew arranged her long hair over her breasts. He studied the contrast of pale skin shimmering beneath the ebony strands.

"It's . . . new." He was a powerful man who treated her gently, she thought, finding the small tremor of fear riding close to her. She closed her eyes; she'd been betrayed and used once. A second time would destroy her. Perhaps men used different skills to betray, one with fists and the other in more devious ways.

"Aye. For me too. I planned to court you slowly. And now that I've tasted you, I don't know if I— Are you sorry?" he repeated, his voice husky and urgent. His fingers found the rapidly throbbing vein in her throat and played over it lightly. He gazed at her tenderly, his hard face softer in the shadows. He touched her as though she were fine china. He trembled. Why?

"They'll all know," she whispered, wanting somehow to move into the shelter of his arms. "That we . . ."

"Aye, they will. But in that knowledge will be joy for us and our new life together." He swallowed, and she felt the trembling of his hands as they lay against her cheek. "You have me now, Becky. I will face them with you."

She gazed up into his face and found it both solemn and tender. But a man's expression could change too quickly. Eric's cruelty was legendary and Matthew shared his blood.

He brushed the pad of his thumb across her bottom lip. "For now, what we have is enough. The rest will come. Trust me, Becky."

Rebecca studied the rugged contours of his face. She shivered, frightened of the future. After Matthew had his dreams, what then? "I do not regret tonight," she murmured finally.

"But I cannot promise—" She looked away, unable to meet the steady probe of his eyes.

After a moment he asked, "Will you let me stay with you tonight, Becky?"

Alarmed, her eyes flew up. "Oh, my! No!"

Matthew looked at her steadily, then took her nightgown from the top of her dresser. He dressed her as carefully as he would a child, lifting her hair free from the folds. "We're married," he said soothingly, his mouth curving tenderly. "But I'll leave early. People will expect us to share a room. Remember that."

While Rebecca decided what to do next, Matthew moved her to the bed. He eased her down, lifted her legs, and tucked her beneath the quilt.

"Matthew, you are pouncing," she accused finally as he began to undress. She had never watched a man in just that way—curious, excited, fascinated by his strong fingers unfastening his clothing.

He rummaged his fingers through the hair on his chest and her breath caught. She remembered the hot feel of his skin sliding against hers, his groans of pleasure.

What had happened to her? She had as much resistance to Matthew's tender look as she did to Maria's hot apple pie!

His teeth flashed within the shadows. "Such big eyes . . . You look like a tired little kitten who needs holding."

She returned his smile shyly in the darkness. Only a man the size of a bear would think of her as a cuddly little kitten. Just then she had the suspicion that Matthew could charm a badger out of his hole. A silver-tongued, Scots-Irishman prowling around her, somehow never accepting her no's. Tonight she was too tired to resist. But in the morning she would have to straighten out Matthew McKay.

Men needed to be studied, she decided drowsily. Sorted out like nails. Eric . . . whose pewter-colored eyes had slid over her as she passed, making her feel . . . dirty, used.

How could two brothers be so different? Or were they?

She closed her eyes against the sight of Matthew crossing the room. She chanced a look at his lean haunches, and suddenly all her senses started heating again. She tingled where she had ached, and in a moment he lifted the covers and slid down beside her.

The bed creaked and she jumped. "Shh! The whole house will hear." Rebecca eased away from him, feeling the feather tick puff up between their bodies.

Matthew placed his arms behind his head. "This is a small bed. We'll need our own."

"Matthew, are you lying in the altogether?" she burst out finally.

He chuckled. "Aye, that I am."

"But don't you think that is indecent?" she whispered, wanting to move into his arms. She was tired to the bone and wanted the safety she had felt to return. "I mean . . ."

The bed creaked again as he shifted on the feather tick, turning to her. "Come here, Becky. Rest in my arms and we'll save all our problems for tomorrow."

"Matthew, about tonight . . ."

"Tonight was a dream, and I'll be gone in the morning. Don't worry so." He snared her gently against him. "We'll work things out tomorrow. Tomorrow."

She'd given herself to his taking, and the restless thought nagged at her. "I was exhausted from logrolling. You . . ."

"I know, you were in a fine temper out there, jumping those damned monsters. Almost made me faint."

He'd made her smile again, she thought. But the sight of Matthew—tall and as strong as a lumberjack—fainting would make anyone laugh. "You . . ."

"It was a grand night, wasn't it? Do you want to put your hand on my chest? You seem to enjoy toying with—"

"Matthew! If you're going to tease me, you can leave. I've had quite enough for one day." The warmth of his body seeped into hers and Rebecca allowed her hand to find its way to his chest. She did so enjoy toying with the hair covering his muscled chest, as she drifted off to sleep.

In the night she heard him groan and move stiffly away from her. Seeking his warmth sleepily, she inched her backside against him and he groaned again.

"Becky, you're tormenting the daylights out of me," he exclaimed roughly, slipping his hand inside her nightgown to cup her breast.

She liked snuggling back against him, she decided as he groaned again, his hand warm on her softness.

"I'll pay you back for this, you little witch," he whispered against her ear.

Just for good measure she wriggled again before settling into a deep, peaceful sleep.

"Good morning," Matthew greeted Rebecca the next morning as she moved slowly down the staircase. Dressed in her trousers and a crisp gingham blouse with ruffles playing across her chest, Rebecca had strapped her Colt back to her thigh. She had her back up, a kitten defending a precious saucer of milk.

Were her kisses as sweet as he remembered?

When he walked toward her, her mouth firmed, as though she were looking for a place to dig in and fight. "Sleep well?" he asked casually.

She glared at him as though he alone had caused the Civil War.

What had he expected? Matthew wondered darkly. Open arms and a good-morning kiss? Yes, damn it all, he had expected just that.

"I'm going to see a lawyer today," she stated flatly. "If you think last night changed my mind about marriage to you—"

"Anything you say, my love," he drawled, admiring the snug fit of her trousers across her backside as she walked toward the kitchen. There was just the slightest swagger in those trim hips this morning. He resisted the urge to tap her bottom affectionately.

She glared at him over her shoulder. "Hmmpf!"

When she thrust open the door and stalked in to take her place at the table, Daniel's sentence trailed off. "Okanogan Mary is washing clothes outside. Her baby is over there in the cradle board. . . ."

Eric rose to his feet, extending his hand to Rebecca. "I believe we met last night, sister."

She allowed him to shake her hand too long, then slid free of his grasp. "We did. How are you, Eric?"

Eric glanced at Matthew. "Why, I'm fine. I'm looking forward to renewing my family ties. And getting to know my sister-in-law."

"Sit down, Becky," Matthew ordered sharply, and Rebecca glared back at him. He hadn't meant to snap at her, but Eric had looked at her as though she were a gold nugget that needed plucking. Or a French bonbon on a silver platter.

"Good morning, Rebecca," Klein offered lightly as she continued to stand, facing Matthew. "It is a beautiful morning, isn't it?"

Matthew pulled out her chair, and when she sat on it, he kissed her cheek. He liked the feel of her silky skin heating beneath his lips and the brightness of her eyes. "It's a fine morning," he agreed, easing into his chair.

Rebecca edged away from him and Eric's alert eyes caught the movement. He met Matthew's dark gaze across the table. "It seems I'll be staying here until I make other plans," he stated slowly. "The Kleins have offered me their hospitality. You see, Rebecca, my father left the McKay land to *his* son, while I am left to make my fortune as best I can."

"There's still plenty of land," Bruno offered.

"There are choice parcels. That's for sure," Eric agreed, looking at his brother. "Aren't there, Matt?"

"For those who work them, yes. I'd like to see you with your own place."

"Sweating like a dirt farmer?"

"Working the land, building a future," Matthew returned slowly. Rebecca glanced at the two brothers quickly. A white-hot thread of danger quivered between them. Why?

Matthew sipped his coffee as his brother watched Rebecca closely. "I can stake you, Eric. Find a plot you like and get the price."

Eric turned to Matthew, his eyes narrowed. "I've picked out a spot. Up the Methow."

"There's good logging country up that way," Klein stated. Twisp is a nice little town nearby, though. The mail runs pretty regular, even in the winter."

Matthew heard a sound behind him and turned to see Okanogan Mary raise a flashing blade. He caught her wrist just as she brought a kitchen knife down toward Eric's upper arm. The knife clattered to the floor, and Mary let out a blood-curdling scream, lunging at Eric.

"Damn sneaky Indian," Eric cursed. He leapt to his feet, raising his hand to slap her.

Instantly Rebecca caught his wrist and slid in front of Mary. "No," she said quietly, her right hand drifting toward her pistol.

Eric's eyes narrowed on her. He breathed heavily, then smiled grimly. "Oh, hell. I wouldn't have hit her."

Mary spat at him, struggling against Matthew's grasp. "*Memaloose*. Him die," she yelled. "McKay bad man!"

"It appears she doesn't like you, Eric," Matthew stated mildly. "Becky, would you mind calming Mary?"

"Of course." Rebecca moved quickly, snatching the baby on the cradle board and thrusting him into his mother's arms. "Let's go now, Mary," she said soothingly, putting her arm around the girl's shoulders.

"Rebecca reaches for that Peacemaker too damn fast. Matthew could get on the wrong end of family squabbles." Eric grinned, sat, and began eating as if nothing had happened.

Bruno cleared his throat, then stood. "They're bringing some new cattle across the river this morning. They may need some help. Do you want to go, Matthew? Eric?"

"Why?" the older McKay asked around a mouthful of eggs. "Those drovers usually make the herd swim everything from lakes to creeks on the trail up from Denver and Montana. They ought to be ready to ford the Columbia by now."

"I'll help." Matthew stood, rolling back his cuffs. "I'd like to get a look at that stock."

"Me too." Daniel jumped to his feet.

Peter Klein stood, holding his coffee cup. "I have to work

on my ledgers. I'm going into the study. Bruno, we could use a few choice heifers, if you see any.''

"Tell Becky I'll be back as soon as possible." Matthew walked to the door. "We're going to the lawyer at Cairo." He looked at Stella, who stood clutching the catalog. "Do you think we might borrow that? I'm afraid I took the liberty of choosing some furniture before I left San Francisco. But Rebecca might want to—"

"*I'll* tell sweet Rebecca for you, Matthew," Eric said, interrupting.

Matthew turned to his brother, saying quietly, "You do that, Eric. And I'll want to talk to you later about your plans. Maybe we should set a time to finalize them."

Eric's eyebrows went up. "What plans? I'm just going to lie back and get a feel for . . . the lay of the land."

An hour later Rebecca stepped out onto the porch. Eric waited, lounging against the corral fence. "What are your plans for the day, Rebecca?" he called. "Want to go for a ride? I'll saddle your horse. My buckskin is raring to go."

She drew on her leather gloves and walked toward the barn. She felt as much need to share time with Eric as she did with a rattler. Eric caused undercurrents to run through her that she didn't like. "I'm going to watch the herd ford the river."

"May I invite myself, Rebecca?" Eric grinned, and for a moment Rebecca saw his resemblance to his brother. The same broad brow, high cheekbones, and strong jaw. But in the bright morning sunlight she noted his puffy eyes and sagging jowls.

Both McKays were large men; Eric was more heavily padded, while Matthew looked and moved like a lean mountain puma.

"If you're up to it." Rebecca adjusted the handle of the Colt away from her body. She'd feared the brutality of a man once, been shamed by her fear. Remembering her thoughts of the previous night, Rebecca sought to separate men as she would nails. But with Eric she had the eerie sense of murky darkness.

Eric flashed another grin down at her as they walked toward the corral. "How's the Indian, Rebecca?"

Okanogan Mary would not reveal why she hated Eric, snatching her baby to her. Rebecca had the feeling she would do the same. "She doesn't like you, Eric. But she's promised not to hunt you on Klein land. You were lucky with that knife this morning."

"Uh-huh. You can't ever turn your back on an Indian. Why are you keeping so many Indians around? They all ought to be kept on the reservation."

Rebecca felt a keen sense of shame for her white blood. Men like Eric weren't concerned about humanity. Was it possible that beneath Matthew's gentle trappings he shared the same lack of sympathy? "This was Okanogan country, Eric. The Nez Percé were forced to move here. They're a proud people, and it sits hard on them to be confined to one area when in the past they hunted and lived as they wished. The other tribes had to make room for them. We're all trying to live in peace." Rebecca whistled for Wind Dancer, looking at Eric from beneath the brim of her hat. "The Indian hating days are over now. You've been gone too long."

For just an instant Eric's cold, steely eyes pinned her. Then he grinned lightly, tightening his cinch on the big buckskin. "I know I have. Who would have thought that you would turn out to be the prettiest woman between Spokane and Seattle? Let me saddle that horse for you."

"I can manage." She didn't want Eric close to her or her horse. Rebecca gathered her saddle and bridle from the tack room and thought of Matthew's sweet compliments. She frowned, wondering again how alike the brothers were.

Eric watched her throw on the saddle and hook the stirrup on the saddle horn, preparing to fasten the cinch. "You know, a pretty woman like you should let men help you. Keeps your hands soft." He paused, his eyes drifting over her. "You don't seem to realize just how you can excite a man. Can you shoot that Colt on your hip, Rebecca?" he asked lazily.

She slipped the bit into Wind Dancer's mouth, then adjusted the bridle. In just moments she had tired of Eric's company. "I can worry about my own hands," she said too sharply, realizing that Rudy, too, had talked about a woman's soft hands. And Matthew had asked her to touch him. "I can shoot my gun."

"It's got the look of a fast-draw gun, Rebecca. Now why would a woman wear a weapon like that?"

She patted the horse's mottled rump. "You know as well as I do, there are snakes around. We hit a pit when we laid out the new apple orchard. We killed almost twenty big ones."

Eric's gaze drifted over her ruffled blouse and rested on her breasts. "What does Matthew think about the gun? And the pants?"

"I don't know. What do you think?" she asked carefully, recognizing a faint recoiling within herself as Eric's stare touched her body. She'd felt differently when Matthew—

Perhaps Matthew and Eric were alike; the thought shimmered and grew. Perhaps Matthew concealed his thoughts better than his brother. Perhaps she had already betrayed herself by listening to his sweet words and giving herself to his gentle hands. Rebecca's lips pressed together, her stomach contracting. Perhaps she had already shamed herself and Matthew was laughing even now!

"I think you're the kind of woman that stirs men up," he returned just as carefully. "I'd be keeping you close—tie you to my bed—if you were my woman."

He stepped closer, and Rebecca looked up at him, leaving her dark thoughts of Matthew. There was something about Eric, something veiled and deadly. "What happened this morning, sister? A little newlywed squabble? You were mad as hell when you waltzed into the kitchen this morning. I was thinking then that I wouldn't mind you taking a little of that temper out on me. If you need someone to talk to . . ." He reached to cup her shoulder, and Rebecca shook off his hand. "Men scare you, don't they? Must be hard on Matt, wanting a proper wife in his bed. If he doesn't treat you right, let me know."

Rebecca stared up at him, realizing just how different Eric

was when compared to Matthew's teasing tenderness. Or was Eric's nasty side what lurked beneath Matthew's loving ways? "We'd better go."

As she stepped into the stirrup Eric's hands circled her waist. His fingers tightened momentarily before he eased her into the saddle. "You are a beautiful woman, Rebecca. It's too bad Matthew got you first. I would have given him a run for his money."

Rebecca stared down at him. "You and I would not have been, Eric. Our ideas don't agree," she stated quietly, knowing the truth of the fact.

Eric's face was expressionless, his eyes opaque and flat. He patted the Appaloosa's rump. "Matt would let you think anything to get you where he wants you and what you own. But then that boyo was never one to let an opportunity pass."

Rebecca held Wind Dancer back, drawing the reins tightly as the stallion pranced. Eric's jaw moved and his lips tightened as he met her eyes. "What do you mean, Eric?"

He shrugged. "Are you ready to ride?"

They rode to the sandy banks of the Columbia, then followed a wagon trail past Brewster. "This country has changed. I think I'd like it here now," Eric remarked, looking at the few houses dotting the sweeping canyons.

"It's growing, Eric. There's plenty of room for you." But somehow she doubted that Eric could adjust to the new times. Rebecca swept back a loosened strand of hair with her glove. She pointed to the cattle being forced into the sweeping, deceptive current. A ferryman hauled the calves across, and their mothers followed, bawling.

Eric looped his leg around his saddle horn. He tugged the brim of his hat lower against the mid-morning sun. "That's a hard way to make a living, driving cows. That and mining." His eyes flicked to her curiously. "Do you know anything about mining, Rebecca?"

She shrugged, scanning the drovers for Matthew. "The gold rush opened up this country. The Chinese left huge ditches from their placer mines and there is still a lot of mining up Nespelem way. And we have an assayer in Cairo."

In the river current Matthew's horse reared, nudged by a sharp horn. He fought to stay on the horse, flapping his hat against the wayward steers. When the horse settled, Matthew leaned over, grinning and patting the animal's neck. Rebecca watched closely, knowing that Matthew was gentling the animal, the same way he had gentled her.

Just then he looked toward her and waved his hat.

The river and blue sky and sand and bawling cattle seemed no more than a few feet away. The wave was as intimate as a kiss, a tender look in the night.

Her heart began to beat more quickly and her body tensed. She clasped the saddle horn to still her trembling hands.

Matthew did have a way about him. . . .

Wind Dancer shifted; the leather saddle creaked. She still ached from their lovemaking, the Western saddle rubbing her tender thighs.

The cattle stepped between the round river rocks to find footing in the sand. They scrambled up a slight slope, the stockmen forcing strays back into the herd. Matthew and the rest of the local men walked their horses around the cattle, studying them carefully.

One of the stockmen carefully separated five cows from the herd. He drove them toward a small group of Indians and left them. When Eric looked at her, Rebecca explained, "The trail boss is part Cherokee."

"Those look like choice cows."

"They would be the best. Wes has his own way of remembering the Trail of Tears."

"Indians stick together." Eric sneered and glanced at her. "What has Matt planned for your land? And the dowry?" he asked softly. "Is that why you two are going to the lawyer later today?"

Rebecca turned to him, her stomach knotting. "What do you mean, my land, my dowry?"

"Why don't you ask Matt?" Eric suggested mildly. "You just might be interested in the answer."

Fighting the sudden chill that swept over her, Rebecca watched Matthew. Was it possible that he was just as greedy as Rudy, using his talents for lovemaking? "Thank you, Eric. I think I will."

He looked at her closely, then smiled. "I've changed my mind. I think I'll look over the stock. Coming?"

"No. I have to get back." Rebecca took a deep breath and began wondering how many sneaky little tricks Matthew Mc-Kay had up his long sleeve. What land and what dowry?

Rudy had been offered the land, but she thought it had been forgotten.

Her father and Matthew had a lot of explaining to do.

Would Matthew make such sweet love to her if she didn't have a dowry?

Would he touch her as if she were silk and velvety rose petals then?

Chapter Nine

"I'll tell you why it matters, Father!" Rebecca slammed the study door. She tramped back to her father's desk and took his plate, placing it aside. "You are not going to eat lunch—even if it is your favorite roast beef and horseradish sandwich—until we have this out!"

"What did it matter, to put the land in Matthew's name? It would have gone to Rudy—"

Rebecca's eyes widened, then narrowed dangerously. She pointed to her chest. "Because I—your only daughter, Papa—do not like it!"

Klein's hands went up defensively. "Now, Rebecca, Matthew would want you, dowry or not—"

"What? How do you know? The man is a sneaky, low-down, conniving son of a—"

The study door opened, the hinges creaking.

"I could hear you through the door, my love. Were you speaking about me?" Matthew asked mildly, behind her.

She pivoted toward him. Breathing hard, trying to hold her temper, Rebecca walked to him; she wanted him within punching distance. Matthew wiped his forehead with the back of his sleeve. "It is warm for July."

"It's going to get warmer," she threatened darkly.

Matthew's eyes sparkled, his lips fighting a grin. "Am I about to see one of Becky's famous tantrums, Peter?"

"I believe you are, Matthew. Ah . . . would it be all right if I ate my sandwich now, Rebecca?" her father asked.

"When I'm finished," she snapped without taking her eyes from Matthew.

"You sure are pretty when you get fired up, woman," he murmured huskily. "Rosy cheeks and rosy lips."

"Pretty as a picture, pretty as her mother," Klein added heartily. "Prettiest girl in the countryside."

"Papa, you can eat your sandwich now," Rebecca tossed over her shoulder. She thumped Matthew's chest with her fingertip, narrowing her eyes. "I just don't know about you. . . ."

She tilted her head, studying him. With his hat tipped back on his head, his black wavy hair clinging to his damp brow, Matthew looked almost boyish. He leaned his shoulder against the door frame and stood grinning down at her, as though he were happy.

Entranced, Rebecca stopped thinking. She ran the tip of her tongue across her suddenly sensitive upper lip.

His gaze darkened instantly. Matthew raised his finger to trail across the softness of her cheek. "What's wrong?" he asked gently, stroking her shoulder with his palm.

She felt herself lean toward him, then she swallowed and stepped back from him. "You stop that."

"What?" he asked, all innocence. He took a step nearer, whispering, "When can I have my kiss? Now or later?"

"Matthew . . . Papa . . ."

"Later, then." He grinned, swooped, and picked her up in his arms.

Her father chuckled as Matthew carefully lowered himself into an overstuffed wing chair. He settled Rebecca on his lap easily. He crossed her thighs with his forearm, holding her still. "Now, what's the problem?"

When Rebecca stared at him, surprised by his sudden move, her father laughed outright. "So that's the way to handle her!" he exclaimed, delighted.

She sat upright, aware that Matthew's body had begun to

harden beneath her hips. "You stop that," she whispered, feeling her face heat.

He rubbed her back with his hand. "I can't," he returned in a husky whisper that she remembered from their lovemaking.

She glanced uneasily at her father, who was watching with interest. "I want to know about the land you took from my father . . . for marrying me."

Matthew's face darkened. He caught her braid in his hand and studied the jet black sheen. "I think you had better explain, Peter." He tugged her braid gently. "And you, my dear, need to realize that we still have much to settle between us. We need time."

"The land?" she insisted, very much aware of Matthew's large hand caressing her back. He touched her as though he had the right of possession.

And for some unexplainable reason she liked his touch. She liked being cuddled and cozened and that odd feeling of being . . . cherished by Matthew McKay.

Why? Why did her body soften against his? Why did she long for that hard mouth on hers?

"I had the deed sent to Matthew two years ago." Klein munched on his sandwich, licking his lips. "Ah, I love good horseradish. Maria grinds it just right."

Matthew's busy hand caressed her arm. He laced her fingers with his, inspecting her skin against his darker flesh. "I thought"—he raised the back of her hand to his lips—"that you wouldn't mind having the deed signed back over to you, Becky. We can do that when we talk to the lawyer. So you see, you can't question my motives for marrying you."

"Did you find any good stock in the herd?" Klein asked as Rebecca once more found herself falling into Matthew's black, velvety gaze. "Matthew?"

"Mmm, what?" His gaze lowered to her mouth, as if he wanted to taste it.

When she nervously licked her bottom lip, Matthew's breath caught. He eased her to her feet. "Ah, would you mind getting me something to eat?"

He turned her hand in his and kissed the very center of it. "Please, Becky?"

Rebecca walked out of the study on shaky legs, wondering how she had agreed to do anything for him.

When she returned, Matthew ate the battered sandwich as if it were fine French cuisine. "Thank you. That was delicious."

And somehow that pleased her. Looking at him, her heart missed a beat.

The July afternoon air was still, the shadows on the mountains already beginning to enclose the river basin. The scent of sagebrush and Matthew's spicy scent drifted around her as she stepped out of George Mead's small board house in Cairo.

At her side, Matthew cupped her elbow with his right hand. She was angry, nettled that Matthew had left her no fighting ground. By signing the deed over to her, he had swept away the foundation of her doubts. She couldn't trust him, that was all. If it weren't for her family, she'd hole up in the mountains until she plotted a way out of the mess. But around Matthew there was just no time to think. Rebecca stepped onto the dry sand of the street, shrugging free of his touch. "Don't touch me, McKay!"

She turned on him, and Matthew lifted his hand, palm up. "More problems?"

"George doesn't think I can get an annulment! Not after last night. He's too anxious to get his hands on your accounts. It appears that you could make him a rich man. All I heard was something about whaler ships and restaurants and money. Apparently timber too. He wanted to know if you needed anything for the new mill. . . ."

She paused, breathing hard. "Did you know that George said he didn't know why any man would want to sign over land to a woman? He wanted me to see if you wanted him to tear that deed—"

"Now, Becky, cool down. Last night didn't happen because of my accounts or your land or for any other reason. It happened because I wanted *you*."

She tapped her boot heel in the dust. "Why did you come back? Surely there are more interesting places in the world. China? India?"

"I've been there. But this is home." Matthew tipped back the brim of his hat. The warmth of his smile touched his ebony eyes.

"You know, if my father had not been so ill, this . . . marriage would not have happened."

Matthew chuckled, his dimple taunting her. "You certainly don't spare my ego. Even with Peter doing some pretty fine matchmaking, a man likes to think his wife wanted to marry him."

"Well, I didn't," she snapped. "I don't. And this whole farce is going to cost my father more than he knows. According to my accounting, he's in my debt."

He ran his fingertip around her set jawline. "I'm certainly in debt to him. What about going for a swim down at the cottonwood slough this afternoon, Becky?"

She jerked from his touch, frowning at him from beneath the brim of her hat. Dressed like a stockman, Matthew had the look that drew women's eyes—lean, broad-chested, and long-legged. Abigail Phillips had all but tripped over her skirts when he'd tipped his hat to her that afternoon.

She tilted her head, studying him boldly from head to toe. Matthew leaned back against the post supporting the Mead porch, his grin lazy as he looked her up and down.

"You look like a rancher—a healthy one. All the time I thought you were sick, dreaming dreams you'd never see come true," she accused flatly, eyeing his worn leather chaps. "You look like a healthy rancher, not a soft-handed businessman. One used to heavens knows what. I've heard stories of gambling dens and men getting shanghaied in San Francisco. There are easy women and fancy parties and—"

Matthew winked. "I'll take you there, Princess. We'll have fun. We'll dance until dawn, and then I'll let you shanghai me."

"I wouldn't want to go." She sniffed, still staring at him. "This . . . marriage is based on my father's deceit. It can't be valid.'' Suddenly visions of ballrooms and gowns and music swirled through her mind. She closed her eyes, almost hearing a waltz. When she opened her eyes, Matthew stared down at her curiously.

"You don't know how to play, do you, Becky?" Matthew asked quietly. ''We'll have to change that.''

Rebecca shifted restlessly, uncomfortable beneath his heavy gaze. He saw too much . . . just like an Indian tracker turning over dead leaves for footprints.

Matthew tipped her chin up with the tip of his finger. His expression was grim; a muscle moved within his cheek, tensing. ''I'm going to find out your secret, you know, Becky. I've got a pretty good idea now—''

She slapped his hand away. He had no right to pry into her life, her fears.

He had no right to make her feel soft and clinging and delicate. To make her feel like a rose among the pines. He had no right to make her blood heat, dancing through her veins.

He'd intruded into her safe world, and for that she'd never forgive him! He could try his skills of enchantment elsewhere. She had no need to be his private quest.

Rebecca glanced down the street. In front of the blacksmith's, beside his high pile of discarded horseshoes, stood a few men, who just happened to be the biggest gossips in the countryside. She could see their wide and knowing grins, and she didn't like them. Men! ''We're planting wire tomorrow. I've got to pick up some nails at the dry-goods store.''

''I'll come with you,'' Matthew drawled, placing the flat of his hand on her back, as though she were entering that ballroom. Oh, he knew how to play the gallant, she decided, stiffening her back and lengthening her stride. He knew just the right touches and looks to make a woman—

One of the men yelled, ''Stagecoach comin' from Wenatchee!''

''Matthew, take your hand off my back,'' she gritted out, under her breath.

He grinned, and she caught sight of his tantalizing dimple.

"Now, Princess, a gentlemen always helps a lady across the street."

"You are thickheaded," she enunciated very slowly. "Dense."

"Now, Becky, couldn't we talk about this down at the swimming hole?" he asked mildly, his eyes sparkling.

"Why do you love to torment me?"

When he lifted her leather-gloved hand to his mouth, Rebecca jerked it away. "Stop that!"

"What, Princess?"

"You know very well what!"

By suppertime Rebecca knew how a cornered bobcat felt—Matthew had shot her meaningful stares at every chance. Once or twice as he helped her clear the irrigation ditches for the grapes and the new trees, his hand had swept alarmingly close to her backside.

She had had to dance around him in the barn, and Matthew's size made that difficult. She had the odd feeling that he'd like to take her behind the haystack and . . .

Washed for the evening meal, Rebecca stared out the window, watching the deer graze in a far meadow. She heard Okanogan Mary croon an Indian song to the baby she had named Little Matt.

Rebecca had taken the only safe recourse, running to hide in her room. The back of her neck tingled as she stared out the window. There was no telling what the man would do if she let him get close enough. He was like a sidewinder, coming at her from all angles—a regular dry gulcher.

She placed her forehead against the cool glass. Matthew had changed everything. Once she'd been so safe, wrapped in the protection of her spinsterhood.

Then Matthew, aided by her father, had torn apart the safety, replacing it with fears. Her lips pressed together. Matthew was a potent danger to her now, but she was on to his game. . . .

Bruno opened the living-room door and came in singing an old cowpuncher's tune, "The Old Chisholm Trail." He grinned at her, tossing his hat on the brass stand. "Wes said he got his start on the trail drives from Texas to Kansas. The trail boss hired him because he could sing the herd to sleep at night, even though he couldn't ride a horse worth a hoot."

When Rebecca continued to stare out of the window, Bruno came to stand beside her. "Problems?"

"None I can't handle."

"That's just what I think. Where's that woman of mine? I want her to meet Wes. He's coming to supper."

"She's upstairs, resting. And Papa said that Emma Schaeffer was napping in the extra room. The hotel is full and he wants her to stay with us."

"Mmm. I remember Widow Jones asking him some time ago. She said the Schaeffer woman was a sister and she wanted her to stay someplace else."

Rebecca turned to Bruno. "Widow Jones runs that . . . that house outside of Cairo!"

Bruno's eyebrows lifted, his gray eyes dancing. "So? Widow Jones is a handsome woman. I'm sure Papa enjoys talking with her."

"Papa? He talks to Widow Jones? Bruno, Widow Jones is half his age."

"Uh-huh. But he's invited her to the settlers' party up the Methow, anyway. He borrowed my boot polish. I'm going up to Stella. Do you think she's doing too much, Rebecca?" He shook his head. "There's just too much canning and preserving now. The other day I caught her lifting a basket of windfall apples. . . ."

"She'll be fine. Mary is helping with the work. I'm more worried about Papa and Widow Jones."

"Mama has been gone a good long time now, Rebecca," Bruno said as he walked toward the stairs. "By the way, is Eric still here?"

"Yes, he's out back, washing up with Matthew and Daniel. Why?" Rebecca sensed that anytime Eric was not in sight, there could be danger.

"That buckskin of his has scars only Mexican spurs can make. His mouth has been torn too. I never liked to see a man misuse an animal that way. Eric still has a mean look to him. If he weren't Matthew's brother, he'd be gone. He's a troublemaker for sure."

Later, seated around the evening meal Maria had prepared, Stella looked at Daniel. "Daniel, would you mind getting Emma?"

"Here I am, all." Emma floated into the room, the scents around her of lilac toilet water and French powder. The men seated around the table stood as the blonde swished to the empty chair. "This is mine, I suppose. Sorry I'm late. But traveling in that open stagecoach just destroys one's toilette."

"Why, Matthew," Emma cooed prettily, batting her long lashes, "how divine to see you here."

Matthew took her extended hand and shook it briefly. "Emma, I understand you'll be staying with the Kleins. I'd like you to meet my wife, Rebecca."

Emma seemed to stop breathing, gazing up at Matthew with wide, blue eyes. "Why, honey, I didn't know the Rake of San Francisco had married. Actually married—imagine that."

Rebecca noted the uneasy glance Matthew shot her way and the grim press of his lips as he introduced the rest of the family. "And this is my brother, Eric, and Wes."

"Ma'am," Eric drawled, his eyes sliding to her plunging bodice.

Wes—his straight, black hair slicked back with water—nodded courteously. The trail boss, in his forties, looked stern, his high cheekbones reflecting his Cherokee heritage. His blue eyes followed Okanogan Mary as she served a heaping bowl of mashed potatoes.

When the men sat, Daniel almost missed his chair. Red-faced and stammering, he glanced shyly at Emma. "Miss Emma."

Rebecca felt Matthew's arm circle her shoulders, and she shrugged his hand from her. She looked up at him and smiled. "The Rake of San Francisco?"

Eric snorted. "That's what I heard. Quite a ladies' man, aren't you, brother?"

"I've settled down now. From now on there's just one lady for me." Matthew grinned and kissed Rebecca's cheek before she could lean away. "My wife."

"Why, that's a downright shame, Matthew. What will all the rest of us ladies do without you?" Emma asked, fluttering her lashes at him. "Becky, you naughty girl. You just up and snatched away the best charmer on the West Coast. Why, la, he can dance and—"

Matthew cleared his throat and Rebecca felt a stab of sheer jealously. "The world's loss." She sighed melodramatically, placing her hand over her heart as she had seen in a traveling show.

Emma giggled wickedly, looking at Rebecca. "The stories I could tell you about this one—"

Matthew cleared his throat again. "Ah . . . did I understand your sister will be coming later, Emma?"

"Oh, yes. Maybelle has to finish cleaning up after supper or some such task. Honestly, of the five sisters, she has had to work like a dog, just to live halfway decent in that little scum town, Cairo."

"Maybelle—Widow Jones—lives decent, Emma," Peter Klein stated indignantly. "She's a fine woman. She's just had a bad turn of luck."

During the remainder of the meal Emma flirted with Matthew. And Rebecca dealt with stabs of jealousy. She felt gauche, rangy as a longhorn caught in a ladies' hat shop. Barely touching her food, she studied Emma whenever possible.

Emma was small and curvaceous, dressed in the style of the day—bustles, corsets, and long ruffled skirts. The blue taffeta silk dress dipped low on her chest and clung to her tiny waist.

When she moved—daintily passing the blue-willow serving dishes—her breasts seemed to flow out of her tight bodice. Scents of lilac toilet water and French powder mingled with the aromas of roast beef and green-apple pie.

Matthew's large palm rubbed Rebecca's stiff back and she glared at him. "Unless you want a fight right here and now, you'll stop that," she threatened under her breath. "I've had enough of your pawing—"

His heavy brows met in a frown, anger tightening his mouth. "Becky, I don't like the sound of that," he warned.

"What are you two whispering about down there, Matt, honey?" Emma asked.

Rebecca rose to her feet. She'd had enough of "Matt, honey" and Emma's knowing glances at Matthew. "I'm going to check on the new stock Wes brought in."

The stockman's low, melodic voice floated over the table. "No need, ma'am. Those dogies are tucked in good."

Rebecca carefully placed her napkin beside her plate. "I think I'll just check on them, anyway, Wes. We had a wolf not long ago. It took a couple calves and some sheep. Maria, save me a piece of pie for later, will you?"

"Make that two pieces. I'll come with you," Matthew added, rising to his feet. He took a sip of coffee, his eyes darkening beneath his lashes as he glanced at Rebecca's rigid face. "I bought some stock, Becky. We'll check on it too."

"Don't bother coming. I'll check the entire herd. Every last cow from here to Mansfield," she snapped, walking from the kitchen.

Matthew's heavier steps followed her out onto the porch. He snared her elbow, and Rebecca jerked back from him. "Let me go!"

His head tilted and his eyes narrowed. "Woman, what is wrong?"

She stalked down the porch steps and glared up at him. Hands on his hips, Matthew looked all male and slightly . . . dangerous. "Becky?" he growled, walking slowly toward her until he towered over her. "You've been dancing around me all day, and I can understand your fears and the fact that you feel you've been misled about my ability to come back. But this temper is another matter."

He swept his fingers through his hair, ruffling the smooth waves. "Look, Emma has always been a flirt—"

"Oh, don't apologize to me." Rebecca turned and walked,

stiff-backed, into the barn. "After all, the Rake of San Francisco has quite a reputation to live up to—"

Matthew caught her at the tack room, her saddle and blanket in her hand. "Just where are you going?"

She didn't like his tone. It was every bit as possessive as she thought he might be. She hadn't invited him to return; she hadn't invited him to do . . . anything. And now he stood there, looking like a cattle baron, demanding an explanation from her. She owed him nothing.

Just for good measure she clamped her lips together and walked toward Wind Dancer. Matthew's deep voice rasped around her like an Indian lariat. "Becky, I'm a patient man, but there are limits. Come back here and we'll talk."

She tossed the blanket and saddle on Wind Dancer's back, only to have Matthew tear them off. He tossed them in the corral dirt. "Becky, I've had enough of this black mood of yours. You are staying put until we have this out."

Rebecca tossed back her braid, placed her hands on her hips, and met his angry stare with her own.

In the moonlight Matthew seemed to loom over her. His eyes glowed in the shadows of his brows and cheekbones, and his jaw hardened. "Becky, my dear," he stated too carefully. "You can be a trying woman. We are going to talk this over—whoof!"

Rebecca shot out the flat of her hand. The blow caught him in his flat stomach and sent him reeling back toward the haystack. Off-balance, he reached out and snared her wrist, bringing her down into the hay on top of him.

Matthew rolled on top of her instantly, pinning her beneath him. He grinned. "Why . . . All you had to do was ask."

When Rebecca squirmed furiously beneath him, Matthew's grin died. "That's enough," he growled, his eyes darkening. "You are a trial—"

"If I don't suit you, leave," Rebecca shot back. Her body had already started melting beneath his weight, and it frightened her. "I'm sure Emma would be glad—"

"Damn! I give up." Matthew placed his lips against her parted ones and kissed her thoroughly. "You're what I want,

Becky. Can't you see that?'' he asked raggedly when she stared up at him, bewildered by the hot urgency rushing inside her.

He smoothed the vein beating in her throat with his fingertips. ''You're what I want,'' he repeated huskily.

He plucked a stalk of hay from her hair and eased to one side, keeping his thigh over hers. ''Such wide eyes, Princess. And such a temper.''

She trembled when his palm cupped her cheek. ''Emma is more your kind, Matthew. Powder and lace and fashionable curls. I've never worn a corset in my life. I've heard you faint if you tie the laces too tight.''

His large hand prowled down her side, fitting neatly into her slender waist. ''Women like Emma need bustles and corsets. You don't.''

He caressed the curve of her waist and her hip, studying her closely. ''I'd sure like a kiss, Mrs. McKay.''

The heat of his eyes caused her heart to start racing again, frightening her. Fighting the impulse to sink into his arms, Rebecca clung to the thought that Matthew could beguile her body, enslaving her. Her body might betray her, but her pride was at stake.

In another instant she had pushed at him and run toward Wind Dancer. Leaping on his bare back, she urged, ''Let's go, boy.''

She wrapped her hands in his mane, and Wind Dancer took the low gate in an easy jump.

''Hell!'' In the shadows of the barn Matthew's throat constricted with fear when the Appaloosa's back hooves sailed over the gate's board. He ran his fingers through his hair and leaned back against the barn. Rebecca—in a mood—was like a miner's quicksilver. She responded so sweetly to him, and just when he thought he was getting close . . . A twig snapped beneath a boot and Wes remarked quietly, ''Nice night.''

Wes moved silently, taking the makings for a cigarette from his pocket. He leaned back against the corral boards and poured tobacco into the paper square. Then he fashioned a neat cigarette by licking and sealing the paper's edge.

Matthew took a deep, steadying breath as he watched the stallion run in the moonlight.

"She's riding Indian-style, Matt," Wes offered in his soft voice. "Saw her take that jump. If she didn't bite the dust then, she'll be all right."

"She's lucky she didn't break her neck." Matthew felt as raw as his voice, his heart beginning to beat again. "Damn fool thing to do."

Wes blew a smoke ring into the night air. "She's spooked—like any filly worth her salt."

"I know that," Matthew clipped out as the stallion slowed to a walk.

"I got a big bay that can match that Appaloosa, Matt. He's half wild, but he's long-winded and he could carry a man your size easily. Haven't had a man who could bust him yet. Are you interested?"

"Maybe. What are you asking?" Matthew liked the soft-spoken cattleman, who offered a distraction from Rebecca's maddening behavior. In another moment Matthew might have run her down and she'd have fought him—he'd have blown his good intentions to kingdom come.

Wes blew another smoke ring. "I'm gonna marry that little Indian miss. Looks like she's as scared as your filly when it comes to men. Thought you might help me along the way. Mary likes you. And your wife. Maybe you could put a good word in for me now and then. Maybe help me get a few purties and such."

"Getting ready to settle down, Wes?" Matthew studied the rangy trail boss, who hadn't spoken this much all day.

Wes shifted uncomfortably on his worn boots. "Maybe. You think I'm too old for the girl? I'd treat her good."

"I know you will. Tell you what, Wes. I think we can do some horse trading . . ."

Wes chuckled. "Son, that bay is an ornery son of a gun. You may want to back out of the deal."

Matthew clapped him on the back. "I don't think so. I don't like eating my wife's dust—as pretty as she is."

The cattleman's hard face softened as he watched Rebecca

walk the big stallion around the herd. He sighed wistfully. "Mary sure is a pretty little thing."

Peter Klein strolled into the corral, following the two men's stares. "She's a little raw now, Matthew. She seems to think I traded her off the way I would a lame mare. Of course, I bent the truth a little for her own good. And I counted on her loyalty to our family. . . ."

Matthew picked up Rebecca's blanket and bridle. "I think we're both in for a fight. But I thank you for my wife, Peter. We'll name a son after you."

Klein chuckled, then roared with laughter. "Boy, you'll have to mend some fences first. And get close to her. That light in her eye isn't exactly loving."

Chapter Ten

Rebecca woke at dawn with a gasp, her legs tangled in the bedding. The nightmare still bound her, the blood-red haze chilling her flesh. For a moment she fought the dream, staring out at the bright morning beyond her window. Her heart surged within her, frantic as a trapped rabbit. What was it that she had to have in the nightmare . . . had to have or die?

Rebecca turned on her stomach, plopping her feather pillow over her head and securing it with both fists. She'd slept badly, searching through the rippling gray water and the red haze of her nightmares. She allowed herself to remember the horror of the lingering dream before coming fully awake.

In the dream her legs fought to run faster, her heart pounding in her chest. Pain lashed at her knees and palms. Cold, stark fear surged through her, the red fog enveloping her, chilling her. She had to reach this something she had to have . . . so close, so far, the wisps of the cold fog threatening her journey, threatening her life. The water was so smooth, so gray . . . faces blurred in the fog, dissolving when she finally reached them. She stretched out her hands and the fog closed around her.

Rebecca threw back the pillow, breathing hard, the fear still vivid within her. She traced the familiar room, drawing her safety from it.

Matthew's tall black boots stood in a corner, the Columbia

sand polished from them. She closed her lids, forcing herself to calm.

She remembered then . . . Matthew McKay's dark face had invaded her dreams, his eyes concerned as he bent over her. He stroked her hair back from her face, trailing his fingertip down her neck to toy with the top button of her nightgown.

Gripping his wrist with both of her hands, Rebecca had lain still, breathing hard, fighting the red haze and her fear. Locking her fingers into his flesh, she had clung to his strength—the warm flesh and hard muscles were her lifeline.

"Sleeping badly, Princess?" he'd asked in that deep voice that caused her to tremble. "Your bed is creaking enough to wake the whole household. Move over," he'd ordered huskily, edging her aside with his larger body.

"I don't want you here," she'd whispered as he moved her into his arms, his hands stroking her tense back and shoulders over the voluminous nightgown.

In the dream Matthew's familiar scents of soap and maleness had seeped into her senses. She'd run her palm across his jaw, feeling the stubble rake at her skin. "Why can't you go back?" she mused softly to the dream. "Why can't things be as they were? I was happy. . . ."

"Were you?" the dream had asked, kissing her fingertips. "You had what you wanted, but were you happy?" His big hand had swept slowly down her body, pausing on her waist and upper thighs. His hard face had fitted into the cove of her neck and shoulder, his kisses warm and sweet upon her flesh. "It's too late now. I've got you—"

Somehow Rebecca had slept, anchored safely by the dream's arms.

The rousing cheers coming through her open bedroom windows were enough to wake anyone, she decided, jerking the pillow aside. The pillow next to hers retained the impression of his head, the scent of his hair. She lay there quietly, hearing the men's shouts build with excitement. "He's sunfishing, Matt! Watch it!"

Rebecca threw back the quilt, leaping to her feet. When a

bucking horse "sunfished," he twisted from side to side, coming down with one side to the earth, then the other.

Wes's shout ran out. "Ride the hay burner, Matt! He's an ornery cuss!"

Rebecca tossed her curtains aside, her heart racing in her breast.

Man and beast locked together, fighting wills and muscles to win the battle. Dust clouds swirled around the horse, his hooves thudding against the corral earth. Teeth bared, the animal snorted, enraged at the man clinging to his back as tenaciously as a cocklebur.

Matthew's coal-black hair glistened in the early-morning sunlight, the bay's coat shining with sweat.

The entire household watched the struggle from the protection of the corral fence, their faces alive with excitement. In contrast, a band of passing Indians watched stolidly. Chelan Sam leaned calmly against a pitchfork while Daniel hopped up on the corral boards, waving his hat in the air.

Matthew, his legs clamped to the big bay's belly, gripped the saddle horn with one hand and swirled his hat in the other. The bay brushed the boards of the holding pen, trying to brush the rider from his back. But Matthew held tight, clearly enjoying the big horse's struggle.

Rebecca quickly dressed in trousers and a light cotton shirt, her fingers trembling. "Well, hell and damnation!" she muttered, drawing on her boots. She was frightened badly, and she didn't know why. Why should she care if the grinning fool broke his neck?

She hesitated as an odd chill ran over her, as cold as ice water.

Fingers trembling, she strapped on the Colt, running downstairs, then out the door to the corral.

She climbed the corral boards next to Daniel, watching Matthew. Grinning, his hair tossing as the bay went into a spin, Matthew's tall body whipped back and forth. His broad shoulders rippled, taut with cords and muscles as he pitted his will against the bay's.

"Watch him, Matt. He's a low-down sidewinder!" Daniel called, slapping his hat against his thigh. "Don't trust him!"

Matthew's broad back rippled beneath the blue shirt, his wide leather chaps slapping the chestnut belly of the bucking horse. He looked like any stockman breaking a horse. But there was a keen difference: Matthew clearly enjoyed the struggle, his teeth flashing in his broad grin. Every muscle looked well suited to the struggle.

Daniel shifted on the fence, allowing Rebecca to perch next to him. He looked at her solemnly for a long moment. "Your hair is hanging down. Looks wild. Doesn't Matt like the braid?"

"If you don't want to be knocked into that corral and stomped to ribbons, you'll close your mouth," she hissed watching as Matthew's lean body seemed to flow with the horse's bucking movements. "He deserves to get thrown," she muttered darkly, trying to still her heartbeat. "That horse needs an experienced rider, not some dandy off the San Francisco wharves."

Walking up to the corral, her father leaned against it. Her father tugged a strand of her hair. "You keep throwing that word *dandy* at him and he's going to prove you wrong. Any man would."

Rebecca scowled at Klein, deciding that of course he'd take Matthew's side. Her father was not only a matchmaker, but also he stirred up trouble in his spare time. "Matthew may have sailed the Seven Seas, but horse breaking falls to experienced stockmen. What kind of a childish game is he playing, showing off at his age and scaring the devil out of everyone? Why, he doesn't have the sense the Good Lord bestowed on a groundhog. McKay needs a good set-down," she said tightly.

The black mane of the chestnut-colored horse stood upright as he landed stiff-legged on the corral floor. Matthew swirled his hat at the bay's flanks and the bucking started all over.

Bruno stood on the corral boards, watching the horse breaking. "That horse is a mean son of a gun. Wes said the animal is a one-man horse, and he'd trotted him up from Denver just to find the right man. The bay is getting winded and it looks like Matt may be the only man to ride him."

He turned to Rebecca. "Your hair is down," he remarked pleasantly.

"I know that, thank you. Daniel has already noted the fact," Rebecca snapped. "What in blue blazes is Matthew doing breaking that horse?"

When Bruno did not reply, she scowled down at him. "Well?"

Her older brother's eyes went over her too carefully, and Rebecca flushed uneasily. He tugged her hair. "He might be the one to do a lot of things around here," he murmured gently.

"Not if he breaks his thick neck," she spat back, gripping the railing. "Look at him, he's enjoying it."

"If he bites the dust," Daniel noted conversationally, taunting her, "the bay will stomp him. Wes said he's already stomped—"

"Oh, shut up," Rebecca snapped, just as the bay charged against the corral, forcing Matthew to lift his leg to keep it from getting crushed. The bay went into a fast spin, forcing Matthew to lean aside, leather chaps flying.

Rebecca could hear her heart beating frantically against her breast, could feel her blood throb through her veins. "He has about as much sense as you do, Daniel," she whispered, unaware that both her brothers watched her taut expression. She could almost feel her blood drain from her body as Matthew momentarily lost his balance. "He'll be lucky if he doesn't get himself killed."

"Nah," Daniel mused, following the bucking horse around the corral. "That buzzard bait is about winded. Old Matt's going to ride him out yet."

"He's a good man," Peter added quietly. "He'll stand the weather."

"Old Matt," Rebecca repeated slowly, watching her husband's intent expression, his jaw set and grim mouth tight as the horse began spinning. Matthew would stick with his plans

until he got his way. He intended to run her life to suit him—
a man moving kingdoms to suit himself.

Her eyes narrowed, watching the cords move beneath the
dark skin of his jaw and neck. Matthew looked tough now,
his big hands strong. His hair, tousled by the ride, gleamed
in the morning sun, and Rebecca felt her stomach tighten.

The bay eased for a moment, and Matthew swatted the
horse's neck with his hat. "He's doing it," Daniel stated
proudly. "Old Matt's about got him broken."

The horse took a few strides, snorted, then began bucking
again. The bay brushed against the corral, crushing Matthew's leg. He grimaced, fastening his leather glove to the
saddle horn as though it had grown there. Rebecca felt her
heart stop in that moment, her fingers gripping the fence
tightly.

The bay quieted again, and Matthew bent toward the
horse's ear, murmuring something. He glanced at Rebecca
for just an instant before the bay went stiff-legged and bucked
once more around the corral. In the instant when Matthew's
eyes locked with Rebecca's, she felt shock ripple through her
body.

Matthew would claim her, fit her into his life, just as he
forced the big black-maned chestnut horse to submit to him.

Without causing her family shame, there was little she
could do to dislodge his hold on her. Her father had hatched
a fine plot, and McKay was set to see it through. With or
without her approval, just like the horse he now rode.

As the horse began to quiet and walked amiably around
the corral, Rebecca's fury rose. Grinning, Matthew walked
the bay up to her.

Rebecca scowled down at him. "You're showing off, Mr.
McKay. You should leave the bronc busting to younger men.
Old bones don't heal easily," she snapped, knowing she had
to lash out at him. He'd caused her to die a little, watching
him wallow in potential danger. She didn't like her heart flip-
flopping around in her chest while he played cowboy. Not a
bit. McKay needed a lesson.

Beneath his Stetson his eyes darkened, his grin easing. "Morning, Mrs. McKay," Matthew drawled.

"You deserve to have your neck broken," she tossed at him, scrambling down from the fence to stalk toward the house.

"Rebecca!" Matthew's sharp voice caught her and she pivoted to see him standing just feet from her.

"Stay where you are, McKay," Rebecca ordered, her hand drifting down toward her Colt. She was angry, recovering from stomach-wrenching fear. Why should she care if the big, daft dreamer broke his neck? His skull was too thick to crack, anyway. "I am not in a good mood."

He'd forced himself into her life and upset everything, just like a cart of apples dumped on the ground.

Watching her, Matthew lifted the Stetson from his head and dusted the brim. "You're as mad as a hornet," he noted pleasantly as he walked toward her. "If you're going to draw down on me, Mrs. McKay, you'd better do it. Because I'm coming for my morning kiss."

"Hells bells! Don't you dare!" Rebecca took a step backward, her eyes widening.

He shifted on those long legs, looking rugged and all Western male in the worn leather chaps. "I dare plenty, Mrs. McKay, where you're concerned. Come here and kiss me proper."

The hair on the nape of Rebecca's neck lifted. If he kissed her, she'd melt—and he'd know that she had worried. "Never."

"Then I'm getting my kiss. You're a pretty sight in the morning, Princess. With your wild hair catching blue sparks from the sun, you turn my mind to soft sighs and dewy lips . . . like the other night." Matthew's shirt gaped across his broad chest; exposing the dark whorls of hair. Her palms itched, as though wanting to rummage across the roughness.

She wanted to touch him, to lock her arms around him. If he touched her . . .

"Ah, Becky. It does my heart good to know you cared enough to run downstairs half dressed, just to see about my safety." Matthew's eyes twinkled. "Why, your blouse is unbuttoned."

When she glanced down, Matthew wrapped his arms around her and lifted her from the ground. "Matthew!"

Pressing her body against the length of his hard one, Matthew chuckled and rubbed her nose with his. "How I love those little ladylike protests. . . ."

Rebecca wanted to lash out at him, but somehow all the fury turned to warm, startling, happy confusion.

In the middle of the ranch yard, her toes dangling inches above the ground, Rebecca felt the warmth of the sun touch her back and shoulders. Another warmth snuggled inside her heart, frightening her.

No one had ever touched her as boldly as Matthew, daring her, challenging her, making her feel, all when she thought she had locked her heart in chains.

But could she trust him or herself?

He grinned, brushing her hot cheek with his mouth. He waited, watching her emotions race across her face. Caught for a moment, Rebecca stilled. She wiped a trail of sweat from his temple with her fingertip. He'd come to her like a victorious warrior, swaggering and boyish and hot with pride.

She traced his rumpled curls, the dimple in his cheek and the lights sparkling in his black eyes.

The softness within her fluttered and bloomed. Was it possible that he really cared?

Holding her tightly, Matthew waited, wanting something from her—and only from her.

"You're lucky you didn't break your fool neck," she murmured gently, stroking back a damp curl from his temple.

"That's what I like to hear—praise from my wife." Matthew shifted her in his arms, placing one hand under her knees and the other supporting her back. He stared at her, long and slow, as though he were trying to see into her head, her thoughts. "You could give me that kiss, Mrs. McKay," he offered huskily. "Wrap your arms around me and show me you would care if I broke my neck."

"No," she murmured, aware of the hard, shifting muscles

supporting her. "Everyone is watching. And aren't I too much weight for a bed-bound invalid who can never realize his dreams?"

There was safety in lashing out at him and no safety in the tenderness she now felt for him.

His mouth tightened grimly, the dark brows meeting in an ominous expression. "Someday, Becky . . ."

The sunlight cut between them, blinding her and she saw a flash of pain cross his face. Regretting having struck at him, Rebecca tried to think of a way to soften her blow.

He grew still when her arms went around his neck. Matthew went taut as Rebecca placed her head against his shoulder.

"Damn," he muttered shakily, his arms trembling as he carried her into the house for breakfast. "That was almost as good as a kiss."

"Imagine Maybelle acting like a girl at her age . . . running off to some settler's ragtag party!" Emma exclaimed, rising from the rumpled bedding that evening. She'd needed a man—hot and ready—tonight, and Eric had been willing, staying at the Klein ranch house with her.

She tugged a silken peignoir over her plump shoulders, then turned and ran knowing eyes over Eric's naked body. Sweat trickled between her full breasts, and she wiped it away with a corner of the peignoir. "Why, la. It's not as if Old Man Klein has anything to offer—like you, sweetie."

Eric propped himself against the bed, biting off the end of a cigar. He spat out the tobacco, lit the end, and inhaled deeply. He blew smoke rings toward the ceiling, watching the wisps dissolve. "Klein has money, Emma. And land. Maybelle isn't so dumb. She'd be set for life if she married Klein."

"Huh! She got tied up with that drifter down in Oklahoma. He landed her out in this godforsaken territory—nothing but half-breeds and poor white trash everywhere. Why, she sat right up on that open coach, right next to that Indian girl and that Mexican woman. Maybelle should have made it to

Seattle—gotten herself fixed up proper with a gentlemen there. She never did have a lick of sense when it came to looking out for herself.''

''And taking care of her little sister, Emma,'' Eric said mockingly, watching as she carefully cleansed her lower body.

''Hush up! I'm only minutes younger than Maybelle, and you know it. I swear, I don't know why I stayed at home with you,'' Emma snapped, glaring at him.

She sauntered to the dressing table, easing her round hips onto the small bench. Brushing her hair around her shoulders, she stared at Eric through the mirror. ''She'll . . . Rebecca will get pregnant if this keeps up, you know. She was blushing like an absolute fool all day. Matt's lost his senses, I do declare. Why, now, he used to be a man.''

Eric blew another smoke ring. ''You don't have a chance, Emma. My brother wants to seed new territory with his holy dynasty. You've been around—''

Emma glared at him throwing down the hairbrush. ''I never would have thought that Matt would hobble himself with that . . . tomboy. Not in all my living days! That girl doesn't know the slightest thing about being a woman. It took the entire family begging on their knees to stuff her into that skirt tonight. She's got a hot-tempered, gypsy look about her that isn't ladylike at all. Then she strapped that gun on just like a heathen gunfighter. I really don't see what Matthew sees in her. He used to be quite a beau with the ladies . . . and I mean *ladies*. To look at him now . . . out there riding that bucking horse this morning just like a paid cowboy. The man must be losing his senses,'' she said fuming. ''Pray to God he doesn't lose all that wonderful money.''

Eric turned, tapping the cigar ashes into a dish on the bedside table. ''My brother always saw things a little different, Emma. Honor and all that. I never could knock sense into him.''

''That Klein family is the same way, holding their almighty name up on high. I could try for the old man, maybe take him away from Maybelle,'' Emma offered, her blue eyes gleaming.

"You lost that one. I'd say the old goat is working up to asking her to marry him."

"La! You don't say?"

"The big cache is up on the mountains, Emma," Eric stated quietly as he stood. "That Chinaman's gold mine is Matt's by way of Rebecca's dowry. It's a strike bigger than Sutter's Mill. It's up there, just waiting."

"It's Matthew, then," Emma surmised softly, wrapping a curl around her finger.

"It's me," Eric corrected walking to her. He drew her to her feet. "With Rebecca dead, I'll be Matt's only living heir. There'll be plenty of money for anyone who helps me."

"I'm your girl, honey. Just take it a little easy this time, hmm?"

At the Moreland cabin raising, Rebecca stepped back from Matthew's outstretched arms. "No thank you."

The flat of her hand slashed the inches between them. "There is absolutely no reason for me to go to Spokane with you. I have no intention of spending that much time alone with you." She primly adjusted the high eyelet collar of her blouse. "You stay on your side of the fence, McKay. Stop watching me, trying to see to the back of my brain. And stop sneaking into my room at night. I was happy before— What are you grinning at?"

Matthew settled back against the cabin logs. There was something comforting in having Rebecca scold him, just a wisp of a promise that she might care. "If I hadn't rescued you, you'd have turned into a crusty old maid, frightening little children and terrorizing a whole new state."

"You flatter yourself, McKay, if you think you can handle me," Rebecca managed tightly.

"I already have—"

"Matthew!"

"Afraid of me, Becky?" he asked softly. He knew a little of her fears from the beating she must have taken. But their tomorrows were at stake and he'd fight for her on any terms.

Her complexion paled beneath her tan. "Afraid of you?"

She looked him up and down. "That will be the day. You're not lacking for nerve. And stop looking at me like that. I feel like a cow up for sale."

"You're a beautiful woman, Becky. Especially when you're laying down the law like any good, caring wife—"

"Oh!" Rebecca said hotly.

Mrs. Peterson stepped up to them. The elderly woman handed them chipped cups filled with warmed apple cider. "Why, she's blushing just like the bride she is. How sweet."

When Mrs. Peterson hobbled away, Matthew chuckled at Rebecca's stormy expression. "Don't take it so hard. Not everyone shares your ideas about marriage."

He wrapped his hand around her neck, stroking the taut cords with the pad of his thumb and wanting to kiss the day-lights out of her.

"I hate skirts," Rebecca began ominously.

Matthew took a deep breath; she had her sights set on one hell of a fight.

Peter and Maybelle walked up to them just as Henry Finnes was tuning up his fiddle. "We'd like to dance, Rebecca—Maybelle and me. Do you think you could start off this shindig?"

"And I hate dancing," Rebecca continued, looking at Matthew. "In fact, I don't know how," she added confidently. "Matthew will have to find another partner."

Peter slid his hand down to Maybelle's tiny waist, holding her against his bulk possessively. "Can you help Rebecca, Maybelle?"

"Papa!"

Daniel bumped into Rebecca's backside. "Hey! There you are. Sally said she'd dance with me, whenever you and Matt start the dance."

"I'll go ask for a waltz," Maybelle said, winking at Matthew. "Stand on his toes. No one will notice, and he looks sturdy enough to me."

Rebecca shot a stricken look at all of them, her face paling before Matthew said quietly, "Give us a moment."

Drawing her into a corner, he placed a hand near her head

and leaned toward her. "I'll make a bargain with you, Becky. We'll dance this once and no more. You can squash my toes as flat as you want, but you'll have to make that trip to Spokane with me. I not only need supplies, I also need to make some business contacts."

Rebecca stared at him. "No."

Matthew fought his rising temper and his wish to carry his bride out into the night. "If you want to play hellcat, I'd prefer it wasn't in front of the whole valley. I won't always be so patient," he ground out, feeling his body tighten. "And you definitely need gentle handling. Maybe it would do us both good for me to make the trip alone," he added, knowing that Rebecca would fight him every mile.

He preferred Rebecca purring and snuggling close. There would be other times . . .

"Well, hallelujah! Now you've finally said something that makes sense." Rebecca dusted her hands, smiling primly. "Are we dancing or not?"

She was pleased about having her way now. But eventually he would have his. "Shall we begin . . . ?" he offered, extending the tip of his polished boot.

Chapter Eleven

Before dawn, Chief Joseph poked a stick in the tepee's small fire, stirring the coals to life. He settled back to watch the flames eat the pine wood gathered by the women. Sitting cross-legged and dressed in beaded buckskin trousers and a patterned cotton shirt, the old chieftain allowed a young woman to adjust the blanket around his shoulders. "Go now," Chief Joseph ordered her.

Wearing a long skirt and blouse, the woman lifted the tent flap. She fastened it back, allowing a wedge-shaped view of the dark gray sky beyond the tent. Dogs barked and a coyote yipped.

Jean Dupres rose from his pallet as gracefully as a mountain cougar. He ran his palm over the small thicket of hair in the center of his chest. The hair was a reminder that he was half white, a symbol marking his fate. Was it the white blood that made the numbers dance in his brain? Jean looked at his fingers, long and slender, capable of writing script or numbers. Did his poetry—songs of earth and animal—arise from his Indian blood?

He shook free his neatly folded cotton shirt and buttoned it carefully. He stretched, straightening the shirt over his buckskin trousers before wrapping his gun belt around his lean waist. Tightening it, he greeted the chieftain. "In-mut-too-yah-lat-lat, the day is good. The sky will be blue."

"The sky is blue for all people," the Indian added solemnly, his voice crackling with age. He sighed tiredly, adjusting the blanket more closely around his aged shoulders. "My bones ache. The summer mornings were warmer in the Wallowa. How I long for the earth of my mother's and father's bones."

Jean chuckled, settling next to him. "You should be living in your government house like the others. It is much warmer than this tent."

"Pah! They have caged us here at Nespelem. The other tribes did not want us here on their land, and there were many fights." The chieftain's lids lowered as he studied the smoke drifting upward to the tent's smoke hole. "I still have the dreams—the old ways live in me. Your father kept the old ways, too."

"But my mother was a French woman, Chief Joseph. I walk in both worlds." Jean's lean brown face tightened as he, too, stared into the smoke. "A half-blood, not wanted by Indian or white."

"There are many such as you, seeking one path or the other, ashamed of the blood flowing in their veins."

Jean took a deep breath, years of pain wrapping around him. "They sent me to school in the East, and the white women petted me like a dog."

Joseph shrugged, taking his pipe and lighting it. "You are a man women like to look upon. Your voice is soft and soothing, making them smile. But the swaying pine still whispers to you, my son. You hear the voices of the birds and the elk. You listen to the spirits of the land. The blood of great chiefs—Ollokot and Looking Glass—flow through your veins."

The younger man, tall and lean, ran his hand through his straight blue-black hair. "I can walk in both worlds but fit into neither."

Joseph puffed on his aged pipe quietly. "In the old days the camas meadows were spread out across the countryside, their flowers blue as the sky. The women dug the roots and made bread. The children were fat and laughed. The people knew me as In-mut-too-yah-lat-lat. My father was Tu-eka-kas.''

Jean listened, watching the old chieftain settle into his memories, his dreams. "After the white man came, rooting in the meadows for gold, there was blood. Cayuse, Flathead, Nez Percé . . . we all fought to hold the land against the whites and the soldiers. The children cried from hunger and cold. I fought, but my heart was sad.''

The old man reached into a buckskin pouch and stuffed crushed leaves into his pipe, puffing at it for a long time. Beyond the open flap, the rising sun turned the sky pink.

"Now we are here—this dry place—and I long for the home of my birth . . . an old man who has fought his wars. I have seen many great things and at night hear the groans of my dying warriors.''

A dog ran by the open flap, carrying a doll in its mouth, and a small girl cried out her protest. The glow of dawn settled onto the chieftain's lined face as he smiled softly. "I fought the white man's school. But I saw that you were a part of the new ways, speaking with paper and numbers.''

Jean drew on his beaded moccasins, then waited, sensing the old chieftain had more to say. Joseph rocked, searching the smoke. "Stay,'' he murmured quietly.

His wife brought food and placed it beside Joseph. She glanced at the chief, nodded, then silently left the tent and closed the flap.

"Two women . . . both white, both seeking. One is strong—she hears the songs of the birds, feels the grass grow, and listens to the song of the deer. Her spirit belongs to the land and she fears her dreams. The other woman is soft but does not know her way. She touches the black panther and follows him. The strong one has a fighting heart that can be killed by the red cloud.''

Chief Joseph shivered, as though chilled beneath his blankets. "Blood runs between two hearts—one good, one bad. The smell of flowers touches them. A shaman woman . . .'' The old man sighed. His lids opened. "It is ended.''

Jean Dupres rose to his feet in a lithe motion. "I must go.

I will see your people get a good price for the Appaloosas at Spokane, In-mut-too-yah-lat-lat.''

Joseph nodded. "They are good horses. It is good you know the white man's numbers.'' He paused, then looked at Jean intently. "You will know both women, my son. And you will be in the river of their lives.''

The younger man placed a black, flat-brimmed Stetson over his hair. "Coming down from Canada, I saw a woman ride an Appaloosa. She rode like a warrior. Is she one of the women?''

The old chieftain stared at him as though seeing beyond the times. Then he shrugged and turned back to study the drifting smoke.

At dawn Matthew studied his sleeping bride, the sweet purse of her lips and the long, intriguing line of her neck. He rubbed his unshaved jaw, feeling as raw as the stubble chafing his skin. He'd slept badly, desiring her, while she had slept as innocently as a child. He tossed his filled saddlebags at the foot of her bed.

Startled by the weight, Rebecca struggled out of the sheets and blankets in a mass of rippling black hair and fiery green eyes.

"When I come back, Princess,'' he stated evenly, "I'll be sharing your bed every night, not just when you have some blasted nightmare.''

While Rebecca dealt with waking up and Matthew's demands, he continued his laying down of the law. He traced her body beneath the voluminous nightgown and bedding. "Don't bother hiding. That tent you're wearing does the job well enough.''

"This is a proper nightgown; there's nothing wrong with it,'' she threw back, brushing the hair from her hot cheek.

"There's plenty wrong with it.'' Taking the collar of her nightgown in his two hands, he ripped it away, baring her to the waist.

"It's come to this, then,'' she whispered, her face going pale.

Fighting for control, Matthew's anger died quickly, replaced by the tenderness he felt for her. He unbuttoned his shirt, took Rebecca's hands, and placed them upon his chest as he eased onto the bed.

"No, this is the way it is, lass." Taking care, Matthew fitted her breasts to the hard planes of this chest. Trembling, fighting his desire, he stroked the long sweep of her back beneath her tousled hair until she eased against him slightly. When her arms lifted to slip around his neck, Matthew closed his eyes. He tugged her hair, easing his mouth to her throat. "Ah, you little torment, you could just drive me mad."

Taking his time, Matthew found her lips with his. When he finished the kiss, Rebecca's mouth had the soft, dewy look he wanted, her eyes drowsy. Matthew ran the tips of his fingers across her breasts and she caught her breath, moving against him.

They stared at each other, testing, probing, until Matthew smiled softly. Sliding down her body, he fitted his mouth over the crest of her softness.

When Rebecca's legs moved restlessly beneath the sheets, he eased from the bed and picked up his saddlebags. He tossed them over his shoulder and grinned down at her. He winked. "Wear my silk shirt and think of me. If we start anything now, it might not end for two weeks. I've got a notion that in Seattle we could bathe each other in champagne for days—never leave the hotel room or those big round beds. I'll lie in my birthday suit and you can parade around in garters and a corset—"

The soft, drowsy look slid into a stormy expression. "You come in here—" she began darkly.

Matthew dipped to steal one more kiss before leaving the room, whistling to himself. Her boot hit the closed door and he hesitated on the stairway. "That's my girl."

A moment later Rebecca raced down the stairs, holding her nightgown closed with both hands. "Matthew, I'm good and mad," she snapped, catching him at the front door. "You come back acting like this and I'm liable to shoot you between those black, no-good eyes."

"Missing me already, are you?" he drawled pleasantly, eyeing the sight of her breasts, heaving and exposed by the torn gown. "Well, I'll savor that thought all the way. Hold it to my heart like a warm memory—"

Rebecca stamped the floor with her bare foot. "Damn you, McKay. You're not fighting fair."

Emma sauntered up to stand beside Matthew. Dressed in an open silk wrapper and a low-cut nightgown that exposed her generous breasts, she looked as dainty as lace. Her blue eyes danced as she looked from Rebecca to Matthew. "Lordy, Lordy, she's all worked up, Matthew. Just like a wet hen."

"Shut up, Emma!" Rebecca hissed, hitting Matthew's bare chest with the flat of her hand. "I suppose you're one of those men who go running off to the—"

"Bawdy houses?" Emma supplied, balancing her coffee cup on its saucer. Her gaze drifted over Rebecca's gown. "Lordy, no wonder he tore the thing. Looks like miles and miles of sheets. Why, a man would have to work himself to death to get through that thing."

"I like it," Matthew drawled, catching Rebecca's hand and rubbing it against his chest. "Gives me something to look forward to—like eating ice cream after all the work of cranking."

"Matthew!"

Emma caught a curl between her fingers and twisted it, looking at Matthew speculatively. "Honey, he's a big one. Why, I surely wouldn't let him go anywhere by himself."

"Ooo!" Rebecca snatched her hand back from Matthew and raced up the stairs to slam her bedroom door.

Looking out of the window that afternoon, Emma waved a silk fan before her face. "La, it's hot for August. And Daniel and Rebecca out there racing in the heat and raising the dust. I haven't felt clean since I arrived."

Coming up behind her, Eric watched the two riders. "She can ride that Indian pony."

"Mmm. She's been worked up for hours. In two weeks she'll have that horse worn to skin and bones."

Eric chuckled, watching as Rebecca lithely dismounted and walked Wind Dancer, cooling him. "She needs taming. Matt may not be the man."

The small woman fluttered her lashes up at him. "And you are? I do declare, you cad."

A full week later Matthew tipped his whiskey glass to his mouth. The tavern talk eased a full day of bargaining. He studied the portrait of a nude woman sprawled above the polished bar.

Rebecca! The scents of pine and roses and the sweet perfume of her flesh beckoned him. He wanted Rebecca, whether as mad as a wet hen or snuggled tightly against him. He took a deep breath and stepped into the clear night air. He remembered his mother's favorite poem and smiled softly. "My midnight rose, my highland heart."

Rebecca was his midnight rose, his prize, and he'd cleave to her.

Matthew saw Wes leaning against the wall, whittling a long stick. Standing near him, he cupped his hands around a match to light his cheroot. "Nice night, Matthew," Wes noted. "There's a lot of people everywhere . . . too many. I like it quiet."

Another man moved lithely from an alley. Tall and arrow straight, the suit-clad man nodded. "You must be Matthew McKay. I'm Jean Dupres."

Wes sliced a wood curl from the pointed stick. "Heard of you. You've got the best Appaloosas in town. They've got Chief Joseph's mark."

Jean shrugged, stepping into the shadows. "They *are* the best, and they're for sale."

Matthew looked at the younger man steadily. "My wife has an Appaloosa stallion. He's the best I've ever seen."

Jean stooped, picking up a long, whittled curl of wood. He studied it intently, running long, lean fingers over the shaving. "Few woman can ride a good Appaloosa stallion."

"Becky rides Indian-style." Matthew's eyes drifted across

a tall, slender woman. His voice softened. "She's something to see on Wind Dancer."

Jean carefully wrapped the wood curl around his wrist. "Your wife . . . does she have hair the color of a raven's wing?"

When Matthew nodded, his eyes narrowing, Jean said, "Perhaps you would be interested in my Appaloosas. It seems my fate to meet the husband of a woman who can ride like the wind."

The first week of August was dry and hot, sapping the women's strength as they preserved peaches and plums. Rebecca found peace in the canning; keeping busy during fall harvest made her too tired to think of Matthew, of her marriage, or of the awful dream.

She wiped her hands on Maria's large apron which covered her to her knees, and leaned on the back of a chair, watching the river drift lazily by the ranch.

Stella sat at the kitchen table, pitting washed plums for jam. She chopped them into tiny, succulent pieces and placed them in the black granite preserving kettle. She wiped a damp cloth across her brow. "It's hot."

Okanogan Mary stirred the kettle on the stove, then lifted the wooden spoon to taste the peach preserves. She nodded, looking at Stella's burgeoning stomach. "Baby come soon."

Maria dipped hot water from the stove's reserves into a bucket, then poured the water into the waiting jars. "Yes. Baby come soon. It move low in her belly."

The Indian girl nodded, smiling softly. "Babies good."

Stella laughed softly, easing her hand low on her back. "They may be, but this one kicks like a mule."

Noting her sister-in-law's pale face, dampened with sweat, Rebecca asked quietly, "Is everything all right? With the baby?"

Stella took her hand, lacing her fingers with her own. "I don't know. I just pray that I won't lose this one too. Bruno is counting on rocking his son in his arms."

"My brother wants you well, Stella. Everything will be just fine."

"I don't know." Stella patted Rebecca's fruit-stained fingers. "Mrs. Peterson said to send a stockman over when Matthew got back. She's got the quilting circle readying for a wedding. Apparently he stopped by the morning he left and arranged the traveling preacher and everything with her. Gave her some money for the store here, then asked what she needed from Spokane for the celebration. Matt and Wes spent most of the morning drinking coffee and eating her home-baked bread."

"The two of them hatched wedding plans? They can marry each other for all I care!" Rebecca placed her left palm flat on the table, studying the ruby ring as though it were a live snake. Matthew was a plotter and she couldn't trust him.

"Now, Rebecca, everyone is just waiting to welcome him here to the valley. He's the new breed . . . business and trade. He'll get good prices, bring in money . . ."

"McKay is a sneaky man, Stella." When the screen door opened and her father entered the kitchen, Rebecca said, "Men of all ages and sizes have their sneaky ways."

Klein's brushy eyebrows lifted. "Did I step into a wet hen's nest?"

"When Matthew gets back, we're all sitting down to clean out this mess," Rebecca stated hotly.

"Fine. We'll wait until then," he returned mildly, reaching for a glass and pouring cold coffee into it. Adding water, he sipped it and gave a long, satisfying sigh. "I think it's safer and cooler working down by the creek."

When the door closed behind him, Rebecca muttered, "He's been running away from me for days, biding his time until his reinforcement arrives—"

"I'd like a cup of cold coffee. Would you?" Stella said, interrupting gently. "And Widow Jones is coming over later with her catalogs. After the canning we can all rest and go through those notions the traveling salesman left at her . . . hotel."

Maria emptied the hot water from the jars, filling them

with peach preserves. She capped them with glass lids and placed them in a kettle on the stove to seal. "Mr. Klein wants a nice dinner for Widow Jones."

Emma waltzed into the kitchen, fanning herself. "La, I feel like melted butter. Did I hear that my sister was coming for dinner . . . again?"

"McKay bring presents for Woman-Who-Holds-the-Lightning," Okanogan Mary stated as she poured cold coffee into glasses. "Want to give his woman pretty things."

Stella shifted uncomfortably, her hand pressing her side. "Oh!"

"What is it?" Rebecca placed her arm around her sister-in-law's shoulders.

"He's strong, like his father," Stella murmured, her face turning pale. "I pray the baby is all right."

Eric entered the kitchen and Okanogan Mary ran to gather her baby to her. She held the cradle board protectively, her round face tight with bitterness.

He studied her lazily, placing a hand on Rebecca's shoulders. "Good afternoon, ladies."

Emma fluttered her fan before her face, eyeing him. "Hot as blue blazes, Eric."

Rebecca shrugged free, aware that Eric's touch caused her skin to chill. She walked to the sink and pumped water over a cloth, then carefully folded it. She patted Stella's forehead and the back of her neck, cooling her.

"How about going for a ride with your brother-in-law, Rebecca? I'd like to show you some land I'm thinking about," Eric said.

"Oh, do go, Rebecca," Stella urged softly. "Pick some pretty flowers for me. Just don't keep her too long, Eric. We've a wedding to plan."

"Who's getting married?"

"Matthew thought it would be just lovely to have all the trimmings," Rebecca snarled, plopping hot fruit into the jars with a ladle. The plum preserves splashed onto the oilcloth-covered table and Maria shook her head.

"A wedding," Eric repeated slowly, watching Rebecca's

scowl. "Yes, that would be just his touch. Wanting everything just right, all the corners tied up. He's like that. The old man was like that too."

"He's something, all right," Rebecca agreed hotly, wanting to race freely through the sunlight. Eric offered that escape for now and she'd take it. "I'm ready for some fresh air if you are."

"Don't be too long, ya'll," Emma cooed as Eric followed Rebecca out the screen door.

Chapter Twelve

Rebecca shifted on Wind Dancer's saddle, watching the shadows of the clouds slide over the blue-green sagebrush flat.

Riding up behind her, Eric said softly, "You don't like being cornered, do you, Rebecca? Well, I can understand that . . . people putting neat little pegs in your life. My brother wants his empire and a powerful woman at his side—one wearing skirts and serving tea to the aristocrats. But that doesn't suit you, does it, Rebecca?"

Rebecca concentrated on the slight breeze that was lifting the damp tendrils at the back of her neck. When Eric talked, she found safety in her own thoughts.

He nodded to a stand of sumac and aspen trees cradled within the thick pines. A doe stood grazing peacefully with her twins. "You're like that deer over there in the sumac . . . wild and free. See them?"

She rested her hands on the saddle horn, scanning Eric's weathered, once handsome face. Though she preferred to be alone, she also wanted to know why Eric had such a keen interest in her life. His nature wasn't to be kindly, and she frequently caught glimpses of Eric's dark emotions concerning Matthew. "I see them. What interest do you have in all this, Eric?"

"I care about your happiness, of course. You like to take

the reins of your own life—do what you want when you want, right?'' he continued, edging his buckskin next to her.

Rebecca felt that her battles with Matthew were private, and if Eric grasped any part of them, he could make trouble. "I think we should talk about something else," she said.

Wind Dancer whinnied nervously, and Rebecca patted his strong neck. Eric ran his glove over the Appaloosa's mane, lifting the coarse hair to expose the Indian brand. "See that? Matt's putting his brand on you, Rebecca. Just like this horse. Oh, his way is slow enough, but he'll get the job done."

"That's enough, Eric."

Eric turned to her, his saddle creaking. He braced his hand on the horse's tan rump. "Why didn't you go with him, Rebecca? Seems to me like newly marrieds would enjoy being alone."

Trying to hold her temper, Rebecca could see Eric's jealousy, his need to hurt and pry. "I'm busy here, Eric. And Matthew had a lot of business to be done. Is this plateau the land you're looking at? This is the old Sorgenson place. The mail carrier uses the cabin in bad weather, but other than that, it has been deserted for years."

He snickered, leering at her. "Changing the subject?" he asked, grasping Wind Dancer's bridle.

"Get your hands off my reins," Rebecca ordered slowly. There was a wild look in Eric's blue eyes, an excited hunger like a wolf hamstringing his prey.

"Easy. You get nervous when a man comes too close, don't you?" He released the bridle slowly, raising his hand for her to see. He patted the buckskin's neck, gazing over the dry plateau. "I've known your family since Ma and I came to this country, Rebecca. I just don't want to see you get hurt."

"You're telling me not to trust my husband, is that it?"

Eric's eyes pinned her. "You're a hell of a catch, Rebecca. And my brother always gets the best. Let me take you to Spokane. You can see for yourself how he does business."

She'd heard of brothers hating each other, yet the strength of Eric's emotions went deeper. Whatever their past, the brothers could not endanger Stella's coming baby, nor the entire family. "You really don't like him, do you?"

After a pause he shook his head. "He's just like the old man, through and through," Eric said with a snarl. "Their way was the only way. Matt even looks like Old Man McKay. In a few years he'll be just as set in his ways."

He dismounted, walking to a small creek. He crouched beside the rippling water, scooping up a handful of sand and studying it. Deep in thought, Eric presented the picture of a lonely man.

For a moment Rebecca felt sympathy for a little boy in a new land, afraid that his mother would be taken from him by a fierce mountain man. Then she thought of what Eric must be feeling about a new baby arriving. She slid to the ground and walked over to him. She plucked a blade of grass and sucked on the sweet end as she knelt beside him. "You look like Matthew. You have the same mother," she said softly, letting her fingers trail through the icy water. "Can't you forget the past, whatever happened back then?"

Eric crushed the sand, letting it flow through his fingers and into the rushing water. Broodingly, he watched the grains settle into the stream bed. "I'm ready to settle down at last, like Matthew. Maybe it is time." He looked down at her. "Maybe I'll find myself a catch just like he did—a beautiful woman at my side, land, money . . . the whole picture."

"Matthew turned the land back in my name, Eric," she informed him gently.

His head went back, as though taking an open-handed slap. The blue eyes burned into her. "Why the hell did he do that?"

"I don't know. But it's legal. I signed the deed of transfer."

Breathing hard, Eric studied her. "So that northeast plat is in your name?"

"Yes." A flock of crows settled down on the plateau grasses, foraging for food. Watching them, Rebecca felt the large man tense, felt his eyes glide over her face, assessing her.

"I'd rather have that old homestead than the Sorgenson place, Rebecca," Eric drawled slowly. He trailed a fingertip down her cheek, lifting it away quickly. "How much are you asking?"

She fought not to rub away his touch, felt his mark chilling her skin. Eric's demons could touch others around him, and she had to protect her family from whatever ruled him now. Taking her time, Rebecca answered carefully, knowing that she didn't want Eric to walk across any Klein land. "It's not for sale. I've always liked that country; it's still wild. The Chinese barely made any mark when they mined it."

"There's a rumor that they left a rich mine up there."

Greed was his demon, Rebecca decided, determined to deal with Eric by herself. He was too dangerous now, hungry for gold. "There are always stories, Eric. They grow through the years—you know that."

Eric stood slowly, then reached down to wrap his fingers around her upper arm. He eased her to her feet, and she sensed his strength. "Let's go up there, Rebecca, explore those old placer mines. Matthew's gone his own way. He'll be living it up in a few days, with you back here."

She unwrapped his fingers, feeling the slight resistance before Eric dropped his hand. "You're free to go if you want, Eric. You can have whatever gold you find."

"Crumbs from the McKay table again, honey?" Eric snarled, his head going back arrogantly in a gesture that reminded her of his brother. "Well, little bride, let me tell you a few things—" He grasped her shoulders roughly, pulling her against him. Eric's hot mouth sought her own. He bit her lip as she fought him, laughing wildly. "Damn, you're wild! I like my women with claws!"

"Eric, she managed, struggling against him, turning her face away from his seeking mouth. Her tongue tasted the tang of her own blood. "Let me go or I'll shoot a hole—"

He laughed coarsely, his arms pinning her to him. "You like it, too, don't you? Ah, you're a wildcat for sure. If Matthew thinks he can put a bustle on you and dance you to his tune—"

Rebecca's nails slid down his neck, leaving four bloody furrows. Eric yelped, freed her, and touched his neck tentatively. "You little bitch—"

"That's enough!" she snapped between her teeth, drawing her Colt as she stepped back.

When he took a step toward her, Rebecca cocked back the hammer with her thumb, each click deadly. "Get off Klein land, Eric."

His face was contorted with anger. "You teased me! Let me think . . . you won't always have that gun," he threatened, his face reddening with anger. "I'll tell Matthew you tricked me, that you wanted me instead of him."

"Tell him what you want, Eric. Just don't touch me again." Backing away a few feet, Rebecca slowly replaced her gun in its holster. Grasping the saddle horn, she swung up on Wind Dancer's back.

Suddenly the breeze stopped and the tiny stream quieted; the earth seemed to still. She closed her eyes and the red haze floated beneath her lids. A chill flowed over her despite the mild, late-summer heat. She shivered, opening her eyes to Eric's rage-distorted face.

"You like it fine, I suppose, when Matthew touches you. That's why he sleeps in another room," Eric jeered, scowling at the blood on his fingers. "I bet he's got marks down his back from a she-cat right now! He's probably throwing up skirts right now, hot as a boar in some wheat field!"

Eric was wild now, shouting whatever obscenities came to his mind. Rebecca trembled with the rage that had returned from her past, when another man had screamed at her, hurting her. To kill him—and somehow to kill the memories of Rudy—would be so easy now. Her fingers ached to slip back to the Colt and kill both men with one bullet.

Rebecca swallowed, breathing the sagebrush-scented air deeply, fighting for control. She had to think of her family, to protect them against Eric's greed. She shivered, fighting the emotions within her. "Leave me alone, Eric, or I'll shoot you like I would a rabid dog."

"Slut! No woman marks me! I'll make you pay for this!"

Rebecca turned Wind Dancer toward the homeward trail, ignoring Eric's threats.

By mid-August, Rebecca felt as taut as a rope on a bull-dogged calf. For two weeks she had fought Matthew's memory. She'd fought his black, gleaming eyes and soft touches in her dreams, her body stirring, aching, and writhing on the hot sheets.

She'd fought the nightmares too. The red haze and the smooth gray water frightened her to the bone, leaving her awake and cold. Why?

Awakening to the last hoot of the great horned owl, Rebecca lay still. The curtain by the open window fluttered, the pine scents slipping into her bedroom. She lifted her left hand, studying the ring on her third finger. The dark rubies sparkled in the shadows, the antique filigree as delicate as lace.

What did he want from her?

She slid her palm down her arm, covered by Matthew's long-sleeved silk shirt. If she had to out-and-out admit it to herself, she did like the soft cloth swirling around her.

When the morning was still, before the household began to stir, she lifted aside her bedroom curtain to watch the dawn. She settled on the small rocker, resting her bare feet on the windowsill. From a small table she lifted a folded length of white lawn and dark green satin ribbon—Matthew's gift to her. "The color of your eyes. Matthew, your husband," he had scrawled boldly on the note.

Stroking the ribbon, Rebecca wondered about Matthew's means to bring her to heel—gifts and soft words and softer touches that drew her hunger.

She answered a muffled knock on her door. "Come in."

Stella entered slowly, a black-fringed floral shawl covering her nightgown. Speaking in hushed tones, she eased onto Rebecca's rumpled bed. She adjusted her heavy body, leaning against the headboard and patting her unborn baby. "That Okanogan stockman grinned from ear to ear when he handed you the parcel a week ago, Rebecca. No wonder, Matthew probably paid him a pretty piece to deliver it. My, that ribbon is just lovely. Have you decided how to cut it?''

Rebecca thoughtfully ran her fingers across the cloth. ''Matthew has experience in giving women gifts. Like a trapper laying out the right bait.''

She sighed, watching the pink glow heighten in the horizon, touching the rugged mountains. ''Stella, this wedding thing is far out of hand. It's his wedding. He planned it. He's a low-down, sneaky—''

Stella whistled, her eyebrows rising. ''Carpetbagger, in the words of our fair Emma?''

''I don't like being herded into this entire . . . flimflam,'' Rebecca stated darkly.

''He's courting you, Rebecca. There's just something so very special in his eyes. Can't you give him a chance?''

''Giving Matthew a chance is like placing Maria's hot apple pie in front of Daniel,'' Rebecca answered flatly.

''Well, anyway,'' Stella said quietly, ''he wants you something fierce, and most women would be proud of that.'' She fingered the cloth. ''Oh, don't roll those eyes. Let's get to work on this beautiful dress—''

''Balderdash! I am so tired of Matthew this and Matthew that.'' At a sound from the doorway Rebecca turned.

Matthew grinned wolfishly beneath a full black beard. His gaze strolled down her body, dressed in his silk shirt. ''It suits you better than it does me, Becky.''

Rebecca grabbed the white lawn from Stella and shielded her body. Leaning against the door frame, Matthew looked big and dark and dangerous. No, he looked hungry. ''What are you doing here?''

Stella eased from the room. ''Mmm, I think I hear Maria calling me.''

''You stay right here,'' Rebecca ordered, watching Matthew carefully.

He swept off his dusty hat, throwing it to the bedpost. ''Morning, Stella,'' he said as the smaller woman swept out of the room, closing the door quietly.

"You stay here!" Rebecca gathered the fabric to her as Matthew took a step nearer. "Stella!"

Big and shaggy and dusty from head to foot, Matthew didn't take his eyes from her. Broad shoulders rippled beneath the faded work shirt, his chest dark with hair. He moved another step closer, his leather chaps creaking. His eyes gleamed beneath the heavy lashes, damp curls lying against his forehead.

Matthew took another step and Rebecca frowned, holding up her hand to stay him. "You stay where you are, Matthew McKay. You've made my life holy hell with all this wedding talk. I don't like being pushed around, like a cork into a bottle, and I'm mad as a wet hen!"

"Let's go swimming in the cottonwood slough," he drawled, taking another step, his grin widening into a blaze of white teeth. "Without a stitch—"

"No! Stay where you are." She backed against the bed, felt the feather tick behind her knees. He was close enough for her to breathe his scent, feel his heat wrap around her.

Matthew's black eyes blazed. "I'm bone-tired, woman. I've thought about those soft lips night and day for almost two weeks. Thought about that silky black hair sliding through my fingers and over my skin. Probably made some bad business deals because my mind was on you . . . and right now, by damn, I want you to kiss me or I'll yell loud enough to wake up the dead."

"Shh, it's bad enough that Stella knows you're here. The way you look, it's a wonder you didn't scare the baby into coming early." Matthew bent over her, eyeing her mouth as though he could devour it. "Matthew?"

"Are you going to put on some clothes to go to the slough, or am I just going to carry you out the way you are?" he asked mildly, playing with a curl beside her hot cheek. He wrapped the strand around his thumb, studying the complement of dark skin and raven hair.

He brushed the back of his hand against her cheek. His eyes narrowed, tracing the rapid pulse at the hollow at the base of her throat. "I rode all night, left two good men with my stock, and crossed the river before light, just to get to my bride. The ride would have done in any horse but the bay, but I'm here," he murmured as though speaking to himself. "And what do I get for my troubles? A reluctant woman who is about to be carried out of the house in front of her family."

"You wouldn't." Rebecca breathed hard, trying to stand, bent backward as Matthew leaned over her. Somewhere within her she resented the rapid beating of her heart, her body warming to his as though enchanted by his male contours. "You stink like a horse."

"That's why I need to take a bath . . . first," he explained slowly. "You and me, down in the cottonwood slough. I've thought of nothing else for two days."

"You've got the whole countryside stirred up over this wedding thing, McKay. I've been looked at like a prize heifer by everyone, and the questions they ask . . ." she protested, leaning farther back.

"I was right. The dark green color suits you." He shook his head, snaking the ribbon around her neck to draw her near. "Mrs. McKay, I do desire to lay with you. Promptly."

"Matthew, I swear I'll shoot—"

His mouth touched hers lightly, tasting her lips. It began slowly and tentatively, the kissing and the tasting, as though Matthew had rediscovered the contour of her mouth. He fitted his lips to hers lightly, skimming their fullness, and then he breathed heavily.

When Rebecca felt she'd fall right into the feather tick, he asked lazily, "Where's the soap and towels?"

"We can't," she whispered, wondering why the world always seemed to slant when Matthew came near her. It seemed she had as much will to deny him as a dandelion puff before a strong wind.

"Why not?" He nuzzled her neck with his jaw, and she shivered, the beard tickling her flesh. "We're married."

"It just isn't done." The tip of Matthew's tongue slid along her jaw, causing her to shiver. "Stop that."

He stepped back, glowering down at her. "If you want a hullabaloo, I'm in the mood, woman. Somehow I had pictured you welcoming me with open arms. But as it is, I'll settle for you coming down to the slough with me while I take a bath.''

Rebecca straightened, trying to gather her wits. It seemed Matthew had found a way of scattering them without her control. "I'm not exactly in a good mood myself, you know," she informed him regally. "At the moment I seem to be the sacrifice for the entire valley. Hells bells, I'm not a sweet, blushing bride, eager to begin her life of slavery, you know. I wouldn't even be in this stew if it weren't for two men in cahoots: one man wanting to pawn off his daughter and the other one wanting her to . . .'' She let the hot statement die, not wanting to complete what Matthew wanted her to do.

Matthew looked at her for a moment, then asked pleasantly, "Are you being difficult, Princess? Let me remind you. You've got two choices: to be carried out of here as you are, or to come along, fully dressed.''

"I thought you were a gentleman," she said tauntingly, feeling her temper rise. He couldn't just come waltzing into her bedroom, wanting her to dance to his tune. "I thought you knew just how to ask a lady.''

A muscle moved beneath his dark skin, his eyes narrowing. His lips barely moved. "Please.''

She had missed him and she deeply resented the fact. He needed to pay for that. Taking her time, she nodded. "Leave the room then, so I can dress.''

Matthew took a deep breath that expanded his chest and widened the tantalizing gap of his shirt. He crossed his arms and turned his back. "This is as far as I go. Make it fast.''

She stuck her tongue out at his shaggy head. "You act like a mountain man. A regular savage.''

"I'm waiting. You have one minute.''

Rebecca dropped the lawn onto the bed and scrambled for her trousers. In the prescribed minute she stood fully dressed, her loosened hair flying around her as she slid the last button through her blouse. She hit him in the back with the flat of her hand. "There. Are you happy now?''

Without looking at her Matthew grabbed her hand and

strode out the door. "Wait, Matthew! I don't have on my boots."

"Don't need them, Becky. Not for what I've got in mind," he growled, forcing her to run down the stairs to keep up with him.

Peter Klein sat on the settee, drinking his coffee. "Good morning, Rebecca," he called. As Matthew drew her after him, Rebecca had a fleeting glance at her father's big grin.

Daniel, waiting at the front door, handed him a blanket roll. "There's soap and towels in here, Matt. See you later."

"You were both listening," Rebecca hissed accusingly before Matthew pulled her out the front door.

Standing on the front porch, Daniel winked at her. "You two would wake the dead, caterwauling like that. I just wanted some peace."

"Where's my horse?" Rebecca asked, just as Matthew placed his hands around her waist and plopped her in his saddle.

"Catch." Matthew threw the blanket roll into her arms. He swung up behind her, wrapping his arms around her to hold the reins. As calmly as she could, Rebecca turned to look up at him. "I always ride my own horse."

"Now you're riding mine, aren't you?" he asked with a nasty tone. "Named him Duke, by the way." Fitted to her back, Matthew's heavy thighs supported her own. He guided the horse toward the cottonwood slough not far from the Columbia River.

The sky was light blue-gray, preceding full light. A buck watering at the river lifted his head. He studied the riders and the horse for a moment before racing toward the alfalfa meadows.

A fat porcupine waddled across the horse path, his quills shimmering in the half-light. Carrying an alfalfa sprout in his mouth, he glared at the intruders, then slid into the underbrush.

Matthew moved his hand, sliding it across her stomach and pressing her back against him. She held her breath, adjusting to the hard muscles claiming her. Somehow Rebecca had forgotten his size and strength, and now, surrounded by Matthew, she trembled. He leaned down, kissing her cheek briefly. "Not scaring you, am I?"

She straightened, glaring up at him for prowling through her private thoughts again. "Not a bit. That will be the day—"

He kissed her soundly, taking time to taste her lips. The bay walked quietly, then stood beside the placid waters of the slough as Matthew's kiss ended. When Rebecca finally opened her eyes, the barnyard rooster crowed and a calf lowed to his mother. The morning mist clung to the water, cattails hovering gracefully in a sheltered cove. Above them, the cottonwood trees created a golden-green cathedral.

"Later, when I can, I'll take up courting again, Becky," Matthew offered huskily as he slipped from the bay. He raised his arms and lifted her down gently. "But right now I'm so damned hungry for the taste of you, I don't think I can."

She watched as he began to unbutton his shirt, the wiry hair springing from his tanned skin. "You're darker—"

He chuckled, sitting on a fallen log to tug off his boots. He stood and began unlashing the worn chaps. "I'm glad you remember something about your husband." He lifted one heavy brow, his hands going to his belt. "Are you watching me drop my drawers, woman?"

Her face flamed as she pivoted, turning her back to him. She threw the blanket to the ground and wrapped her arms around herself. "You're positively crude."

Matthew's arms closed around her, his fingers unbuttoning her blouse. While Rebecca dealt with his busy hands, somehow Matthew undressed her and waded into the slough, carrying her.

"Matthew, there's a catfish in here as big as a whale," she screamed before he let her drop into the chilly water.

When Rebecca struggled to her feet, tossing back her mass of wet hair, Matthew grinned down at her. He handed her the bar of soap, then turned his back. "Scrub."

"I'll m-make you eat this!" she stammered, her lips quivering with cold. "I'll cram it down your throat!"

When he looked down at her over his shoulder, Rebecca

sank into the murky water up to her neck. "Turn around, you bully."

"Are you going to scrub me or not?" he asked mildly, his eyes drifting to her shoulders.

"You turn around, Matthew McKay—"

"And you'll scrub my back like any good wife?" he pressed, seeking her breasts beneath the water.

"Oooo . . . yes, I will."

"Ah, good. I've been waiting for my woman to take care of me for two long weeks." Matthew slid to sit on the sandy bottom, presenting his broad back to her.

Hesitating, Rebecca placed the large bar of homemade soap against Matthew's dark skin. Then, slowly, she cupped water with her free hand and dribbled it over his flesh. Rubbing the soap until it foamed, she found she liked Matthew resting quietly beneath her fingers, liked the steely, hard feel of his muscles as he stretched like a petted cougar. "Ah, that's good," he murmured. "How about my hair, woman?"

He ducked underwater, then sighed heavily, enjoying every minute. "Well?"

She eased to her knees, tentatively scrubbing his hair with the bar of soap. Wet and clinging to her fingers, the strands were as silky as a baby's, black against the mounds of suds. "You need a haircut," she murmured, noting the strength of his neck as he turned sideways to allow her to work up a lather.

"Uh-huh. Soap my beard," he ordered softly, drowsily. "I could get used to this, Becky. You touching me, your breasts brushing my back—"

"They are not!" She pushed his head underwater and Matthew came up spitting out water.

He grabbed her and plopped her on his lap. Taking her hand and the bar of soap, he rubbed it over his chest. "All of me, Becky. And stop squirming, or you'll wake up that big catfish and we'll have a lot of explaining to do if he sticks our backsides."

Between her teeth Rebecca gritted, "You have nerve, McKay. This water is freezing." But her fingers worked the lather into his chest, sliding the soap over his muscled shoulders.

She really did like that mat of hair covering his chest, treating it to a slow, intense cleansing.

Matthew's gaze darkened, surveying her averted face. "Did you miss me a little, Becky?" he asked huskily, lifting a damp strand back from her bare shoulder.

Avoiding his question, Rebecca soaped his left shoulder, studying the tendons and rippling muscle as he caressed her hip with his palm. "I don't like being handled and forced against my will, Matthew. And you've done just that this morning."

"I know," he agreed softly. "But I don't frighten you, do I?"

She touched his beard, working the lather into it. "No, I can't say that you do."

"That's what's important, Becky," he murmured softly, pressing his mouth against hers. "I don't want to frighten you."

The slough had quieted, the mists drifting around them. Matthew's lips left hers. He smiled gently, kissing her fingertips as they followed the line of his mouth. "Do you like the beard? I could trim it, keep it just for you—"

She tilted her head, studying the hard shape of his face and the coal-black beard, covered with soap lather. "It tickles. I've never been kissed by a man with a beard before."

Matthew's large hand flattened on her back, supporting her as he bent her backward. Leaning over her, he brushed his lips against her throat, tracing the tendon that ran toward her ear. "Now Matthew . . ." she began, finding that her arms had slipped around his neck.

He rubbed his beard against her neck, the foam sliding down her skin. Matthew's tongue followed the bubbles, trailing over her to tease the crest of her softness. He tasted her gently, supporting her easily as she gasped, closing her eyes with the sweetness of her emotion.

Gently his hands moved over her beneath the water—warming, sliding, seeking.

She quivered, feeling the softness wash over her, feeling the rising need enter her as sweetly as honey.

Matthew breathed heavily, heating her throat with his open mouth, easing her breasts against the hard planes of his chest. Leaning back, he rubbed side to side against her softness, watching her.

"Your lips are soft as rose petals, Becky . . . and as sweet as the morning dew," he whispered, dark eyes flowing over her heated face. "I dreamed about you lying in my arms like this."

Rebecca ached for his mouth, lifting her lips for his taste. The waters stirred between them, lapping gently around her breasts as Matthew closed his eyes in pleasure.

Rebecca felt feminine, cherished, as Matthew stroked the length of her body. Shyly, she eased her head against his shoulder, allowing him to touch her delicately. His hands trembled, fitted to her curves, then swept on slowly.

"This is sweet, Becky," he murmured at last, shifting her hips to his left thigh. "But you're driving me mad," he finished roughly, taking her hand and easing it between them.

The instant she touched him intimately, Rebecca stiffened, reclaiming her hand. "Hell and damnation, Matthew!" she exclaimed, looking up at him. "We're in the middle of a slough and it's broad daylight now."

He chuckled, tugging her hair. "Ah, someday, my fine raven-haired witch, you won't care where we are. And if my dreams come true, you'll be doing the touching."

She forced inches between them, aware that Matthew's eyes instantly sought her foamy breasts. "Women don't do such things, Matthew. And there's a name for those who do."

He closed his eyes and sighed tiredly. "You're a hard woman, Becky."

"And you're positively . . . randy!" She squirmed, fighting his loose, slippery grasp.

"Shh! I hear something," he ordered, wrapping his arms around her. Sitting on his lap, Rebecca could feel him thrusting boldly against her.

"Hold still. There's horses coming," he whispered, holding her hips against him. "Stop squirming."

"Matthew, I swear . . ." she promised darkly. "You are so full of tricks—"

He glared at her from beneath soapy brows. "Do you want the whole countryside to know where you are? It wouldn't bother me, but you're such a prude," he whispered.

The approaching horses whinnied and snorted. Through the white, rough trunks of the cottonwoods they watched two men lead a string of Appaloosas and pack mules.

One of the men, handsome and of native American heritage, lifted his black Stetson and waved it toward the cottonwoods. "Hey, Matthew! How's the swimming?"

Rebecca's hands flew to her hot cheeks. "He knows you're here. What if—"

"Go on to the house. They're expecting you for breakfast," Matthew called, edging his fingers between Rebecca's thighs.

She grasped his wrist, scowling at his devilish grin. "Stop that this instant!"

"Merely testing the water, my dear," he returned with a kiss.

"You are no gentleman," she finally managed as he stood, drawing her to her feet. "Kindly look the other way."

Rebecca couldn't any more stop her eyes from drifting downward than she could have stopped the winter snow. Blushing furiously, she closed her eyes, crossing her arms over her breasts when he laughed outright. "Well, I was curious."

He patted her chilled bottom affectionately before stretching his arms high and yawning. "That's an improvement, Becky. You're showing signs of being a good wife already. Go on, get dressed. I'll finish up in a minute."

"You close your eyes, Matthew McKay," she ordered, walking toward her clothing.

He threw a rock that caused cold water to splash up her backside. "Not a chance! A man doesn't come home to a sight like that every day!"

Chapter Thirteen

"You've embarrassed the holy mortification right out of me, Matthew McKay!" Rebecca marched straight toward the kitchen.

Matthew followed, admiring the sway of her hips. Everyone at the kitchen table turned expectant faces toward them as Rebecca took her chair. Matthew held the back of it, easing it beneath her as though seating a grande dame at a ball. He lifted back her long hair, smoothed it possessively, then seated himself at her side. "I guess everyone has met Wes. This is Jean Dupres. Jean, this is my wife, Becky."

"Hello, Jean." Rebecca snatched back her hand from Matthew's fingers, glaring at him.

Jean's black eyes sparkled as he acknowledged the introduction. "Mrs. McKay, you're every bit as lovely as Matt's description. Congratulations, Matthew."

"She's getting prettier day by day," Peter Klein stated. "Being married seems to agree with her."

"Just wait until she wears her new dress with the green ribbons," Stella offered, sipping her coffee and easing back in her chair, close to Bruno. "It really does match the color of her eyes, Matthew. Such a lovely emerald color."

Wes watched Okanogan Mary refill coffee mugs. When she came to him, Wes lifted his cup and said boldly, "Hello, Mary. Nice morning, isn't it?"

The Indian girl looked at him, nodded, then continued to pour. Wes shot Matthew a look of frustration, then jammed his fork into the pancakes.

Rebecca traced the oilcloth pattern with her fingertip. "About this wedding . . ." she began after clearing her throat.

The door opened and Emma drifted in, dressed in a pink lawn ruffled dress. A tiny spray of white baby's breath shimmered in her blond curls as she nodded to the members of the family. "Lovely morning. Just lovely."

The men half stood, waiting for her to be seated, but Jean walked to her chair. "Allow me, ma'am," he murmured with a white-toothed smile.

Emma's blue eyes drifted over him, from blue-black hair to dusty boots. "La, who's this lovely man? Such manners." She settled her skirts and bustle with an air of a queen settling before her court. Filtering glances at Jean as he returned to his chair, Emma sipped her coffee. "You're a half-breed, aren't you?" she asked baldly after a moment.

Matthew's voice was cool and hard. "Jean just sold me some fine Appaloosa stock for Rebecca's own line, Emma. He's agreed to help me set up my businesses, keeping tallies and so forth."

"She does not offend me, my friend," Jean murmured. "Miss Emma is far too beautiful. Does my presence upset you, *ma chère*?" Jean asked softly. "If so, I will leave, but my heart will ache never again to see such beauty—"

"You're staying," Rebecca interrupted quietly as she buttered her pancakes. "She's a guest in this house, the same as you."

Emma gasped, and Matthew leaned back in his chair, watching the two women come to a silent understanding. His wife went on eating as though she hadn't spoken, while Emma's blue eyes darted nervously toward Jean. Rebecca, Matthew decided, would indeed be a good mate—he'd have to remember that soft, deadly edge to her voice.

The small blonde licked her lips, playing with her cutlery. "Well, I didn't mean to be discourteous. You know me. . . ."

Rebecca's cool green stare drifted over the members of her family. "About the wedding," she began again, shifting her thigh away from Matthew's encroaching one. "I think all this fuss is out-and-out foolish. The marriage by proxy was good enough." She looked at each family member, pinning them with her gaze. "If you all don't stop ordering me around, I'll do something drastic."

Matthew stroked the taut tendons in his wife's neck, smiling easily as her anger focused on him. "She's right. Being a bride must be almost as difficult as being a bridegroom."

Rebecca shook free of his light touch, leaning toward him petulantly. "What are all those packs on those mules? And who asked you to buy me horses? And what right do you have to come traipsing in here—"

Matthew couldn't resist kissing the drop of maple syrup that clung to her bottom lip.

"La!" Emma exclaimed softly as Rebecca blushed. "He sure knows how to hush her up."

In the next three days Rebecca decided against running away and dying on the spot. Matthew prowled around her like a possessive husband, and everyone else grinned so much that their teeth were probably as dry as the sagebrush flats.

The quilting circle descended upon her like a flock of hungry ravens, fashioning a white lawn dress despite her protests. Rebecca had been pushed and pulled, her very flesh pinned into the material. Yet the night before the "shindig," the dress hung in her room, completed, the green satin trim shimmering in the light of the kerosene lantern. The bustle Matthew had purchased in Spokane fit perfectly beneath the skirt's panels.

Escaping into her room after the evening meal, Rebecca found the huge family tub filled to the brim with hot water. The tin monster must have taken four men to haul upstairs into her bedroom. "Huh!" she said with a snort, glaring at the steamy water. "Just what the sacrificial lamb needs."

With a sigh, Rebecca undressed and eased into the tub. She leaned against the high back, closing her eyes. She felt like a ship in a tidal wave, buffeted by the entire populace of the valley, pushing her into the "biggest shindig this country has ever seen," according to Mrs. Peterson.

From the front porch the strains of a flamenco guitar sounded, the music passionate and soaring into the night air. Then Jean's soft voice carried over the softer strains, a soothing French ballad.

The bed creaked and Rebecca opened her eyes to see Matthew sprawled across her bed amid mounds of lacy garments. His black eyes sparkled as he watched her slide beneath the soapsuds. She glared at him, crossing her arms across her breasts and sinking up to her chin. "For the past three days, I have been pushed and prodded, jabbed with dressmaker's pins until I bled. Every last woman in the country has offered me her recipes for everything from jams to cough syrup to hard cider, and now, just when I have a moment's peace, you turn up."

Matthew's dark brows lifted. "You have been ignoring my presence for the past few days, Princess, so I thought you preferred the privacy. Had I known you desired my company, I would have obliged."

He wrapped a delicate length of silk around his hand, rubbing it with the pad of his thumb as he studied her. "You've been about as gracious as a scalded cat to all these nice people."

"A scalded cat!" she repeated, blowing a mound of bubbles away from her chin. "How do you expect me to act?"

He tilted his head, lifting and inspecting a length of lace carefully. "Gracious. Yes, that's the word—gracious. Pleased with the efforts of the community."

"Balderdash! Hell and damnation! *You* be pleased. This is your wedding. *You* thank everyone. But for now you get out of here."

Matthew flicked open his shirt, exposing the dark wedge of hair covering his chest. "Tomorrow, Becky, you are going to act every bit as pleased as I know you really are. You are not going to throw all this work back at the well-wishers.

That nasty little temper had better change to purring. Do you understand?''

Her eyes narrowed. ''I really don't like your tone, Matthew. Perhaps you had better leave.''

He stretched, sliding a silky, lacy garment across his hard cheek. ''This may surprise you, sweetheart. But I want tomorrow to be one of the high points in your life. It seems you need reminding that we'll be sharing a life and a bed. I just thought the wedding would be a commemoration—''

''I have no intention of sharing a bed with you, McKay, let alone a life. Get out.'' She was angry now because she wanted him to hold her. But her pride stood firm and she had to defend it.

Matthew sat in a lithe motion, stripping his shirt from him. He threw it amid the mounds of lace and satin and stalked toward her. ''Mrs. McKay, before I leave this room tonight, you're going to change your tune. At least to the rest of the world.''

''What are you doing?'' she asked just before he pushed her head under the soapy water. When she surfaced, sputtering, her hand grabbed his collar. ''What—''

''Merely washing your hair,'' he answered grimly, plunging her beneath the sudsy water again. ''I can play the lady's maid when I have to.''

''You're drowning me, McKay!'' Rebecca gasped, blowing a mound of bubbles from her nose. ''You're trying to kill me!''

Matthew's face thrust against hers, his eyebrows forming a straight line across his brow. ''You would try the very devil, my dear.''

''You *are* the devil! Everything was fine until you started shoving people around. You've practically incited the whole territory. Women from fifteen to eighty are falling all over you—''

''You know, Becky, you remind me of an old buffalo hunter I used to know—too set in his ways to change with the times. He rode his horse right off a cliff to his death rather than change.'' Matthew started working soap lather into Rebecca's wet hair, piling the mound atop her head and studying her intently.

He cupped her face with his hands. "It's too bad you're bound and determined to ruin everyone's good time. The ladies' circle has worked hard for days making that dress. The least you can do is wear it with grace."

"I did not ask for the dress, McKay," she reminded him stiffly after blowing a mound of bubbles off the end of her nose.

He plunged her beneath the water, rinsing her hair. Taking the damp strands in his fingers, he eased her head back. "No, but by damn, you've got it, woman. And you've got me, like it or not. You may terrorize everyone else here, but you're still going to act like a lady tomorrow. You're going to say thank you so many times, your tongue will ache. Your face will ache from smiling. But so help me God, you're not going to throw all this work back into these folk's faces. For some reason—unknown to me—this entire valley thinks you're their little princess . . . and you're going to act the part."

So he was going to try to shove her around, was he?

He plunged her beneath the water again, leaving her sputtering. Lifting a bucket, he poured warm water over the top of her head. A muscle contracted in his jaw as he stood glaring down at her furious expression. His eyes narrowed as he nodded toward her Colt, hanging from a wall peg. "You'd like to reach for that gun, wouldn't you?"

"I'd like to shoot a hole in you . . . yes, McKay," she hissed. "I'd really like that. You're an evil, conniving, sneaky—"

"I'm your husband, woman. Probably the only person alive who knows how much of a woman you can really be—when you set your mind to it," Matthew stated quietly, distinctly. "On the other hand, when you set your mind to it, you're pure hellion. I wanted to spare your family and neighbors, and I've kept smiling while you acted like a spoiled child."

He wiped his damp chest with a towel, throwing it over a chair. "But I'm coming to the end of my leash."

Rebecca grabbed a towel, mopping her face. Good. She

had him as angry as he'd made her. Perhaps it would be a fair fight, after all. "You probably visited all the . . . the houses in Spokane and back again."

Matthew's jaw tightened as he placed his hands on his hips. "Nasty as a riled hen, aren't you? I guess it's left to me to treat you like Sir Galahad. Everyone else is tiptoeing around you, whispering bridal nerves. At first I thought that too. Now I think it's just plain bad temper." In the next moment Matthew plucked her from the water, despite her struggles. Holding her upper arm, he swished a towel down her body as impersonally as if she were not his wife. Wrapping a towel around her head like a turban, Matthew grabbed a delicate garment from the bed.

He thrust the bright fuchsia silk at her. "Here, wear this."

Rebecca grabbed her nightgown from the bedpost, grasping it in front of her. "Get out, McKay, before you really make me good and mad!"

"Why, you close-minded, hardheaded little snoot! You're not even making an effort to please anyone but yourself. I brought back a number of gifts from Spokane, Becky. And, by damn, you will wear them!" He glared down at her, his face rigid with anger.

With a sudden movement he swept lace and silk garments before her. His big hands crushed the delicate fabric. "Drawers. Women's drawers. Silk from China and lace from France . . . gifts from a husband to his wife, Becky. I ordered them from back East some time ago and had them delivered to Spokane. I had some idea that you might like them."

Rebecca glanced at the soft garments, crushed in his fists. He wanted to remold her, tearing her apart from herself. And he'd done just that, her body following his sensual demands until it seemed he commanded her very skin to heat at just a look from him! "You want me dressing like one of those fancy women, don't you? Your own private—"

"Don't say it, Becky," he warned tightly. "You know all about pleasing a man instinctively, but you're so wrapped up in fighting the past that you'll take out your revenge on an entire community—"

"You don't know what you're saying, McKay. I've lived here all my life. You don't know anything about this valley or these people—"

"The hell I don't." He breathed hard, towering over her. "I've got a nasty temper, myself, Becky. And you've pushed me just about as far as I'm going." He threw the clothing to the bed, then ran the flat of his hand across his mouth.

"Get out, McKay," Rebecca ordered quietly, catching the scent of liquor. "You've been drinking."

"So I have—a bridegroom sharing a brandy with family and friends. I've got some addleminded notion that my bride is a hell of a woman beneath those claws. Only a willful child would spoil all the work of these good people, Becky."

"I didn't ask for a thing, Matthew. And I didn't ask for you," she snapped, edging around the bed, holding her flannel gown like a shield. She resented how he made her feel—shy and soft, and at his command.

She'd fight to protect her emotions, her vulnerability.

"You could be carrying my child, Becky. That's a fact I don't take lightly," Matthew growled, taking a step toward her.

Her eyes widened. How dare Matthew pry into her body. "Oh, I suppose you're going to throw that at me now—the fact that you've had your way with me!"

He stalked nearer, snatching the damp towel from her head and tossing it onto a chair. "Who has had whose way, my dear? Well, guess what I'd like to do now—"

"Now?" She gasped, suddenly realizing that Matthew did indeed hold himself on a tight leash. He looked like a man ready to . . . "There's a houseful of people downstairs."

"Making love might remind you of the circumstances, Becky," he drawled, arranging the long, wet strands around her bare shoulders. "I am already your husband, whether tomorrow's festivities take place or not."

His large, rough palm glided over her shoulder, cupping it. "Take care. I'm not the man to be pushed this way and that."

As his lips neared, Rebecca questioned the softening within

her. She had fought with him so hotly, now it seemed she merely wanted his mouth touching hers. "Is that a threat, Matthew?"

He brushed her mouth with his, looking deep into her eyes. "That is a promise, Mrs. McKay," he whispered. "You keep looking at me with those big green eyes and I won't be able to resist."

She couldn't give him his way after he'd acted like a brute. If she started letting him set the pace, there would be no telling where his demands would end. She edged back a step, tilting her head. "I'm not too sure you're acting proper."

He chuckled, picking up a hairbrush from her bedside table. "Proper—now that's a word. You've got me so hungry for you, I'm on fire."

He lifted a long, curling hair and studied it beneath the kerosene lantern. His gaze lifted, pinning her. "I want your love, Becky. And I intend to have it, despite any barbed-wire fences you intend on planting between us. But if you ruin tomorrow for these good folks, I won't be held responsible."

He wanted her love? "You are threatening me, McKay—"

He scooped her high into his arms, then settled in a large chair with her on his lap. Matthew caught her wrists, pinning them with one large hand. "I am promising, my dear. Now hold still while I brush your hair. It's as willful as you are."

"Maria can help me." Rebecca struggled, suddenly flushing when she realized his mood had changed suddenly. He was too dangerous, his black eyes gleaming and his body so near.

Matthew breathed heavily, arranging her hips over his. He brushed the long strands carefully, allowing her to adjust to his rising hardness. His skin heated as he raised and lowered his hips rhythmically. Throwing the brush to the bed, Matthew groaned, lightly running his free hand over her thighs. "Oh, Becky."

He trailed his fingertips down her left breast, circling it with his large hand. Gently supporting the soft weight, Matthew searched her face. "You're quite a woman, Mrs. McKay," he murmured huskily.

"Don't—" Rebecca wanted to move away. Yet she wanted to be near, ached to be close. . . .

"Don't what?" He kneaded her breast gently, his palm flattening, lifting the creamy mound upward. "Touch my wife? I have to, it seems," he whispered. "Come here, Becky."

Taking great care, he eased her thighs over his. Rebecca began to tremble, forcing her palms against his bare chest. Somehow her fingertips foraged through the hair there, seeking the hard warmth of his chest. Matthew slipped his arms around her, hands cupping her bare buttocks. Lifting, easing her closer, he fitted her over his male desire.

Hands sliding, caressing her along the length of her back, Matthew's dark gaze held her questioning eyes. "Hold me," he ordered softly. "Wrap those silky arms around my neck and let me feel you against me, woman. Give me a taste to keep me going."

Breathing lightly, Rebecca could not have denied him. Slipping her hands over his shoulders, she allowed her breasts to settle upon his hard chest. Matthew stiffened, trailing his hands lower, sliding his palms over her thighs and upward.

"Matthew, I don't think this is at all proper before the wedding," she protested as his fingertips played amid the curls above her thighs.

"Of course it is," he whispered raggedly against her ear, licking the lobe with his tongue. "Quite proper under the circumstances."

Rebecca rested her hot cheek against his, her breasts aching as Matthew slowly, inch by inch, trailed kisses along her bare shoulders. "What are you doing, McKay?" she managed, feeling the muscles of his thighs grow taut.

He chuckled, nuzzling her long neck with his rough chin. "Not nearly what I'd like to be doing. Merely tasting . . ."

Rebecca timidly traced the planes of his back with her fingers. It was strange, as though she held him within her power.

"You don't have any idea what you're doing to me, do you?"

He pressed the flat of his hand against her back, flattening her breasts against him. Rebecca shifted, her blood heating as Matthew began to caress and kiss her. Slanting his mouth against hers, he eased his tongue within her mouth.

She trembled, her hips instinctively pressing down against his rising manhood. Matthew groaned, his eyes closing, his fingers slipping upward, and gently he entered her. Delicately he traced patterns upon her flesh, slipping a gentle fingertip higher.

Rebecca stiffened, leaning back. "Just a taste, my love," he said huskily, his lips closing on hers once more. Using his tongue and his hands, Matthew set a gentle pace that drove her to seek him hungrily, moving upon him as though she were riding Wind Dancer.

When she moaned, rising and falling against his touch, Matthew's face darkened with desire. Taking his time, carefully sucking on her breasts, he lured her to a passionate crest.

Heart beating furiously, her body throbbing, aching, Rebecca hungrily fitted her mouth to his. Her hands roamed down his sides, flattened and prowled through the thick hair covering his stomach.

Matthew's fingers wrapped in her hair, easing her head back until her throat was exposed to his lips. Kissing the silken length, Matthew murmured, "You're wanting more, aren't you? If you purr any louder, the whole house will know I'm in here."

Somewhere within her a voice cautioned Rebecca, causing her aching body to still. "Hmm?"

Matthew placed her palm over his thrusting male desire. Pressing down the layers of clothing separating them, her flesh tingled with the need to really touch him.

"I said, if you become any louder, everyone will know we're making love."

Rebecca was trembling, warm and damp with passion. She breathed lightly, resting her cheek on his shoulder. Matthew cupped her breasts, caressing them gently. He smiled at her warily. "I think that tomorrow night we had better be alone, Princess. You can be quite noisy . . . and demanding."

The heat seeping through her chilled slightly. Realizing she had strained against Matthew's hard body, wanting him, Rebecca began to breathe rapidly, denying her need for fulfillment.

"You were teasing me, Matthew," she managed carefully, beginning to feel the first fine swell of anger surge through her. He was trying to control her, bend her to his will by sheer torment.

He leaned back, resting his head against the back of the chair to view her from beneath his lashes. "Brides need warming, I'm told."

She trembled once, feeling the rage heat her now. "You have the experience to . . . touch me. But that doesn't mean you can bring me to heel."

"I have no intention of breaking that fine spirit, Becky. But you have the passion in you to drive a man mad, and it's time you recognized what you feel."

A strain of Jean's flamenco guitar invaded the room, the sound as hot and passionate as Matthew's lovemaking.

"Women do not seek out men for their . . . lusts, Matthew," she began hotly.

"No? What have you been doing, Lady Godiva?" he taunted in a tone that brought the hair on the back of her neck upright. He tilted his head, searching her flushed face. "Or perhaps you really feel something for me. Is it possible, I wonder?"

Rebecca began to tremble with anger. She eased to her feet, drawing on the bright pink robe and lashing the belt around her waist. While she dealt with her unsteady emotions Matthew rose and cupped her jaw. He trailed his thumb across her swollen lips. "I could have you now, Becky. But I want more."

His scarred eyebrow rose. "I have a fine temper too. Tomorrow isn't just for us but also for the people who love you and who have watched you grow into a woman."

Rebecca tossed back a strand of hair from her temple, glaring at him. "I will repay you for this, Mr. McKay . . . if it's the last thing I do."

He laughed, trailing a finger down the warm crevice of her breasts. "I hope you do. I'll be waiting."

When he stepped out of her bedroom, closing the door quietly behind him, Rebecca stormed, "McKay, get back in here!"

In another moment the crash of broken crockery sounded, bringing Emma's fan to her startled face. Seated on the porch, she frowned at Jean. "That girl has a beastly temper. Matthew surely has his work cut out for him."

Jean strummed a few cords, his grin wide. "They suit each other, *ma belle.*"

"Why, they don't, either! Just like oil and vinegar. She's just as wild as this country. Rides like a man and wears a gun like one too," Emma answered quickly.

"And Matthew?" Jean's long fingers played the intricate chords of a flamenco. "What do you think of him?"

Emma's blue eyes softened above her fan. "Now there's a man. A gentle man clear through. All polished manners . . . and he has money too. He could buy and sell anyone in this entire uncivilized state."

"Ah, the money. That is what draws you to him," Jean murmured softly.

"Well, honey, money doesn't hurt a man. Not at all." Emma gazed out into the moonlit night, studying the silvery Columbia River.

"You are a woman who needs a man, my Emma," Jean stated softly, his black eyes glowing beneath their lashes.

"I've had my share." Emma smiled, smoothing her bobbing curls with her fingers. "Surely you've known a few women?"

"I have been waiting for someone like you, Emma," Jean said, watching her small face grow still. "I have known many women, but none like you."

She frowned, confused. "Oh, my. Why, that's impossible. I mean . . . you're—"

"A half-blood, *ma chère*? Yes, I am." His black eyes pinned her blue ones. "You have not yet loved a man, Emma. One day you will love me as deeply as Rebecca loves her Matthew."

Emma's small hand fluttered to her bodice, her blue eyes wide. "Jehoshaphat! I will not. You and my sister, Maybelle, have the strangest ideas." She stood, swishing past Jean, tucking her skirts carefully aside so as not to touch him. "The very thought makes me ill, sir."

Jean stood, sweeping his arm before like a courtier. He bowed from the waist, then straightened. "Thoughts of you, mademoiselle, make me dream of soft lips and warm nights."

"Well, I never! You'd better not go spouting off your dreams to the men hereabouts, Mr. Dupres. They're not about to let their womenfolk get carried off by the heathen savages," Emma snapped. "The very idea! I never—"

"You are a beautiful woman, Emma. Surely you cannot blame me for wanting you." Jean slipped his hand over hers, raising the small palm for his kiss. "Your beauty haunts me."

Her eyes widened as she snatched her hand away. "Haunts you? I am offended, sir. Calling me a nightmare? Good land sakes!"

Jean leaned over her, placing his lips on her forehead. Emma's hand flew upward to slap his cheek. Her eyes blazed at him. "Don't you dare take liberties with me!" Her gaze scorched his beaded leather moccasins. "Straight from the reservation. Ready to take scalps, no doubt."

Jean rubbed his cheek, smiling softly. "The sweet was worth the punishment. Perhaps it is my scalp that is in danger."

Matthew walked toward them, carrying a bottle of whiskey. He lifted it toward Jean. "Looks like it's going to be one hell of a long night, Jean. Care to join me?"

Jean's eyes sparkled. "Will you excuse me, Miss Emma? Duty to a white brother calls."

"I wouldn't think of stopping you," Emma hissed, storming inside the house. She slammed the screen door. "You stay away from me, Mr. Dupres."

Matthew watched Emma's skirts swirl up the stairs. "The women in this house are nasty-tempered tonight," he remarked mildly.

"Her claws are not for me," Jean said softly. "She is beautiful . . . soft as a lamb, I think. Her eyes are as blue as the camas flowers."

Wes slid from the shadows to lean against the porch post. He lit a cigarette before speaking. "You were right. Mary likes the hat, Matthew. She's a sweet little thing. If we'd had more time, I'd ask the preacher to say the words over us tomorrow."

Jean chuckled. "Ah, love. When there is a wedding, it starts working on the old bachelors."

Wes blew smoke into the night air. "Young ones too. Eh, Jean?"

"She is my vision," the younger man answered softly, following the flight of the great horned owl across the night sky. "The white dove will settle by the panther's side."

In the quiet hours of dawn, Emma awoke with a start, her long blond hair sliding against the satin pillowcase. She breathed quietly, listening to the quiet. She frowned suddenly, noting the curtain fluttering at the open window. But she had closed it just before going to bed.

The shadows in the room moved, and a tall, slender man stalked quietly toward her, as quietly as a panther prowling through the night.

Emma parted her lids, drawing breath for a scream, when suddenly Jean's face lowered to hers. Her feather tick mattress shifted as he sat beside her. His hand covered her mouth, his voice low and husky. "*Ma chère*, do not be frightened. I will not hurt you."

She leaned back against the satin-covered pillow, her eyes wide. In the small path of moonlight Jean's dark face softened. A swath of midnight-black hair crossed his forehead. From beneath long lashes Jean's eyes trailed over her loosened hair and unpainted face. "You are lovely, *ma petite*," he murmured. "As beautiful as I knew you would be."

"What are you doing here, Mr. Dupres? What in heaven's name are you doing here?" she hissed, pressing back against the pillow.

He shrugged a bare shoulder, his hand reaching out to stroke her cheek. "The panther prowls in the night, seeking his mate. It is my fate, I'm afraid."

"Well, good heavens! If the Kleins catch you here, we're both in a kettle of hot water," Emma exclaimed, pulling up the sheet to her neck. She jerked her head away from his fingers, glaring at him. "Stop playing with my hair. Get out that window, just the same way as you came in. You savages have no sense of privacy."

Jean continued to play with her hair, untying the ribbons that held its long, sausagelike curls. Emma snatched a ribbon from him, then another. "What are you doing?"

He wrapped a long curl around a lean finger, watching it. "What color is your hair before you whiten it like bones bleached on the desert?"

Her eyes widened indignantly. "It's a ghastly shade of light brown. Looks like old brown leather. Now you—"

He nodded. "Ah, the rich pelt of the doe in winter. Perhaps a little red like the coyote."

"Lord Almighty! Who cares?" Emma did not like Jean's close inspection. "Listen, the Kleins are nice people, and if you think for one minute that I'm going to . . . well, play with you, you're wrong, mister. Why, I'd be wasting my time."

Jean's eyes darkened savagely. "You have spent it with McKay's brother freely enough. And others before him. But now, my white dove, your wings will flutter for only me. You are a maiden from this day on, clean and new. I will kill any man who comes near you."

Emma straightened, then sat upright, braced back against the headboard. "Don't get any fancy ideas where I'm concerned, Jean Dupres. You're not at all what I want." Her eyes narrowed, watching him. "You've been drinking with Matthew, haven't you? I swear it's true! Give an Indian firewater and he goes all haywire. . . ."

Jean trailed a lean finger down her full white breasts, circling the crests until they thrust at the embroidered muslin bodice. "It is true . . . I have shared a drink with my friend."

"Good Lord, I thought there was a law against giving Indians whiskey."

"Emmaline. The name flows over my tongue like honey. I will taste you like the bee tastes the honey, you will take my seed, and we will have sons that will grow strong and straight."

"Land sakes! You savages turn poetic when you're skunkdrunk, don't you?" Emma breathed, her eyes wide. "Not a man alive has wanted children from me."

Jean's hand cupped her full breast, his eyes closing. "You are sleek and plump. It is good to hold you. When we become one, we will fly to the skies, mating—"

She pushed at his hand, her bodice loosening in his nimble fingers. Jean's hungry eyes drifted slowly downward, staring at the quivering softness. "No other man," he reminded her through his teeth.

With shaking fingers she retied her bodice. "Good Lord, you've got fast fingers . . . and crazy ideas."

Jean touched the cloth over her breasts lightly. "You will nourish my sons at your breast, Emmaline. But first my lips will possess you inch by inch, until you will not look at another man."

"You are possessed. Simply possessed. Or crazy. I've heard Indians go crazy when they drink."

"You will live by my side all the days of our lives, Emmaline," Jean murmured softly, touching her hair. "I have brought you a courting gift."

Solemnly he reached into his belt and placed leather moccasins into her hands. "You cannot be made lovelier. Please accept my humble gift."

Emma trembled with an unknown fear. Men had wanted her for her body, and she had been paid. "A courting gift?" she repeated slowly, her fingers trailing over the pattern of the beads covering the moccasins.

"When the snows come, you will warm my furs," Jean whispered. "I will treasure you all the days of my life."

"Oh, no. No . . . no. Now, listen, Mr. Dupres. You've had a little too much celebrating tonight. And I am honored by your visit." Emma took a deep breath. "But I understand. Tomorrow we'll talk . . . you'll feel differently then."

Jean smiled, his teeth gleaming in the shadows. "Tomorrow we will talk, Emmaline. Mother of my sons."

She glared at him from beneath her lashes. Why in the name of blue blazes did this half-blood make her tremble?

"I suppose you have a whole flock of Indian women and half-breed children tagging after you," she shot at him.

"I have not allowed my seed to enter the womb of any woman. I will have my dove alone swell with my child," Jean answered steadily as he rose. In another moment the room was empty.

Emma threw the moccasins at the open window. "La! I'm not about to become your woman, Jean!"

His soft laughter floated back to her.

"Heathens!" she hissed, turning on her stomach. "I can just picture myself dressed in skins and tending the cook fire in a tepee."

Chapter Fourteen

"I'd like to speak to the bride and groom privately, Peter."

The next morning Jacob Edwards glanced around the Kleins' study. The short, rotund preacher tucked a well-worn Bible beneath his arm. "This wedding is special to me. Aye-ya, watched the girl grow up, I did. Where is she and the boy?"

"I sent Daniel up to get Rebecca a good half hour ago, when we first spotted your mule. I should tell you, the two start sparks flying off each other. He's a good man with a dream, and everyone but Rebecca can see her fitting into his plans. Matt is checking his stock with two good men, Wes and Jean Dupres."

"Dupres? He's no stockman. He's a wealthy man," Jacob said, surprised. "What's Dupres doing here, I wonder? He's like the wind. Oh, he's a good man, don't get me wrong."

Jacob glanced at a wagon unloading a cluster of children of various ages. "He's got a spread up in Canada but never spends any time there. Seems like he's looking for something . . ."

Matthew entered the study, dusting his Stetson against his chaps. "Good morning, Peter."

After introductions Jacob handed Matthew a cup of coffee, watching the younger man settle into a chair. "Rebecca's special, Matthew. Has something in her that is as wild as the wind but as sweet as the blueberries up on the Cascade Mountains."

When Matthew nodded, Jacob added, "She needs a lot of rein, boy. But only so much."

"I'll tend her carefully," Matthew said quietly, looking at each man.

Then Rebecca entered the room, dressed in boots, trousers, and a threadbare workman's shirt. She glared at the three men, then flung herself into a chair. Her hair swirled around her, the strands settling on her shoulders like a rippling mantle of black silk. Ignoring Matthew, she threw a strand of hair back from her throat and crossed her boots at the ankle. "I'm here."

Jacob's cherubic face warmed, his eyes twinkling. "So you are. Lovely as ever. I've waited a long time for your wedding. Seems you waited a long time, too, but you got a good man in your lariat."

Rebecca flicked a glance at Matthew. "He's got some high-handed notions. People from the city usually do."

Placing his hands behind his head, Matthew stretched like a mountain puma, the long line of his body taut. His wife didn't like being pushed and prodded, but neither did he. "I'm a hard-working bridegroom, Becky. I've been out branding our cattle and horses and am well warmed and ready for my morning kiss."

"You'll not get one, McKay," Rebecca shot back at him, tensing. She straightened, her eyes flashing, her cheeks flushed with anger. Matthew decided that perhaps he should have made love to her to keep her temper sweet as she continued. "*Our* cattle . . . *our* horses. That's how you see this whole thing, don't you? As a branding—"

"Rebecca!" Peter stormed, throwing up his hands. "Show some respect. It's your wedding day, and Jacob has traveled for miles to do the honors."

Her breath caught, and she swallowed as though reining her temper. Then, forcing her eyes from Matthew, Rebecca forced a smile that grew into genuine warmth. "Is that Bible the one with the pistol in it? Or is it real?"

Jacob lifted the Bible's front flap to expose a Colt pistol. He closed the flap, patting it affectionately. "Sometimes the Lord just needs a little help."

Peter excused himself to greet the visitors, closing the door just as Jacob began, "This is a solemn event you are undertaking."

For a moment there was silence, then Rebecca exclaimed, "Hell and damnation, talk to him!"

Whistling, Peter closed the door to the study. Spotting Maybelle at the front porch, he walked straight toward her. He badly needed the small woman's softness after Rebecca's thunderstorms. For just this once he decided to hide behind a woman's skirts if necessary.

"Honor and obey!" Rebecca's outraged cry sliced through the fresh morning air. "I will not take a vow like that one, Jacob!"

"Morning, Peter," Maybelle's soft Southern tones spread over Peter like a sweet herbal balm. "I baked you a special pecan pie. 'Course, I had to cheat a little bit and make do with walnuts and oatmeal. . . ." Maybelle smiled, lifting the tea towel covering her pie to tempt him.

Suddenly Peter looked into Maybelle's twinkling blue eyes and forgot about his daughter's willful ways. She was Matthew's concern now. . . .

Waiting on the riverbank, Jacob reached into his pocket and took out his gold watch. It was almost eleven o'clock—wedding time. A small layer of clouds skimmed the blue sky over the river basin, their purple shadows sliding over the sagebrush and the new orchards.

The wedding guests gossiped beneath a stand of pines, enjoying the cool breeze rising from the icy waters of the Columbia. The river looked sluggish, almost placid, yet the currents were enough to drown an able-bodied man. He'd seen one or two canoes turn over in his time, seen log rafts torn like twigs when the Columbia went on the rampage. Jacob skipped a small, flat rock three times across the river's surface before it sank. He thought of the old-timers, fur traders, and gunslingers who had lived and fought for the land.

He scanned the rugged, mountainous horizon surrounding the river basin. It was a new land, tough and untamed, taking lives and yielding little but heartbreak. Yet the wagons came, filled with children and dreams. Someday it would all come true . . . every blessed dream, making the waiting worthwhile.

He breathed the scents of sagebrush and clean sand, scanning the crumbling basalt bluffs lodged within the mountains surrounding the Columbia River. This land cried out for men like McKay and Dupres—strong men with new ideas. It took a special breed to claim the land, and now the land demanded seasoned businessmen to deal with the railroads, the burgeoning crops.

Jacob watched a small boy prod the river gravel with a stick. He bent, plucking tiny freshwater mussels from the icy water. The boy beamed, showing his treasure to his sister. So it was, Jacob mused, that the fortunes were ripe for the taking. . . .

A new state filled with settlers that built water flumes for the new orchards and fields and raised a fuss over where their children would be schooled.

August was a fine time to marry Christians, Jacob decided as he scanned the Kleins' neighbors. He stuffed the watch back into his pocket and glanced uneasily at the Klein home. He'd never seen a woman as riled as Rebecca McKay, or a man as calm and determined as Matthew. "Marriage is like breaking two good pulling mules to harness. Takes work to get 'em pulling together. Not worth a damn if they both can't keep step," he said to himself as he strode to the Myers family. "I hear that someone's needing a baptism here. . . ."

Picnic tables spread beneath the pines were laden with food and drink. Settler women fussed about handcrafted gifts, exclaiming with delight at the intricate crocheted doilies and embroidered pillowcases. Children played, running between the wagons and the waiting groups. And a group of Indians watched in the distance, wrapped in their reservation blankets.

When he saw Rebecca leave the house, Jesse Daniels stopped talking to the men. Spreading an accordion wide, he began playing the Wedding March, directing all eyes toward the rocky path leading to the Klein house.

Fancy Denning, a small girl missing her two front teeth and dressed in a pink gingham dress, carried a huge bouquet of sweet grass, roses, and wildflowers. She grinned, casting a shy glance back over her shoulder at Rebecca.

In the late morning Rebecca slowly and stiffly began her wedding walk. Her green ribbon shimmered in the bright sunlight, her lawn dress elegant and clinging tightly to her. The low-cut bodice molded her breasts, the tiny pearl buttons trailing down to her slender waist. Holding a bouquet of red roses, black-eyed Susans, and huge daisies laced with baby's breath, Rebecca paused. Her heart thudded slowly as the crowd turned toward her.

In the hushed silence she felt the hot, dry breath of August wash across her face. She'd watched other brides walk toward their marriages, but now, walking slowly toward Matthew, his black waves glistening in the brilliant sunlight, she trembled. She felt him around her, beckoning her. His gaze flowed over her, melting the coldness within her.

The slight breeze moved a strand of her hair, sun-warmed and feather-soft, against her cheek. She took a step and the delicate scent of the baby's breath in her hands drifted over her. Her silk-and-lace underwear slid against her legs, cool despite the summer heat.

The mountains surrounding the Columbia River were dry in August, shades of brown and blue sweeping down the canyons. Trees studded the mountaintops in the distance, the sound of the water lapping at the smooth river rocks.

At one time a glacier had passed, scarring the granite riverbed, and the land had never been the same. Would *she* be the same person?

In the distance Wind Dancer whinnied, prancing around an Appaloosa mare. What did Matthew want? she thought as the stallion nipped the mare's hindquarters.

What did he really want?

Stella sniffed into her handkerchief as Rebecca passed. Stretching out her hand, Stella clasped her fingers for a moment, her eyes shining with tears. "I'm so happy for you, Rebecca," she whispered as a tear slid down her cheek.

Stella smoothed the green ribbons resting on Rebecca's ebony hair and reverently touched the sprays of baby's breath crowning the bride's head.

Rebecca glanced at the expectant faces. Matthew waited beside Jacob. In his dark suit he looked little different than when she had first seen him, but now the passion in his face stirred her, making her hesitate on the rocky path to the shelter of the pines. Matthew's eyes wandered down his bride, heating as they touched. She met his eyes, caught by the dark fire and the promise lying there.

The determination hardening his jaw almost frightened her. yet there was something else in his expression that lured, beckoned her as surely as a hungry doe to the sweet meadow grasses of the high country.

When she stopped beside him, Matthew took her hand. He lifted it to his mouth, kissing her palm. ''All the days of my life,'' he promised huskily, gazing into her eyes. His eyes grew gentle, moving over her face as though imprinting it forever in his memory.

He touched her hair, lifting a strand to the sun, then smoothed it against her back. Mrs. Peterson's loud sigh of enchantment swept over the gathering. Peter's grumble sounded suspiciously like a choked sob as Stella sniffed into a handkerchief.

The lines beside Matthew's eyes deepened. ''Shall we begin, Mrs. McKay?''

He'd gazed at her as though she were his happiness, and the thought startled her. A tingle ran through her, warm and comforting. When she glanced up at him, he winked.

His hand touched hers, the tremor surprising her.

She allowed her fingers to slide between his, allowed his strength and warmth to encompass her as Jacob began, ''Dearly beloved, we are gathered . . .''

A few moments later Matthew placed a new wide gold band on Rebecca's left hand. Taking the ruby ring, he slid it onto her right hand. Jacob ended with ''I now pronounce you man and wife. You may kiss the bride, Matthew.''

Rebecca caught the dark glints in Matthew's eyes just before his head lowered and his lips touched hers. Holding her carefully, Matthew leaned her back over his arm and kissed her until she couldn't breathe.

When his lips lifted, Rebecca's fingers dug into his upper arm, her eyes dazed with the sweetness of the kiss. She'd expected a hot possession, but instead his gentleness surrounded her like soft, warm velvet.

Still holding her, Matthew smiled tenderly. "You're ice cold, Becky," he whispered. "Don't be afraid. I'll be right here beside you."

"That's just what I'm afraid of," she returned, allowing him to hold her against him a moment longer. "I want this whole thing to be over and done with."

"Why," he said teasingly, before the party swooped down upon them, "this should be the happiest day of your life."

"I'll pay you back for this if it's the last thing I do, McKay."

"I long for the day. In fact, I anticipate the very hour. I have a feeling that once you and I are alone, the Indian wars will look like child's play. By the way, there's an inscription on your new ring."

His gentle tone and the warm stroking of his eyes, as though he . . . loved her, caused Rebecca's nerves to quiver. Uncertain, feeling as though she'd been cornered, Rebecca took the safest route—anger. She glared up at him. "I don't like being marked as your possession, Matthew."

His fingers tightened around hers. "You'll wear this ring, Rebecca."

Jean Dupres stepped up to Rebecca, glancing at Matthew. "May I, my friend?"

"Of course. Just return her to her rightful owner." Matthew hugged Stella, grinning widely just before Jean's cool kiss touched Rebecca's cheek.

"You are a lovely bride, Rebecca," Jean murmured. "Perhaps one day I shall have a bride too."

Feeling as though she had to throw something at Matthew, and since Jean was the closest "something," Rebecca kissed him quickly on the lips. She winked at Jean, who winked back, then grinned at Matthew's scowl. "She is a playful kitten, no?"

"She needs . . . care," Matthew began in a low growl.

Emma slid through the well-wishers and wrapped her arms around Matthew's neck. "A kiss for old times' sake, Matthew?"

Matthew eased her arms down, then kissed her cheek. "Thank you for your good wishes, Emma."

Rebecca glared at Matthew, his hand resting on Emma's tiny, cinched waist. Emma flashed a wide smile back at her, just before Jean took her hand to kiss the back of it. His eyes flowed down her yellow dress and low, eyelet-edged bodice. Emma breathed shallowly as he stepped closer, dark eyes glowing. "You are as lovely as an ermine in winter, Emmaline," he murmured huskily. "No jewel could enhance your beauty."

She stepped back a pace, glaring at him. Dressed in a dark suit with a snow-white silk shirt, Jean looked every inch a gentleman, down to his polished black boots. When his gaze touched her tightly laced, overflowing bosom, Emma burst out, "Now listen here, Mr. Dupres. Don't you start on me today!"

Jean's hand shot out to Matthew. As they shook hands he said, "She is distraught over losing you, my friend. I shall try to console my little white dove."

Emma's blue eyes widened. "You come near me, you savage, and I'll scream the house down, wedding or not."

Jean's dark face lightened almost boyishly. "She cannot wait, my friend. Soon you will be congratulating me—"

Emma gasped. "Don't you dare say things like that, Jean. I don't want people to think I'm consorting, being friendly to a savage!"

Jean's lean finger touched her parted lips, his eyes sparkling. "Shh, my pet. Would you like to dine?"

"With you?" Emma spat, shifting her skirts away from his long legs. "Never!" With one last glare at Dupres, Emma bunched her skirts together and marched to the food-laden table.

Jean winked at Matthew, then strolled after her, whistling the "Marseillese."

Standing beside Matthew as the well-wishers passed by, Rebecca gritted her teeth, "I can't stand much more of this, McKay."

His hand tightened on her waist, drawing her against the support of his body. "Chin up. Marriage to me can't be all that bad. Think of cool, green meadows. Of roses. Think of babies and kisses." Matthew kissed the side of her hot cheek. Mrs. Peterson oohed, pressing her hands to her bosom while Rebecca flushed wildly. The man was a disaster, setting a course to torment her.

"I'm thinking of the year I promised Papa. You can't handle me like . . . like a piece of merchandise, Matthew." She tried to straighten from his side, just as Ole Sparks handed them cups of hard apple cider.

Ole nodded to Matthew. "Folks said you was an empire builder. Knew how to cut a neat fortune for yourself. This part of the country needs some of that, for sure. I'm a pretty good freighter, Matt. If you need a helping hand . . ." Ole offered staunchly.

"Sounds good, Ole. Rebecca and I are going to spend the winter up there, planning for next year. But I'll keep it in mind."

"I got my own team. Six of the best pulling cayuses from here to Coulee City."

After Ole wandered off, Rebecca stiffened, leaning away from Matthew's grasp. "Staying up there this winter?" she asked, frowning.

Matthew kept charting courses that interfered with her life. She liked to make her own decisions. He could have asked, and then she would have known how to counter him. "I have no intention—"

Matthew silenced her with a quick kiss, his eyes darkening. "I'd really love to carry you off right now, woman."

"I will not winter up there with you," she said.

Bruno, his arm supporting Stella, ambled up to them. "I see the sparks flying. The women are waiting for you two to begin the dinner. After that everyone will take a little rest and we'll begin the dancing later. Emma has agreed to lead the new dances. She's suggested Matthew as a partner."

Rebecca remembered the blonde's white arms twining around Matthew's dark neck and blurted out, "Emma can go climb a tree."

She flushed beneath Matthew's questioning stare and wondered why she had gotten so angry. No doubt Emma knew the latest dances; no doubt she could dance until the floorboards began to burn. "I am not going to dance on top of your toes again, Matthew. I was humiliated enough that night."

"You hated leaning on me, depending on me, didn't you?" he asked quietly. "Someday you'll see that I'm not going to hurt you."

Mrs. Peterson swished up, slipped her hands through their arms. "Really, you two. You have a whole life ahead of you. Don't you think you can spare a little time for the rest of us? Now come on down to the gift table. Everyone is waiting."

"Mrs. Peterson," Rebecca said, "I would really like to—"

"Nonsense," Matthew said, interrupting smoothly. "Of course, we're coming, aren't we, Becky?"

Mrs. Peterson beamed, clasping her hands over her bosom. "He's so handsome, so masterful, so gentlemanly-like. I just know you'll be the happiest couple in the Territory. Why, I can just see the love sparks flowing between you. It's so romantic," she said, gushing. "A proxy bride and a dashing husband off to a new life. Jacob will be baptizing those babies one a year."

Rebecca closed her eyes, for once allowing Matthew to lead her.

He placed his arm around her shoulders, whispering, "Cheer up, Becky. Only few more hours of torture." Then, lifting his cup of hard cider high, he proposed a toast. "To the queen of my heart."

Women began to weep softly. And Rebecca forced herself to sip from the cup he held to her lips, her eyes furious over the rim.

Emma stared at them boldly, her yellow dress pinned to her by the slight breeze. Jean came up behind her, bent to whisper in her ear, and Emma jumped back. She spoke heatedly to him, her finger wagging in his face. Jean grinned, lifted the finger to his mouth for a kiss.

"Now that's a pair," Matthew whispered in Rebecca's ear.

He looked down at her intently, the dark stare warming her until she blushed.

While the crowd chattered all around them, Rebecca turned to face him squarely. "I do not want to winter up there with you, Matthew. No telling what sort of debauchery you're planning—"

"Debauchery?" He laughed outright. The scarred eyebrow lifted as he leered. "My dear, I will do my best to please."

Matthew slipped his arm around her waist, pressing his cheek against hers. He leaned closer to whisper, "Are you wearing those silk drawers, Becky? The ones with the lace?"

When she looked away, blushing, he relented and smoothed her hot cheek. "Poor Becky. Captured and tossed into an unwanted marriage. I think this moment would be appropriate to give you my wedding present."

The crowd was hushed as the pearl necklace slid around her throat, a large emerald settling between her breasts. When she opened her lips, Matthew sealed them with a quick kiss. "You're mine now, Mrs. McKay. A man needs to give his wife gifts. It's a matter of pride. And something else too."

Rebecca felt fluttery and light, wanting to settle into his arms like a dove in the nest. When she wanted to be as bold as brass, fighting him, he caused her to be shy. "I haven't a thing for you, Matthew."

"Sweet Becky McKay, you're all I want and more," he returned huskily, taking her hands in his.

Chapter Fifteen

"Just look at her, the belle of the ball," Emma said with a sneer that evening as the dancers circled the Kleins' living room in a fast polka.

She ran the tip of her tongue over her lips, tasting the Kleins' red wine. Jean followed the movement as Emma continued. "She's had everything she's ever wanted and no idea at all how to use it. Why, Matthew did a lot better than her down in San Francisco."

"He seems quite happy holding his lovely bride, Emmaline." The music—a combination of Jesse's accordion, a fiddle, and a Jew's harp—began to play "Comin' Through the Rye." On the perimeter of the dance, children clasped hands, laughing as they mimicked the grown-ups.

Emma fingered her ruby eardrops. "La, the girl never wore a fancy dress until today. Doesn't even know how to walk in decent shoes, she's so used to boots. And dancing . . . huh! I'll bet Matthew's toes ache from her stepping on them. All that loose hair, swinging around—she should have twisted it up, put a roll in it. She looks like some half-grown gypsy girl."

"She is radiant. Surely you can put aside your anger on such a day, my dove." The music changed and Jean took her glass, placing it on the table. "Shall we waltz?"

Emma's blue eyes widened. "Good Lord, Jean! I'm an

unmarried woman. I have to be careful who I talk to, let alone dance with some half-blood!'' she exclaimed, backing away a step.

She bumped into Okanogan Mary, and the girl smiled timidly. Emma hastily swished aside her skirts. ''Indians everywhere I look. I thought the government had taken the whole passel and locked them up on the reservation.''

Jean swept her out onto the floor, swirling her amid the dancers. He laughed, leaning down toward her furious face. ''This savage will not be happy until his dove smiles.''

Executing an intricate step, he swept Emma beneath his arm, then close against his lean body. Holding her tightly, Jean guided her stiff body with such elegance that she relaxed. ''Jehoshaphat! Where did you learn to dance like a white person?''

''But I am part white, Emmaline,'' he returned easily, flashing another smile down at her. ''You feel like a feather in my arms.''

Emma flushed, avoiding his dark, knowing eyes. ''La, you certainly know what to say to a woman.''

''Did you like my gift of last night, *ma petite*?'' he asked softly, drawing her close to him.

''The moccasins? I am not about to wear them,'' she answered hotly. ''Don't you dare creep into my room again, you hear?''

Jean's eyes darkened, stroking her small, upturned face. ''Nothing can keep me from you, Emmaline. You are in the river of my life—''

Emma missed a step, then stamped her small foot angrily. ''I think this has gone far enough. I'll shoot you on the spot if you come near me again.''

Jean's long fingers wrapped around hers tightly. He drew her palm to his mouth, kissing the soft center. ''These pretty hands using a gun? I think not.''

''Oh!'' Emma exclaimed after she caught her breath. ''Oh!''

''Mother of my sons, you are the moon—white and round, filling my empty heart.''

"Land sakes!" She gasped, staring up at his dark, intent face. "How you do talk!" She stopped dancing, sweeping out of his arms. Glaring at Jean, Emma marched up to a big German farmer, and lifted her arms in a dance position.

Standing nearby, Wes nudged Jean's shoulder companionably. "She's a scared little heifer."

Jean stared at Emma's blond curls, bouncing as she danced a fast polka with a wheat farmer. "In the winter she becomes mine," he promised quietly.

Wes looked at the younger man sharply. "She's mixed up with Eric. One of the Flathead Indians brought her a message from him today. Don't know what the note said, but Eric killed a big Dutchman in the North Half—up on the San Polls River. Lost an eye doing it."

"Eric . . . the mad wolf," Jean murmured quietly, sipping his wine. His gaze slid to the petite blonde circling the room. "Emmaline is mine."

Rebecca laughed as Matthew moved her gracefully into a box waltz. "I didn't know dancing could be so much fun! It's just a matter of counting."

Matthew drew her against him, flattening his large hand low on her spine. "I think you've had too much champagne."

She missed a step, feeling weak and warm and suddenly the most beautiful woman in the countryside. "You had cases of it hauled up from the steamboat landing."

She tilted her head, allowing him to lead her through the stately waltz. Matthew moved her as easily as his own body, circling the floor. He made her feel as though she were dancing on clouds, as light and as free as the wind. Once she had gotten used to the guiding press of his hand on her waist, she'd forgotten her stiffness.

Matthew twirled her until she suddenly felt light-headed. With his collar open and his black hair curling across his brow, Matthew looked handsome. She ran her finger down his jaw slowly, liking the prickly sensation of his new beard.

Matthew's gaze stroked her dreamy face, darkening as she

toyed with a dark curl resting on his collar. She traced a tendon beneath the dark skin of his neck. "You've had more to drink."

His eyes drifted downward, stroking the emerald nestled between her breasts. "Hmm. I didn't know you were paying attention. You've been dancing with every man here," he murmured, placing his lips against her temple. His arms tightened, drawing her closer. "I want you alone."

Rebecca sighed, closing her eyes as he kissed her lids. Matthew had to learn the rules of their duel, but for now he just seemed so . . . sweet. Tomorrow she'd have to straighten out his commanding nature and keep him away from the heart of her. "I feel just like a puff of dandelion weed riding on the wind."

He chuckled, leading her out onto the porch. "If we don't get out of here soon, we're doomed for a shivaree."

He whistled, and the bay trotted out from the shadows. He snorted and stamped impatiently, his reins neatly tied by a length of mane. A blanket roll had been neatly tied around his neck.

Somehow Rebecca found herself seated in front of Matthew on his horse's bare back. He had placed her as though she were an English lady, riding sidesaddle.

Holding the reins before her, Matthew guided the horse toward the low, pine-covered hills. Rebecca breathed the fresh air, her head as light as a feather when she placed it against Matthew's broad chest. She wriggled, getting comfortable as his arm tightened around her. When his fingers prowled along a corset stay, she giggled. "I feel like an apple squeezed into a cider press."

Rebecca kicked off her shoes, allowing them to drop to the path. She wriggled her toes, lifting her legs straight out to study them. She tugged up the skirt, exposing long, slender legs. "My feet hurt. . . . The wedding wasn't half bad. Everyone seemed so happy."

"Not bad? You were beautiful. You made Emma and every other woman there look dowdy." She began to slide from the bay, and Matthew's arms tightened, rearranging her before him. His hand slid beneath her skirts to warm her thigh. He caressed the soft skin above her knees. "If you're not careful, we'll both end up on the ground."

She leaned against him. "Just as long as you're the one that lands first. I wouldn't want to get crushed."

If they were all happy, so was she, Everyone was happy and laughing and enjoying the get-together. She leaned back against his broad chest, her head resting against his shoulder. "Where are we going?"

. She didn't really care. Matthew leaned down, nuzzling her lips with his. "There's a little knoll overlooking the valley. They won't find us there," he murmured, easing his big hand across her stomach, flattening it.

She sighed, liking the feeling of being cherished and handled so carefully. Placing her hand over his, she wriggled her nose against the hair covering his chest. "That tickles."

His forearm tightened, his hand rising to cover her breast. "My dear, you are slowly driving me mad."

She giggled. "I think I like that, Matthew." Tormenting Matthew could be fun, she decided.

Lifting her skirts, she turned in his arms. Placing her legs over his thighs, she circled his neck with her hands, leaning back. The moonlight caught on his harsh face, his eyes shadowed. "I know what I'm doing. You deserve a little tormenting since you came in here and stirred everyone up."

"Oh, do I?" His hand slid between them, easing the folds of the dress aside. Cupping her hips, he lifted her closer to him. "That's better. I've been wondering all day if you'd wear these silk drawers." His fingers trailed over the lace edging, then slid beneath to stroke her upper thigh.

Entranced by the ragged tone to Matthew's deep voice, Rebecca slid her fingers through his hair. She traced his eyebrows and lashes slowly, then carefully palced her palms over his cheeks. "You're hot. Do you have a fever, Matthew?"

"Not one you couldn't cure." He flicked open the pearl buttons, his fingertips trailing down to the valley of her breasts. He toyed with the lacy chemise, then met the restrictions of the stiff corset. For a moment he breathed unevenly, then asked politely, "I suppose you're wearing the full female uniform?"

"I am wearing everything," she pronounced airily, waving her hand. "Everything a lady is supposed to wear, from garters to drawers. Even a chemise and a corset . . . buttons and lace and bones from head to toe. I almost passed out while you were teaching me to polka. Hell and damnation, I couldn't breathe."

"Damn!"

"What's wrong? That's what you wanted, isn't it? Now, Matthew, the whole valley worked themselves into a frenzy just to make you happy."

Matthew cupped the back of her head, placing his lips over hers. His tongue slipped into her mouth, enticing her own. The sweet, heady kiss heated Rebecca, her arms tightening around his shoulders. He tasted of champagne, his scent a dark, intriguing musk.

The kiss sought her essence, igniting the golden cords within her, stirring. . . .

Then suddenly the taunting changed into hunger, the tip of her tongue gently sliding along his lips. Matthew's broad chest pressed against her softness, and she slid her palms over him, knowing him. His mouth slanted, brushing hers, nipping on her lips, taunting her. . . .

She wanted Matthew then, wanted to play his teasing game of touching and heating.

Rebecca leaned back, sliding her hands over him. His muscles rippled beneath the hair-roughened skin. She trailed a fingertip down his inner arm feeling the muscles leap at her touch. She liked touching Matthew, pleased as his skin rippled and heated beneath her touch. Unbuttoning his shirt slowly, she stripped it from him, dropping it to the rocky earth.

Rebecca's gaze surveyed his chest lazily. She'd longed to touch him for hours, and now she finally had him beneath her fingertips.

"We're leaving quite a path. It wouldn't take a tracker to

follow us," Matthew warned in a dark sensual drawl. "What are you up to? You look like the cat who stole the cream."

"Don't complain, I'm only making you comfortable." She smoothed the taut skin across his belly, watching it ripple as he held his breath.

Trailing her fingers along his belt, she continued. "I've worked hard today, Matthew. It was hot as blazes dressed in this garb. My bosom, according to Maybelle, needed to be emphasized by a tiny waist and she kept tugging and tugging. What do you think of my bosom?" she asked seriously, frowning up at him. "Do you think it's fashionable?"

Matthew nodded. "I've appreciated the delightful sight all day, though I'm sure you've suffered."

"Hell's bells! I'll probably be scarred for life. I'm not ever wearing such a thing again, do you hear? High bosom in fashion or not." She sighed, lids drifting closed as she lifted her face to the moonlight. "The night air feels good. Smell that? The mountain air and the pines . . ."

Rebecca shifted, adjusting her bare legs over his hard thighs. Matthew tensed, breathing heavily as she pushed her skirt aside, her lace drawers resting intimately against him.

"Comfortable?" he asked in a husky rasp, the moonlight stroking the harsh planes of his face, his eyes gleaming within the shadows.

"Quite comfortable, thank you. Are you?" She lay back folding her arms behind her head to rest on the bay's muscled back. Regarding Matthew from beneath her lashes, she shifted her hips, lifting them toward him. He definitely needed tormenting.

"I've never worn garters before . . . they're tight." She lifted her left leg and the skirt raised, revealing the smooth length.

"Allow me to assist you, Princess," he drawled after a moment. He rolled the garters and black silk hose from each leg, smoothing it with his hand. He rubbed the delicate indentation caused by the garters. "Is that better?"

"Much." Taking care, she scooted toward the horse's

neck. Lazily she lifted her toes to rummage through the hair on Matthew's chest.

He caught her ankle, circled it with his fingers. Taking his time, he lifted her leg to kiss her inner calf. With his lips against her skin he said reminding her, "We're on the back of a horse, you know."

"I was raised on the back of a horse," she returned slowly, her flesh tingling from his kiss. "Why did you kiss me there?"

Matthew slowly caressed her inner thighs. "I'd like to kiss you all over. Has to do with tasting one's wife."

She idly studied his deep-set eyes and strong jaw. "Do people really do that, Matthew? I mean . . ." Suddenly shy, Rebecca looked up at the stars. "I like when you kiss me on the mouth."

"Do you really?" Matthew's fingers edged beneath her lacy drawers. "Are these uncomfortable?" Untying the knot, he eased the silken garment from her. The breeze pleasantly cooled her lower stomach and thighs. With the bay's muscles surging beneath her back and Matthew's large hand stroking her hips, Rebecca closed her eyes. She liked being petted and soothed by the strong, sure sweep of his touch.

In the moonlight Matthew's eyes flowed over her as if he wanted to memorize every curve and hollow. In the shadows the enticing hair matting his chest seemed to shimmer, catching the bare light. His shoulders rippled as he leaned forward to place both hands on her waist. "You little cat," he drawled huskily. "You're enjoying the hell out of this, aren't you?"

"Why, I don't know what you mean." Rebecca placed her hands on his forearms, lightly scoring the hair-roughened, supple skin.

Matthew's fingers nimbly unbuttoned the bodice of her dress. "I mean that when you get your claws, you'll be deadly."

The bay whinnied as Matthew lifted her against him for a rough, searching kiss. "Is that what you wanted?" he asked unevenly as she leaned against him, smoothing his chest with the flat of her hand.

"Yes," she whispered truthfully. She liked stirring Matthew's dark, savage moods, testing the gentleman's veneer with her claws.

"A little later, Becky, you'll learn that tormenting a man on the back of a horse is not the safest thing to do," Matthew stated carefully, smoothing her long hair and twining it around his fingers. "There are better places."

When they reached the moonlit knoll, Matthew slid from the bay. He spread the quilt, placing the small sack beside it, then returned to Rebecca. "Aye, come here, woman."

She slid from the saddle into his arms. "I was perfect . . ."

"You were the perfect bride, Becky. But I still think you're a little tipsy." Matthew stood her on the blanket, then lifted the lawn dress from her. He regarded her for a moment, long-limbed and slightly drowsy. "Tipsy and beautiful and wild."

"What are you doing, Matthew?" she asked as he began unlacing the French corset.

"We are saving my sanity, my dear," he returned, stopping to unknot the bustle from her waist, "preparing for a deed that needs doing . . ." Muttering when the knot did not give, he tore the strings apart.

Impishly she grinned up at him. "It took Stella, Maybelle, Maria, and Mary to get me into this rig," she announced, tugging at the strings of the corset. "I haven't been able to breathe all day. Damn, idiotic thing . . ." She plucked at the laces futilely while Mattthew's able fingers completed the task. "Trussed and hobbled . . ." she muttered as the corset flew into the bushes.

A coyote howled and a barn owl careened through the night sky as Matthew unlaced the chemise. He lifted it from her carefully, allowing it to slide to the blanket.

Rebecca stood still, listening to the rough sound of his breathing over the night sounds. She trembled, wanting to move against him but wanting a sign from him.

"There is more to this than the giving," he said after an endless moment. Sliding his fingers through her hair, he carefully removed the bridal flowers. His hand trembled when they touched her again, drifting over her throat. "Touch me, lass, because now I cannot wait.'' He groaned, his eyes pleading with her. He needed her—needed the source within her more than her flesh.

She knew that he trembled in his need, aching with it, but that with a word she could bind him. Given the choice, Rebecca touched his hard jaw, smoothed the stubble covering it. He'd claimed her body once, cradled her in his arms after the red haze of her nightmares.

She wanted to touch him, to feel his skin heat beneath her touch, to feel him tremble. She skimmed the breadth of his shoulders, the rippling muscles trembling, controlling his desire. She wanted to take and to give. To enter his body with her soul, to take him within hers.

The dark heat began low in her stomach, her heart beating quickly for the moment of their joining. Sliding her hands from his shoulders, down his chest to his stomach, Rebecca leaned back. Feather-light, her palm drifted lower, causing Matthew to catch his breath.

His hands slid to her breasts, gently warming the soft weight until she eased down to the blanket. Reclining beneath the silvery moonlight, Rebecca lay on her side, waiting, her hair rippling over her breasts and smooth shoulders.

A moment later Matthew joined her, his hard, naked body pressing against her softness. Beneath the canopy of the pine boughs, his mouth sought hers. Her arms twined around his back, her fingers pressing against the taut ridges of his muscles. Matthew's large hands moved on her swiftly, hungrily. His palms cupped her hips, pressing her against his trembling, hardened body.

Easing over her, Matthew kissed her face feverishly, his new beard scratching her cheeks.

Rebecca closed her eyes, luxuriating in the hard length of his body pressed intimately against her. Her breasts, aching and tender, dragged across the hair covering his chest. She moved closer to him, holding him tightly. Feeling his heart throb against her, she caressed his chest with her softness, his lips with her own.

Matthew groaned, his tall body taut with desire. Gently, carefully, he eased into her waiting moistness.

The silken entry caused her to gasp and tighten around him. Then, adjusting to him, cradling him with her hips, Rebecca knew a moment of absolute serenity before the storm.

Matthew's lips slid down over her breasts, his breath warming her flesh. Taking the very crest of her softness within his mouth, he treasured the delicate taste. His hands slid over her, caressing her stomach, then moved lower, stroking her thighs.

The sweet hunger throbbed through her, heated her bones and flesh as he moved within her, seeking. . . . She sobbed as the wildfire began to sweep through her, wild and free, rousing, heating, needing. Lifting her hips to meet him fully, Rebecca began the passionate ride.

Matthew's tongue played with her own, dancing, stroking, loving, as his palms cradled her hips.

She gasped, the throbbing within her growing as Matthew whispered against her throat, urging, teaching, praising. He groaned as the crest of the wave swept over her, her body taut, accepting his own gift deep within her.

The height took her to the golden meadows, to the dainty flowers, to the sparkling streams. Savoring the wild tempo of their joined bodies, Rebecca ran with Matthew to the starburst and the slow path drifting downward.

Matthew sighed raggedly against her throat. His heart beat furiously, pounding heavily on her breasts. He kissed her ear, her hot cheek tenderly. "My wife."

She trembled, the cool night air drifting over her damp lashes. Matthew's body pressed snugly to hers, resting after the storm. She touched his cheek lightly, feeling the heat of his passion brushing her fingers. He kissed her swollen lips, easing aside to cradle her to him.

Allowing her thigh to slide between his, she accepted his cherishing—the soft movement of his lips in her hair, the strength of his arms surrounding her. She needed his gentling touch after the wildfire, needed the easy stroke of his hand on her shoulder.

Upon his body lay the patterns of the moonlight passing through the pines. She felt his gentleness surround her and wondered about his passion, the driving search for the heavens that swept her outside herself. Beneath her palm, his heart slowed, beating heavily. His hand stroked her hip and thigh, warming her.

The bay whinnied, munching on wild grass as Rebecca lay in the security of Matthew's arms. Beyond the heat of their passion, there was another peace, a satin swathing of tenderness and sharing and a meeting of souls.

Rebecca allowed her fingers to wander over Matthew slowly, carefully, until he groaned. Shifting her to lie above him, he smoothed the tangled hair back from her face. "You've got that secretive look about you, Mrs. McKay."

Propping her elbows on his chest, Rebecca studied him. The canopy of her hair shadowed his face. "You planned this," she accused huskily, drawing a spray of baby's breath down his darkly matted chest.

"Guilty as accused," he murmured, toying with a silky strand. He wrapped it around his dark finger. He smiled, and she saw his eyes reach into her, questioning. His mouth was softer, their kisses leaving it less grim.

"You're a devilish man, McKay. Full of all sorts of tricks," she accused once more.

"A fitting match for a witch, don't you think?" he drawled. When she tossed her head, the long tendrils brushing his throat, he added, "Because that's what you are, a beguiling, tormenting, silky-skinned, raven-haired witch . . . half-willful sprite and more than enough woman to wrap me around your finger. I'll have to watch that—those flashing emerald eyes and soft lips. You'll have me jumping through hoops like a trained seal."

She trailed the spray of tiny white flowers across his tanned throat. "Not likely." Peering at him through her lashes, she smoothed his bottom lip with her thumb. "You've sharp teeth, McKay. And you've a hungry shark look about you."

He shifted beneath her, sliding his palm down her backside. "I admit to developing a certain hunger." He caught the emerald necklace with his teeth, tugging it gently. "Come here, I've a taste for more," he whispered, settling her over his desire.

Rebecca lazily stroked his bulky calf with her instep. "You have hairy toes, McKay. What makes you think I'd consider another . . . mood?"

He laughed, drawing her astride his need. "Because, Princess, we took the journey a mite too quickly. There are more leisurely methods—"

Rebecca tossed back her head, her hair settling around her shoulders and breasts like a mantle. "So certain of yourself, McKay?"

"Come here," he murmured, smoothing the silky hair about her. "Torment me at your leisure."

"Oh, I'll have my revenge, McKay." She rose, settling next to him. His full measure touched the heat within her, and she lightly scored his chest with her nails.

"Becky," he said with a groan as hot waves swept over her. She heard his deep voice tremble, the hard beat of his arms enfolding her, drawing her down. Suddenly, there was not time for play, for torment. Nothing but the hunger of bodies and souls, the soaring, the savage beat taking them to the heights of fulfillment.

Later she lay upon his chest, drowsy and warm. He nuzzled her hot cheek, kissing her swollen mouth. "Tired?"

She sighed, arching and stretching like a well-petted cat. She nipped his shoulder lightly, the moonlight gleaming on her long black hair as it crossed his chest. "You can be quite . . . the pleasant companion, Matthew."

Eyes closed, Matthew caressed her supple waist. "Mmm, the prize was worth the waiting."

She plucked a hair at the base of his throat. "You're pleased with yourself, aren't you? Luring me here to this deserted hill, having your wicked way with my innocence."

He rolled his head toward her, opening one eye. "Are you baiting me, Becky?"

She gazed upon his high cheekbones, the hard line of his jaw, and the dimple of his cheek in the moonlight. His body was leisurely sprawled across the quilt. He moved against her with certainty, graceful, adept at pleasing. Her gaze drifted over his taut hips and the shadows of his thighs. He'd been in women's arms before, and a niggling doubt slithered across her drowsy peace.

"I'm not up to playing your games," Matthew warned carefully, wrapping his fist in her hair to bring her face to his. "What's going on in there?" He tapped her forehead gently. "You're frowning, Becky. Why?"

She licked her lips nervously, and his gaze followed the movement. "I didn't know . . ."

He smoothed a tendril back from her damp cheek. "It's not always like this between a man and a woman, Becky."

"You know so much," she began huskily. Was she lacking in lovemaking? Why did she ache to hold him all through the night? The answer nettled her, caught her broadside, and sent her emotions tumbling: She cared for him.

She'd betrayed herself, given her body to a man who wanted her bound so firmly to him. What was it Eric had said? That Matthew had his ways?

"Come here." Taking her in his arms, Matthew lifted her chin with the tip of his finger. "There are feelings between us, Becky. Those feelings make us want each other."

She'd soared to the moon, gathered stardust in his arms, and floated back to earth. Was that how he intended to rule her, to make her obey his commands?

Fear raced inside her like a hunted fox, shuffling for a secure foothold. She had no idea how to be the woman he wanted. No idea how to . . . She wanted to set her own pace, exploring Matthew until she understood him better. But when he touched her, she forgot how to protect herself, forgot the pain of opening her heart.

Matthew had said he wanted her love. And then that he'd have all of her. And she wasn't ready to follow his path just yet. He'd have to learn patience or she'd have to teach him.

Tonight she'd had too much to drink, allowing it to dim

her senses. Then Matthew had come close to being her love, the husband she'd wanted as a young girl. But now she had to protect the very heart of herself.

It was safer to fight him now than to surrender what she didn't fully understand.

"I'm not a child needing explanations," she said flatly, shifting away from him to cover her breasts with the crushed dress. Her head pounded from the champagne; she hadn't known her body could betray her pride, bending it. "But if you keep up with this . . . madness, I'm certain to . . ."

She scowled at him darkly, and Matthew's hand shot out to wrap around her wrist. Testing her strength against his for a brief moment, Rebecca glared at his grim face. "You're an evil man, McKay. You're out to get me with child, aren't you?"

He frowned, sitting up. Tugging her wrist, he brought her nearer. "Why, you narrow-minded little witch. You can't believe for a moment that you wanted me because you felt something for me, can you? Admit it, damn you!"

"I was forced into this whole tangled plot!" Rebecca's anger swept over her. Matthew was making her feel things she didn't want to feel, like life was all new and clean and spread before her. Those were dreams that could rip her safety from her and she wasn't ready just yet to run into them. Matthew would have to learn that she set her own terms and his prodding ways would have to stop. "You have me drink champagne, then I fall into your waiting arms. I'd never get away from you with children."

"That's true enough. I'd never let you walk off—with or without children." He breathed heavily. "You're missing a point or two, aren't you?"

She didn't want to be reminded of her taunts, her newborn feminine instincts. Why did he insist on spreading everything before her, such as the hot way she had answered his passion? "Quite the gentleman, aren't you? Let me go, Matthew," she ordered carefully, shaking with anger.

"Not now. Not with those crazy notions stirring you up." He paused, catching her other hand before the blow. He rolled back, pinning her beneath him, shackling her wrists beside her head. "What we just shared was as close to heaven as I've ever been, woman. Accept it. Stop looking for fault." He breathed heavily, glaring down at her. "I swear, you'd try the patience of Job. You've got nasty little claws, Becky. They leave scars. I'm your husband, like it or not. Think what you want, but you're not running away from me."

"My lord and master," she hissed angrily. She resented his easy strength, her pride binding her. She wanted to bend, but her nature would not allow it; she ached to settle the matter, but to give in easily would cost her.

And Matthew needed to know her own strength. That he could not always have her on his terms. When she was ready, she would meet him on equal footing, without the clinging reminders of how she'd been forced into marriage, with nothing from the past between them. But not just yet.

He caught her hair, tangled his fingers in it, bringing her lips to his. In the moonlight his smile was dangerous. "Someday, Princess, I swear you will tell me you love me."

Rebecca breathed heavily, trying to force inches between his hot flesh and her own softness. She quivered, hating her weakness. "That day will never come, Matthew."

"Lass, someday you will fight for me as fiercely as a wolf for her mate."

Chapter Sixteen

"We are not the only ones enjoying the McKay wedding night." Jean slid from Emma's clinging arms. She protested drowsily, reaching out to him. In the predawn shadows, Jean chuckled as he drew on his pants. "While I long for your warm bed, my dove, I must leave."

Emma turned in the rumpled sheets, watching Jean draw on his shirt. Her lazy gaze drifted over his lean body, rippling beneath the fine fabric. La! The man could love sweetly . . . but she knew better than to get tangled with a half-Indian. Still . . . she'd known a man or two since she was twelve, and the black-eyed demon had just wiped out every last one of them. "I ought to shoot a hole straight through you. That or send the sheriff after you for a hanging."

"Oh? You were so unhappy in my arms? Was my performance lacking?"

Emma tossed her tangled curls, her body still warm from his passionate lovemaking. He'd taken her quickly, then soothed her trembling body with the gentlest touch. Watching him glide to the open window and stretch, Emma's body contracted, wanting more.

The savage had treated her like a lady!

"You had no business sneaking in here and waking me up." She wanted him back, damn him! Wanted the sweet feeling that he gave her, as though she were a girl with her first beau. That all-new feeling. Damn his half-blood hide!

"You were sleeping so prettily. I could not resist your charms."

"You'd better be resisting them! You could get hanged for rape!"

Jean laughed, his lean body silhouetted by the bare light coming in through her bedroom window. "But you were so cooperative, melting against me."

"Land sakes, you didn't give me a chance, Jean. For a minute I thought you were just a bad dream. Imagine creeping through windows and sliding into a lady's bed. Just like savages, I guess, not to respect an upstanding lady. Why, back home, you'd be horsewhipped. Or gelded."

Her eyes widened with the thought of the lash touching Jean's smooth dark skin. She chewed her lower lip, watching him roam the room like a caged animal. Her fingers curled on the musky sheets, remembering the fluid, steely feel of his body encased within hers. His body had a certain feel to it, as though it belonged with hers.

Emma stretched within the warm muslin sheets, knowing that she should rise and cleanse herself, yet somehow she could not summon the life to stir.

He touched her perfumes and powder cases, then lifted aside the curtain to her closet to look inside. "Just what are you doing?" she whispered. "You have no right to go prowling through my things!"

"You do not need all this, my dove." Sauntering back to her, his dress shirt a white flag in the shadows, Jean sat on her bed. He toyed with the curls flowing across her pillow, arranging them on her white shoulders. "Your beauty draws me until I cannot resist."

"Well, resist anyway!" She breathed heavily as his black eyes went prowling over her face, his hands sliding beneath the covers to cup her breasts. La! The man could take her breath away when he looked at her like that . . . as though she were the only woman in the world and he'd die for her.

Beneath his touch, she barely breathed, wondering about his gentleness, his passion which raised her own.

He slid the blanket from her, his lids narrowing as her plump breasts shone in the shadows. Holding them, he slowly lowered his head to place his open mouth upon her.

Emma could no more have resisted him than a slice of sweet, down-home pecan pie.

His straight hair slid upon her skin like silk and she knew she'd forever remember the touch. Reluctantly her fingers speared through his hair, holding him closer as his mouth moved to her other breast. Drawing from it, Jean lifted his head to stare into her eyes.

His hand slid to her hips, caressing the roundness beneath the blankets. "You carry my seed, Emmaline. In the warmth of your body it will be nourished and then my child will be born."

Emma's heart stopped beating, her fingers sliding down his smooth chest. She closed her eyes, feeling the heavy throb of her heart begin. Jean tangled everything up inside her, just with a few words. Lands!

His hand slid over her stomach, his palm resting over her womb. "Do not run from me, Emmaline. It is our destiny to make a child."

"Let me up," she whispered. The thought of Jean's black-haired child nursing at her breast caused her pain. She wasn't meant for children.

His palm pressed down and she almost felt his child stir within her. Opening her eyes, she begged, "Jean, you've got to go."

"I would like to take you again," he murmured, kissing her palm. "Hear your soft cries of pleasure—"

"Good lands, get out of here before someone discovers you." Emma felt the fine lash of new panic. What if someone did find him in her room?

He placed a fingertip on her lips. "Shh! It is before the dawn, the house is at rest. There is only you and I talking Emmaline. Your voice is like the music of the birds." He stroked her cheeks, caressing the fine bones with his thumbs. "When we are married, I wish you to sing to me—"

Emma shot out her hand to push him away, then her fingers strayed, caressing the smooth skin of his shoulders. She felt her nail marks, the marks of her passion crossing his skin. "You're crazy," she whispered shakily.

He laughed and she found herself grinning back like a fool.

Quietly, he said, "When we are alone, before the baby comes, we will have many good times talking like this. I have waited long for a woman like you, Emmaline."

Emma's heart stopped utterly. She went cold then hot. Jean meant what he said, the silver-tongued savage absolutely meant what he said about babies and weddings! "No!"

For just a moment Jean's expression changed, hardened. Emma saw it all then, the French-Indian heritage, the savagery and the passion. His determination frightened her. "We have mated, my little fox. I will share you with no other man now."

"You're crazy as a loon. I can have who I want . . . do what I want! I always have."

Jean took Emma's wrist, opening her small hand with a stroke of his thumb. He dropped a chain into her palm, then pressed his lips against it. "Heart of my own," he murmured tenderly.

Emma found herself looking into the black eyes of her destiny and trembled in fear.

In another moment the curtains fluttered, and she was alone.

She opened her hand and the gold chain slipped to rest on her stomach. "I've got to get a grubstake and get the hell out of here," she whispered achingly, feeling soft and fragile.

In the next instant she remembered his long hands fluttering over her beauty powders. Leaping from the bed, she inspected the various assortment of bottles and tiny cans. Her hands flew to her cheeks. "He took my *Blondine*! The lowdown Indian took my hair coloring! It will take weeks—months, maybe—to get another bottle."

She plucked a tiny mirror from the empty place. The delicate filigree wound about the perfect mirror, another gift from Jean.

"The next time I bed down after a wedding, it won't be next to a cottonwood slough," Wes drawled, patting the Appaloosa mare's rump. He squinted in the late-afternoon sun, his lids shielding the humor dancing in his eyes.

"Hmm?" Matthew had his mind on his bad-tempered bride, not conversation. Rebecca had squared off at him, challenging him with dark looks. She was determined to set her own rules and take her own time doing it.

When a man wanted his wife as badly as he did, a woman's intricate mind could nettle like hell.

He could wait her out; there was a softness in her now that hadn't been there before.

Damn!

Wes tightened the ropes around the animal's packs. "Seems the night critters start moving about dawn. Kept me awake."

The cattleman carefully checked over the string of tied horses and their packs. He glanced at the small herd of Appaloosas waiting in a corral. "We're about ready to start for the high country, Matthew. Seems Jean has a thing or two to take care of at the house, and then we're off." Wes dipped behind a horse to shield his grin.

Matthew stared at Rebecca, who stood waving to a wagonload of departing neighbors. Amid the well-wishers, Rebecca was the gracious hostess, seeing to the comfort of her guests. Knowing she avoided looking his way, he felt as raw as a boy needing his first girl. He tugged a sliver of grass from its stalk to suck on the sweet end. They should still be in their bridal bed, her long legs curled around him.

But he wanted more . . . the same soft look as when she had stood in the rose garden, the laughter shining in her as she'd played with the children in the meadow.

Rebecca moved, bending to lift a horse's hoof for her inspection. Her trousers tightened across her hips and Matthew's whole body went taut.

Wes followed his friend's dark, thoughtful gaze. "Jean and me are going on ahead, Matthew. We'll work on the house up on the homestead first. Get it as ready as we can, maybe see what we can do about rounding up some winter hay for the stock."

"I bought some sweet, dry grass from a rancher. If he turns up before I do, you might have him put it in the barn." Rebecca talked to the big German wheat farmer, and Matthew's jaw tightened. When she laughed up at the boy, Matthew wanted to start breaking bones.

"I'm taking Mary and the boy with me, Matt." Wes looked at Rebecca. "Jean and me can batch it alone, but. . . ." His cheeks flushed beneath his dark tan. "I'll pay her good for her time. I got her a good pony and some clothes for the boy . . . she can clean and such. I just want the pretty little critter near me. I'm getting too old to waste any more time trying to catch her alone here."

"I know just what you mean," Matthew answered slowly. "I'm not in a sharing mood myself."

"Don't imagine you are. I heard Stella's having trouble and is past her time. The women were talking about it this morning." Wes nodded toward Rebecca. "You staying here for long, Matthew? Becky might want to see this thing through, you know."

"We need to be settling in for the winter. I've got two freighters bringing up household goods and tools from Coulee City. If I need to, I'll go up with them . . . Becky can come later." Rebecca turned, her braid bobbing down her back. When their eyes met, her head went back proudly before she turned to another departing family.

Matthew took a deep steadying breath. She was in a bad mood, was she? A champagne headache and lack of sleep didn't make her any sweeter, he decided. Half siren and half vixen, she could easily drive him mad. It was the sweetness that came flowing over him like honey, that bound him. When Rebecca decided to make love to him, there was nothing as sweet.

He wanted to carry Rebecca straight up on the mountain.

Wes interrupted his thoughts. "Ah . . . I heard there was another cabin up there, Matthew. Old Jake's place." The trail boss dusted his hands, staring at his callused palms. "I've got a dollar or two . . . what would you take for it and a few acres?"

"I think we can arrange a fair price, Wes."

The cattleman extended his hand for a handshake. "That's good. Think it over. Jean will be moving on, once you and Becky settle in. He's got some business up north, then he'll be back. But my old bones like a good warm stove in the winter." Wes's eyes followed Mary as she carried a stack of blankets to a settler's wagon.

He kicked a stone with the toe of his boot. "Ah . . . I'd appreciate it if you'd bring a case or two of canned milk up with the freighters, Matthew. My packhorse is plumb caved in with cooking pots and blankets and such for my own place."

"I'll take care of it. I might even throw in a length of calico and some thread," Matthew added.

Wes grinned, looking years younger. "I'd appreciate that. I think I'm about to get this courting business figured out." He shook his head, laughing. "From the looks Becky is sending over here, you might need some help with this marriage business. She looks like she's got a burr under her saddle."

"She's not the only one." Matthew had had enough of Rebecca's dark, forbidding looks. He crushed the stalk of grass in his fist, then threw it to the ground. "Tell Jean I set up an account for you at the general store. He can sign for what he needs, ledgers or papers. . . ."

"We'll be needing plenty of soda for the winter, salt too . . ." Wes's voice faded as Matthew stalked toward his bride. Wes grinned, shaking his head. "That filly is feeling her vinegar this morning."

Matthew slipped his arm around Rebecca's shoulders, felt her body tense against his. So she was out to make him pay for her headache, was she? He nodded to the elderly ranch woman. "Good morning, Mrs. Peterson. Have a nice trip home."

She beamed, pinching his cheek. "You have a nice marriage, son. Make sure those babies get proper baptisms when they come along. I'll remind Jacob to check in with you now and then."

Rebecca took a deep breath, edging away from Matthew's arm. He tugged her closer. "We hope the first one's a girl, just like my Becky. Pretty as a princess."

Matthew helped her climb slowly into the hack's seat. "Thank you, Matthew. Your man has such manners, Becky. You are the lucky bride, I do declare." The old woman's wrinkles settled into a concerned expression. "You'll watch Stella, won't you, Becky? Her color isn't good, and she's having some trouble that can only be helped by the Lord. This baby is taking too long to come into the world. Stella's had some pain in the night, and she's to keep off her feet."

"We'll take good care of her, Mrs. Peterson. You just be careful going home," Rebecca returned, stepping forward for her kiss on the cheek.

"Have a good marriage, honey," Mrs. Peterson whispered against her cheek. "He's a handsome devil, he is. And eyes only for you. Makes me think of my man years ago. Why, once you two are alone . . ."

Within the circle of his arm Rebecca trembled. She waved a last good-bye to Mrs. Peterson, then turned on him. "Stop pawing me."

"Your nerves are showing, Princess," he drawled, fascinated by her blush. "But then, brides are sweet, shy, nervous creatures by nature."

"Damn your hide!" She tossed her head, the braid whipping against his arm.

Matthew felt the keen edge of his own anger. "Have you ever played poker, Becky?" When she continued to glare at him, he added, "When I sit down at a big game, I play to win."

By late afternoon the last of the well-wishers had piled into their wagons, counted their children, and begun the trek home. Emma, silent and brooding for once, had quietly packed her bags, said her thank-yous, and left with Maybelle.

At the evening meal Rebecca was subdued, the shadows deepening beneath her eyes. When Matthew reached to hold her hand, her fingers slid through his, tightening.

His thumb rubbed across the back of her hand and she looked at him tiredly. There was something so soft passing between them that he wanted to reach over and tuck her head against his shoulder.

But Rebecca's pride wouldn't allow the trespass, and he settled for the slight clasp of her hand within his.

At midnight Matthew lay on Rebecca's bed, his arms behind his head. The leaf shadows danced on the wallpaper, and he listened to the house settling down for the night. Throughout the day Rebecca had smiled brightly and accepted heartfelt congratulations. But he noted her sloping shoulders.

Stella had needed help in the evening, and Rebecca had stayed long hours tending her. Now Rebecca murmured softly in the hallway, and Bruno rumbled, "Go on now, Becky. It's my turn."

Matthew breathed lightly, his nerves tensing. Would she come to him or would she go to Emma's empty bed?

His mouth tightened. He'd been strung tight as a fiddle string all day, and if Rebecca opposed him tonight . . .

The door swung open and Rebecca quietly slid into the room. Leaning against the closed door, she stared at him through the shadows. For a moment Matthew stopped breathing. The curtains fluttered at the open window, the coyotes howled, and cattle lowed, all disturbing the peace. She could have slipped into another room, so why hadn't she?

In the slice of moonlight crossing her face her eyes looked like large, smudged shadows on a too pale face.

She had come to him, needing him, and with that knowledge Matthew's heart skipped a beat. Without a word he rose from the bed and walked toward her. "Come here, Becky."

Lifting her face to his, Rebecca sighed tiredly. Matthew

cupped her cheeks between his palms, feeling the fragility of
the bones and the coldness of her skin. He ran his thumbs
across the fan of her lashes, then stroked her temples. "How's
Stella?"

Rebecca's slender fingers rose to rest on his wrists. "She's
so tired, Matthew. The baby seems so large."

Taking her carefully, Matthew rocked her in his arms and
she rested her cheek against his shoulder. She'd come to him
for comfort, and the knowledge sent his hopes soaring.

When her arms slipped around him, her hands pressed flat
against his back, Matthew kissed her smooth temples, soothing the tendrils back. "Aye, that's it, Becky. Come to me."

She sighed again, resting heavily against him. "I read the
inscription on your ring, Matthew. 'My Rose—1902—M.' "

Lifting her in his arms, he carried her to the bed. Tugging
off her boots, he gently began undressing her. He kissed the
crest of each soft breast reverently. "In the words of my
mother's favorite poem—'Bewitching lass, my heart's true
luve . . .' "

Her hand touched the back of his as it curled around her
neck. "I'm too tired to fight you, Matthew."

"I know. Now is my chance to have my evil way with
you," he teased softly. He slid his silk shirt over her and
buttoned it. Taking the collar in his hands, he drew her up
for his soft, gentle kiss. "Let me help, Becky. You haven't
slept in hours."

She tilted her head back, looking at him from beneath her
lashes. "I have an idea you're going to help, anyway."

"Aye," he agreed huskily as he sought the tip of her braid
to unravel the binding ribbon. "That I am, Becky."

Rebecca yawned, her eyes closing. "Call me if Stella needs
me, Matthew. Bruno tries, but he's badly frightened. Stella
doesn't need to worry about him just now too."

Matthew unbraided her hair, combing the tangled length
with his fingers. "I'm proud of the way you saw to everyone's
needs, making them comfortable." Taking the brush from
her bedside table, Matthew brushed the long strands until

they rippled down her back. Then, easing her into the sheets, he slid next to her and took her into his arms.

"Stella isn't well, Matthew," she murmured after a moment. "The doctor just left. He's says there's nothing to do but wait now." She sighed tiredly, allowing him to stroke her hair back from her face. "I'm so tired."

Her fingertips found the hair on his chest as she drifted off to sleep.

The blood-red haze swirled around her, men moving in the water . . . fighting. Rebecca cried out, running toward the smooth gray water, her heart bursting with pain. She was ice cold, her lungs hurting, fighting for air. She had to run to them to help, but she couldn't move. Fighting her rage and fear, Rebecca awoke, lifted her hand, and gestured to the shadow-men who were no longer there.

Shivering, she nestled closer to the warmth sharing her bed. She rubbed the cold sweat from her forehead against the warm pelt of fur.

For a moment she was able to breathe quietly, forcing the fast beat of her heart to slow, forcing the panic and the fear deep down within her. The red haze clung behind her lids, waiting for her to sleep.

Matthew sprawled across her bed, his long, nude body wrapped in the early-morning light. His arm and leg bound her to the bed possessively, his face pressed against her ear.

She listened to the heavy sound of his breathing and knew he was awake.

"You've been dreaming again, haven't you, Becky?" he asked in a voice laden with sleep. His palm cradled her left breast. "Want to tell me about it?"

Sitting up, he propped the pillows behind his head, stroking her hair. "Come here. Tell me about it."

She shook her head firmly. She didn't need him prowling through her dreams. Matthew had a way about him—a bull-headed way that saw straight through her. "I've got to check on Stella."

"You've got to sleep. Come here." Matthew drew her up

to rest against him. "You came to me last night, Becky. Put your trust in me. You can do the same now."

She rubbed her temples, fighting the red haze that lingered there. For an instant she smelled old lavender and crushed rose petals; she sensed the dream had something to do with Matthew. "It's nothing."

"Like hell. You clawed me in your sleep. Look." He pointed to the red marks scoring his shoulder. "Tell me."

"It's a silly dream." *The nightmare concerned Matthew!* In a lithe movement Rebecca leapt from the bed, gathering up her clothes. She could feel the cold rasp of fear still on her skin. Why? "I'll dress in the other room. I'm going to Stella."

He settled back against the pillows. "I'm getting to the bottom of this, Becky. I promise."

Chapter Seventeen

Rebecca scanned the foothills and the Columbia River snaking slowly through the basin. The scent of ripe apples drifted in the mid-September breeze, a sweet perfume.

Stella's increasing difficulties had allowed Rebecca a measure of time and she had stayed behind. In a few more weeks, the first snow would touch the mountains.

Matthew had been gone for two weeks, and she remembered his parting kiss . . . right smack in front of the freighters waiting up on their wagons. They'd hooted and made the eight-horse teams prance, jingling the bells on the reins. Bending her back over his arm, Matthew had pressed his taut body against her softness. She'd had to cling to his neck or fall straight to the ground, and the devil knew it!

His hand had slipped beneath her blouse, cupping her breast, running his thumb across the crest. "I'd like to kiss you there.

"Aye, you'll do," he'd murmured huskily, stroking her long hair down to her hips. Out of sight of the freighters, his broad palm had molded her curves beneath the trousers, caressing her. "Don't get any ideas, you little savage. I'll be right on your heels if you take off."

Hell's bells, he knew he'd leave her aching, wanting him. Her breasts felt fuller, sensitive now. He had the experience,

and his black eyes danced with promises as he swung up on
Duke, the big bay.

Later, an old trapper had passed through, asking for
"McKay's woman." He'd handed her a parcel, spat a stream
of liquid tobacco to the ground, and loped off, leading his
pack mule.

She had unwrapped the brown paper carefully in her room.
Matthew's bold scrawl across a note slipped from the lacy
camisole in a spray of dried lavender flowers: "Come to me.
M."

He still wanted her. Why?

Now, in the middle of September, the first apples were
ready to be picked, sweet enough to ship out on the steamboats and freighters. Apple slices were drying on every flat
rooftop, covered with muslin to protect against insects. Her
father had send three barrels of his best early apples up the
Methow for Matthew.

As a wave of sheer loneliness washed over Rebecca, she
found herself watching the road that led to the Chiliwist.

" 'Bewitching lass, my heart's true luve . . .' "

That night Daniel hadn't returned from Cairo with Stella's
laudanum. Wanting time to herself, Rebecca had suggested
she ride into town, looking for him. Gramophone music
floated from the parlor as Wind Dancer carried her from the
ranch yard.

The lilting melody was a sign that Maybelle was visiting,
as she often did now, and that Peter was enjoying a dance
with her.

Riding along the Columbia, she thought of Matthew. He
wanted an empire and he wanted all of her, body and soul.
She shivered in the night air, riding beneath the stars and
moon. " 'My heart's true luve . . .' "

She smelled the smoke of the cook stoves before she saw
the lights of Cairo. Riding into town, she noticed Daniel's
pony tied to the saloon's hitching post. Someone banged on
a piano while some of the men let out shouts of rowdy laughter.

Swinging down from Wind Dancer and tying his reins,

Rebecca frowned. When she entered the saloon, neighbors shielded their faces. Amid the smoke and whiskey fumes, Daniel leaned against a bar, supported by Eric.

Slowly Eric turned to her, his eye patch glistening in the lantern light.

The bartender shook his head, catching Rebecca's slashing glare. "I told him to get on home. But the boys bought him a few rounds and—"

Rebecca grabbed the bottle from Daniel's hand, plopping it on the polished counter. Eric moved to support him better and Rebecca snapped, "He's had enough, Eric. He's pie-eyed now."

Owlishly Daniel tilted his head down at her. He squinted, his head weaving on his shoulders like a cobra mesmerized by flute music. Her arm circled his waist, and when she stumbled under the weight, Eric almost carried the boy to the door. "I'll help you."

Rebecca nodded curtly. Now was not the time to stage a scene; she already had a full-blown mess on her hands. She could handle Eric, just by staying within drawing distance of him. The other men shuffled their feet and studied the sawdust with sudden intense interest. She turned to the barkeeper. "What does he owe?"

"Not a thing. Once he got started, everyone wanted to see how much he could hold. I'd have had to use my gun to stop them." He shrugged, wiping the counter with a damp cloth. "He's a boy, Rebecca. They all do it sooner or later. Better here than behind the barn where they can get robbed."

Once outside the saloon, Eric supported Daniel's weight easily. "He's not hurt, Becky. Stop looking as if you'd like to shoot someone, though there was a time when I deserved your bullet. I'm sorry for that."

Daniel moaned as Rebecca studied Eric's eye patch. His expression seemed earnest. "I didn't know you were back."

"I've been around. I came across your high and mighty husband—he doesn't want me near his precious bride. Outside of fighting that boyo, I've decided to be the considerate brother and keep my place."

He eased Daniel to the hitching post, leaning the boy against it. "Here, hold on to this."

Daniel retched, moaning. "Help me, Lord, I'm dying!"

"Good. Help me put him on his horse, Eric. We'll tie him to it. He can sober up on the way home."

Eric ran his fingers through the hair on his chest, scratching it thoughtfully. "I hear Matt went on up the Chiliwist. Is that true?"

"He's gone. Getting settled in for the winter." She held Daniel's head as the boy's knees started to fold.

Daniel groaned loudly, holding his head. "Laudanum's in my pocket. I think I may need some."

Rebecca placed her hands on her hips, shaking her head. "I ought to just let him sleep it off right there in the street."

Eric stooped, picking up Daniel in his arms and carrying him like a child. "Bring the horses. I'll help you sober him up over at Maybelle's. They're used to this sort of thing at all hours." He turned when she hesitated. "Well, come on. He's not fit to travel, and the girls there won't say anything. Emma won't tell Maybelle and the almighty Klein name will be as fresh as a newborn babe."

"Eric, I don't know—"

Leading the way to Maybelle's, Eric said, "The boy needs a bed right now, not the backside of a horse. You can quit worrying about me, I've learned my lesson."

Eric carried Daniel straight into the brightly lit house, leaving Rebecca to take care of the horses. Shaking her head, she tugged them around to the rear of the house, bedding them down in the customer's privacy stable. Rebecca shook her head, pressing her lips together as she marched into the back door of the establishment.

Entering a small sitting room, Rebecca glanced at the ornate, carved furniture and Oriental rugs. Emma, looking frightened, hovered in the brightly lit hallway. Dressed in a silky robe and little else, the smaller woman's blond hair had darkened at the roots. When Rebecca's stormy gaze touched Emma's hair, she reddened. "I've been hiding out here, just waiting for a tinker to come through. I look just awful, my roots coming in that awful red-brown color, makes me look like a squirrel—"

"Where's my brother?" Rebecca demanded, glancing around the narrow hallway.

"He's in the Parisian room." She pointed toward a closed doorway. "There. Eric's cleaning him up. Oh, Rebecca, I'm so embarrassed," Emma cried, following Rebecca's long-legged stride. "I'm just going to have to hole up here, hiding like an old hag."

Rebecca swung open the door and found Eric holding Daniel's head over a washbasin. He placed the groaning boy back on the satin pillows and tugged off his boots. Lifting Daniel with one arm, he jerked the thick comforter from beneath him.

"Maybelle would have cats if he soiled her bedding," Emma said with a sniff, wiping her eyes with a rumpled handkerchief.

"I'll need a fresh pitcher of water and some rags," Rebecca ordered grimly. "Would you get them, please, Emma?"

Emma clasped her hands before her dramatically. "Of course. Of course I will. But first, tell me . . . you haven't seen that awful Jean Dupres lurking about have you? The man chills me to the very bone."

"I'll help you, Emma, " Eric offered slowly, rising and following her out. "The boy is going to need some rest, Rebecca. And some good strong coffee. I'll help . . . because I'm blood and all. And because I figure I owe you one." His blue eye slid over her face. "Matthew didn't take you with him, then," he drawled with some satisfaction.

Eric seemed sincere, and for now Rebecca had to take him at his word. Moving toward Daniel, she answered, "Stella's been sick. She needed me."

His expression was thoughtful. "Hmm. I thought maybe you two had . . ."

Sitting on the bed beside Daniel, Rebecca smoothed his hot forehead. "He's burning up, Eric."

"He's no different from any other lad away from home.

We'll get the coffee and the wash water. Come on, Emma.''
Eric closed the door just as Daniel moaned loudly and leaned
over the bed to the washbasin.

Three quarters of an hour later Emma was hovering in the
shadows of the room, her blue eyes darting between Eric and
Rebecca. "Rebecca, you can share my room if you want,"
she offered timidly, glancing at Eric, who was sprawled across
a chair in the shadows of the ornate room.

"I'll stay with Daniel."

Emma's indrawn breath sliced over Daniel's soft moan.
"Oh, but I don't mind . . . really I don't. La, the bed is big
enough for . . ." Her eyes slid fearfully to Eric, then to Rebecca's face. The small woman's face turned pale. "I mean
. . . you're welcome to stay if you want."

Emma lifted a dainty cup and saucer toward Rebecca.
"Have some. It's a special brew of Maybelle's, for her cus-
tomers. I mean . . . it's delicious, really it is, and it'll make
you pert and feeling like new."

Rebecca ran her hand across her eyes, feeling every inch
of her night ride. "Thank you, Emma. I think I will."

Emma handed the saucer to her, her hands trembling until
the liquid sloshed over the rim of the cup. She glanced fearfully at Eric's scowl as Rebecca sipped the hot coffee. "This
is good, thank you. We'll be all right, Emma, if you want to
go to sleep."

The smaller woman ran her fingers through her hair, her
eyes sliding toward Eric. "Maybe I will. Just maybe I will
. . . but I'll check back with you."

When her cup was empty, Rebecca felt light-headed. She
sensed Eric taking the cup from her hand. He lifted her from
her chair as easily as a child, carrying her from the room. In
a haze, she felt him strip her, running his hands roughly over
her breasts. She protested weakly, fighting the weights surrounding her as he breathed harshly, his fingers probing her
thighs, bruising. . . .

"Fight me, damn you, you gypsy witch!" Eric growled,
his teeth nipping her throat. She felt her body fall to the bed

as light as a leaf drifting to the earth. For a moment there was silence, and then a hushed fight in the shadows.

"You're hurting me, Eric. Stop it," Emma pleaded in the distance.

She cried out as Eric snarled. "Tell her, you bitch. Tell her now, when she can hear, or so help me, I'll snap your neck."

Emma mewed softly, "Matthew and I . . . he's been with me, Rebecca. We . . . I'm carrying his brat!"

"That's enough. I'll tell her how Matthew and you rolled in his bed, wanting it. Get out or join me, you slut," Eric said with a sneer.

She heard her own groan, the bed creaking beneath his weight, his hot mouth hurting her breasts. She couldn't move, pinned beneath his weight, couldn't breathe as his teeth nipped at her throat.

He growled his pleasure, working his way down her cold body. Holding her hips as he nuzzled her stomach, his fingers bruising, hurting. . . . "Fight me, witch!"

Then the void came, encasing her in soft black velvet, replacing the pain.

She awoke before dawn, the red haze chilling her, swirling around her. Eric's head rested on the pillow beside her head, his nude body sprawled across hers. An empty whiskey bottle lay against him.

Rebecca shifted, her stomach knotting. *Matthew and Emma!* She carried his child. . . .

He'd betrayed her, using her, toying with her while he visited Emma.

She felt dirty, remembering Eric's curses, his hands probing, hurting. Breathing quietly, Rebecca eased from beneath his arm. She dressed quickly, untangling her clothing from his, her fingers shaking.

The tears of shame came creeping softly from behind her lids. She'd almost forgotten the pain at Rudy's hands, and the shame that stalked her soul. Now it came back, as painful as the lash of a bullwhip.

Matthew and Emma. Her stomach churned and she held her fingers to her mouth. Emma carried Matthew's child!

She retched silently. He'd had Emma, they'd used each other. . . . He'd betrayed Rebecca after all the promises, and she had believed him.

She closed her eyes, envisioning Matthew's dark body sliding down into Emma's white, plump one, easing himself in her arms. He must have laughed at her own attempts.

She strapped her Colt to her hip, fingering the butt for a moment. She could kill Eric now and start the valley gossiping about Matthew and his brother sharing her. She pressed her fingertips to her aching head, trying to think. Eric had raped her, she was certain of it.

She pressed her palm against her knotted stomach, sickened at the thought of him entering her body.

As Matthew had taken Emma . . .

Her knees began to buckle, her stomach turning. Of course, why hadn't she seen him for what he was? He wanted a "woman of the country," and he wanted his toy, giving him pleasure.

She gasped, pain shooting through her chest. ". . . my heart's true luve . . ."

The McKay brothers were a deadly pair. Perhaps Matthew's method was even more unsavory than Eric's. He'd been so loving. . . . Her lids tightened grimly, her body ice cold.

She wouldn't be used by either man. The two of them badly needed a lesson on how to treat women, and she might just give them that taste of revenge.

Her tongue flicked across her lips, tasting dried blood. For now she had to protect Daniel and her family from gossip. She pressed her fingers to her swollen lips tentatively. She'd been through enough pain to last her a lifetime.

Matthew had taken her and every other female in his sight. He was no more bound by the marriage by proxy than a buck in rut. He'd wanted her as his wife, did he? If he came close to her again, she'd use her gun.

She pressed the backs of her hands to her eyes, her stom-

ach rolling like a log caught in the current. Matthew and
Emma . . .

She'd find a private way to deal with Eric, away from town.
She'd track him down.

She closed the door quietly, glancing down the hallway.
"The Parisian room," Emma had said, and Rebecca quietly
opened one door to find Samuel Smythe pulling on his long
johns, his naked backside a snowy white. "Sam, you help
me get Daniel on his horse and I won't say a word to your
wife, or your Indian woman, let alone the twelve children in
between."

Samuel's face went stark white. He glanced uneasily at the
sleeping woman sprawled in the rumpled bed. "Rebecca,
you can't just come hunting through these rooms for Daniel
. . . he's a grown man now. This is a man's territory."

His cheeks reddened beneath his large handlebar mustache. "Now, Rebecca, you wait a minute. A lady doesn't
come to a house like this, even after her brother—"

"Button up, Samuel," she hissed. "Your drawers and your
mouth. I meant what I said about telling your wife and your
Indian woman. The way I see it, one would scalp you while
the other gelded you—"

Moments later, Daniel, tied to the back of his horse,
groaned as Rebecca led him out of town at a fast trot. "Anytime you feel you can sit on that saddle, Daniel, let me know.
Right now I don't care how you're feeling."

Pausing beside the bank of a tiny stream, Rebecca helped
Daniel to his feet. "You'd better clean up. I'd have a pretty
good head on me when Papa starts asking questions, let alone
Bruno."

Daniel held his head, weaving on his bare feet, while Rebecca turned on her heel and marched upstream. Hidden by
cattails, she stripped and stepped into the icy snow water,
washing Eric's touch from her with trembling hands. She'd
cry later, she promised herself as her lids burned with tears.
But not just yet, not until she had Daniel safely home and
Stella resting easily with her laudanum.

"Laudanum," she whispered as a dry rake of fear widened

her eyes. A doe sidestepped the rocks bordering the stream, drinking from the fresh water. "He used laudanum."

Chilled by the icy water, Rebecca thought of her wedding night and Matthew's champagne. *Each brother has his method of dealing with me, it seems.*

Rebecca dried her aching body with her shirt, replacing it and dressing quickly. She clamped her lips closed, gritting her teeth as she strode back to the horses. Eric had marked her, and she'd remember his shaming touch until she died. But she'd kill him first.

But it was the other brother who had hurt her pride, taking her with promises while he laughed upon Emma's plump breasts.

She wiped her hands over her bruised thighs, trying to cleanse Eric's touch from her. Eric was a dead man—but at the right place, at the right time.

Her revenge on Matthew needed planning. She wanted deeper, more wounding justice. She'd cut him off where it hurts—his almighty, manly pride. He'd ride out of the country without his dreams.

Inexplicably, hot tears brimmed over her lids. Damn his soft, raspy voice, which weakened her knees! Damn his melting, smoldering stare and magical touches. . . .

Rebecca slashed the back of her hand against her cheek, shivering with conflicting emotions.

She'd meet him on his own terms and tear the very guts out of him with her sweetness; she'd ply him with every dram of her new femininity, then find her niche and have her revenge.

Matthew needed a special revenge, one that would last him into the eternity of hellfire. "Daniel, are you ready?"

Chapter Eighteen

Rebecca rode ahead of Daniel, her back ramrod straight as they approached the ranch in the dawn.

Her flesh felt weary and dirty, the ache within her growing. She'd aged a century since meeting Matthew McKay, and she would have her revenge on him as surely as winter followed autumn. It was just a matter of timing—no matter what length of time—until she had her complete revenge.

McKay wanted a wife in the high country, did he?

Well, she'd give the black-eyed devil his due, then take her pound of flesh at the right time. The taste of her revenge would be as sweet as honey and McKay would feel the fine lash of humiliation.

Wind Dancer began to prance. He scented his early-morning oats, waiting for him in the Klein barn. He wanted to run, wild and free through the snappy morning air, while Rebecca wanted him to take her back into yesterday, when only Matthew's touch had lain upon her skin.

She shivered, remembering his betrayal. Her fingers tightened on Wind Dancer's reins, the smooth feel of the leather reminding her of Matthew's rippling back. How she had clung to him. . . .

Hell and damnation! McKay belonged in hell, and she was just the one to put him there!

The ranch yard was strangely quiet as she rode into the

barn to unsaddle the stallion. Chelan Sam stopped raking hay and began to curry the stallion as he ate from the grain trough. "Baby *memaloose*."

The fear raked Rebecca's taut back, forcing her own pain back. "Whose baby is dead, Chelan Sam?"

But she knew before the old Indian answered. "Big man's. *Skookum* brother." His eyes, enfolded by wrinkles, pinned Daniel as the boy rode into the barn. "Big, good brother, Not *kultus*—bad one."

Daniel flinched, aware that Indian word traveled fast. Shoulders hunched, he swung down from the saddle. "I'll be in later."

Rebecca ran toward the house, her heart pounding with fear.

Peter, holding his head in his hands, lifted his weary face at the sound of her boot steps. He nodded, acknowledging her presence dully. "It happened early this morning. Stella won't let them take the boy from her room."

He shook his head, collapsing onto the settee. "It happened so fast. She screamed once, and the baby came before the womenfolk could even get to their room. Bruno can't talk to her—she won't listen. He's out back chopping wood like he's possessed."

"I'll go on up." Gripping the oak railing for support, Rebecca took the stairs slowly, her stomach knotting.

Opening the bedroom door slowly, Rebecca sought Stella in the darkened room. "Oh, come see him, Rebecca," Stella crooned, holding the tiny bundle. "He's just like Bruno. You're an aunt at last. Shh now, come here."

Rebecca eased down on the bed, sitting beside Stella. Her face was radiant, her brown hair curling around her shoulders. "Let me see him," Rebecca whispered gently, easing back the fold of the tiny blanket.

She forced herself to smile, despite the trembling inside. Stella had so wanted the baby.

"Isn't he beautiful?" Stella rocked the tiny bundle, her eyes shining with tenderness.

"Can I hold him, Stella?" Not knowing what she would

do, Rebecca was prepared to take the baby by force. The longer Stella held the dead child, the harder it would be for her to give him up.

Stella frowned, clutching the baby tighter. "Bruno tried to take him from me. He said awful things about his firstborn child . . . awful things." She shook her head fiercely, denying the baby's death.

Maybelle slipped into the room, carrying a tray with filled teacups. "Chamomile blossom tea, anyone? Stella, I've prepared a special cup for you." She looked at Rebecca meaningfully, then indicated the cup by a nod. "I put just a little something in it, especially for the new mother. You see that Stella drinks it, won't you, Rebecca?"

"My milk is coming in. Why I'm fairly dribbling through my wrappings." Stella hummed, rocking the baby. "He'll wake up just any minute and want to eat. He'll let out a squall that will raise the dead." She frowned, clutching the baby tighter. "There, there, little man, I won't let them take my boy."

"He's a beautiful baby, Stella." Rebecca nodded at Maybelle, who slipped out of the room as quietly as she had entered. "I'm so thirsty for a good cup of tea. I've heard it's nourishing for new mothers. You're going to drink yours, aren't you?"

"La . . . le . . . la . . . le," Stella singsonged. "He's such a good baby."

Rebecca fought the tears, burning behind her lids. Maybelle had a reputation for knowing the powers of special herbs, and she wanted Stella to have her tea.

Remembering another drugged brew, Rebecca's hand trembled as she handed Stella her cup of tea. "Here, Stella. We don't want to offend Maybelle, do we? Let's talk about the baby's name while we drink our tea."

Stella chattered happily away until gradually her lids began to droop, her hold on the baby less fierce.

Maybelle peered around the corner of the door, then moved toward Stella, who slept deeply. "Good. You take the baby downstairs and I'll tend to her. Shoo!"

Peter waited at the bottom of the stairs, his eyes filled with tears. For a heartbreaking moment he cradled his grandson, then tenderly placed him in a tiny pine-board coffin. "It's the way of the Lord."

Rebecca slipped out of the kitchen door to find Daniel standing, his fists at his sides. He began to shake with silent sobs, and she wrapped her arms around him. She held him tightly, leaning her forehead against his. "You made a mistake, Daniel. But you didn't cost a life doing it. Go on upstairs and clean up. Go on."

When she was alone, Rebecca sat, her back against a tree as she watched Bruno chop wood, working out his pain.

"Oh, Matthew," she whispered to the night breeze, the aching sound surprising her.

The baby was buried later in the morning in the family cemetery. The tiny grave was marked by a wooden cross and a rock, protected by a white picket fence.

The neighbors sent pies and sympathy for the next two weeks, while Bruno's haggard face reflected his agony. Stella's wails awoke them in the night, and she cried all day, refusing to leave her room.

Matthew held the rose gently, the frozen petals flying away in the October wind. He rubbed a frost-bruised petal between his thumb and forefinger, reminded of Rebecca's smooth flesh.

He wanted her!

Laughing green eyes . . . the tipsy, delighted way she giggled on their wedding night . . . her ability to entice him on the backside of a horse. . . . Few women had touched his heart, yet his wife had wrapped her golden fingers about him.

He breathed the crisp Methow wind, his hair whipping around his face. The tantalizing, lingering scent of the rose swirled around him.

"Come to me, lass," he whispered, rubbing the petal across his lips.

* * *

The second week of October, Peter took Maybelle's hand at the breakfast table. "I've asked Maybelle to marry me. I want her here every day, not just to visit or to take care of Stella. Emma's gone, didn't leave a note where she was going, and Maybelle's all alone. The Simpsons are buying her place for a hotel."

Bruno nodded slowly. "That's good. A man needs a woman."

Maybelle kissed his cheek. "We can wait until Stella is better, Bruno."

"She's been this way for weeks now. I don't see her changing." Bruno cupped his coffee, his shoulders hunched. He glanced at Rebecca. "I sent word up to Matt that we had trouble. You'd better make your plans to go to him. It snows up in the high country in early November."

"I'm staying here." Rebecca toyed with her pancakes, separating the tiny chunks of apples from the dough.

"Rebecca—" Peter began, just as Bruno raised his large hand.

"I thought you were past the fighting stage, Rebecca," her elder brother said quietly, his eyes watchful.

"Stella might need me—"

"Stella has a husband—me—and I'm speaking for the both of us now. I don't want to see your marriage fail because of our loss, Rebecca." Bruno touched her shoulder, shaking it gently. "He'll be coming after you soon. Don't stay because of us."

Rebecca clamped her lips closed, her stomach churning. "I'm staying as long as she's like this, Bruno."

"The mountains are plenty cold now, Becky. He'll be coming down."

The frost came on the third week of October, killing the last of the settlers' roses. Stella hovered between sanity and the shadows, crying out for her baby in the midnight hours.

Rebecca took long walks, picking the dried thistle and baby's breath into large bouquets to place over the baby's grave.

In the night the red haze tormented her, left her clinging

to a pillow Matthew had shared. Eric's grimace and eye patch hovered over her; the scent of his unwashed body clung to her nightmares. She opened her mouth to scream, fighting the gray waters, and awoke to hear Stella's sobbing.

She couldn't ever love Matthew now. Something that had budded within her was slowly withering. She'd fought him, fought the tenderness he demanded from her. . . .

She'd use his tricks, then leave him as high and dry as a piece of driftwood on the riverbank.

The memory of Eric's heavy body weighted her dreams, the feel of his hands hurting, though the bruises had long since healed.

In a quiet ceremony Peter married Maybelle, taking her to Wenatchee for a honeymoon.

At the midnight hour on the first of November the low damp clouds of the Columbia River Basin promised the first snow. Standing by the corral, Rebecca watched the clouds glide across the full moon. She patted Wind Dancer's neck. "I hope they're happy. Papa has waited a long time."

The cold breeze lifted her loosened hair, playing along her neck. She drew the collar of her coat higher against the cold, damp air. She wanted Matthew's arms locked around her and his husky voice whispering encouragements in her ear.

She wanted the sweet, cherishing taste of his mouth on hers. . . .

The night chill sank deeper into her. Matthew had betrayed her, while his brother had left her with a filth that wouldn't fade. He'd taken her like a mad dog, ravaging her because of his jealousy.

She turned, facing the high country. Matthew was up there. . . .

The breeze riffled the dead leaves at her feet, the pine boughs over her head swaying. The hairs at the back of her neck tingled, chilling her. She'd been stalked by a cougar once, and now the feeling was the same—a fine edge between curiosity and fear.

A coyote howled and a wild dog answered him, the dark clouds trimmed with silver moonlight.

She shivered, aware that someone stood in the shadows of the barn watching her. She slid her hand to the butt of her Colt, tense, waiting. The pungent scent of tobacco wafted over to her.

"You're taking your own sweet time coming to me, Princess." Matthew's quiet tone wound around her like the lash of a whip. The orange tip of his cigar sailed a high arc into the frozen ranch yard.

She turned, her hair flying wildly in the wind. The strands clung to her throat, settled down around her back. He'd come for her. "Matthew!"

He sauntered from the protection of the shadows. "I've been waiting."

"I'm not going with you." She breathed heavily, following his lithe stride toward her, like that cougar stalking her. She hadn't planned on his coming down from the high country so soon—too soon.

His thick brows shadowed glittering, deep-set eyes, a heavy beard covering his jaw. In a long deerskin coat, the fur turned up around his throat, Matthew's long hair caught the wind, lifting it from his brow.

Dark and savage, his eyes held hers.

From beneath his coat he drew a small pink rosebud, lifting it to the moonlight. The delicate fragrance hovered between them as she leaned her head back, watching his shadowed face. "One last rose. '. . . Wi' thorny ways and dewy lips . . . Yet 'round my empty heart she curled . . . My midnight rose, my highland heart . . .' "

Lifting a swath of her hair, he eased the bud behind her ear. "I've trimmed the thorns, but not before they marked me. Just as you have, my lady of the emerald eyes. I've not slept, dreaming of you. Waiting for you."

His soft, rich voice held her entwined, the scent of the rose playing around her face. "I dreamed of your hair, wrapping around me, catching blue sparks from the sun; your flashing green eyes when you're angry."

Rebecca ached, felt his heat surround her, staving off the

fears. How could her heart warm at the sight of him? How could her hands tremble with the need to hold him close?

How could he have betrayed her?

The taste of her bitterness soured her tongue, even as something within her wanted to walk into his arms.

He'd done that to her—making her want him.

Could she make him want her as desperately?

Could she own his flesh, making him desire her?

Could she take her revenge?

He stretched out his hand, trailing his fingertips along her rigid jawline. "Smooth as a rose petal, just like I remembered. How's Stella?"

Rebecca shivered, the hard warmth of his flesh rough with calluses. He'd come to claim her, his eyes tracing her lips hungrily. "She's better. I don't think she'll ever get over the loss of this baby."

"I'm sorry. I was hoping by this time we'd . . ." He wound his hand through her hair, studying it, letting the strands slip through his fingers. "The cabin's ready. Wes and Mary are settled in their own place, and Jean's lit out for up north. It seems he has his eye on a choice fox pelt. He says it's his dream." He rubbed the silken texture with his thumb, tugging her nearer. Beneath the fringe of his lashes his eyes glittered. "I've been waiting, Becky."

Her throat dried as she thought of Matthew alone with her for the winter. Her plans for revenge shredded before the lash of panic. "I'm going to Seattle, Matthew. Aunt Elizabeth is ailing."

"No, you're coming up on the mountain with me."

She threw off his hand, backing away. She'd had other plans for their first meeting. Matthew had a dark, quiet, intent look that frightened her. He wouldn't want her if he knew about Eric, would he? "I've had enough of you telling me what to do, Matthew. I'm calling it quits."

The even line of his teeth shone against the heavy black beard. "I always liked your fire, Princess. But I like it better when you melt against me. Like it or not—"

Eric had wanted her to fight him. "I've had enough," she

shouted, dancing back from his outstretched hand. "I didn't want this marriage and I still don't!"

A man cleared his throat in the shadows, and Bruno stepped to share the patch of moonlight. He nodded to Matthew, then searched his sister's furious expression. He rolled his heavily padded shoulders like a grizzly sensing a fight. "I've had enough yelling in the night. Leave her alone, Matthew. Go back to the high country. If she wants to stay here, she can."

"She's my wife, Bruno. Don't mix in this."

Bruno tilted his head back, measuring Matthew's determination. Standing between the men, Rebecca placed a hand flat on her brother's chest, staying him. "I don't want any trouble, Bruno. He's leaving—"

"Not without you I'm not. I have certain rights, brother or not." Matthew wrapped his fingers around her upper arm and tugged her toward him. "I'll help you pack. That or I'll take you as you are."

"Take your hands off my sister," Bruno rumbled, stepping closer. "I wouldn't want to hurt you."

The two men glared at each other over her head. Matthew's hand tightened on her arm. "It's been a while since I've been in a good brawl, but I think I can hold my own."

"You think so, Matthew?" Bruno's fist shot out, catching Matthew's jaw.

Releasing her, Matthew stumbled backward, caught his balance, then planted both long legs wide, rubbing his jaw. The wind whipped his hair around his face, the fur-lined coat flapping about his thighs. "Now that wasn't at all brotherly. It's a fight, then. Make it good, Bruno."

"You'll have to go through me to get to Rebecca, Matthew," Bruno answered evenly. "Anytime you're ready. . . ."

"You Kleins are a hardheaded crew." Matthew stripped the heavy coat from him, flinging it to the ground.

Bruno crouched, raising his fists, and Rebecca's blood froze within her veins. He'd beaten Rudy into unconsciousness. He couldn't hurt Matthew . . . *her Matthew!*

She'd wanted him hurt, but not this way!

"Stop this now!" Rebecca ran between the two men just as Matthew pushed her out of the way.

She stumbled, then quickly regained her balance.

"Try pushing me," Bruno taunted dangerously. "Or is it women you like to fight?"

Rebecca's flesh raised in goose bumps, Bruno's deep growl reminding her of another time.

"Bruno, stop it!" The two men stepped together, the force of their meeting taking them to the ground. Bruno, the heavier, pinned Matthew, clamping his knees to the leaner man's hips. Matthew grunted, pushing free. He leapt to his feet agilely, his fists raised.

"Let's have it out now, Bruno. Your sister's been giving me a bad time since I came, and someone has to pay for it," he said with a snarl. "I won't stand for interference between my wife and myself."

Bruno charged, lowering his shoulders to catch Matthew in the midsection. They rolled to the ground, just missing Wind Dancer's prancing feet. The dry dust swirled about the thrashing men. The big stallion reared, hooves pawing the air.

"No! Easy, boy." Rebecca ran to the horse, calming him, holding his mane as the two big men rolled across the corral. The sounds of blows and grunts chilled her. "Bruno! Matthew!"

Then it was quiet, the echo of the blows ringing in her ears. Bruno staggered from the shadows, wiping blood from his mouth. Rebecca stifled her scream, her palm covering her mouth.

Bruno swept his hair back from his face. "What do you want me to do with him, Rebecca? We can leave him there or I can tie him on his horse."

"You hurt him! Did you have to hit him?" she cried, running toward Matthew. Crouching by his side, she touched his face and he groaned loudly.

Bruno watched her closely. He rubbed his knuckles. "He'll live."

"You get him into the house this minute."

"Why, Rebecca, I thought you wanted him gone."

"Pick him up and carry him up to my room, Bruno. Or you'll wish it were you lying on that cold ground."

A corner of his bruised mouth lifted, his eyes gleaming. "You're as mad as a wet hen. Why?"

"You hurt him, that's why." She cradled Matthew's head on her lap, probing his beard. "Oh, we'll have to shave him to see if he's got any cuts."

"Does it matter?" Bruno asked lazily.

"Of course it does." She stroked Matthew's hair back from his temple, then bent to kiss his forehead. She'd meant to torment him, not to see him mauled!

Matthew groaned loudly, turning his face into her coat. Bruno made a noise and Rebecca rounded on him, eyes blazing. "Proud of yourself, are you? Stop that grinning and help me get him into the house."

Bruno bent, easing Matthew to his feet. "You'd better take his other side, Becky; he can't stand. I must have hit him harder than I thought. I probably broke a rib or two."

"Yes, and you're going to pay for it too!" Matthew's head lolled to her shoulder, his lips brushing her throat when he groaned again. He needed her! "Shh," she whispered, kissing his cheek.

"Women!" Bruno laughed softly, then walked to the house carrying his brother-in-law. Rebecca followed until Matthew lay sprawled on her bed.

"You can go now," she ordered with a toss of her head. "No telling how much more damage you would do if you stayed. Don't you dare touch him again."

Bruno touched his bruised lip tentatively. "You're saying you care for him, then."

Rebecca's lips parted to deny his statement, then she glanced at Matthew's torn face. Dabbing a cloth at his lip, she paused, sifting through her emotions. "I've come to know him," she whispered. "Go on now, see to Stella."

Matthew groaned, twisting his head against her breasts. Rebecca held him closely, smoothing his shoulders as she rocked him. She kissed his brow, unaware that his arms had drifted around her.

He shifted, drawing her closer. "Becky?"

"Shh, my love, I'm here. Rest now."

He breathed deeply, his warm breath sweeping down into her blouse. His hand spread upon her buttocks, caressing her. "Matthew, lie still. You're hurt."

"Aye. Wounded by your great bear of a brother. But I'd do it again to have you hold me." He nuzzled the fragrant softness with his lips. His beard swept along her skin as his head slipped lower. He flinched, leaning back against the pillows, an arm thrown over his face.

"Oh, Matthew," she crooned, dabbing a cloth in the washbasin. He was hurt and it was her fault. She'd wanted revenge but one of a different nature. She hadn't asked for broken bones and bleeding flesh! She lifted his arm, letting it slide down her back. The warm span of his hand caressed the small of her back. "Let me see."

Matthew's black eye gleamed through a swollen lid. "My mouth, Becky, it's crushed beyond repair."

Instantly, she dabbed the cloth over his lips, pressing it to the cut. Leaning near, she felt Matthew's indrawn breath against her cheek.

Taking a wild chance, Rebecca chose to try her first tentative revenge. She delicately kissed the cut, feeling him stiffen instantly.

She felt a tiny ripple of pleasure. Perhaps the way of her revenge would be slower than Bruno's fists, but much, much more effective in its pain.

Once started, she caressed the hard line of his cheekbones with her mouth, unaware that his hand had crept to her waist. She pressed kisses along his black lashes, heavy brows, and warmed, tanned skin. "Is this better, Matthew?"

Somehow his nimble fingers had slid between them, opening her blouse beneath her coat. Tugging the tiny ribbon of her undershirt, he eased his fingertips within to caress her softness.

Revenge forgotten, she found his mouth with hers, taking of the gentleness, then the hunger.

In a lightning-quick movement, his hands worked quickly, seeking, riding her hip, sliding between her thighs to press insistently against the cloth. He breathed harshly, lashing her flaying hands in one of his. Then, lowering his head slowly, he pushed her blouse from her shoulder, trailing kisses to the rising mounds of her breasts.

"Matthew . . ." She warmed, wanting him within her, her body heating. *How could she want him so desperately?*

"My sweet rose," he murmured, the hard mouth tasting first one pink crest, then the other.

With his mouth he caused her to burn, wanting her palm to trail down the flat belly to his hips.

He shifted, his weight pinning her to the bed as his lips took hers, his tongue sliding within her mouth.

Rebecca longed for the sweet touch, welcomed it, her tongue edging forth to trail across his hard lips. Then, nibbling, tasting, her eyes closed, she trembled, waiting.

Her fingers curled, wanting to slide along the hard arc of his body, wanting to tug his head closer.

Suddenly his head lifted. "So you did miss me, Princess."

Stunned by his change of mood, Rebecca slowly opened her eyes. She had just the glimpse of his triumphant grin before he wrapped a cloth around her mouth, then quickly bound her wrists.

Rebecca kicked, weighted by his hard thighs. He chuckled, quickly buttoning her blouse and the jacket over it. He grinned, leaping from her. Placing his hands on his hips, Matthew's grin widened as he surveyed her kicking the bed, rumpling the blankets with her boots. "There, there. You're angry. How I love those flashing eyes, your lovely breasts straining the buttons."

She fought the cloth over her mouth, making muffled, furious cries. Matthew bent, kissing her forehead and slid his hand upward to taunt her womanhood. "Aye, you're in a temper, Princess. Those long silky legs have better uses than kicking a lifeless bed."

Fighting her bonds, she kicked out at him, barely missing his upper thighs. Matthew's brows lifted teasingly. "It's a long ride ahead of us, and I don't want to be disabled at the end of it."

In the next moment Matthew had wrapped her in her blankets and carried her downstairs. At his whistle Duke trotted into the moonlight, followed by Wind Dancer.

Carefully seating her on the bay, Matthew tucked the blankets around her, then swung up behind her.

Taking Wind Dancer's reins, Matthew turned to Rebecca. "Say good-bye, Becky. We'll visit in the spring."

Furious, her curses muffled by the cloth, Rebecca tossed her head, her hair swirling around her.

She held onto the saddle horn, her body stiff within Matthew's arms. She leaned forward, hating the easy strength with which he held her.

He laughed, tightening his arms to draw her back to his chest. He nuzzled her cheek. "We're in for a long ride, Princess. You'd better relax."

She twisted furiously, only to find herself snared against him. How could she have forgotten for a moment his sneaky ways? She should have let Bruno—

Matthew's breath warmed her cheek, his hand sliding beneath her coat to flatten on her belly. "Aye, I've missed you like blue blazes, Becky," he whispered huskily. "I'm needing the sweet scent of my rose."

She had known he would come. The tiny warmth within her grew, even as the first snowflake came drifting across her hot cheeks.

Chapter Nineteen

"Becky, say something!" Rebecca hadn't said a word in hours, and just before dawn, Matthew's temper began to flicker. She sat astride her stallion like a haughty princess, careless of the snow swirling on the mountain trail. Sheltered within the folds of the blanket, her face was rigid, deathly pale.

His gaze flicked to her set mouth. Punishing him, was she?

Matthew rolled his shoulders uncomfortably beneath the weight of her silence. She was his. When would she come to him, giving in to the tenderness within her . . . ?

Elbowing aside Rebecca's left boot, Matthew checked Wind Dancer's cinch. He flicked a tuft of snow from his collar, hunching against the arctic wind. The cold had long ago seeped beneath his fur-lined coat. He'd chosen the mountain trail instead of the wagon road because it was faster, but in the thigh-high snow, crossing was slow and dangerous.

He reached up to wrap the quilt closer to her head, tucking it about her thighs. "Here, keep this tight around you then, you ill-tempered little cat. I won't be responsible for you deliberately getting frostbitten." For just an instant her eyes lashed out at him, her face pale within the shadows of the cloth. So she was damn angry, was she?

A wolf pack howled in the distance, the sound blood-chilling. The horses moved restlessly, frightened. Matthew wondered briefly if the male had had to fight for his mate.

"They've found their food for the night already, boyo." Patting Duke's neck, Matthew moved his toes experimentally within his damp boots. There were dry moccasins and boots at his cache, as well as a haunch of roasted deer meat wrapped in an oilskin slicker. But Rebecca's cold disdain caused him to want the warmth of the cache's whiskey more than dry clothing. He'd heard of women driving men to drink and now knew the truth of it.

Taking Wind Dancer's reins, he began to break trail for the horses toward his cache. Pine boughs broke beneath the weight of the snow, falling to the white drifts below. An eerie blue-gray blanket weighed down the heavy thickets. A dead tree, its juices frozen, cracked open—the sound like a rifle shot—and fell into a high drift of snow.

Matthew covered his hat with a thick woolen shawl, wrapped it around his nose and mouth, then knotted it at his neck. Hunching his shoulders to tuck his face deeply within the collar of the deerskin coat, Matthew felt the cold seep into him. The horses followed, their breath like small white clouds torn apart by the vicious wind.

At dawn they reached the cache, a stone cairn covered with brush and snow.

Matthew waded back to Wind Dancer, raising his hands to lift Rebecca down. "Only a maniac would try this route at first snowfall. Don't touch me, McKay," she gritted through her teeth, swinging down. She stamped her feet, warming them.

Rebecca tossed her head, the black strands of hair shining in the soft light. They fell like a mantle around her stiff shoulders. She patted Wind Dancer's forehead, brushing a tiny clump of snow from his mane. Her eyes, luminous in the fragile oval of her face, cut through the curtain of snow at him. "I hope you are genuinely happy, McKay."

The cool, deadly tone echoed loudly in the wind.

"Don't touch you?" Matthew said, feeling a white-hot anger wash over him "Oh, I'd like to touch you." He'd been tired and frozen before, but never this angry. She was his wife and she had curled up in his arms, sated and loving. He needed her, her ill temper and pride and the warmth of her laughter.

He wrapped his fingers around her arm, drawing her to him. "I'd like to make you burn as you did on our wedding night—"

"Here? In the snow?" She jerked away from him, arranging the quilt over Wind Dancer's back and rump. "I doubt even your abilities extend that far."

He studied her frown, the fiery challenge of her eyes, and the straightening of her shoulders. "You'd like that, wouldn't you? A reason to hate me."

She brushed a fat snowflake from her cheek. "I have good enough reason now, McKay."

He shifted his weight to one leg, crossing his arms. Frozen to the bone or not, Rebecca could cause him to heat with anger. "Spit it out, then. There's nothing that can't be said between a husband and a wife."

"A faithful husband, bound by his marriage vows, caring for his wife. . . . In my own good time, McKay." Tired and frozen, Rebecca wouldn't give an inch. Snow drifted between them like a lacy white veil, clinging to her lashes.

He wanted to shake her, to drag her from that drift of snow and take her soft mouth under his.

Thinking better of it, Matthew glared at her, then marched to his cache. Flinging away concealing branches, he dug out an oilskin bundle, carrying it to a log. He unwrapped the cache carefully, then stripped off his sodden boots and stockings. Jamming them into a leather pouch, he drew on the soft moccasins and fresh boots as Rebecca watched from the shadows of the snow-encrusted pines.

He unwrapped a cape of bear fur to find a small cloth sack of oats and a bottle of whiskey. Matthew cupped oats into the palm of his hand, offering it to Wind Dancer and the bay.

When they finished, Matthew stomped his feet, feeling his toes warm within the boots. He drank from the whiskey bottle, welcoming the liquid fire flowing through him.

Offering the bottle to Rebecca, he wasn't surprised when she glared at him. "So you had this all planned out, did you? You're a kidnapper to boot, then . . . a man with many skills."

A branch, heavy with snow, swayed beneath the weight of a bird. The snow plopped to the earth near Rebecca, falling between them like a wooden mallet. "I should have let Bruno kill you."

He unwrapped the cooked venison, tearing off a chunk in his teeth. He chewed, felt the food warm his stomach and washed it down with another long drink of whiskey. 'You're not in a good mood, then, Princess."

"Hardly. I haven't been in a good mood since we met. I've been kidnapped, you know, and I'm frozen clear through. You should know better than to take the high country at first snowfall. Especially at night."

"You're in a fine temper." Matthew jammed a seaman's wool cap over his head, then waded back to her and placed one over her head. He stuffed the length of her hair beneath it. Mad as a wet hen or not, Rebecca's slant-eyed beauty still held him. He trailed his knuckles down her cold cheek. "Did you think I wouldn't come for you?"

Her head snapped back as his flesh grazed hers. "I had my hopes."

"Sorry to disillusion you, Princess, but I'm a man who likes his woman with him. And since I haven't heard any word from you, I decided to take matters into my own hands."

"The enforced bondage for a winter? Matthew, you should know me better. I'm hardly the helpless lady riding sidesaddle. I'll ride out when I wish. But first . . ." There was just the slightest edge to her voice, her eyes glimmering up at him. "I think I'll count coup. I just haven't decided how yet."

Matthew lifted an eyebrow, mocking the usage of the Indian term "counting coup." If Rebecca wanted his scalp dangling from her slender waist, she'd have her opportunity the coming winter.

He touched a wayward tendril, felt her warmth linger against his skin after she moved away. "You knew I'd come—I'm not a waiting man."

Her tawny brows shot up. "And I'm not a forgiving woman. Are we camping here for the day or not? I'll build a fire if we are."

"I'd like to build our own fire, but I'm afraid you'll have to wait. Here, chew on this for a while. I'm tired of your nagging tongue." Matthew handed her a chunk of the roasted meat and watched as her sharp teeth tore into it hungrily. She licked a tiny sliver from her upper lip, and Matthew's body heated despite the freezing temperature.

He threw a heavy bear robe over her, adjusting the hood around her head tightly. Rebecca chewed on the meat, watching him. Snowflakes clustered on the tips of her long lashes and she dusted them away impatiently with the back of her hand. "You're going to need your strength. You'd better have some whiskey, Becky. It'll keep you warm."

"I'm mad enough to keep hot all winter," she answered, swinging up to the back of her horse. For a moment Matthew stood still, savoring her saucy look when another woman might have been crying.

The lush fur stroked her cheek, and from its depths she probed deeply into his eyes as though trying to see his soul. He caught her gaze, wondering at her silent questioning. Then she looked away and the moment was gone, buried like a fallen leaf beneath the snow.

"Dare I hope, Princess?" he drawled, throwing the oilskin over her head and adjusting it around her legs.

By midmorning the temperature had dropped to form a heavy crust on the snow. Coming to the steep canyon before the house, Matthew paused, looking at the smoke drifting from the cabin. "We have visitors."

He glanced back at Rebecca, her body slight under the folds of the grizzly pelt. She looked like a young girl. If anything happened to her now . . .

A new path, wider than the old one, led to the cabin. Matthew moved slowly onto the snow-covered path, holding

Wind Dancer's bridle tightly, leaving Duke to follow. The
Appaloosa slipped once, and Matthew's glove wrapped itself
in the thick mane. "Steady, boy. Becky needs you now."

The sunlight on the snow blinded Rebecca, and she finally
closed her eyes, dozing. She was tired and frozen despite the
pelt and the oilskin. Too tired to think, she smelled wood smoke.
Beneath her Wind Dancer pranced, sensing food and rest.

A big dog barked excitedly, but she was beyond caring,
her fingers locked stiffly to the saddle horn. She huddled
deeper into her coat, dozing.

Birds chirped happily as she slid more fully into sleep.

Matthew's hushed tone greeted the dog, the animal running circles around the tired horses. "Shh, now my lad.
You'll meet her soon enough. And you'd better be on your
best manners, because she's a lady with her temper up."

The dog whined, and Matthew's tone lowered. "We'll have
to let her sleep or she'll put us both through our paces, I'm
afraid."

Sleep. She fought the heaviness of her lids, barely roused
by Jean's call. "Welcome, *mes amis*! Here, I will take the
horses."

Rebecca dozed, aware of the momentary stillness, of
hushed men's voices. In another moment she'd slide down
into the soft, welcoming snowdrift to sleep.

"Your Becky . . . she is well?"

Beside her, Matthew cursed. "She's tired and mad."

He lifted Rebecca from her saddle, carrying her into the
warm cabin. Her lids fluttered, fighting the sleep beckoning
her.

"Becky?" His rough, urgent whisper against her cheek
and his strong arms tightening around her caused her to rouse
briefly. Above her, Matthew's grim expression hovered for a
moment before she fell into the soft, waiting clouds.

She stirred, felt the hard warmth cover her. Snuggling deep
in it, Rebecca dreamed of Matthew's lips moving sweetly
over hers, taking, touching, giving.

His lips prowled along the line of her cheekbones and she reached to lock her arms around him, drawing him nearer. She smoothed the sleek, rippling muscles of his back, the kindling warmth arching her against him. His weight slipped over her and she welcomed the tender joining of his body to hers.

The sweet, dark storm took her, and she cried out in her need as the tempest grew.

"Aye, Becky, love. Like that," her dream urged huskily, drawing her deeper into the white-hot heat.

His mouth moved over her, drawing her into a quicker journey. Riding to the crest, Rebecca clung to her dream and urged him on.

When the sweet pleasure burst, Matthew caught her, soothed her as she fell, tucking her closely to his side. She rubbed her cheek against the damp planes of his shoulder and lifted her lips for one lingering, sweet kiss before she drifted off to sleep.

When she awoke fully, Matthew lay stretched out beside her on a huge brass bed. A large white dog lay watching her from a braided rug on the plank floor.

The large room was separate from the main room, scented by fresh timber, with a potbellied stove in one corner. Orange flames danced within the grate, the fire crackling. The scant light of day glimmered at the small windows.

A huge, tall carved golden oak wardrobe occupied one side of the room. Rebecca turned her head on the fluffy pillow to see a lady's dressing table with a tiny matching carved chair. A huge oval mirror over an ornate dresser caught the bare light, shooting tiny rainbows around the room.

Rebecca stirred, feeling Matthew's arm slide possessively over her. His slow, deep breathing changed, his right hand opening to rest upon the ridge of her hip. His fingers stroked her thigh as his breath swept across her cheek. He nuzzled her neck, his lips gliding beneath the lace to kiss her throat.

"Becky . . ." Asleep, shifting his head to her breasts, he kissed the soft, fragrant flesh. "My Becky," he murmured, wrapping her possessively in his arms.

He breathed quietly and she knew he was sleeping. The weight of his head upon her breasts was a sweet torment, her fingers wanting to smooth the rumpled waves. How long had she slept? Was it day or night? In the quiet of dusk or dawn, she listened to the fire crackle, her husband's rough cheek pillowed upon her chest.

In that moment she allowed her hand to slide across the width of his shoulders, allowed herself to think of Matthew as hers alone. He'd never know the tenderness she felt for him while he slept. Her teeth tore at her bottom lip as the tender emotion filled her. She was content at last, wrapped with Matthew as if in a silent, silken cocoon.

She remembered the strength of his arms holding her as she fell, and the tender dream of his lovemaking.

She stirred, uncomfortable with the freshness of the dream, as though it were a reality. She'd torment him, play him, but hell and damnation, he'd pay for Emma through the teeth! She'd count coup on that fine black mane of his and leave him drooling.

Her jawline tightened, the tender tendons crying out.

Matthew's large hand spanned her stomach, a heavy warmth. Lazily his fingers slid to press a full breast, and Rebecca tensed. "It's morning. Sleep well, Mrs. McKay?"

Remembering Emma's confession, Rebecca slashed at his hand, sliding from the massive bed.

In a fury she dragged the heavy coverlet across her body, shielding herself, while he grinned, careless of his naked body. She turned away, closing her eyes against the vision of his dark skin and pale, lean haunches. "Cover yourself, McKay."

Gritting her teeth and clenching her fists deep under the coverlet, Rebecca turned back to him. Sprawled across the white sheets, resting back upon the pillows, Matthew lounged like a pasha waiting to be served.

The bare light coming from the window washed across his tall body, catching the brawny length from glossy head to long, muscular legs. The wedge of intriguing hair played across his chest and narrowed down to his belly. Her eyes widened as he turned. "McKay!"

"Aye?" he asked innocently, before chuckling and drawing a sheet across his hips. "You're blushing, though I'd thought you to be past that stage."

"Is it any wonder?" She backed away, glaring at him through her tumbled hair. She felt a wash of heat rise to her cheeks. She was angry, wanting to wipe that arrogant grin from his face. Play with both Emma and her, would he?

He'd forced her to keep to the marriage, taking his pleasure with her. Then he had turned to another— She slashed him with her eyes. No doubt he had tired of her feeble efforts at lovemaking.

"Your breasts are fuller, Becky. And there's a softness lurking about you, though you're acting like a sulky child," he said quietly, watching her face. The black eyes gleamed, noting her high color. He chuckled, opening his arms to welcome her back. "Come here and take all that ill temper out on your waiting husband. Use me as you wish."

She tossed her head; he could wonder about her until water flowed uphill.

The huge white dog padded across the floor to her. His big feet crushed the coverlet, pulling it from her grasp. The cloth slid down Rebecca's bare shoulders. "Get off!"

The dog's squarish head tilted with curiosity as she scampered to draw the blanket around her.

For a moment Matthew was treated to an enticing display of his wife's fuller breasts and round hips. Turning, tugging the blanket from the dog, he saw the gentle sweep of her backside and it caused him to warm. The creamy softness of her hips trimmed down to the slender length of her legs. "Let go!"

The beast plopped his bottom to the coverlet, watching her with curious, yellow eyes. He gave a low, inquisitive growl, then slid to lay at her feet, forcing the coverlet from her grasp.

"Oh!"

The dog whined, tilting his head as Matthew laughed

aloud. Rebecca crossed her arms in front of her, shielding her breasts. "I hope you're enjoying this," she tossed at him angrily, glancing around the room.

Her hair danced, shimmering in the soft light, the triangular nest above her long thighs beckoning.

"In the wardrobe," he managed from a dry throat, his eyes darkening as he rose from the bed to walk toward her. He'd take his chances with his wife's temper for one sweet taste of her dewy lips. "There are nightgowns and robes for you, but not just yet."

Rebecca backed away a step. She threw open the wardrobe, catching a bit of lace in her fist and snatching it out. "You stay away from me, McKay. Go back to Emma."

He paused in mid-stride, his expression alert. "Emma?"

Rebecca clamped her lips closed. She glanced at the off-white satin wrapper, jamming her arms in the Oriental sleeves and wrapping it tightly around her waist. The fabric clung to her, accenting her body.

She glared at him, placing her fists on her waist, her long legs spread apart defiantly. He noted in a long appraisal the gaping part of the silk that exposed her inner thighs to that sweet nest. "Matthew, stop leering. I'm warning you . . . you take another step closer and I'll—"

"What's this about Emma?" he asked quietly, wrapping his fingers around her wrist. The pad of his thumb traced the smooth skin of her inner wrist.

"You should know." Jerking her wrist from him, Rebecca backed away a step.

Flattening her back against the wall, Matthew placed one hand on either side of her head. Women wanted to play games at odd times, and he had no idea what Rebecca meant by throwing Emma at him now. He lowered his head, looking down into her face. "I'm not in a good mood myself. I've been too long without my wife. Perhaps you'd better explain before we go back to bed."

Rebecca flinched, her eyes darting to the tumbled bed.

Sitting up, the dog tilted his head curiously and whined.

"Becky? I'm waiting," Matthew growled. Then, when she

hesitated, he scooped her up in his arms and walked to the bed. Dropping her amid the sheets, he placed his hands on lean hips. "Well?"

The soft strains of a Spanish guitar floated through the tenseness and Rebecca moistened her lips. "Jean's here?"

"Aye. But he won't disturb us. He probably thinks he's lending to enhancing our lovemaking." Matthew's eyes traced the thrust of her softness against the satin and down to the gaping folds. His gaze warmed as it flowed over the slender length of her legs. She could feel him pause, taut heat rising from him.

"There's better use of the morning than to argue." The husky rasp of his voice reached inside her and started that strange tingling.

"No! You're not having me, McKay!" she lashed out. So he thought he'd collect her after playing with Emma, did he? Perhaps the man wanted to father a score of babies across the countryside!

"What?"

In the next instant Rebecca threw a pillow at him, scooting off the bed. She ran to the tiny dressing table and hefted a crystal perfume bottle, threatening him. "Get away, you. . ." The correct word failed her and she searched a moment, then lashed out. "You male tart!"

"Rebecca McKay! What are you saying?" At Matthew's maddened roar, the soft guitar music stopped.

She threw back a long strand of curling, ebony hair. "Oh, that may not be the right phrase. But it suits you just the same."

Matthew's thunderous expression darkened. "I understand the meaning . . . not the cause."

For a tense moment Rebecca glared back at him. Oh, he knew the cause. Or perhaps he thought he deserved a wife and a mistress! But she hadn't decided how to play her revenge just yet. "All in good time, Mckay. When I see fit."

He stared at her blankly, his jaw working. "I want you to tell me now. You're jibbering—"

"Jibbering?" With the boldness of a brass ape Matthew

had played with two women. Now the adulterer wanted
more. . . . Her chin rose defiantly.

Matthew cursed, and the dog rose to his massive paws
instantly, growling, his hackles rising. Matthew loomed over
her. "I want an answer now."

In that instant Rebecca felt the fine lash of fear. She'd
roused the beast that slept quietly within Matthew. Black-
eyed and black-tempered, Matthew stood naked before her.
He ran his fingers through his heavy hair, leaving a wild trail
of curls.

Despite his raging anger, Rebecca knew deep within that
she could match him. She couldn't allow him to touch her
again; her pride demanded to have the argument out.

Her knees weakened at his dark, intent look, and she
thought better of lashing out at him.

Perhaps in a cooler moment, one in which she had the
upper hand.

Rebecca felt the door latch behind her, carefully edging
her hand toward it. When Matthew took one step, she jerked
open the door and ran straight into Jean Dupres's arms.

Jean stepped back with the force of her body, glancing at
Matthew's dark, angry face. The French-Indian stepped back,
releasing Rebecca with a wry grin.

His gaze strolled down Matthew's towering, taut, naked
body, then Rebecca's flushed and stormy face. He cocked an
eyebrow, then sauntered to the couch. Dressed in fringed
buckskins, he sprawled across a red velvet tufted couch. His
fingers danced delicately across the guitar strings, finding the
melody of "Greensleeves."

"You have frightened your bride, Matthew. Perhaps a less
savage expression. . . ."

Matthew glowered at Rebecca, his lips drawn back across
his teeth. Jerking on his trousers, he stepped into the main
room. "Rebecca, you will answer me or I'll—"

"That's it—beat me." Bolstered by Jean's presence, Rebecca clenched the wrapper about her legs and squared her
shoulders. Damn McKay! *Her* heart bore the wounds; *she*
needed to make him pay.

Crossing her arms in front of her chest to still her quickly beating heart, Rebecca glared back at him. Innocent as a newborn lamb, was he?

As Rebecca paced across the room, her long black hair streamed down the cream-colored wrapper. She thumped Matthew's bare chest with her finger. "Emma's with child."

The room was too quiet. The dog's nails sounded against the planks as he rounded Matthew's spread-eagled legs. The animal padded toward his bowl. He lapped the water noisily, the sound quieter than Rebecca's heartbeat.

Matthew frowned at her and Jean slid to his feet.

Matthew's chest lifted and fell slowly, his gaze thoughtful. A muscle slid across his jaw and down his muscled neck before he spoke. "Becky, you can be so . . ."

"Emma carries a child?" Jean hung the guitar band upon a wall peg, meticulously placing the instrument against the logs. His long, slender fingers stroked his jaw.

His gaze swung from Matthew's hard face to Rebecca's furious expression. "The baby is mine and no other's."

Matthew shook his head as if to clear it.

Jean chuckled wickedly. "My little white dove has stirred up a hornet's nest, it appears. Is she well?"

Rebecca's temper wavered. Emma had been badly frightened by Eric, her shrill cry of pain ringing through the darkened room. While the smaller woman had wounded Rebecca's pride, she did not wish her harm. "If you care for her, Jean, I suggest you go to her."

He nodded solemnly. "I had affairs to settle and merely rested the night in my friend's home. I will go to her . . . and my son."

Rebecca tossed back her hair, glaring at Matthew. "Jean, would you please tell my family that I lived through the ordeal? *They* would be concerned," she threw at Matthew.

Matthew's black eyes swept across Rebecca's mouth hotly. "I'll help you pack. Don't worry about my bride, Jean. She has claws that bite deep."

His lips tightened grimly. "She can protect herself."

Chapter Twenty

In mid-morning Rebecca stood at the cabin window tracing the snowshoe trail Jean had left, leading to the mountains. The snow drifted across his prints as she watched.

Shielding her eyes against the blinding glare of the sunlight on the snow, she searched for Matthew. The winter wind howled around the snug, warm cabin, causing her to draw Matthew's flannel shirt more closely to her. She had gathered his trousers to her waist with a strip of leather, rolling the long legs to better fit her own. After a moment she turned back to the beautifully furnished main room.

The dark cedar logs were newly chinked with clay and the windows were shuttered against the winter cold, yet the room seemed light.

She measured the room, deciding that it had been lengthened, a cluster of windows added near the cooking area. An immense iron-and-enamel stove occupied one corner, her damp clothing hung on a peg nearby. A glass-enclosed china cabinet, filled with dishes, stood near a window draped in lace. Oriental fringed carpets covered the lacquered floors.

The couch and upholstered chairs were elegant, carved woods and red velours. English globe lamps with huge clusters of flowers added a cheery effect to the heavy furniture. A rolltop desk, cluttered with papers, rested near a treadle sewing machine.

Filled with space and light, the room beckoned to her as she wandered around it. Here and there she noted their wedding gifts.

For just one pendulum swing of the carved grandfather clock she allowed herself to remember Matthew's expression as she walked toward their wedding. His gaze had washed over her possessively yet tenderly.

The door burst open and Matthew entered in a blast of wind and snow. He tramped the snow from his boots, stripping off his woolen mittens. Standing unnoticed in the muted shadows, Rebecca watched him unbutton his thick coat and hang it on a wall peg beside her own.

His hand drifted over her coat, a light caress before he sat to tug his boots free. She breathed lightly, uncertain as to his mood. He'd been angry, then quietly cold.

Was Jean really the father of Emma's baby?

Matthew paused in the midst of drawing off his boot. He turned toward her, his eyes meeting her own. "You could help."

"I think not." She protectively wrapped her arms around herself. He'd carried her off like a sack of meal and then expected her to serve him!

Matthew dropped one boot to the floor, then yanked off the other. He rose, walking toward her. "That's it. Keep your moods to yourself, like a sullen child. Let me know when you want to talk."

His eyes held a dark, empty pain that chilled her. His hand rose to touch her hair, hovered in midair, and fell to his side.

"Do you like the house?" he asked quietly, studying her. She wanted to move into the shelter of his arms, dismissing Emma's child. But she could not; her wounds were too fresh.

He wanted something from her, something so deep and so savagely wild that it tore at her heart.

When she didn't answer, he cupped her cheek, trailing his thumb across the smoothness. His smile was tender. "You're a sight, sweet Becky McKay . . . all dressed up in my clothes."

"Mine are still damp." Feeling suddenly shy with him, she lowered her head, allowing her hair to shield her face.

Matthew's hand swept around the nape of her neck, cupping the back of her head. He searched her face. "Aye," he murmured, the burr rolling deep in his throat. "You're a sweet sight to come home to, lass."

The wanting ran through her so strongly, she trembled, aching to embrace him. Instead she moved away to the stove, bound by her pride. "Jean made stew and biscuits. Do you want some?"

Matthew nodded. "I'd like more substantial fare. But food will do for now."

Shaking, she ladled the venison stew into the soup bowls. Matthew watched her quietly, then sat in a chair. "Stop hovering like a lost bird, Becky. This is your home now; you might as well be comfortable in it."

She sipped her coffee, her hands trembling.

Matthew's large, rough hand encased her slender one, his fingers lacing with hers. "Take care, lass. Guard your heart well, for I am out to have the whole of you," he whispered.

Rebecca slept until the afternoon shadows slid into evening, the wind whipping around the cabin. Dozing beneath a crocheted afghan on the huge bed, she sensed movement in the room. Holding still, she peered through her lashes to find Matthew standing beside the bed.

He bent, tucking the afghan around her feet and smoothing it on her legs. Unaware that she watched, he stared at her with such sadness and longing that she ached to reach out to him. Tiredly he turned, motioning for the huge dog to follow as he left the bedroom.

When she rose, Matthew had gone. The dog whined, padding to her and then to the latched door. He repeated his path, barking sharply. Minutes later Rebecca stood outside, dressed warmly as she watched the dog leap and frolic on the thick snow, headed for the barn.

Leaning into the winter wind, Rebecca followed Matthew's long strides in the snow to the barn. The pungent scent of hay and horses filled the frosty air, the Appaloosas milling around the large shadowy space, their mottled coats eerie shades of dark and white.

Matthew crouched beside a mare, wrapping a cloth above her hoof. His hands ran knowingly over the mare's leg, his voice soft and gentle as he spoke to her. "Becky is a handful, just like you, Beauty. Proud as blazes and fiery when she's mad."

Lured by the deep croon, Rebecca eased around a pony toward him. "There now, Beauty." He stood, digging into a grain sack. "Have some oats for your pain. It will pass."

The mare turned, looking at Rebecca with soft brown eyes. She whinnied, and Rebecca stepped closer, intrigued. Matthew turned, his eyes darkening as he saw her. "This is Beauty. She had a nasty scrape from an old fence post staple."

"What are you doing for her?"

"Touching her, salving her wound. Letting her get to know me," he answered simply, his eyes flowing over her face like black satin. "Trust me, Becky. Just as she does."

Trust. The man wished for her trust after lusting with Emma. Or had he?

Taking her chances, Rebecca decided to begin her game. She rubbed the mare's forehead. "I've been forced into a marriage I didn't want."

He nodded, waiting. "Aye, a courtship would have been better suited to you, Becky. But once seeing you, I decided to take my chances."

"I've been kidnapped," she accused, watching his arrogant head tilt down toward her.

He crossed his arms. "You're as stubborn as a mule, Princess. And I'm not the waiting kind. Just what do you want for your pound of flesh so we can go on with our lives?"

Rebecca wrapped her arms around the mare's neck, watching Matthew. She licked her lips, moistening them, and instantly Matthew's eyes began smoldering. He'd had his way since the beginning; now it was time to have hers. "I want your promise that you won't touch me . . . until I say."

His expression hardened, the tendons in his jaw tightening. "I'm your husband."

"I'm unwilling, Matthew. Give me your promise and I'll stay for a while, or else I'll leave. As simple as that."

"You're a hard woman, Becky," he growled, leaning down toward her. His breath touched her cheek, warming it in the cold building. "And if I play this foolish game of yours, what then?"

She took a deep breath, steadying her shaking fingers by wrapping them in the mare's black mane. "I'll stay . . . for a time," she murmured simply.

His head went back arrogantly. "I see. Be warned: If you leave, I'll come for you."

"Is that a bargain?"

"It's a hard bargain. I had other plans for the winter." He shifted his weight on his long legs. "I'm not a man to be led around by his nose, Becky. But I've got a hunger for the sweetness you hide away like a miser." He nodded, patting the mare. "I'll play your game, Princess. But beware that you don't get tangled in your own web."

"It's a bargain then?"

"Aye. For a time, until you come to me with your love fully given, as you did this morning."

"I did not!" The tender, loving dream swept before her, the hunger and the delight.

"You did. You curled beneath me, hot and loving the daylights—"

Her hand slashed up toward his face, only to be caught a hairsbreadth away from his cheek.

Matthew allowed her palm to rest against his jaw, watching her. "You just can't believe that you could come to love me, can you? That you're as eager for me as I am for you? Whatever you've got in your craw is poisoning you, and sooner or later you'll tell me what it is," he gritted through his teeth before releasing her wrist and stalking from the barn.

Rebecca sighed, turning in her sleep. Her hand fell upon Matthew's bare chest and stilled. He breathed lightly, feeling his body harden, as it had for two days each time she came near.

Her fingers moved slightly, rummaging through the hair on his chest, and Matthew gritted his teeth. She had bathed, and the scent of her hair wafted around him, the silken strands sliding upon his shoulder. Even in her sleep she played with him, taunted him with golden delights.

A chill ran across his face and he realized he'd been sweating, forcing himself not to make love to her. *She was his wife!*

Warm and soft, the fullness of her breasts nestled against his arm. She wore his silk shirt, and it slid up her thigh, baring the smooth skin to his hair-roughened leg.

The fire crackled in the heating stove's grate as her palm flattened, smoothing the planes of his chest. Damn!

He'd had a taste of her, the soft cries of her passion echoing in his ears as a heavy mass of snow slid from the roof. He wanted her, to feast upon what was rightly his.

He'd promised in anger, knowing a secret Rebecca had yet to discover. The softness of her breast nuzzled his arm as she stirred, and perspiring, he closed his lids. Rebecca had yet to admit she cared. Their child lay nestled in her womb.

When they had made love, he'd noted the slight changes in her body—the fullness and tenderness of her breasts, the softness lurking around her hips. He eased his hand over her womb, his palm warming the child he knew slept within her.

Rebecca's arm slid across him, her fingers seeking his throat to prowl along the muscled length.

He wanted all of her! Yet some shadow had crossed their love, angering her. She'd tossed Emma at him like a hot branding iron, then went on. After Becky he was hers, heart and soul, and she'd have to trust—

The shirt's buttons gaped open; the tantalizing fullness of her left breast nestled against his chest. Rebecca's fingers toyed lazily with his hair, her face nuzzling his shoulder.

A man torn by passion, Matthew groaned inwardly. In her sleep Rebecca wanted him, seduced him with her soft touch. How long could he resist the torment?

Finally, when the fire had burned to coals, Rebecca lay almost atop him, her face tucked into the warmth of his shoulder and throat. "Matthew?" she purred drowsily, stroking his hair gently.

The perfume of her hair beckoned him, urging him to wrap himself in the silken masses, binding them together.

Her palm drifted downward, skimming his body, leisurely, yet he knew she still slept by her easy breathing. Tormented, wanting, Matthew lay beneath her touch, aching for full possession.

Groaning, taking care not to disturb her, he eased away, turning her in his arms. She sighed, nestling against him like a kitten that wanted petting, then finally stilled.

It was almost dawn before Matthew slept, holding her close.

Her scream shattered the silence of the new day.

Rebecca's hands clutched at him, her body trembled, her legs fighting the covers.

"Here now, lass," he murmured, wrapping her in his arms.

Her face pressed against his chest, and he felt her damp lashes, the coldness of her cheeks. "Hold me, Matthew. Hold me tight."

For a long moment she lay trembling against him, her arms locked around his neck. He smoothed her hair away from her face, whispering to her. "It's the dream, lass. Nothing but a dream. It's far away now, and nothing can hurt you. Shh . . ."

She swallowed, clinging to him. "I'm sorry."

He felt the power of fear about her, felt her fight the unknown.

Kissing her temple, Matthew drew the blankets close around her. "We're safe, lass. Tucked in our own nest with Wolf guarding the door."

The fearsome beast hovering by her seemed to yawn and quiet, Rebecca's fingers less taut around his neck. Matthew stroked the long length of her back, the tight muscles easing beneath his touch. "Shh, now, lass. Gently, now." With one last ragged sigh Rebecca's cheek settled to his chest.

"Tell me about your dream?" he asked.

She shuddered within his arms. "I can't. Nothing makes sense. Just a silly dream."

She sniffed and Matthew tilted her chin up with his fore-finger. He kissed the softness of her lips lightly. "What are husbands for then, lass, but listening to silly dreams?"

He'd toss away the world to have her look at him like that forever, he thought hazily. As soft and as trusting as a kitten, lying quietly against him like his other half. Their flesh blended, hard and soft, smooth and rough, each fitting neatly against the other.

After a long moment her eyes began to sparkle. She wriggled her toes. "You keep my feet warm."

He returned her impish grin. "Aye, that's one purpose of marriage."

Lingering in her arms, Matthew leashed the keen edge of passion stalking him. "Have you forgiven me, then, for my unknown sins?"

He stroked his palm lower, resting on the rise of her buttocks. "May I touch— Is the promise forgotten?"

The shadow crossed Rebecca's face as she considered him thoughtfully. He felt the give-and-take of her emotions, wished for the soft warmth to come flowing back.

"That promise must be kept," she whispered, moving away from him.

Matthew stared at her across the width of the bed, feeling the rage boil within him. "What have I done, then?" he asked carefully, rising from the bed, uncaring of the chill flowing over his naked body. "The condemned surely has a right to know his guilt before he's hung."

He jerked the blankets from her grasp. "Tell me!" he roared, tossing the blankets to the floor. "Tell me, you cold-hearted witch, or by heavens, I'll take you now—the promise be damned!"

She tossed back her hair, rising to her knees. "Take me, then—I won't fight you," she threw back. "I never had a chance, locked in this . . . bondage."

"Bondage?" So his wife still held their marriage against him.

Brushing back a wayward strand of hair, Rebecca folded her arms in front of her chest. The softness of her breasts surged upward beneath the silk, tempting Matthew even as his temper raged within him. The faint light shone upon her thighs as she knelt, her eyes lashing accusations at him. Her lips parted, then closed firmly. "Well? I'm waiting."

She glared up at him as Wolf whined and placed his head on the sheets near her. She turned slightly to pat his head, the movement baring one full breast to Matthew's gaze.

Seeing her eyes lower and widen, Matthew jerked on his trousers. "There's no hiding the fact that I'm hungry for you, lass, but not demented enough just yet to break my promise. You'd hold that against me with that cold heart of yours."

He stalked to the bureau, jerking open the drawers. "Here." He plunged his hands into the silken contents, tossing the tumbled mass on the bed. "You could wear these and not tempt me, play the woman for once, and I wouldn't break that blasted promise. Because I know what a lock you've got on your heart, Princess. It's all frost and snow beneath those flashing green eyes—you gave me just enough of a taste to drive me mad! You'll hold your ideas of bondage to you like a wall of ice. Bondage! This is a marriage before man and before God!"

Matthew rummaged through the hair on his chest. His hands clenched at his sides, wanting to wrap in that mass of silken hair, draining her mouth with his.

His wife clung to her walls; taking her now would only build one more barrier.

A mound of snow plopped from the swaying pine boughs to the cabin roof, then slid to the snowdrifts with a muffled sound. An ember crackled within the stove and Wolf whined. Still the man and the woman battled silently.

Rebecca's pale lips moved, her voice low and crisp and imperial. "Leave me."

Matthew nodded curtly. "Aye, your majesty. It's a woman

I want in my arms. The one you can be when you don't hold your love so tightly.''

Within her anger-pale face, Rebecca's green gaze flickered. "Love? I don't remember that in the bargain.''

"Aye, you wouldn't. You'd bury it beneath those men's pants you wear.''

Rebecca's chin rose. "That's enough, Matthew.''

"You couldn't make me break that damned promise if you tried,'' he spat out. His black eyes blazed for a moment before he stalked out of the room, slamming the door.

"Oh, couldn't I?'' she asked softly after a long, thoughtful moment. Wolf whined again, nuzzling her hand. She stroked the dog's coarse pelt, her eyes watching the bright sunlight cut through the glass window.

"Ignore me for a week, will he?'' Rebecca stalked across the bedroom, the lantern light outlining her shadow against the cedar timbers. In the night the wolf pack called the huge dog, and he padded restlessly about the bedroom, listening.

"They're out there, wanting you to run with them, aren't they?'' she whispered, rubbing the dog's head. "But you're needed here. At least I've got you to talk to.''

The dog's eyes met hers steadily, his yellow-white head angled to one side as he listened to the long, chilling howls. "You stay,'' she ordered, rubbing his ears. "Matthew said there are bounty hunters out there waiting for you.''

Rebecca glared at the closed door. "He's sitting out there, wrapped in his papers and his plans. Then he comes to bed and turns his back on me as though I didn't exist.''

Matthew's broad, tanned back had tempted her for enough nights. Once she had awakened, curled around him like a clinging vine, her hand flat upon his chest. His hard, naked buttocks had fitted neatly against her stomach, calming the uneasiness she had begun to feel.

Within her arms he had breathed deeply, sleeping. Rebecca had rubbed his scarred back with her cheek, aching for him. As he slept, she had kissed the scars, the tears creeping behind her lids. Then, forcing herself to remember Emma, she had eased to the bed's cold, empty space.

Now she felt raw, snowbound in the cabin with a husband that preferred his dog's company. Something within her screamed in anger.

Taunt her, would he? Challenge her ability to make him drool as Emma had?

Wolf whined, padding to a window to listen to the howls as Rebecca stood in front of the full-length oval mirror studying herself.

She turned to the side, smoothing the flannel shirt to her waist and the heavy braid swung down her back as she viewed her backside. The trousers had tightened slightly across her hips, clinging to her curves. "So I couldn't make him want me—I suppose I'm not woman enough!"

Oh, he had been polite enough as they shared the daily routine. But his manner cut at her, wounded the delicate softness within.

She jerked open the chest of drawers, lifting out a green gown and a matching wrapper. "He needs to pay. Acting like an innocent, Wolf. Jean was just protecting him."

The green silk drifted down along her flannel shirt and trousers. "Likes lace, does he? He's promised not to touch. I should be quite safe enough to parade around in this. Maybe then he'll look up from his papers. After all, I am a woman. Hell's bells, the man needs tormenting!"

Unbuttoning her shirt, she tossed it to the floor, the remainder of her clothing following. In the light of the stove, she slid into the low-cut, clinging gown. She tied the tiny strings at the bodice, turning in the mirror to note the curves displayed there.

Her breasts felt heavier, more tender . . . and she noted she had gained weight in the time she'd been in the cabin. After all, she'd developed the appetite of a horse, stuffing herself with Matthew's sourdough biscuits and melted butter.

Rebecca sat at the dainty dressing table, unwinding her braid. She combed her fingers through its length, draping it over her shoulder.

She met the reflection of her half-closed dark emerald eyes. "He's had his game. Now I'll have mine."

She'd torment the holy daylights out of him, then settle in for a nice sleep.

Rebecca ran the flat of her hand across her uneasy stomach, regretting sneaking from Matthew's taffy jar.

Wolf whined and she looked over her shoulder to him. "He talks of love, then runs to Emma's bed. I'll show him what he has left behind."

Taking a deep breath, Rebecca tightened the wrapper around her waist. She studied herself in the mirror, then decided to let the wrapper hang free.

Matthew had a badly needed lesson to learn, and she might as well start now.

Studying a mound of papers, Matthew ran his pencil down a sum of numbers. Working over the new house plans, he wondered if Rebecca would ever turn to him. He'd rechecked the figures several times in the last hour, distracted by her restless movements in the next room.

The wolves were howling in the snowdrifted meadow, calling for Wolf. No doubt his mate called him to her.

His lips tightened. Mate . . . Promise or not, Rebecca's softness enticed him as had no other woman. Her scent lingered around him every minute. The sight of her body turning, twisting, fighting Wolf for the blanket, tormented him night and day.

He closed his lids, allowing his tired eyes to rest. The sunlight had touched her hair today as she frolicked with Wolf in the snow. Like a child, she'd fallen back into a drift, waving her arms and legs to make a snow angel. She'd laughed wildly when Wolf's cold nose touched her face.

Matthew rubbed his forehead, leaning back in the desk chair. Later Rebecca had sat cross-legged on the red velvet couch, looking like a child as she flipped through a catalog.

She'd sent him questioning glances, then lowered her lashes quickly. It took all within his power not to sweep her up in his arms.

Promise or not. He was daft over the hardheaded lass. With a look she could stun him. With a touch she could take away his pride.

The whisper of silk and the scent of French perfume floated around him. When he slowly opened his eyes, Rebecca held a brandy glass out to him.

Matthew's gaze trailed slowly down the clinging silk, her long slender throat flowing into the fullness of her bosom. The gown fell to her hips, caressed them lovingly, then swept on to her bare toes. She moved, and an enticing curve of soft thigh and calf slid from the gown.

Raising his eyes, Matthew's heart skipped a beat. Within the frame of ebony hair, her eyes slanted down at him, her mouth softly curved.

A temptress from head to toe, Rebecca boldly met his gaze. She lifted her own glass, exposing the length of her slender throat. Then setting her emptied glass atop his papers, Rebecca sauntered to the couch, her hips swaying enticingly.

With the graceful air of a courtesan she settled amid the pillows, leaning back and closing her eyes.

Matthew drained his glass, wondering at her game. He settled back in the chair, watching her. As she lay on her side the wrapper slid to one side, exposing a slender thigh and the generous curves of her breasts. A curling lock rested enticingly within the deep, soft crevice, jet black against the pale silky flesh.

From beneath her lashes the slanted green eyes were mysterious. She rummaged through the catalog restlessly, flicking glances at him.

Playing the wanton, was she? Tempting him into breaking his promise . . .

Matthew settled back, linking his fingers behind his head and placing his stocking-covered feet upon the couch. Her eyes flickered over his bare chest, then down at the book.

Rebecca had the air of a child at play, the sight intriguing Matthew. The intricate facets of his wife never failed to excite him. He decided to follow where her game would take them.

"You look quite lovely, Princess." Matthew could feel her

passion tug at him as she swept back her hair. The strands caught the lantern light, glistening. "The gown suits you."

"Thank you." She turned another page, absently licking her bottom lip.

"Playing the wanton on a long, boring winter night, Princess?" Matthew's body hardened as she met his bold stare.

"I have no idea how a . . . a woman like that behaves."

Matthew had never been one to sidestep an opportunity to hold his wife. Just for a precious instant he needed the sweet torture of her nestled against him. "For a start, she'd come sit on my lap."

She closed the catalog, studying the cover. "I see."

"Of course, she'd allow me to touch her—quite intimately. Perhaps a kiss or two on the shoulders and neck."

"It's a cold night," she murmured conversationally.

He half smiled, knowing she felt her way uncertainly. "Aye, that it is." He poured himself another brandy from the decanter and tossed it down. "For warmth," he explained. "A man likes something warm on a night like this."

A flush ran up her cheeks, her fingers trembling on the cover of the book. "Umm. This woman—the wanton—what then?" The husky timbre of her voice stopped his heart.

"Well, it's hard to describe." He settled back, crossing his arms behind his head once more. He had all the time in the world to let Rebecca play seductress. "She might ask his preferences."

Her eyes widened. "Preferences?"

"Every man likes to be treated differently. Different touches, different . . . styles."

"I see." Rebecca ran her palm across the velvet upholstery. "I could sit on your lap. But you'd have to keep your hands to yourself."

"I wouldn't think of touching you without permission. Why, it would break my promise. And I'm a man of my word."

"Hmm. You wouldn't touch?"

"Aye. Not even a kiss."

"I don't trust you."

He shrugged. "Well, then, I've these sums to attend to. . . ."

Rising, Rebecca crossed to him. She eased into his lap, sitting primly, her hands clasped. "Like this?"

He nodded, watching her carefully weigh the situation.

Lord, she felt wonderful, close to him, scented of roses and her own sweet musk. Her eyebrows rose. "And then?"

He shrugged, the soft weight of her hips enchanting him. "It's the touching. The woman's role is to entice, you see. Do you like touching me, Becky?" he asked huskily, locking his fingers to keep them from her.

The blush rose from her neck, staining her cheeks. Her lashes fluttered down, hiding her eyes. "That's beside the point, Matthew."

Her fingers fluttered up to his chest, the slender tips just touching his shoulder. She skimmed the heavily padded muscles of his shoulders and chest, then slid to his neck, watching him. "What are your . . . preferences?"

Her shy blush caused his blood to heat, to throb through him. He stared at her lips. "I like a woman's mouth on me. Perhaps nibbling at my earlobe, her breath warm against me."

Their eyes met, the longing within her shaking her. How could he hold so still? Didn't he want her?

She hesitated for one tick of the grandfather clock. Then, placing her cheek against his rough one, she tugged at his lobe with her teeth. "Like this?"

"Aye, lass. Like that and more. . . ." Her perfume surrounded him in the velvety mist, her darkened gaze finding his own.

Slowly, carefully placing her arms around his neck, Rebecca closed her eyes and fitted her lips lightly to his unyielding ones. The taste of the brandy and smoke lingered on his mouth, drawing her nearer. She flicked her tongue across his bottom lip, feeling his breath warm her cheek.

"Remember when we first came here and you lay with me, listening to my stories like a child?" he asked huskily.

The memory warmed her. "Aye."

His lips curved at her tease. "Here's one more tale."

Watching the light sweep across her face, the emerald-green eyes studying him, the tender part of her lips, Matthew stated his case in his mother's favorite poem. The words slid across Matthew's lips like an old friend, accented by his childhood burr.

> Wi' night-black hair and emerald eyes,
> The bonnie maid did so beguile.
> Wi' thorny ways and dewy lips,
> O'er highlands she ran free and wild.
>
> Yet 'round my empty heart she curled;
> I lured her to my fern veiled lair.
> Wi' whispers soft and tender kiss,
> I wooed fair lass of raven hair.
>
> Bewitching lass, my heart's true luve,
> 'Til stars do fall; and sun burns cold.
> Our kindling fire shall rise in flame,
> Consuming all our hearts could hold.
>
> Through rivers rage and cold snows deep,
> I come to her, my luve, my own.
> My midnight rose, my highland heart,
> Wi' emerald eyes she calls me home.

He breathed heavily, entranced by her. Would she listen with her heart? Would she care enough to place her vow aside?

Matthew caught the damp brightness of her eyes before she lowered her lids. Her teeth tugged at the soft bottom lip he ached to kiss.

"I've missed you, lass," he whispered coarsely. "You're in my blood."

Denying her revenge, Rebecca felt the rose bloom within her, her heart warmed as though embraced by summer sunlight. "You may touch me, Matthew."

The scarred eyebrow rose, the dimple creeping into his

right cheek. "Thank you, Princess. But soon touching won't be enough."

"I know," she murmured, smoothing the strong line of his jaw with her palm.

He eased his arms around her, felt the woman within warm to him. "There's more than this, lass. Much more."

"Show me."

Rising, lifting her in his arms, Matthew carried his wife into the bedroom. For now he had her; later he would fight her wars.

Chapter Twenty-one

The middle of November, the season of the McKay truce, was warm. A Chinook wind—the wind melting the snow—swept across the valley.

There was a softness blooming within Rebecca, one she could not deny. Matthew spent each hour tugging skillfully at her heart. Yet he watched her cautiously, and she in return studied him.

Did he father Emma's child? The doubt lingered between them, despite the long, tender lovemaking.

The marriage grated on her still yet was dimmed by Matthew's tender care.

Matthew took her in fire and in need, yet tended her carefully, skillfully, always cautiously.

When she woke screaming in the night, he held her possessively, the flat of his hand resting over her stomach. Where was her pride? she thought. Where were her grand promises to "count coup"? Somehow, when Matthew came near, she threw those things to the mountain winds.

Matthew felt the fine blade of time twist against him. She hadn't given herself fully to him, clinging to her fears. Unknowingly Rebecca cradled his child within her womb; he was certain of the fact. Forced into this marriage, would she deny the child? Would she deny the love bonding them together daily?

And the nightmares that made her damp with sweat, her frantic cries, her fingers clutching at him . . . why?

Three weeks had passed since Jean's departure, a time for playing and for making love. Matthew and Rebecca watched the Appaloosa herd roam the white expanse, nipping at exposed bunchgrass. He tucked the deerskin hood more tightly around Rebecca's head, placing his arm around her shoulders.

She laughed up at him, leaning against his side. "You were right—Wind Dancer was in danger of becoming an old bachelor. He's frisky as a colt now."

Matthew raised his eyebrows, leering at her. "I know how he feels. I feel as young as an untried boy when you set your mind to it."

She giggled, and Matthew hugged her closer, enjoying the sweet sound. "I thought your eyes would fall from their sockets when I wore that corset, though the laces were far too tight."

Matthew gazed down into her face, knowing that she hadn't yet realized she was going to have a baby. He'd been badly frightened by that damned, tightly laced corset, her chemise barely covering her burgeoning breasts. He'd felt panic lash at him, taking care to ease the restriction from her gently.

He'd touched her reverently, realizing the woman's pride in her needed to tell him that he had fathered the baby. Still, her doubts lingered. Matthew knew he had never played a deadlier game with time than now.

He kissed the tip of her cold nose, watched her lashes close in pleasure. Beautiful, her wildness gentled for a time, Rebecca had set her silken web around his heart.

There were things to be said, promises to be made, easing the way for the child. Another stroke of time slipped by while he gazed into her green eyes, drowning in the sheer pleasure of watching her tender smile.

While the snow clouds promised overhead, Matthew slipped his arms beneath Rebecca, lifting her. "Matthew!"

"Aye?" He wanted to hold her against him in the heat of

the cabin, feel that last softness yield beneath his hands as she gave herself reluctantly to her passion. They had this, at least—the sweetness and the pleasure of their bodies.

Rebecca trailed a damp mitten down his nose. "Such a gallant."

He cocked an eyebrow, leering, making light of his desperate need for her, the softness waiting to soothe him. "Merely taking care of you, Princess. There are things that need doing in the cold of a November afternoon." He tossed her lightly, taking care even in his play.

"I thought we discussed 'needs' last night and this morning. Surely you're tired."

"Worn to the bone, a mere skeleton. But I'll recover, you wanton." She giggled, leaning back against his shoulder to flick him that saucy, knowing look. The look caught and lingered, warming him.

A long wisp of gleaming raven hair escaped the deerskin hood to catch the sun. He lifted it, brushing the strand across his lips. She raised her hand, touching his cheek lightly, tenderly. "I'll have to feed you better then, McKay . . . if you're a mere skeleton."

Tucking the strand inside her hood, Matthew lowered his head to kiss her lips. "Apple dumplings?"

She had yet to come to him trustingly, he thought as her eyes darkened and the pink blush crept up her cheeks. The tip of her tongue crept out to moisten her bottom lip. Entranced by this feminine play, Matthew felt himself grow weak.

Wolf suddenly gave a long, deep-throated howl. From the wagon road another dog answered, then several dogs began barking excitedly. Wolf leapt through the snow, running toward the sound of the dogs.

"It's Jean. He's running his dogsled." Matthew scowled, carrying her toward the house with a long stride. "Trust him to interrupt a good afternoon's rest. . . ."

Rebecca squirmed in his arms. "Aren't you going to meet him?"

"Not a chance. Hold still or we'll both end up in the snow.

Jean's not exactly welcome right now," Matthew answered darkly, glaring at the edge of the snow-covered forest. "The Duchess should have taught her son better manners."

"Duchess?"

"His French mother." His black eyes cut toward the wagon road. "Damn!"

"Matthew!"

He marched up the steps, pausing only to unlatch the door. "You've had enough cold wind and snow, Becky." Once inside the cabin he placed her on her feet, then unbuttoned her coat. "You don't need a cold."

Rebecca stamped the snow from her boots on the thick braided rug. When he took her coat to hang it from a peg, she glared at him. "Rest and eat . . . don't get too cold, don't . . . don't . . . don't!"

Matthew lowered his brows, taking off his coat. "Don't argue with your husband, woman. We're a long way from any help if you do get sick."

"Hah! Playing at lord and master again?" She punched his lean stomach before he bent to draw off her boots. "I think I'll serve Jean two apple dumplings and give you—"

"A kiss?"

Rebecca caught the dark, knowing excitement racing between them, felt her heart begin to beat more rapidly.

"Aye?" Matthew pressed, his tone low and husky. "I'm waiting, lass. What will you give me? Your heart?"

She turned away to hide her blush, knowing his eyes followed her hungrily. Matthew wanted her, not concealing his need of her. For now she couldn't give him everything, not just yet. Still, he deserved a tiny slice of torment.

For good measure she allowed her hips to sway just a tiny bit more within the tightness of her trousers, and was rewarded with a male growl of frustration. "Becky . . ."

Hearing Jean's footsteps upon the steps, Rebecca merely winked. "You'll have to wait, you lecherous—"

"I'm a famished man, lass," he returned, stalking toward her, his eyes lighting. "I'll bolt the door. Jean will understand. . . ."

There was the excited barking of dogs, stilled by a man's low command just outside the cabin.

"Rescued!" she squealed with delight, dancing outside his grasp to open the door.

Jean was carefully unwrapping Emma from a furry nest within the seven-foot-long birch sled. The eight running dogs already rested in the snow, their white eyes startling in their black-and-gray pelts.

The French-Indian handled Emma as carefully as a grand lady entering a ballroom on a suitor's arm. He grinned, pushing back his hood. "It was a good fast run, Matt. Emmaline will make a fine dog puncher."

Matthew returned the wide grin, placing his arm around Rebecca's shoulders and shaking his fist at Jean. "You blasted Canadian! Get back on that sled! Rebecca and I were just about to—*whoof*!"

Rebecca smoothed her hand over the lean ribs she had just pinched. ". . . waiting for company, Jean. Come in. I've just baked some apple dumplings."

Wolf bolted through the doorway, shaking the snow from his pelt and almost knocking Rebecca aside. He plopped down on the crumpled rug to watch Jean and Emma enter, both wearing long, lush capes of buffalo fur.

Emma's small face peeked out from her ermine-trimmed hood, her glance at Rebecca fearful. "We're married, Rebecca . . . the baby is Jean's."

The words came out in a soft rush, closing around Rebecca with the force of a vise. She'd blamed Matthew for the child, believed Emma—

She heard Matthew curse softly before she fainted into the strength of his arms.

"La! You gave us all a fright," Emma said soothingly, tucking the quilt closely around Rebecca. Sitting on the bed, she dabbed a cold cloth across Rebecca's forehead. "Matt's out there, prowling like a caged tiger in a sideshow. Jean said Matt would scare the daylights out of you, acting like that. I had to promise him I'd call him the minute you woke up.

The man's in love with you, honey. And you've scared him out of ten years just now. Why, I thought he'd faint too. And a man Matthew's size would be a hard one to tote!''

Dressed in a white-beaded doeskin tunic and trousers with fringe, Emma was radiant. A soft red-brown cap of curls covered her head, and freckles crossed her nose. Her face was fuller, her blue eyes shining with concern. ''Matt said he's 'daft' over you,'' she whispered. ''Isn't it divine, knowing that the father of your baby loves you?'' she asked with the tone of a conspirator. ''Jean has all sorts of fancy French ways to say it.''

Emma ran her hand across the small bulge of her stomach, outlined by the soft white doeskin. ''La! I never fainted, though . . . well, just once—when Jean marched into the hotel at Wenatchee looking like a savage dressed in his buckskins. He scared the clerk, threatened to burn him at the stake in that French lingo. La! It sounded like a scalding. He grabbed a thin sword off the hotel wall and started slashing curtains, demanding to know my room number.''

Rebecca settled back against the goose-down pillow, fighting the nauseating churning in her stomach. ''Jean is the father?'' she repeated carefully, aware that the soft strains of Jean's guitar had entered the room.

The fire crackled in the small corner stove, just as it had the previous day. Yet her world had turned around completely.

Emma glanced uneasily at the shuttered window. ''Yes, he is. I loved him even then, I just didn't know it.'' She blushed prettily. ''He wants babies . . . lots of them, he says. My babies only. He says I'm in the 'river of his life until the end of his days and beyond.' Isn't that something? Me and only me. Lord, how I love that man.''

Rebecca traced Emma's dreamy face with her gaze. ''Emma, that night at your sister's . . . when Eric—''

''That varmint!'' the smaller woman snapped. ''I was a fool, scared out of my wits that night. I'd have said anything. I came back, you know. Eric knocked me senseless. Honey, I didn't know who to ask for help. By the time I found a shotgun and came back, you were gone. He couldn't have been intimate with you—you were drugged, and Eric wants a woman to fight him or he can't . . .''

She took Rebecca's limp hand, rubbing it with her own. "Oh, honey, don't you see? Eric hates his brother . . . hates him bad, he wants to take the most precious thing from him— and that's you. He could see Matthew had eyes for no one else. Lord, how he hates him—has to do with something that happened way back.''

Tears filled her lids, her eyes pleading with Rebecca. "Jean is my man, the baby's father. He can make me feel like I'm walking on clouds. Matt never touched me, not once.'' Her lashes swept down, the tears trickling across her cheeks. "Forgive me, honey,'' she whispered brokenly. She brushed the back of her small hand across her lids, attempting a timid smile. "You think you can?''

Rebecca closed her eyes, settling back against the pillows with a tiredness that flowed like lead in her veins. *Matthew had not fathered Emma's child!*

Jean's music floated softly into the room, the fire crackling in the stove's grate. Rebecca felt so tired; she'd fought Matthew, accusing him unjustly. She turned her head toward the window, watching the icicles catch the late-afternoon sunlight.

Emma smoothed a tendril back from Rebecca's temple. "You look so white, Rebecca. When's your baby due?''

Barely hearing Emma's soft musical voice, Rebecca carefully placed her hand over her stomach. *A baby!*

Her fingers moved tentatively over the trousers' tight waistband, sliding lower. *A baby!*

Deep within she had questioned her body, but then Matthew hadn't given her time to think lately. Dazed, feeling the soft glow wash over her, she looked at Emma. Her companion's small hand rested over hers lightly. "Why, honey, you really didn't know, did you? Why, I could tell right away. You've filled out and you've got a glow a mile wide. La! I've heard of women . . . How far along do you suppose you are? I mean, before Matt left, do you suppose . . .''

Rebecca concentrated on the drop clinging to the very tip of the icicle, adjusting to the new knowledge. *When?*

"Eric," she murmured on a breath as dry as the desert wind. She felt the first stirring of doubt, remembering that night at Maybelle's. What if Emma were wrong about Eric taking a drugged woman?

"Shoot! That lily-livered skunk left me with a bruise that lasted for weeks. I thought he'd broken my jaw! He went on a rampage! The lawmen all over the countryside are looking for him. He's gone mad, crazy as a loon."

Rebecca closed her lids, feeling her blood run cold. She'd denied Matthew with her heart and her body.

The door creaked, and Matthew looked sheepishly around the corner. "Emma?"

"See?" Emma whispered to Rebecca. "He's been doing that about every minute or so." She winked, then turned to Matthew. "She's just a little tired, Matthew. Whatever have you two been doing up here by yourselves?"

Ignoring Emma, Matthew came to stand over Rebecca. His face, lined and shadowed, was gaunt. His large hands hung limply at his sides. "Lass?" he asked in that soft burr that tore at her.

Mocking him tenderly, she answered, "Aye?"

Emma closed the door softly behind her, leaving them alone.

For a moment he hovered beside the bed, searching her face. "You're feeling better, lass?"

"Aye." She traced the rugged features, the broken nose, the scarred eyebrow, the long, silky lashes. How she'd hated him . . . the man who had touched her with gentleness, tormenting her into loving him. Stretching out her hand, she touched his fingers, tugging him down.

He knelt on the floor. Taking her hand, he pressed the back of it to his mouth, kissing her knuckles. Then, with trembling hands, he turned her hand to press his face within her palm. She could feel his rough breath on her wrist, and her other hand crept to touch his hair, smoothing the disheveled curls.

Against her flesh he whispered roughly, "It's hard for a

man to win his wife and salvage his pride beneath the noses of the whole countryside, lass. Alone up here, I thought to soften your heart toward me.''

The clock counted the minutes, ticking loudly as Matthew knelt by the bed. When he looked up, torn by pain, she felt the tearing within her. His eyes searched hers, waiting.

''Matthew, I'm going to have a baby.'' The words slipped from her lips as easily as the spring wind flowing through the pine boughs.

He nodded slowly. His deep voice bore a husky note of possession and pride when he spoke. ''My son. Don't hold it against the baby, love . . . that I forced you into this marriage.'' His hand turned her face to his, the tips of his fingers trembling against her skin. ''I love you, Becky. I love you enough for the both of us. Hate me if you must. But just don't hate the boy.''

''It could be a girl, Papa.'' Rebecca traced his craggy features, watched them slowly change back to his old arrogance.

His fingertip followed the edge of her jaw, his eyes growing soft. The dimple on his right cheek slid out, the sight capturing her heart. ''Aye, a saucy little gypsy beauty like her mama.''

She touched the scarred eyebrow. ''You knew then, Matthew.''

He stretched beside her, sharing her pillow. His large hand slid down her stomach, resting over the baby. ''You've changed.''

His fingers plucked at her shirt, exposing her lacy camisole. Sliding his hand beneath the fabric, he pressed lightly against her softness. ''You're tender there, lass. Fuller too.''

He caught her chin, turning her blushing face up to him. ''Aye, you're the rose of my heart, Becky. The thought of you carrying my child has been a hard secret to keep. I've waited for the day . . .''

Her lashes fluttered down, shielding her glistening eyes. He kissed the soft slope of her hot cheek. ''We were bound to get caught, lass.''

Matthew unbuttoned her trousers, smoothing her tight belly

beneath the bright pink drawers. "When you came seeking me, soft and fluttery, my strength deserted me. I tried to refuse you, but you insisted, spreading those rosy charms before me until my tongue nearly hung to the floor—"

"Matthew!" she breathed, leaning back to study his grin. "I came seeking you?"

"Tormented me with silk nighties and fancy corsets . . . toyed with my affectionate nature, so to speak." His thick eyebrows rose, taunting her, his teeth shining in the darkness of his face. "Keeping after me day and night, thrusting your bosom like ship's high mast before me, your aft side swaying in these tight britches."

"Matthew!" Rebecca felt the sun burst within her, his teasing gaining him a light punch in the ribs.

"Aye?" he asked innocently, leaning back upon the pillows, cradling his head in his arms.

She trailed a finger down his open shirt, toying with the hair covering his chest. "Sure of yourself, aren't you?"

"Pleased as a bear in a honey cache." He turned his head, suddenly serious. His black eyes smoldered within the depths of his lashes. "I'm daft over you, lass," he admitted roughly. "You have my heart . . . take my child with the same love I have for you. You're my rose, the sweetest of my life."

Within her the warmth bloomed, trembling and aching and sweet. Matthew had paid dearly for Emma's lie, yet admitted his love freely. She ran the flat of her hand across her stomach, still caught by the wonder of the child. Matthew watched her quietly, studying her features intently. "You're happy then, Becky . . . with the baby—my baby?"

"How long?" With lightly probing fingers Rebecca touched her stomach. She'd forgotten to count her days, caught by their play.

As though reading her thoughts, Matthew murmured, "We'll have to wait and see, since the mother hasn't kept track of her times," he teased lightly. "She'll know better when the other babies come along."

Taking her hand, he rubbed it against his cheek, smiling wistfully. "You're a beautiful woman, lass. Am I forgiven?"

he whispered, kissing her temple. "For forcing you into marriage?"

She trembled lightly, shy with him now. He pressed on huskily. "Will you take the child to your heart, Becky? Warm him with your love?"

"And his father?" she returned in a whisper.

"Can love enough for the both of us, my rose." Deep with emotion, Matthew's voice flowed over her. Taking her face within his warm, rough palms, he lifted her for his searching kiss.

He tasted, asking . . . always searching for her answer until her lips began to move beneath his. When she was breathless, drowning in his caresses, he asked huskily, "You'll take my child to love then, Becky? I have to know."

"Aye." She nibbled at his bottom lip, feeling him tense.

His hand cupped her right breast, massaging the fullness. With darkening eyes he turned her, resting over her lightly. His hips moved against her, the male demand strong and full against her thighs. "Well, then, Princess, shall we seal the bargain?"

Rebecca blushed, looking away from his questioning stare. "We have company."

Matthew cursed softly. He arranged her hair, letting it winnow through his fingers, and studied the strands shimmering in the half-light. One curl fell to the hollow of her throat and he bent to kiss it. Nuzzling the soft spot behind her ear, he whispered hoarsely against her skin, "I'm dying, lass. We'll latch—"

A soft knock on the door brought Matthew's head up sharply. "What?" he roared, looking as fierce as a wounded grizzly.

"Matthew!" she whispered, rubbing his rough cheek with her open hand. "They're our guests."

"Guests!" he muttered darkly, easing from her. He glanced at her, then drew the corner of the blanket across her disheveled clothing. "They could have picked a better time for visiting. You've yet to come after me, lass . . . I was about to experience my first taste of your wifely submission.''

Matthew had all the markings of disgruntled husband, his fur ruffled. The look was endearing, and she cherished him at that moment. Soothing him, Rebecca caressed the nape of his neck. He looked at Rebecca like a small boy caught with his hand in the cookie jar. "I'm not happy about this at all, Rebecca," he growled. "First I have to keep secret the fact that I'm visiting my wife's bed in her father's house—"

She tugged his head down to hers, brushing her lips across his firm ones. "I'll make it up to you later."

Matthew breathed shakily for a moment, the color rising in his cheeks, then traced the warmth in her own cheeks. He grinned, rising from the bed to smooth his clothing. He briskly tucked his shirt into his pants, all male arrogance. "Hmm. See that you do, wife."

Rebecca watched his broad shoulders, the confident swagger of those hard buttocks and long, hard legs as he walked toward the door. She fully intended to make good her promise, but just now Matthew's highhanded, dominating husband role needed a bit of trimming.

"I'll be a moment," she purred, stretching. The camisole's fastenings yielded, the lace falling aside to reveal her tempting breasts. Lifting her arms behind her head, she stretched like a cat waiting to be petted. She ran the flat of her hand down her side to rest upon one rounded, jutting hip. "Tonight . . ."

Matthew's eyes fastened on the rosy crests, his big body tensing. His gaze ran down her rounded curves, then up, tasting them. "Becky, you tempting little witch, you'll pay for that," he groaned, shaking his head before he opened the door.

"Aye?" she questioned softly, blowing him a kiss.

His breath caught sharply as he cursed and softly closed the door behind him.

Matthew stole glances at Rebecca as she and Emma cleared away the evening meal. Dressed in a soft cotton dress with blue sprigs of flowers and white ruffles, Rebecca had left her hair down and it swayed around her waist.

It was the long, soft looks Rebecca threw him that knocked Matthew sideways. When he caught her at it, she blushed, turning away. Now he barely heard Jean's low voice above the guitar music.

"Eric has two friends now, Matthew. Both wanted by the Royal Canadian Mounted Police. Mean sons of bitches."

"Sounds like the type my brother would choose," Matthew answered, distracted by the sway of Rebecca's hips beneath those enticing skirts. Hell, the more clothes she wore, the more he thought of the satin skin beneath. He swirled his brandy in his glass, wanting his bride to himself.

Rebecca laughed, the tantalizing sound drifting over the music. Matthew settled back into the chair, crossing his taut legs at the ankle. Tonight, she'd promised, and he could feel his desire rake at him. But she clearly enjoyed the visit, playing the perfect hostess. There was a pride in her voice as she described his plans for hauling to the railheads and the way station. To have Rebecca's love, he'd wait an eternity.

"Beware, my friend," Jean continued softly, meeting Emma's enticing gaze. "I will kill your brother if he comes near my wife. I would hunt him down now, but Emmaline wants this baby safe. I'm taking her to my spread in Canada."

Jean's lean fingers floated across the guitar, and he studied them. "If he crosses my path, he is a dead man."

"What are you two talking about?" Emma's soft Southern voice floated over them. "I can tell—it's getting all serious man talk when we want to visit. Play something sweet, Jean, honey."

Giving Matthew a meaningful glance, Jean smiled at his wife. "Only if my Emmaline will come here."

"Naughty boy," she said teasingly, giggling as she padded over to him. Caressing his sleek, black hair, she sat, leaning against him. "I'm here."

He kissed her briefly but with care. Looking on, Rebecca was caught by the fond intimacy between two such different people.

Untying her apron, she hung it on a peg to find Matthew's black eyes pinned hungrily upon her. He wanted her heart, he'd said. And he wanted the child. Holding his gaze, she felt herself move toward him, beckoned by the flame that drew them closer each day.

Placing her hand in Matthew's outstretched palm, Rebecca allowed herself to be drawn to his lap.

His gleaming eyes held hers boldly, making promises for a night, for a lifetime. She heard Emma sigh wistfully in the distance as Matthew's arms comfortably closed around her.

"Tired?" he whispered as she allowed her arm to settle across his broad shoulders. He shifted easily, the warming thrust of his desire against her skirts.

"Emmaline needs a good night's rest, my friend," Jean said softly. "Where . . . ?"

Stroking her palm along Matthew's strong neck, Rebecca played with the thick hair at the nape of his neck. She kneaded the tense muscles beneath his dark skin. Matthew would have to wait for another time. As his wife it was her duty to see that their guests were comfortable. "We'll sleep together, Emma. The men can share the floor out here."

Both men stared at her, their faces blank.

"By all that's holy!" Matthew snorted a moment later. "By next year our house will be standing with enough beds to accommodate the whole countryside!"

Jean's roar of laughter followed Matthew straight out the door.

Later Rebecca woke to Emma's urgent whisper. "Wake up, honey! Wake up, you're dreaming . . . and scaring me half to death!"

The smaller woman patted Rebecca's shoulder. "There. Better now? Lord, honey, you'd scare even my Jean. What's all this about red clouds and water?"

When Rebecca shuddered, forcing the nightmare away, Emma tucked the covers more closely around them. "La!"

Rebecca breathed heavily, listening to the crackling fire. The fear rose and devoured her. The baby . . . whose baby? She ran her palm across the blanket covering her belly. *Whose baby? Which brother?*

Chapter Twenty-two

The Columbia River ripped the sheets of ice from the rocky shoreline, forcing them into the strong current.

Standing at the window of his study, Peter Klein watched a large sheet smash against a boat wedged in the ice at the landing. Broken into smaller pieces, the ice then swept on downriver. He turned to Maybelle, who sat curled in a big chair. "It's the week of Christmas. I wonder how she is."

"Rebecca? Why, honey, she's just fine, bubbly as a new bride should be." When Peter settled on a footstool in front of her, she smoothed his hair tenderly. "You'll worry about that child when you're in your dotage, Papa."

Peter took her small hand and turned it within his rough ones. His wife's gentle strength had seen him through Stella's screams and Bruno's steady drinking.

"You know what we need, Peter? A party," Maybelle said. "I want to dance while I can. When I'm as fat as an old sow I'll watch you."

He smiled gently. "You'll never get fat."

Maybelle grinned, pressing his hands to her stomach. "Twins, sugarplum. With Emma and Jean and Matt and Rebecca, you menfolk are going to be toting babies . . ."

When Peter began to smile, slowly and widely, Maybelle kissed his cheek. "Don't you worry, honey. I'll cut the heart out of anyone who teases you . . . because there's always next year.''

By the first of the new year, snow covered the McKay valley. The morning sun reflected on the snow, blinding Rebecca. She shielded her eyes with her hand, tracing Matthew's path to the barn.

It was a beautiful, clear day. Though she had promised Matthew to take care, the urge to ride Wind Dancer was too strong. She grinned, lengthening her stride. Matthew was hunting with Wolf and she needed the fresh air.

She tugged the beaver cape to her, her mittens running over the lush, dark fur lovingly. The cape had been a Christmas gift from Matthew, one he had fashioned in secrecy. She rubbed her cheek against the fur, remembering how his eyes had darkened when he'd given it to her. ''Give me your heart, lass,'' he'd whispered roughly, drawing her to him. ''I'll tend it until the end of my days.''

His kisses had trailed warm and beckoning across her flushed skin, his lips plying hers with mere brushes. ''Yield to me, Princess. You give me only so much and no more. Your dreams . . . tell me your fears.''

When she hadn't answered, he'd run his hand across her taut belly, warming the gentle mound. ''We've a baby between us, lass. One that needs no secrets between his parents . . .''

How could she tell him about Eric? About that night?

Opening the barn door, Rebecca entered the shadows, then closed the door against the biting wind. Drawing off her hood, she turned slowly, her thoughts locked upon Matthew's harsh face, his fleeting, hurt expression.

''Well, well. What have we got here?'' a male voice said. ''The high-and-mighty Lady McKay comes to visit her stables.''

Eric emerged from the shadows of a stall, tapping a quirt across his open palm. A patch covered one eye, his long red hair and untended beard filthy above his buffalo cape. His stench reached her as he came close, leering.

''I've just given that mare over there''—he nodded toward

Beauty, who whinnied and pranced nervously around her stall—"a little taste of these good manners."

He tapped the quirt lightly on Rebecca's shoulders. "My women don't leave my bed until I tell them to. Remember that in the future."

"What are you doing here, Eric?" she asked, struggling to keep her tone even. She clenched her hands, fighting to still her quickly beating heart. Preying animals scented fear, and Eric would pounce at the first sign. Within her mittens the fingers of her right hand flexed, instinctively seeking the butt of a Colt, but she had stopped wearing the gun long ago. Rebecca knew that her only chance for survival was to remain calm. She had her baby to protect, and she feared that Matthew would return and be vulnerable to Eric's attack.

She moved toward Beauty, smoothing the quirt marks across the velvety muzzle and crooning to the frightened mare. Scenting his mistress, Wind Dancer kicked the boards of his stall. "It's all right, boy," she murmured.

Eric grabbed her upper arm, jerking her around. "Don't ignore me, Miss High-and-Mighty." He raised the quirt and brought it across her backside. The heavy cape shielded her from the blow.

Rebecca pivoted, her chin lifting, eyes flashing. "Matthew would kill you if he knew about that night."

Eric's one eye pinned her face. "So you haven't told him. Well, I wouldn't expect you would," he said with a sneer. "Come on out, boys."

Two men, dressed in heavy bear capes, emerged from the shadows. A smaller, older man eyed Rebecca. His grimace served as a smile, showing a row of rotting teeth. "So this is 'er, is it?" he said, walking around her. "What do you think, Billy?" he asked a tough-looking youth who leaned against the stalls.

The boy stripped her with his stare and moved to stand in front of her. His dirty hand crept out, caressing her cheek. "She's got that hot gypsy look—she'll keep us warm, that's for sure."

"Get your hand off her, Billy," Eric ordered coolly. "She's mine."

The older man sneezed, wiping his nose with the back of his sleeve. "Blimey! Let's get 'er in the cabin if you want to play . . . we're freezing our butts off out here."

Eric slashed the quirt against the wiry man's cheek. "Shut up, Pickins."

Pickins rubbed the bloodied welt on his cheek, hunching away from Eric's temper. "Well, me bones are cold," he whined, turning toward Rebecca. "Want to ease your butt on a bed, gypsy?"

"No one goes in that house."

"What about grub?" Billy asked, slinging a cloth bag in front of Eric. He shook it. "We've got one can of beans here. I need food in my gut."

Eric grabbed him by the throat, half lifting him from the floor. "I say no one goes into the house." He threw Billy from him, glaring down at Rebecca. "There's a root cellar out back. Take what you need from that."

"That house ain't haunted, Eric. There's hot coffee and whiskey inside." Pickins crouched by the door.

"Say another word and you're a corpse, old man," Eric growled. "Now I'll keep the girl here, and you two take what you need from the root cellar. Cut a wide path around that old rose garden. It's not to be touched."

"Ha! And I reckon you'll be taking what you need in the meantime, right?" Billy asked, rubbing the front of his dirty trousers and leering at Rebecca. "I can wait for you, slut. I've got something here that women beg for—"

"Get out," Eric said softly. At the deadly purr both men glanced meaningfully at Rebecca, then fled the barn. The door slammed shut and she jumped back from Eric's outstretched hand.

"Come here, you green-eyed whore." Eric wrapped his hand in her braid, winding it until her face turned up to his. The roots of her hair stretched painfully, but Rebecca met Eric's stare impassively. "So we're alone at last, my lovely sister-in-law. I trust you have fond memories of our night together? Answer me!''

Molding her against him, Eric fitted his mouth over hers, his tongue penetrating her mouth. She bit down hard, and he reared back, furious.

He struck her with the back of his hand, his eye rolling like a child's blue marble.

She sprawled backward unto a pile of hay, stunned by his blow. Through the pain she feared for her child. Hers and Matthew's.

''Getting a nice soft spot for your backside, dearie?'' His eye darkened, his smile menacing as he threw off his coat. ''I like it when a bitch fights me,'' he said, snarling. ''I've been wanting to have you for a long time. No wonder my brother has kept you up here. He's always had the best, and I remember you lying beneath me, begging for it. Spread your legs, whore, or I'll beat the living hell out of you.''

Beauty whinnied nervously, fighting her tether. Wind Dancer screamed, kicking the door of his stall with his rear hooves. The other horses pranced within their stalls. The barn door opened, the bright sunlight shafting into the muted shadows. Without turning, Eric said, ''Get out of here, boys. I'll call you when I'm through.''

A dog growled low in his throat, and Wolf's white pelt shimmered in the blinding light.

''You're through *now*.'' Matthew's hushed, deadly voice was a roar in the silence. ''She's mine. Stay, Wolf.''

''You!'' Eric pivoted, half crouched, his expression filled with hatred. Drawing and cocking his pistol, he leveled the sights on Rebecca. ''Back off, Matt. I've already had her. You won't mind sharing for a time—''

Through the smoky shadows Rebecca saw her husband pause. His eyes cut at her, pinned her back to the hay. His silhouette, outlined in the doorway, seemed to grow, the sunlight shining through the wide spread of his legs.

Rebecca raised her hand to her mouth, wanting to cry out her innocence. She could feel him breathe, inhaling her guilt like a tangible thing. She felt his silence lash out at her, condemning her and Eric.

The baby stirred within her sleepily, and she tugged the cape across her stomach protectively. Remembering Emma's statement, Rebecca knew it to be true. "You couldn't have taken me that night. You want women to fight you or you can't—"

"Shut up!" he screamed wildly.

She'd had Matthew's love. Now she would have his hatred.

"You lash out where you can, don't you, Eric?" Matthew asked slowly. "You can't bear that she's mine."

"She's not, I tell you!" Eric raged. "She's mine."

"She wouldn't have you, Eric." Matthew's face was savage, his knuckles showing white. "I'm going to beat the hell out of you for even coming close to her."

Wolf growled again, circling Eric, the fur on his back bristling. He stood beside Rebecca, his four legs stiff and ready to spring. He bared his teeth at Eric.

Rebecca stretched out her hands, grasping the dog's cold fur. "Stay, Wolf."

Eric flicked a glance at the dog. "That cur! The old man's dog whelped with the wolf pack, then. I'd heard rumors from the Indians that there was a white wolf up here."

"Pa's dog, Ghost, was a mastiff, Eric. And from the looks of Wolf, I'd say he's out of Ghost." Matthew tossed his snowshoes to the floor, then closed the door quietly. "Do you believe in ghosts, Eric?"

"Ghosts," Eric muttered. "Some say there's a curse on the cabin. Of course, I don't believe it." His eye slid to the house fearfully. Uncertain, he wiped the back of his hand across his mouth, muttering, "Ma brought those witch chants with her. She had a potion for everything, turning those damn tarot cards at night, seeing the future."

Matthew paused, watching his brother carefully, thoughtfully. "Aye. But you never believed them."

"They were both crazy as loons, Matt. And you're of the same blood." Wolf growled low in his throat and Eric eyed him. "I'll shoot the dog dead in his tracks, Matt."

"Rebecca has him," Matthew ordered softly, watching his brother's face more closely. "Show Eric how you can talk with animals, how they listen to you."

Eric's blue eye widened, his skin paling as Rebecca crouched to her knees, wrapping her arms around the dog's neck. Wolf licked her cheek, then sat beside her like a well-trained puppy.

"She's got the touch, just like Ma, Eric," Matthew whispered, prodding. "I've seen a doe walk right up to her and eat from her hand." Meeting his brother's wild, frightened stare, Matthew tossed his hunting rifle to the haystack, then stripped his fur cape from him. He threw it over a board, his black eyes slashing Rebecca's pale face.

"A witch woman." Eric snarled. "I might have known you'd hitch up with one."

"She's my woman, Eric. My wife."

The older brother laughed coarsely. "She's got a strawberry mole on her right hip. Oh, she knows witchcraft, all right—flat on her back!"

Matthew turned slowly to his brother. In the semidarkness his face mirrored Eric's—savage, dark, and primitive, barely bound by civilization. Ready to kill each other, their resemblance was pronounced. Rebecca felt then the sheer power of Matthew's rage, the depth of his feeling for her. In another second he'd be at his brother's throat.

She shivered, fearing the high temper within him. Matthew was as she'd never seen him, wanting to beat his brother. That same look had been on Bruno's face when he'd beat Rudy. It was the killing face. . . .

Matthew and Eric had stepped back into another time, and instinctively she knew that once begun, their battle would be to the death.

"Are you all right, Becky?" Matthew's voice was a soft, raw whisper.

"Yes," she croaked, realizing for the first time that Matthew did not wear a gun. A large hunting knife nestled against his ribs. She wrapped her fingers in Wolf's coarse pelt, taking his strength. Matthew would hate her!

Eric fitted his hand around his gun butt. "I'm feeling kindly today, brother." He sneered. "You've just got time to hightail it back to that warm house you've been nesting in. The old man's house . . . hell, the place is seeped in him, even stinks like him."

"It's warm in the house, Eric. Would you like to come in?" Matthew asked, and Rebecca recognized the dangerously cool tone. He fought Eric on two planes, she realized slowly, curious as she watched Eric pale.

"No!" Eric crouched, circling his brother. "Anytime you're ready, Matt, I'll have her over your dead body."

"Why won't you come into the house, Eric?" Matthew asked, prodding, backing into the shadows. He placed himself between Rebecca and Eric. "What are you afraid of—Ma?" His voice dropped softly. "The day she died, she placed a curse on you, Eric. You feel it, don't you?"

Rebecca sensed Matthew would protect her with his body and wits, felt him searching for Eric's weakness.

The red-haired man spat into the straw, pointing his sights at Matthew's stomach. "I found Ma's bags of sticks and leaves hanging from the porch after the old man died. The hag had torn up one of my shirts and cursed me with her witchcraft. It was always you."

Just then the baby kicked strongly against her side, and she gasped, fitting her hand over the new life. Eric's eye followed the motion, traced the slight bulge beneath her loose shirt. "A brat!"

"My son," Matthew corrected, inching in front of her. "Why won't you go into the house?"

Leering, Eric turned to Matthew. "Whose brat rests in Mrs. McKay's belly, I wonder?" He cackled wildly just as Pickins and Billy entered the barn with filled gunnysacks.

Grinning, Eric raised the gun, poking Matthew's stomach. "Boys, I've spawned a few brats in my time, but she's got one in her belly that I'll keep. We can use the woman right up to her time."

Wind Dancer's hooves thudded against the door of his stall,

his wild whinny echoing in the large, eerie barn. Surprised, Eric pivoted with the sound, his pistol poised.

Matthew's fist shot out, hitting his brother's jaw with the solid crash of muscle and bone. Stumbling backward, Eric hit a post. His pistol fell to Rebecca's knees, and she snatched it up just as Pickins and Billy grabbed Matthew's arms.

"Hold him, boys," Eric yelled, moving toward his brother.

Wind Dancer kicked the door of his stall, breaking it. Eric turned, and in that moment Matthew leapt free of Billy and Pickins. His hand jerked the hunting knife from its sheath and he threw it into Pickins's chest just as he fired.

The bullet ripped through Matthew's left shoulder, tearing skin and muscle. Stunned, he slumped back against the wall. Wind Dancer trotted around the barn, rising up on his back hooves, pawing the air. Dust and hay swirled in the shadows.

Rebecca ran toward Matthew just as Eric hit his brother. Both men fell to the floor, and Wolf wove in and out, barking excitedly as the men rolled. The sound of grunts and fists hitting flesh mingled with Billy's cries as Wolf attacked him.

Rebecca moved around Wind Dancer. "Easy, boy. Back now," she crooned softly, trying to get closer to the fighting men. Matthew rolled on top of Eric, hitting him with his good hand.

Eric's hands rose to Matthew's throat, choking him.

Wind Dancer pawed the air, forcing Rebecca back against the wall. His feet came down inches from her face. When she screamed, it was Eric who turned toward her, his eye wild with fear. "Banshees!"

In that second Matthew's hand found a broken pitchfork, and he held the deadly points to Eric's throat. "Becky?" he called sharply. "Are you all right?"

Through the swirling dust she could see Matthew's wounded shoulder. A dark red stain spread across his flannel shirt.

She felt weak, barely able to breathe. The barn's dust became the nightmare, sweeping the cold red haze around her. It clung with icy fingers to her skin, chilling within her bones. It weighed down her shoulders. She could almost feel the blood dripping from her own flesh, and she wrapped her fingers around a rough barn board, felt a sharp sliver enter her thumb. Dazed, she looked at the blood seeping from the wound. She closed her eyes once, and then the mist lifted.

She trembled, caught by the unknown.

"I'm all right," she managed, stroking Wind Dancer's muscled neck. "Be careful."

"Banshees!" Eric muttered, his eye rolling with fear. "Holy Mother, they've come for me!"

With a scream Billy tore out of the barn, Wolf running after him. Matthew stood, lifting his brother but keeping the pitchfork at his throat. "Becky?" he asked more softly. "Come here, lass."

With unsteady legs she walked to him. Matthew glanced at her white face and down at the gun held in her limp hand. Eric breathed heavily, watching her with a fearful eye. "She's one of them witch women," he said, babbling.

Matthew held out his palm. "Give me the gun, Becky."

When she placed it in his hand, Matthew glanced at her fleetingly. "Put Wind Dancer back in his stall, Becky." She obeyed his soft directions, still claimed by the red haze, feeling it chill her spine.

She returned, standing near Matthew. The stain upon his shoulder grew, and she watched it, fascinated. Matthew's blood and the nightmare wove into each other, beating down upon her. She touched the wet circle, felt his blood glide on her fingertips.

Rebecca's head throbbed; she pressed her fingertips to her temples, easing the voices—*Brother against brother*—the woman's scream echoing in her brain. *My sons* . . .

"Let him go, Matthew," she whispered huskily.

Matthew glanced at her just before she fainted. With the gun he motioned toward the door. "You heard her, Eric. Don't come back or I will kill you, blood or not."

Wolf trotted into the barn, his ears lying close to his head. He snarled at Eric, showing his bloody fangs and mouth. Eric backed against the wall. "Call him off," he said.

"Wolf . . . stay," Matthew ordered in a low tone. "Billy won't be coming with you, Eric. Get out of here."

Eric gathered his cape, stopping to kick Pickins's dead body. "Useless scum!"

He turned at the doorway. "Another time, brother. Away from here. Your bitch carries my brat in her belly." He snarled, his eye glittering. "I'll be back for my son."

Rebecca awoke in the huge brass bed, a cold cloth on her forehead. Outside, the night wind howled, curling in the corners of the cabin. She closed her eyes, pressing her temples. In the barn she'd heard a woman plead for her son's life; she'd seen the swirling red haze wrap around Matthew as clearly as in her dream.

"Becky?" Matthew's slightly rough voice wrapped her like a silken caress. His warm hands smoothed her temples, his breath falling quickly upon her cold face. "Becky, wake up, lass."

When she looked at him, he bent over her, his dark eyes filled with uncertainty. *Matthew was here! Alive!* She clutched his shoulders and he half raised her into his arms.

"It's the dream, isn't it?" He stroked her hair, holding her tightly against him until the shuddering quieted. Rebecca's pale face seemed luminous in the lantern light, her eyes huge and haunted. She'd frightened him badly, having crumbled into a heap at his feet.

When she'd crossed the barn floor toward him, he'd seen her expression. Her lips had seemed like soft, pink petals, her green eyes flashing with fear in a too pale face. Matthew had seen that expression on another woman's face—his mother's. The hairs covering his body had risen when Rebecca's gaze had flowed over him, as though she saw something he could not.

Whatever bothered her lingered still. Her fingers clutched at his clean shirt. He forced himself not to wince as she grazed his wound. "So much blood . . . you were hurt."

"The bullet barely scratched my shoulder."

She plucked frantically at the shirt. Fearing that the sight of his injury would recall her dream, Matthew caught her fingers. He kissed them, then placed a cup of hot tea in her hand. "Drink this, lass. You need it. You can see my scratch in all its glory later. It's nothing, lass."

Her shimmering, fearful eyes watched him like a doe caught in a bear trap. "Hold me," she pleaded softly, lacing her cold fingers with his own.

He touched the back of her hand with his finger, insisting she drink the hot, strong tea. Over the rim of the cup Rebecca continued to gaze at him, the soft tendrils catching the light like a halo.

She finished the tea, allowing him to take the cup. Her fingers clutched at his shoulder, her nails sinking into his flesh. She trembled, leaning toward him. "Eric drugged me that night, Matthew," she began urgently. "I fought him, but . . ." Her lashes closed, shimmering with tears.

He brushed a solitary tear from her cheek, following its trail with the pad of his thumb. "Not now, lass."

Matthew forced his hands to steady, his hatred for Eric rising hotly within him. Brother or not, he'd kill him the next time they met. But for now, he had to tend to Rebecca's fears. He closed his eyes briefly, enclosing her shaking shoulders with his arms.

She trembled, seeking the shelter of his neck with her damp face. Gently, wrapping the afghan around her, Matthew lifted her into his arms to carry her into the front room. He sat on the large oak rocker, holding her against him like a child.

Rebecca's arms wound around his neck, holding him tightly. "Eric is gone, lass. He won't hurt you again," he murmured into her hair. Rocking her tenderly, Matthew gritted his teeth. Eric had to pay, and later he'd track his brother down, killing him on the spot.

In broken whispers and sobs Rebecca told him what happened that night, and he questioned her softly.

His rage grew, the slow, steady throb of his heart mingling with her pain. Forcing himself to calm, Matthew tucked her head beneath his chin, harboring her in the shelter of his body.

Matthew felt the fine bones tremble beneath his palm as he stroked the length of her taut back. When she gave her last, heaving sob, settling tiredly against him, Matthew cupped her chin. He lifted her worn face to his, placing his other palm possessively over the baby that rested within her womb. "This is my son, Becky. And no other's. What happened that night is past, and you're to forget it as you would a bad dream."

The child stirred against his hand, and Matthew's tears seared his lids. "My child," he repeated softly, kissing her lips lightly, tasting the salt of her tears. ·

Rebecca's hand covered the back of his, her fingers trembling. "I wanted to tell you . . ." she whispered achingly.

He trailed kisses across her cold cheeks, feeling her warm beneath the caress. "You have more to share, my love."

She leaned back against his arm. Her fingers gently traced the lines of his face as she whispered unevenly, "You'll think I'm crazy."

"Don't deny me now, Becky, love. What did you see out there in the barn when you looked at my blood?"

She lifted her fingers, staring at the washed, trembling tips. "So much blood." She lay back against him weakly. "I think you have something to tell me too. Eric's fear of the banshees, your mother . . ."

He smoothed her hair, lacing her golden fingers with his darker ones. "Aye. Perhaps I should."

He tucked Rebecca within the folds of the afghan, rocking her. The winter wind howling about the cabin, Matthew opened the memories that he had long ago forgotten.

"Ma was a believer in spells and potions of the light. Some say she had the 'sight.' Eric believed it." He shifted Rebecca easily, gathering her close to him. "In the Gaelic folklore a banshee is a female spirit that warns a family of death."

She caressed his throat, sighing tiredly. "So that's what you meant—"

"Aye. Ma was a gentle woman and well loved, but she had her ways and kept to them. Some called her touched."

By her drowsy weight and the easy breath stirring the hair

upon his chest, Matthew knew his wife slept. She badly needed the rest, and he feared for her drained strength.

His lips tightened, the rage running like hot steel through his veins. Eric had had the look of a mad hound, and he would return, keeping his promise.

Matthew closed his eyelids. The vision of Eric's body crawling upon Rebecca's sickened him. Trembling with hatred, he gathered his precious burden against him, felt her heart throb softly into his side, the gentle press of her full breasts nestling against him.

He felt their child stir against him and closed his eyes, leaning back against the chair. "This baby is mine, lass. As are you, till my dying day."

Chapter Twenty-three

The late March breeze swept through the pines, carrying the scent of fresh-cut timber across the small glade. Bumble-bees droned over the petals of the nearby buttercups. The tiny, waxy flowers grew through the patches of melting snow, welcoming spring. On a patch of sunlit ground Wolf sprawled like a king holding court.

Matthew pointed toward the trees bordering the valley and the snowy peaks of the mountains rising in the distance. "Have the loggers start on that stand of timber, Wes. Make that team of Percherons earn their oats. They can pull better on that steep grade than the Indian ponies."

Wes glanced at the big-boned draft horses, pulling logs to the new McKay mill. "At first, I thought they were just another of your fancy ideas, like the taffy-pulling machine you ordered for the way station."

Matthew breathed deeply, surveying the newly plowed fields. "The land, Wes, it's waiting."

"It's like a woman, isn't it?" Wes asked slowly. "Wild and beautiful, promising and fertile. She can make or break us on a whim."

Matthew chuckled at that. "So be it. We'll love her and she'll love us back."

"We'll keep her safe. And Mary, too," Wes added softly.

* * *

Rebecca tipped the bottle of linseed oil against her dusting cloth, her gaze roaming over the grazing Appaloosas and the two men in the distance. The baby kicked her side, and she placed her hand over it lovingly. The pressure had eased beneath her breasts, the baby positioning itself for birth.

She frowned, remembering the viperous nightmare that recurred more frequently. Eric had claimed the child, promising to return for it.

Straightening a crocheted doily on the dresser, she brushed the cloth across the carved cherry-wood dresser. Outside, the pine boughs swayed in the wind, and the sun slashed brightly through the window, touching the old mirror.

She had come to love the small mirror, hung on cedar logs. Enchanted by the hues of blue sky, green pine, and golden sun, Rebecca traced the dusting cloth across the walnut frame. The fabric caught on a sliver of wood, and when she tried to loosen the threads, the frame suddenly split apart at one corner.

A tattered yellow ribbon, wrapped around a tiny sheaf of aged paper, tumbled onto the dresser. Tarot cards, yellowed and frayed, spilled over them. Carefully Rebecca touched the frame, examining the tiny niche in the old clay. A thin gold band rested on a rough peg in the clay, and two small leather bags hung there like peas in a pod.

Gently she removed the ring and the tiny bags, placing them on the dresser. On an impulse Rebecca slid the ring onto her finger. She untied the ribbon, easing the old paper to read a woman's delicate handwriting.

"I've lost track of time. I go to my saints soon, having spent my life with my dear Abraham. Beloved man, he refuses to listen to my tales, my fears. 'Blarney,' he says of my Gaelic faith. Some call me mad, but the Indians believe in my powers. I know the truth of what can be. The future can be seen, my sons. How I will miss you both."

The black ink was blurred, as though from a falling tear.

"Eric, my firstborn. Brought from the Emerald Isle. I see nothing for you but the devil and the death cards. How I prayed to the Mother Mary for you, then to the voices that tell me the future.''

Rebecca felt a chill move up her spine, tingling strangely in her throat. It lingered, then passed as she continued reading. ''I feel,'' the woman wrote. ''I see in dreams that come by day or at midnight. I saw my firstborn kill my two babies in the dreams. I saw him grown into a fine red-haired giant of a man. I saw his father, the high-and-mighty gentry, throw me to the ground and have his crude way.''

The next line, slanted and trembling, swept Rebecca's air from her lungs. ''A seer, they called me when they cast me from the village. A witch woman. Perhaps it is true, but the gift has not failed me in my life. It rings true. The cards tell all. There is power in seeing the future and there is pain. The velvety black-haired child that nursed my breast is my true son, given to me by Abraham. Abraham, my heart, my blood. The dark, laughing son will mate with one such as I, a seeress. She denies her gift yet it serves her well. Beware, for the red son must kill the dark or roam forever with the banshees screaming for him. The red must devour the heart of the dark or die—the key to both lives lies within the midnight rose. Nancy.''

Rebecca closed her eyes, forbidding the vision to come. Yet it came, stirring to life with the soft scent of crushed rose petals. She felt cool satin slide across her cheek, a warmth tingling on her shoulders like an embrace.

She gave herself to the dream, opening to the beckoning that settled around her like a warm, soft cloak.

A wolf, foaming at the mouth, its matted pelt shaded blood-red, leapt out at her, fangs bared.

Matthew's pale face shimmered beneath a thin sheet of ice, then was gone. A baby whimpered and the wolf turned toward it.

Rebecca gripped the dresser, her heart thudding like the beat of Indian drums. Within her the baby moved, pressing against her ribs. Her husband's scent drifted around her.

She shivered, forcing herself to breathe. Eric would return for the child. He would kill for her. . . .

Alongside the note the woman had written in tiny script as though it were an afterthought, "I love both my sons and my faith. But by the Holy Mother, there is another side."

With shaking fingers, her heart beating wildly over her unborn child, Rebecca unwrapped one of the tiny pouches. A red curl tied by a black ribbon and dried grasses fell against her finger, pricking the tip slightly. From the other bag she slid a wedge of dark doeskin, wrapped around a raven-black lock of hair and crumbling rose petals and scented herbs. *My true son . . .*

Pressing her fingers to her mouth to keep from crying out, Rebecca met her own reflection in the old mirror.

Another woman had dreamed and feared. And saw.

She remembered the poem; Matthew had called her his "midnight rose."

The red mist swirled around her, rising, cloaking her in a chill.

"Jean's seed orders are being shipped from Seattle. We should have a hauler in here with fruit trees and hops any day now. The man has a large family. If he wants lumber instead of cash, give it to him. Tell him we'll supply room and board if he wants to send his boys. I'll keep an eye on them." Matthew looked up, pausing in his directions to Wes.

In the sun-mottled morning shadows of the firs he spotted a yellow skirt. "Damn, I thought Becky was resting."

Ignoring Wes, Matthew strode toward her. He rounded a red-barked pine just as Rebecca grinned up at him impishly. Placing his hands on his hips, Matthew shook his head. "I thought the doctor told you to stay off your feet, with the baby due any day. Now *I'm* telling you."

"Yes, sir, Mr. McKay," she agreed meekly, her eyes twinkling. She tilted her head back and closed her eyes, pursing her lips. "I brought you a piece of taffy."

The candy lay in her slender hand before she tucked it behind her back. "I came for my kiss."

Rebecca stood amid the buttercups in the patch of sun filtering through the tall pines. Her raven hair drifting alongside her face, to curl around her hips, she seemed no more than a young girl.

She wore his coat now, allowing for her burgeoning stomach, and Matthew reached out to button it against the cold, piercing wind. He'd remember her, round with his child, the pink of her cheeks, for eternity.

"Hussy," he murmured, pleased by the saucy way she could stop him in his tracks. He brushed his lips across hers lightly. "Are you happy now?"

Her eyes opened, flashing green up at him. She plopped the candy in his open palm, then licked her fingers with an innocence that caused him to heat. Matthew chewed the candy, yet thought of sweeter fare as she turned aside to study the valley.

His shirt stretched across Rebecca's full breasts as she brushed her hand down a pine branch. "I should say not. The high-and-mighty Lord McKay ordered me not to ride while I'm carrying his child. Yet he rides where he wants and all the farmers' wives roll their eyes. I'm not blind, you know. I saw Maudie Langtree making eyes at you."

She plucked at a button on his shirt, wedging her fingertip between the cloth to stroke the warm planes of his chest. Slanting a glance up at him, Rebecca nuzzled the exposed area. "Laying down the law, indeed . . . and my father backing you on his last visit. Wind Dancer needs riding—he's too fat and getting half wild. It's time to start breaking the ponies to the bit. The whole countryside is watching me like an egg about to hatch. I'm fat, I waddle like a duck. You smiled back at Maudie, Matthew. I saw your dimple . . . and the flash of your black eyes."

Matthew brushed his lips across hers, smiling at her play. A man could be proud when Rebecca McKay came calling for him. The lady had ways to make him feel like jelly. After the child she'd make him pay at her leisure.

"You've kissed the Blarney stone, Mrs. McKay. Maude or any other woman doesn't hold a candle to my wife."

Matthew cupped the full weight of her breasts, savoring the strong current of desire washing over them. "You're my heart, lass. Bearing my child has made you even more precious, more beautiful to me.''

Sighing, Rebecca slid her arms around his waist. Holding him tightly, she rested her head upon his chest.

His son moved between them, protesting the cramped space, and Matthew's hands encircled her. He smoothed her back, rubbing the low ache gently, then slid his palms to rest lightly upon her stomach. The new life rippled a tiny elbow or knee, and Matthew felt the awe spread over him.

Against her temple he murmured, ''You hold my child, Becky. You've wound yourself around my heart.''

The slight breeze lifted a silky strand of hair, winding it around Matthew's sun-warmed neck. She raised her soft, parted lips to his. ''How I fought—''

''Aye, that you did.'' He lifted her face higher, studying her lightly tanned skin, her high, slanted cheekbones, tugged the soft lobe of her ear. ''You still fight me, in your way.''

Her lids lowered, the tips of her lashes gleaming in the sunlight, and a blush stole softly up her cheeks. ''Matthew, I've baked pies and mended socks. I've even scrubbed your back.''

''Aye. And then I scrubbed your back and your—''

''Matthew!'' Her hot cheek rested against his, her fingers covering his lips.

Matthew chuckled, remembering her wild temper when he'd forbidden her to ride Wind Dancer. Locking her in his arms, he kissed her forehead, felt her sigh. It pleased him when she drew on his strength, leaning against him. He kneaded her spine, feeling her arch against his touch. ''You've been the perfect bride. But you keep your dreams, lass. The circumstances of our marriage still chafe your pride. The baby will be here soon, and you haven't given yourself to me fully.''

She rested a moment, the stillness of the glade wrapping around them. Slowly the flat of her hand skimmed his lean stomach, and Matthew knew he'd been fenced from her secret bowers.

He groaned, his body hardening at her light touch. ''There

will be time for wanting later . . . when my son is sleeping in his crib and not in your soft body. We'll celebrate with that trip to Seattle," Matthew murmured, drawn by the sweet scent of her hair. He twisted a loose lock around his finger, watching the bright strand catch the sun.

It was then that he saw her naked fear, felt her hands tremble upon him. Taking her face in his hands, he stroked her face. "What is it, lass? Is the baby coming?"

She swallowed, the thrust of her swollen stomach between them. "Eric will come back," she said.

Matthew shook his head, yet knew that his brother would return. "No, lass. You're safe."

"It's the baby he wants," she whispered in a tone so soft, the slight breeze blew it away.

A large tear seeped from her lashes, the tiny prism catching the sun as it slid down her cheek. "And me," she added, the words torn from her.

"A madman makes promises," Matthew murmured, fearing for her. Rebecca was too close to having the baby. He lifted her into his arms, a precious burden.

She sniffed against his shoulder, resting lightly in his grasp. Dabbing her damp lashes with his collar, she whispered, "You'll strain a muscle, Matthew. Put me down."

"Hush now, woman." For once she settled against him, her arms looped around his neck. Above her shining head, Matthew's expression was grim. Eric had vanished like a nightmare, no rumors marking his passing.

The spring breeze was scented of freshly turned earth and newly cut timber. An ebony tendril caught against his bottom lip; another snagged against his rough, hard jaw. Only death could prevent Eric from returning.

Rebecca shivered, clinging to him, her face pressed against his neck. Matthew's arms tightened possessively.

When Rebecca was out of harm, his son nursing at her breast, he'd hunt Eric down like a rabid dog.

Emma eased her round body onto Jean's lap as he watched the embers of the evening fire. Kicking off her moccasins, she ran her hand across the soft buckskins covering his chest. La! There was just something about the man that would enchant her until the end of her days. "What are you thinking about, honey? Moving down to the Methow?"

As always, his palm found her stomach, resting possessively over the child. She smiled secretly, smoothing his sleek hair back from his temple. Jean was her man until the end of her days, but as smart as he was, he didn't know that she carried two babes within her womb.

She traced the black lashes, the long, narrow face of her lover. He'd given her life, a deep happiness she'd never thought possible. He kissed the tips of her fingers in his courtly manner, and she felt the wild blush tinge her cheeks, as it always did at his touch.

Jean had given her so much. It would be her gift to him, the two babies.

He drew a soft blanket across her against the night's chill, tucking her head beneath his chin. His silence worried her.

"Jean?"

"Yes, my dove?" His melodic voice carried a note of aloofness, his fingers toying with her auburn locks. "Are you comfortable?"

She giggled, leaning back to look up at him. "You're the squashed one, honey. I'm as fat as a hog ready for market."

He continued stroking her hair, watching the red-orange embers thoughtfully. Emma watched him a moment, then settled down to stare at the coals. Jean had that closed Indian look, the one that spelled trouble.

"You're worrying about Matt and Rebecca, aren't you, Jean?" she asked quietly, sensing his withdrawal. "You've been like this ever since that chief stopped by, talking about the big red-haired man coming down from the Yukon. Honey, that could be anyone . . . not only Eric. There are plenty of men with red hair."

"It's Eric," Jean stated quietly, his fingers tightening in her hair. "The red wolf comes to claim his cub."

Shivering, Emma gathered the blanket around her. "Jean, please don't talk that Indian dream nonsense. La! It makes pretty words, but you can scare the woolies out of me when you get so serious. And besides, Matt is pretty handy when it comes to fighting.''

Jean wearily leaned his head against the rocker. ''When the time comes, Matthew will not be able to kill his brother. Another must cut the throat of the wolf.''

Emma sat upright, her blue eyes wide. ''Jean, don't you think for one minute that I'll let you go alone. I'm not about to let you mix that crazy redskin medicine with Eric's madness.''

''Ma chère,'' Jean murmured, opening his eyes. ''He must be killed.''

Her freckles shone on her pale cheeks, her mouth trembling. ''If you go, Jean,'' she began in a low, husky tone, ''don't look for me here, because I'll be right on your tail.''

''Rebecca is in the river of my life, too, my dove.''

''River of your life?'' Emma scooted off his lap clumsily. She faced him like a cornered, spitting kitten. ''She has her man—Matthew! He'll take care of her *and* Eric. Don't you dare go traipsing off, Jean. I warn you. Up to now I've let you lead me around like a mule after a dangling carrot—you and your Frenchie sweet talk—but by Jehoshaphat, you won't go anywhere without me.''

She tossed her curls impatiently. ''Not now. No! Not ever, Jean. You're not leaving me.'' Stamping her foot, Emma wagged her finger at Jean as he came lithely to his feet. ''River of your life or not, I'm going with you, Jean. And I don't want any back talk.''

For once Jean was quiet. Emma shook her head once, then straightened her hair with elaborate dignity. ''You heathens think you know all there is to know about this 'river-of-life' falderol. Well, Emma Dupres doesn't let her man go easy. Like it or not, you overgrown savage''—she sniffed haughtily—''I have some say in things, and I like those two people too. I owe them one.''

''But *chère*—''

Emma's chin rose. ''You just figure out the hows! Stay or

go, but I'll be at your side, and if I have to crawl through a swamp of alligators—''

"*Chère*, be reasonable. Our child comes—''

"Fiddlesticks! You men think you can just pack up and go when the notion hits you . . . free as the breeze. Mind me, now, Jean: Okanogan Mary said she saw Indian women drop their babies in the hop fields, wrap 'em up, and just keep on working. If you think I'm one whit less than any of your people, then you can go to blue blazes!''

Emma's face flamed as she trembled, trying to reclaim her dignity. "You're my man, and where you go, I go. I'll start packing now. We'll take the baby's things with us.''

Knowing better than to argue with Emma in her aroused state, Jean watched with pride as her rounded hips swayed beneath her skirts.

She turned, glaring at him over her shoulder. "Don't you dare start thinking you can sweet-talk me out of this, Jean. I'm as mad as a hornet, so get crackin'!''

Chapter Twenty-four

From the forest high above the McKay valley, Eric watched Rebecca wander in his mother's rose garden. His single eye squinted against the afternoon sun, pinning his sister-in-law's burgeoning body.

The March wind wildly whipped his long hair against his head and Eric impatiently brushed it aside. Placing his shoulder against the trunk of a pine, he lifted the field glasses from their leather pouch.

Large patches of melting snow glistened in the bright sunlight as Eric focused on Rebecca. She tugged the large coat closer to her, the rounded bulge of her stomach evident.

"It's my brat she bears, not his," he raved to his companion, a burly seaman with lank hair and a round, pockmarked face. "I had Her Royal Highness screaming for it. Aye," Eric muttered, slapping the red bark of a lofty pine. "That's my child resting in her belly, not Matthew's."

The seaman rolled his hunched shoulders beneath the dark blue jacket. His teeth protruded when he twitched a toothpick between his thick lips. "Forget about the bitch, Eric. Let's get to the Chinaman's gold."

"Shut up! Don't you see? By rights the woman is mine, her land—the Chinaman's gold—is mine too," Eric said with a snarl. "Once Matthew is dead, she'll sign everything over to me just to keep the brat. It's just a matter of time, Boswick, before she sees things my way. Why settle for half a loaf when you can take it all?"

Down in the ranch yard, Mary crossed to Rebecca, carefully holding a rolled sheaf of paper. Watching Mary, Eric's tall body went taut.

He spat a stream of tobacco into the budding green thicket. "Those damn thorny sticks? Roses. So she's taken up all of Ma's fancies. Witches, the both of them, with screams like banshees. Aye, she'll be screaming all right." He sneered, turning his glasses toward the two men riding toward the house.

"That cowpuncher and Matthew. Look at that." His mouth curled into an ugly grimace. "Riding up across my land just as pretty as you please, taking what is rightfully mine. Everything from the new mill to the fields will be mine, as well as the mill—*my* empire."

Boswick picked his teeth calmly. "Let's dig out the Chinese gold pokes, then head for calmer seas, mate."

Eric turned on him, enraged. "Damn your worthless hide! The gold is up here, but no one knows where the mine is for certain. My mother knew but died before I could get it out of her. She kept her secrets, but they're locked in the house if I know Ma. That bitch in Matthew's bed is of the same mold. She'll scent out the map like a hound after a fresh kill."

He breathed heavily, his hand reaching for Boswick's whiskey bottle. "Here, give me a swig of that." He drank deeply, wiping his lips with the back of his sleeve. "She's found Ma's secrets by now. She'll know where to find the gold mine. Listen, Boswick: That Indian woman is going to walk on the mountain trail over to the old Baroque place after their lunch hour—I've been studying her habits. Bring her and that papoose to me."

"Ah, Eric . . . I ain't in the mood for red meat."

Eric's smile was cold. "She's bait, my friend."

Rebecca folded the small wedge of tanned leather around the black lock of hair, tucking it carefully back in its hiding place. A warm draft slid across her fingertips like a caress as she replaced the concealing walnut frame.

Leaning against her thighs, Wolf whined as he looked up at his mistress.

"Nancy stitched a map on the deerskin, Wolf. She marked the old Indian trail crossing Papa's north quarter . . . and the creek marking the land for my dowry. Then the one gold Indian bead between the markings. Why?"

She skimmed the mirror with her fingers, wondering about the other woman who had touched Matthew's life. Just then the last slice of the day's sunshine crept through the window. The beam touched the silvered surface in a rainbow of hues. "I'll keep him safe, Nancy. Your son grows more precious to me each day," she whispered, hearing a rustling noise in her front room. "That may be him now. Come, Wolf."

Okanogan Mary stood inside the cabin door, wringing her hands. Her huge brown eyes turned woefully toward Rebecca, tears spilling over her lids. Her round cheek bore a darkening bruise; a bloody scratch ran the length of her throat. She gathered her blanket around her, shivering despite the warmth of the room.

Rebecca padded to the Indian girl, wrapping her arm around her shoulders. "Mary, what's wrong? Where's Little Matt?"

Mary touched her cheek, wincing. "I fall. Leave Little Matt." Mary glanced around the cabin fearfully. "Wes get *moos-moos*?" she asked hoarsely.

"Wes and Matthew went to trade for cattle just after lunch, remember?" Rebecca hugged the smaller woman, feeling her shudder beneath the blanket. "Come in, Mary. It's only twilight. They'll be back later tonight. I'll send Wes straight on home."

Mary's eyes rolled wildly. "No. McKay man hurt in mountain, want Woman-Who-Holds-the-Lightning. Mary bring help to him."

"Matthew is hurt? Where is he?" A cold draft entered the room, chilling her. The logging crew was four miles upstream, camping out for the night. The nearest neighbor would take hours to reach at night.

"In mountains. McKay man hurt. No Wes . . . come." Mary looked away from Rebecca. "Him say dog stay. Come . . . help."

Within minutes Rebecca had saddled Wind Dancer. Packing a warm blanket and salve, she tucked a tiny bottle of laudanum within her saddlebags. Dressed in Matthew's loose shirt and his rolled-up trousers, she eased herself gently up into the saddle. Mary ran into the darkness, beckoning for her to follow.

Taking a deep, steadying breath, Rebecca tried to soothe the prancing stallion. "My time is too near, Wind Dancer." She leaned to rub the velvety ear as the great horse quieted beneath her. "Take care."

She felt each smooth stride as the Appaloosa left the ranch yard. Wolf loped easily beside the stallion's hooves. "Go back, Wolf," she ordered. "Stay."

Whining, the great dog paused. "Stay," she repeated firmly. "Matthew must be afraid of the bounty hunters."

Leaving the valley, rising to the foothills, Rebecca gathered Matthew's greatcoat around her against the evening chill. Her fingers gripped the saddle horn, easing the jostling of her unborn baby.

Mary rounded a clump of thicket, and Rebecca followed her trail, picking around the empty holes left by the pulled tree stumps. Wind Dancer whinnied wildly, rearing on his back hooves.

Two men leapt out of the bushes, the larger man gripping the stallion's reins.

He held a lantern up to his leering face. The grotesque shadows outlined Eric's heavy jowls; his shiny, leather eye patch. "We meet again, dear sister-in-law. The slut who crawls from brother to brother."

He clamped a bruising hand around her wrist, jerking her from the saddle. She fell heavily, the greatcoat exposing her rounded stomach as she lay on a small, soft bush.

Dazed by the fall, she barely felt Eric's fingers pull her

braid, bringing her to her knees. "Ah, that's where you should be. Down on your knees and begging to spread your legs for me," Eric crooned madly.

Drawing his knife, he trailed the flat edge of the blade down her cheek. The baby lurched within her, and she barely felt the cold steel slide along her skin. "Look at this, Boswick. Skin like mother's milk."

The baby stirred again, folding tiny elbows and knees within her womb. She groaned, feeling the pain surround her. "Missing me, beauty?" Eric asked softly, drawing her to her feet.

His hand roamed down her body, seeking the full curve of her breasts. "Aye, hair like the midnight hour, and skin soft as rose petals. You're a beauty, all right, the midnight rose," he murmured softly in a tone that reminded her of Matthew's deep voice. Fleetingly his hand curved upon her abdomen, feeling the tiny, restless life within. "My brat," he whispered in gentle awe.

Surprised by his proud possession, Rebecca wondered about the crooked trails of Eric's mind. "Where is Matthew?" she managed through dry lips.

"Matthew?" Eric roared, the night animals scurrying for safety. "Ah, she wants my brother, Boswick." Lowering his voice, he loomed over her. "You'll see him soon enough. But not just now, witch."

Wind Dancer pranced, fighting the reins held by Boswick. Eric crouched, snarling. "Quiet that damn animal or I'll shoot him through the head!"

Fearing for the stallion, she obeyed. "Wind-Dancer, easy . . ."

A child whimpered, and Okanogan Mary ran toward Little Matt. Clutching him in her arms, she ran into the thickets. Eric fired one shot into the darkness, cursing. "Boswick, find that damn Indian bitch and kill her! She's trouble!"

The heavily built man tore through the night, his footsteps crashing in the brush. Another pistol shot cut though the starry night. Eric scowled in the direction of Boswick. "He'll be a while. She can run like a deer."

''Where is Matthew?'' Rebecca repeated softly, her fears chilling her beneath the heavy coat.

Eric's furious expression beat down upon her. ''It's always him—the favored son, the beloved husband! You'll forget about him soon enough, my fine, bonnie bride. Once we're married, I'll treat you like a queen, giving you anything you want.''

Rebecca grew still, feeling the cold wash of her fear rise. Eric had gone completely mad. His eye tenderly surveyed her face. To protect her baby she would give her soul. To protect her husband she would give her life. ''What do you want, Eric?''

''That's better, my fine lass,'' he crooned almost tenderly. She shuddered when he leaned down to her, kissing her cheek. ''Aye, you have that woman smell—the clean scent of roses and fresh-baked bread clinging to you. My lass and mine only. How's my child?''

Stunned by his gentle conversation, Rebecca couldn't answer. He shook his head as though trying to clear it, then gazed down at her for a moment. His eye seemed to deepen in its socket, its hot stare at her condemning. ''Where is the mine, the Chinaman's mine of my mother?''

He trailed the cold steel down her face once more. ''You would have found the map by now, witch woman.'' He snarled. ''You have the sight, just as Ma did. Where is the mine?''

Rebecca closed her eyes against the cold, swirling red mist. Behind her lids the tiny wedge of tanned leather appeared, each detail clear.

Eric's large thumb rose to press a threat against her throat. ''It's on your land, the northeast quarter of the Klein spread, isn't it?'' he asked too softly. ''Up in the rocks where the Chinese ditches are? Well, I've been all over those rocks and haven't found a sign. Where is it, damn you?''

His voice lowered menacingly. ''Then we'll wait here and I'll shoot Matthew the minute he comes into my sight. I've been wanting to do it, anyway—for a long time. In fact, I once put a price on his head, but the bastard lived, anyway.

Ma charmed him, you know—didn't want him smothered to death like the rest of the McKay litter. Ma rolled beneath that old black-haired bastard, let his pups suck at her paps. Pushed me aside, Ma did . . . whoring for the old man.''

Feeling Eric's pain and hatred enfold her, Rebecca knew she had to protect her child and her husband. "I do know where the gold is, Eric. I'll take you there.''

He took one heavy breath, studying her darkly. "It's only to get started, Rebecca. Once that gold is in my hands, I'll make you rightly mine. I can do it then . . . you'll see," he said, raving softly, winding his hand in her hair. He studied her single braid intently, then the knife flashed in the lantern light, cutting the binder.

Eric tenderly eased her hair free of its braid, weaving his fingers through the heavy mass. He arranged it lovingly around her shoulders, his intense expression reminding her of Matthew for a moment.

But Eric had gone mad. That single thought caused her to grow still, draw from her inner strength—she had to protect the child and Matthew at her own risk. Matthew would find her; she had to play for time.

Eric's face hovered over hers, and she forced herself to raise her hand, placing it alongside his bearded jowl. "We'll get the gold, Eric. Just as you wish," she whispered calmly. "But we must be careful of the child . . . your child.''

As though dazed, his eye prowled down to her rounded stomach. "Aye, lass, the child," he repeated, as though re-membering something from long ago. He dropped to his knees, wrapping his arms around her thighs. Placing his head against her stomach, he rubbed the mound lovingly with his cheek.

When the baby stirred, he grinned up at her almost boy-ishly. "We'll all go to Hawaii, live like kings until the land is mine. My midnight rose and our son.''

Fighting to still the nausea within her, Rebecca forced her-self to smile. "But first the gold?''

He rose, buttoning her coat. "You must keep warm, Re-

becca, for the child. Yes, I need the gold, and you'll take me
to it now, my sweet?''

When she nodded, he bent to kiss her cheek with hus-
bandly tenderness. She ached to rub her skin clean of his
touch, forcing herself to smile again. ''Aye, that's a good
lass,'' he crooned. ''Here, let me help you onto your horse.''

Lifting her as lightly as a feather, Eric placed her on Wind
Dancer. He shook out a blanket and gently draped it on her
thighs. Looking up at her, Eric watched the moon rise over
the crest of her head. He studied her for a long moment, the
silver light touching her rippling black hair. ''Aye, the Ma-
donna,'' he whispered, taking the stallion's reins in his hand.
''The midnight rose.''

Mounting a sleek Arabian stallion with prancing feet, Eric
asked, ''Which way, Rebecca?''

A wolf howled from the mountain as the moon rose higher.
The pine boughs formed a lacy curtain between the silvery
disk and Rebecca. It was then that a warm, soft summer
breeze swept across her stomach as though a woman's loving
hand had touched her womb. Rebecca drew on the touch,
needing the strength against Eric's insanity. She smiled, lovingly smoothing her hand over the baby.

Eric paused, watching her in the bright moonlight. ''You're
so like her,'' he murmured huskily. ''Matt doesn't know,
does he, my midnight rose? He doesn't know about your
gift.'' He lifted his head proudly. ''Only me. I know what
you can see. Shall we go?''

Through the next three hours Rebecca fought the strain of
riding the mountain trail. The lantern swayed in Eric's grasp,
casting an eerie light upon the rough trunks of the pines.
Periodically he dismounted and led Wind Dancer through a
dense thicket or a blue-white patch of snow. The stallion, as
though sensing the danger to Rebecca, was easily handled.
Within her the baby settled into a peaceful slumber.

''Go along the creek, Eric.'' Rebecca twisted in the saddle
uncomfortably, her body protesting the strain.

The stars twinkled above the pine boughs as the wolf pack

howled, their song chilling. The warm wind became strong, curling around Rebecca and carrying the howls to Eric.

Walking on the smooth path, Eric tensed, looking toward the sound. "Pa had a dog that sounded like that and could call the wolves from their dens. One of my boys shot one of the monsters, and the pack tore him apart like so much deer meat."

Small animals scurried into the brush, and Eric stopped, his head tilted as he listened closely. "Aye, the pack is hungry like that night," he whispered. "How much farther?"

"There's a rock slide coming up, and then the Chinese mine." Rebecca tensed, aching. "Tell me about your mother, Eric," she said, feeling the baby stir and angle for a better position within her taut abdomen.

"It's cold up here. Smells like death," he muttered, shooting uneasy glances into the forest. "She was like you."

"Me? I thought she was small and redheaded."

Eric pivoted, his fists tense at his thighs. "It was always the bastard's brat she favored, never me. Once I had her, then he took her . . . and she laughed as he—" Throwing back his head, he roared with a tormented laughter. "I saw them. She thought I didn't, but I did."

At once Rebecca saw a slight breeze lift Eric's wild hair. In a lightning-quick flash she saw a young boy's pain, his longing to be the single love of his mother's life. "She loved you," Rebecca whispered, watching Eric's tormented face.

He laughed coldly. "Aye, but she loved the old he-goat more. Enough to bear his brats. I let one of the litter live, and I always regretted that. Matthew has been her curse to me."

Eric looked sharply at her, his hair tossing wildly. "But I have what he claims is his—what was his, is mine now—the true son. By taking his heart he'll die. Ma told me that once. You think he'll come for you, don't you? I'll have you now to seal the bargain—my son won't mind sharing."

He moved as though to take her from the saddle and Rebecca drew Wind Dancer back. She needed more time; she knew Matthew would follow. "The mine is not much farther. It's behind the bent tree."

She swallowed, touching her lips with her tongue. The warm wind touched her cheek like a kiss, and Rebecca followed her instincts, trusting her senses.

Perhaps she'd heard about the Chinese cache; perhaps Nancy's thoughts had become her own. In the wispy vision that floated before her, Rebecca saw gold hidden by brush and rocks.

Eric paused, torn between her and his lust for the gold. Stoking his greed, Rebecca urged, "You'll have to pry off the brush. The old placer mine is marked by a rock wall, and there's a wooden door covering the stash."

He nodded briskly, speaking softly, reverently. "Aye, you're like her—a witch woman seeing dreams. Soon, my lass, we'll have it all."

Leaving her, he ran a few steps and paused, scanning the moonlit scenery. He placed the lantern on a large, flat rock near a rippling stream. "It's there—the tree—just as you said."

Running back to her, Eric held up his arms. "Come . . . rest. I'll fix you a pallet to rest upon while I dig for the gold."

"I don't like this, Matthew," Wes said quietly. Letting his horse follow Duke up the mountain trail, he scanned the eerie stillness. "Rebecca had no reason to take Wind Dancer out on a night like this, especially since the baby could come at any time."

Following Wolf quietly, Matthew felt the warm wind lift the hair at his collar. Rebecca had seemed happy enough, waiting for the baby. Was she happy, or did she still hold their marriage against him?

His fingers laced though Duke's reins so tightly that they ached. The warm Chinook wind was melting the snow, yet one wrong step could send Wind Dancer plummeting down a steep cliff.

The wolves howled beneath the silvery moon, and Wolf paused, lifting his head for an open-throated lament.

Waiting for Wolf to continue, Matthew lit a cheroot and settled back in his saddle. The Chinook caught the smoke, swirling it around his face as he wondered about his wife.

The mountain trail was dangerous, yet the fastest route to the land that was Rebecca's dowry— Matthew felt a cold chill despite the warmth of his sheepskin-lined leather coat. The rough, rocky land was unfit for anything but mining. Mining! One man wanted that land—Eric.

The thoughts of his brother and Rebecca caused Matthew's belly to knot. Yet every sense he possessed told him that Eric's hand lurked in the mystery. He wanted the Chinese miners' gold.

When Wolf moved, Matthew felt his blood freeze. He tossed the cheroot into a patch of snow. "Let's go, boy," he urged softly. "Let's find Becky."

Both men remained silent during the next half hour. Then Wolf stopped, sniffing a muddy clearing. Dismounting, Matthew and Wes searched the dark, wet earth and the nearby brush.

Wes crouched, motioning for Matthew to follow. He struck a match, the sulfur smell sharp in his nostrils. "Big men moving around here. From the looks of it, they were here some time. One has new boots with a fancy heel; the other has worn heels."

Wolf padded to the crouched men, leaning against his master's broad shoulder. Matthew traced the footprints with his finger. "A woman's boots . . . an Indian woman's moccasins too." He nodded toward a bush. "Someone landed in that, broke the limbs. The moccasins lead off in that direction . . . one man ran after her."

Wes met the younger man's knowing stare. "There's more than wolves and coyotes out there, right, Matt?"

"Those are Becky's boots."

"And Mary's moccasins," Wes added, studying Matthew's dark face intently. "She wears the right one a mite thin at the heel. Let's have it, Matt. What have you been chewing on since we started to follow Wolf?''

''Eric. He's big enough to make these tracks; he'd be wearing specially made boots.''

''Damn crazy bastard.'' Wes spat into the brush, wiping his lips with the back of his hand. ''What's he after this time?''

Matthew stood, drawing his pistol from his shoulder holster. He checked the cartridges, then shot a hard stare at Wes. ''I suggest you do the same. My brother doesn't know what mercy means.''

Wes nodded, examining his gun. ''Rebecca is with him, and so is Mary.''

''Looks that way. Let's go, Wolf. Find her.'' Settling into Duke's saddle, Matthew's face was grim. If his guess was right, his brother would have to die this time.

In another hour the moon slipped behind a cloud bank. The two men moved more slowly, alternately taking the lead to walk through the dangerous patches. Wolf moved ahead, restless and disturbed as the pack called to him.

''The dog is part wolf, Matt. How do we know he's not leading us on a wild-goose chase?'' Wes asked quietly.

''He won't,'' Matthew returned curtly. ''He's on the scent of a trail.''

''Good enough. I'll kill the bastard if he's touched my Mary.'' Just then Wolf stopped, lifting his nose to the wind. Lowering his head, his tail wagging, he slid into the underbrush.

''He's got something,'' Matthew whispered. He stroked Duke's muzzle, quieting the uneasy bay as he dismounted. Tying the reins to a limb, Matthew drew his pistol, following Wolf.

Before Wes could enter the brush, Matthew stepped back onto the trail.

In his arms Little Matt looked at Wes drowsily. Matthew handed the baby to Wes, then laid his hand on Wes's shoulder. ''It's Mary,'' he said quietly. ''She's not pretty. But she managed to wrap the baby in a warm blanket before she died. It was a big man wearing worn heels.''

Locked in his pain, Wes felt Little Matt's chubby hand wrap in his hair, tugging it. He glanced down at the round-faced toddler, who sucked his thumb, watching him with sleepy eyes. "How's it going, little fella?'' Wes asked softly, feeling the baby snuggle against him. "It's just you and me now.''

Matthew swung into his saddle. "I'm going on, Wes.''

Wes looked up, his eyes damp. "Give me a minute and I'll be along.''

"You can't. You've got Mary and the baby to tend to. We'll be fine,'' Matthew added softly. "Little Matt might cry at the wrong time . . .''

Wes nodded sadly, the tears trailing freely down his cheeks. "Work the bastard over good before you kill him, Matthew. For Mary.''

With a grim nod Matthew turned to follow Wolf. "Go on, boy.''

The dawn had not yet come, yet the birds stirred restlessly in the shadowy pines bordering the mine. The damp night chill clung to Rebecca's coat and blanket, and she shivered. The ropes, wrapped expertly around her wrists and ankles, chafed against her torn skin. Her burdened body ached with fatigue, yet she found herself dozing almost peacefully.

The cry of the wolves had ceased, the animals in the underbrush moving quietly as though not to disturb her. The Chinook played around her now, lifting her hair gently, soothing. . . .

She watched Eric chopping at the small brush with a small ax. He was close to the mine now, swearing when he dug through a rocky slide to the underbrush.

Several times during the last two hours he'd come to rest at her side. He held her like a tender lover. He stroked her wild river of hair, wrapping his fingers in silky strands.

"My midnight rose," he crooned in an oft-repeated litany.

She shivered again, closing her lids to will Matthew to her side. He had to come, for her sake and their baby's. She turned her face to Matthew's collar, searching for his scent. The scent of his cheroots melded with another scent that reminded her of his dark eyes—loving eyes that caressed and warmed.

Rubbing her cheek against the rough wool greatcoat, Rebecca curled her legs higher to provide a warm nest for their child.

She dozed, seeking a heat that followed her spine, as though Matthew's body lay against hers. Eric swore sharply, and she roused momentarily, forcing her lids open. He chopped feverishly now, tearing in the brush.

At her back the warmth shifted restlessly, then curled around her again. A huge gray muzzle rested on her knee, watching her with yellow, slanted eyes. The wolf's companion, a small female, nestled against Rebecca's back and head. The female provided an intimate warmth that touched Rebecca's face.

A thought went scurrying around her brain, snagging and drifting away—the wolves were friends, guarding her.

Too weary to care, Rebecca allowed herself to slip back into sleep.

Minutes or hours passed, then a man's roaring curse sliced through the sounds of the new dawn. Boswick crashed through the brush, panting. His eyes rolled back as he fired shots into the underbrush near Rebecca.

Struggling to sit, she tossed back a wild strand of hair and saw Eric running toward Boswick. His fist crashed into the heavier man's jowls, sending him staggering into a thicket.

Boswick aimed the pistol at Eric menacingly. "Your bitch was laying with them wolves," he said with a snarl. "She's as crazed as you."

Eric crouched, his eye flashing in the pink shades of dawn. "She's not to be hurt, Boswick. Harm her and I'll break every bone in your body, one by one."

Boswick paled. "You would too. I seen you do worse."

His gaze slid fearfully to Rebecca. "Why is she sleeping with those wolves? Why ain't you shooting 'em?"

"They're keeping her warm, you daft bastard!" Eric roared, as if the other man were an idiot. "She's got the powers, the same as Ma!"

Boswick shivered, his hand trembling as he held it up. "You've gone 'round the bend, mate. Let's get the gold and leave the slut."

"Aye, we'll get the gold," Eric agreed too softly. "But you shoot a wolf, and its mate will tear out your guts and leave you to strangle in them!"

Boswick shivered again, backing away from his companion. "I'll help you get the gold, then I want it split right here."

"Agreed." As though nothing had happened, Eric turned his back on the pistol and returned to chopping the brush. "Drag this aside, I'm almost there."

Following him and glancing uneasily at Rebecca, who sat motionless, Boswick reholstered his pistol. "She's the one the Indians call Woman-Who-Holds-the-Lightning, ain't she?"

"She's handy with a gun," Eric agreed, throwing a large clump of brush at the seaman.

Boswick pitched the clump aside. "I killed that Indian bitch. But not before she said you were her brat's pa. Something about catching her in the Yakima hop field."

Eric paused momentarily, then returned to chopping and tearing aside the brush. "I've spawned a few brats in my time, but the midnight rose alone bears my son."

The burly seaman leered at Rebecca. "Ain't you the gentleman, now? Protecting your lady's honor—"

Eric straightened, sending Rebecca a wild, possessive stare. "I'd kill for her," he stated softly. "She's my only chance."

"Chance for what, mate? You've got the gold within your reach."

"None of your business. Get to work!"

Rebecca closed her eyes, willing Matthew to her.

. . . I come to her, my luve, my own . . . Wi' emerald eyes she calls me home.

"Come to me," she whispered softly, "my love."

Chapter Twenty-five

"You've got it, mate!" Boswick yelled triumphantly as Eric's ax sank into a rotted wooden door. He fell on his knees, tearing at the wild grapevines tangled over the planks. "Here, let me in there!"

Working feverishly, the two large men grunted and cursed, ignoring Rebecca, who had come fully awake by now. In the bright morning sunlight a hawk shot through the blue sky, screaming in its descent. Buttercups, elegant ferns, and wild grass spread across the tiny glade bordering the old mine.

A mist hovered in the center of the blue-green glade, dew clinging to the blades of rich grass. Wild strawberry plants clung to mossy banks, a delicate balance of gold-green hues.

The flat rock caught the warmth of the sun, soothing her aching limbs. The baby moved restlessly within her taut stomach, a tiny elbow protesting the hard rock. The wind lifted Rebecca's hair; a sunlit strand slid along the length of her cheek like a caress.

Shielding her eyes with her tied hands, Rebecca's gaze wandered over the old Chinese mine. The workers had once dug with picks and shovels, placing the gold-laced earth into a wooden sluice. Dead cattails stood in a dried, rocky creek bed that once had held water for the mine's sluice. In this manner the dirt had washed away from the heavier gold. The precious grains settled into shallow bowls carved within a rock wall.

"Ugh!" Boswick grunted, tugging the rotting planks aside. "There's human bones in there, Eric! Probably a nest of rattlers too."

Eric thrust a stick into the crumbled building, raking out the remains of several skeletons. He sank to his knees, digging with his hands. "The snakes haven't woke up yet. Help me get these sacks out."

Rebecca heard a rustling noise behind her. Turning slightly, she met Wolf's yellow eyes as he rested, concealed in the brush. Two more sets of yellow, slanted eyes shone in the shadows.

Wolf's pink tongue hung from his lips and he panted, evidence of his hard run. The Chinook wind caused the pine boughs to sway above Rebecca, and a restless tingle played along her spine. "He's here, isn't he?" she asked the dog and the gentle wind. "He's coming."

Boswick stood, holding the decaying sacks of gold high in the sunlight. A tiny trickle of gold seeped from a torn corner to drift, sparkling upon the wind. He laughed wildly, kicking the enormous pile of sacks at his feet. "There's more where that came from! Plenty more!"

Wolf growled low in his throat as Eric stood, ax in hand.

There in the sunlit glade, Boswick crumpled over the Chinese bones, the ax head buried in his chest. "Time to divide," Eric murmured quietly, reaching down to wrench the sacks from the seaman's grasping hands. "Mine and mine."

Boswick's gurgling noises lasted a moment before he shuddered and died.

Eric's hot, possessive stare pinned Rebecca to the rock. Within her she knew: A primitive man, Eric had killed; now he wanted release in her body!

Taking two of the old bags, Eric sauntered to where she rested, his eye glittering coldly. "And now we begin," he whispered coarsely, sprinkling the gold dust on her from head to toe.

He's from another time, a pagan time, she thought as the tiny mound of her stomach contracted momentarily.

Closing her eyes, she saw Eric clad in a fur loincloth, lifting a carved dagger. The red mist swirled around her, the water splashing upon her as men fought—then Matthew's velvety eyes gazed down at her lovingly.

Forcing herself from the image, she opened her lids to see Eric tenderly smiling down at her. He reached to pluck some buttercups and then arranged them gently around her face.

"My heart, my true love," he whispered hoarsely. "My midnight rose."

Taking the big knife from its sheath, he cut the ropes binding her ankles. He rubbed her boots gently, stirring her circulation. His gaze flowed over her long hair, the gold dust glittering in the rippling raven strands. "I'll have you now," he crooned, easing his fingers up her thigh. "To seal the bargain . . ."

He placed the tip of the blade beneath her throat, lifting her chin. Crouched over her, his nostrils flared as he rubbed her intimately. "When you're ripe with my spawn—"

Then suddenly he was lifted free. He sprawled backward, then regained his balance, and found he now faced his brother. His fingers tightened around the hilt of the knife, slashing it at Matthew. "You!"

His back to her, Matthew stripped off his jacket, wrapping it around one hand. His muscles rippled beneath the woolen shirt, his long legs taut within his trousers. With one hand he unbuckled the shoulder holster and tossed it at Rebecca's side. "We meet again, brother," Matthew said quietly. "And this time will be the last."

Eric slashed the air between them quickly, tossing the knife into his other hand. "She's going to see you die . . . then it will be only me. Think of it, boyo. Her hot and wet beneath me, crying . . . begging for it."

"Matthew, be careful," Rebecca warned softly. "He's—"

"I know," he answered as quietly. "I think I always knew. He's mad."

Incensed, Eric danced closer, the blade glistening in the

bright sunlight. Wolf rose to his feet, his hackles rising as he stood next to Rebecca. "Stay, Wolf," she commanded, knowing that one wrong move could cost Matthew's life.

Restlessly the other wolves prowled in a circle around the two large men—one with long red hair and the other with blue-black waves.

A sudden pain surged through Rebecca's abdomen, the baby shifting to a lower position.

The next pain caused her to gasp, a warm, wet circle spreading beneath her hips. The trousers were soaked and stained when she managed to reach the pistol, clasping it in her fingers. Lifting it, she aimed at Eric. "Now, Eric . . . stop!"

A gentle hand touched her shoulder. Dressed in fringed buckskins, Jean knelt by her side. His knife slid between her wrists to cut the cords. "Don't shoot, my sister. This wound has festered long and deep between the brothers. Let it be settled."

"That damn half-breed would have to turn up!" Eric said with a sneer. "I'll bet he's had her too."

He glanced at Rebecca, snarling. "She's a witch woman, like Ma. Full of secrets and seeing dreams."

He laughed wildly, tossing his matted, red hair back from his face. "Only I knew then, boyo . . . Ma made me promise not to kill you like the other brats she bore that black-haired bastard. In her dreams she saw the way I laid the pillows over them in the cradle. She charmed you, boyo. Or else I would have had your ear on a platter by now."

Matthew lifted his forearm, wrapped in the heavy coat as Eric's knife slashed at him. "I've noted one or two knives coming my way. Now I know the cause. But my wife is mine, and you made your last mistake by coming back—"

"Hah!" Eric continued advancing, slashing as Matthew danced backward. "She's got the gun on me. But she won't shoot—I know her too well. She sees you in me, and me in you. Look at the bitch, Matthew. Her eyes are as round as her belly. Her time has come to whelp."

"I will take care of your wife, Matthew," Jean promised

solemnly, placing his arm around Rebecca's shoulders. "If he does not kill you, Eric, I will."

Matthew hesitated for a split second, and Eric pressed his advantage. The tip of his blade sliced across Matthew's chest, leaving a crimson streak on the sliced fabric. Matthew grimaced, stepping back. "I have to ask this—"

"Mercy? Tell her to put down the gun, Matthew. We'll play by the old rules."

"Will you give yourself up?" Matthew continued, watching his brother closely. "Face trial?"

Eric dropped the knife, his hands at his side. "By our mother's grave, aye, I will. If you take me alive—"

"Matthew, don't—" A rippling pain shot through Rebecca as she forced herself to her feet, aiming the pistol at Eric.

He glanced at her carelessly, unbuckling his gun belt. He tossed it over the pile of gold, a mark of his possession. "It's her time. Will the brat have red or black hair?" he taunted. "Or will it be a redskin?"

"Rebecca, sit down. Jean?" Matthew murmured softly. His eyes blazed fiercely, and she obeyed clumsily, waiting. Knowing she stood outside their bonds of blood and childhood, she bit her lip to force down another cry. He turned to Eric, throwing his coat toward Rebecca. "Put that over you, Becky. Rest a moment."

In a fleeting second he sent a silent question to Jean, who nodded. He arranged the coat around Rebecca, then sat back on his haunches. "The red wolf is crazed and must be killed. His time has come."

"Hah! You trained her like a dog, Matthew. Good work. She's the prize, you know!" Eric shouted wildly. "Not the gold or the land . . . but her. She is the heart—the midnight rose. See? The gold dust glitters in her hair like stars in a midnight sky."

"Yes," Matthew agreed softly, crouching, his fists raised. "I remember now how one brother would have the midnight rose and one would die. Do you remember Ma's prayers, Eric? You'd better start praying now—"

"She's mine! She's special, like Ma. But this time she's

mine!'' Eric scooped up the knife, snarling. ''My blade has tasted your skin once or twice, little brother. Remember the delicate nicks here and there?'' He slashed the blade at Matthew's grim face. ''That eyebrow there—it bears my mark.''

Rebecca closed her eyes, willing the pressure low in her womb to ease. So the baby had chosen now to enter the world! The gun fell from her fingers and Wolf whined softly as she gave herself to the rigid pain circling her body. She splayed her fingers across the hard mound, pressing, waiting for the moment to pass.

From far away she heard the low growl of men's threats. Bone crashed against flesh, she heard grunts of pain and curses and the sound of breaking limbs. Wolf nuzzled her cheek and a soft mist settled quietly over her.

Jean patted a cloth across her damp forehead, drying it. He took her fingers, laced them in his, and bore her tight grip. ''Rest, sister of my dreams. Bear your child.''

When the pain had passed, Rebecca wiped her wet lids with the back of her hand. The red mist swirled around the two fighting men, the icy water splashing upon her as they fell into the creek.

The time has come to win the prize, a woman's lilting, yet sad whisper said, carried on the wind.

Rebecca felt Jean move from her side. There was a hiss and dead thud. Then Eric's wild shriek tore through the glade: ''You've killed me, boyo!''

Twisting to see past the heavy ferns, Rebecca felt a searing pain just as she saw Jean pull his knife from Eric's bloody chest. Matthew stood aside, his face ashen.

The hawk soared high into the blue sky again, screaming. And then the glade was quiet.

Her belt of pain grew, taking her. ''Matthew!''

In an instant Matthew crouched over her, his wet curls clinging to his brow. He took her hands, kissing the bruised and chafed flesh tenderly.

Beneath the heavy brows and lashes his gaze was tender. ''Our son is as impatient as his mother,'' he teased gently, easing the greatcoat from her.

She pressed her hand against his scratched cheek. "Matthew?"

"Eric is gone, Becky. Jean is taking care of him and his friend. He thought you'd want only me," he murmured quietly, loosening and tugging her wet trousers from her legs. He spread the greatcoat across the rock and lifted her easily to lie upon it.

He gazed at her tenderly, his fingers stroking back the tendrils from her damp face. "You'll have to trust me now."

He brushed her mouth with his, green eyes meeting black ones in silent understanding. They were going through a dark passage and he would take care of her; she would trust him to keep her safe. "You are my love, my life. Lean on me now."

She felt his large hands tremble, easing up the loose shirt. "Becky," he breathed in husky awe, his eyes glistening damply. When had she come to love this tender conqueror, tears flowing down his dark, beloved cheeks?

Another pain shot down her, a high-pitched scream rending the glade. Was it her own?

"Shall we begin, Princess?" The burr clung to his deep voice as his hands gently probed.

Through clenched lips, Rebecca forced the words she had to say. "Have I told you of my love?"

For a moment his hands grew still upon her. His kiss upon her lips was salty with tears, his and her own. Mouths clung sweetly, tenderly, taking and giving promises that would last forever and beyond.

Just before noon Rebecca's black-haired son thrust himself into the fern-draped glade. He pushed free of his mother and fell into his father's waiting hands.

"A boy!" Kneeling beside Matthew, Jean nodded approvingly. The baby squirmed, naked and dripping, his tiny fists and feet thrashing. When he wailed hungrily, Wolf jumped aside, his tail between his legs.

"Let me see your son, Matthew," Rebecca whispered weakly, her fingers still clinging to Jean's.

Matthew swallowed, handing the baby to her. In his large,

strong hands the infant looked tiny, his head covered with a thatch of blue-black curls.

Jean handed Rebecca a clean towel from his saddlebags and she wrapped the baby in it, nestling him against her side. She smiled at Matthew's awestruck expression. "Well, Papa, haven't you anything to say?"

He forced a swallow, gazing at her shining face, his newborn son sheltered in her arms. His brow furrowed, his eyes darkening.

Sensing the private moment, Jean rose silently, leaving them alone.

"Will you take him to love, Becky . . . despite the errors of his father?"

The tiny fist curled around Matthew's dark finger. Rebecca watched the wonder spread across Matthew's harsh face, softening it. "Aye, I'll take him," she whispered huskily. "And his Papa too."

Matthew's dark, concerned eyes searched her glowing face. "I took you against your will, Becky. Forced you to carry through with the marriage when you fought me."

She took his hand, placing the warm, rough palm to her cheek. Laying her hand over his, she whispered softly, "I do love you, McKay. Until the day I die."

Chapter Twenty-six

In the faint light of the early June dawn Matthew sank his ax blade into the tree. The damp mist swirled around his bare torso, cooling him. He closed his eyes, remembering the way Rebecca had curled next to him in bed earlier, her palm roaming his chest. He had slid from their bed to stalk to the creek for an icy bath.

He withdrew the blade and threw it back into the wood. His wife had yet to come to him after their son's birth. It had been three months, and he could feel the hot, feverish need rise within him. Each night her scent tantalized him; a silken strand slipped across the pillow to snare his cheek.

Yet he could wait until Rebecca came. . . .

When Sean was born, she'd cried out her love, but now Matthew needed to know that without the pain, her love ran true—Rebecca had promised her father a year but Matthew wanted a lifetime.

A hummingbird darted by, a flash of green and red. The mist clung to the lacy ferns, then dripped to the lush grass. The small glade had quieted suddenly, and Matthew sank the blade into the wood once more. The back of his neck tingled and he sensed another presence as he turned, leaving the ax sunk in the wood.

Standing near the white trunk of a birch tree, Rebecca watched him, a single blood-red rose in her hand. The scant light touched her hair as it rippled down around her bare shoulders to the gathered Mexican blouse. From her slender waist a long cotton skirt fell to slender ankles and bare feet.

Matthew's heart skipped a beat as he looked at his wife. The new dawn tangled in the jet-black mane, creating a halo around her. Within the shadows of her hair Rebecca's green eyes glowed, bewitching, beckoning him.

He walked toward her slowly.

As he crossed the glade to her, Rebecca's gaze slid down her husband's tall body. She'd hungered for him and felt his blazing hunger in return . . . and now it was time.

With Sean tucked in his crib, attended by the Dupreses, Rebecca had chosen the dawn to come to Matthew.

Moving toward her through the dappled shadows of the clearing, Matthew's broad shoulders were darkly tanned, the enticing vee of hair sliding down to his waistband . . . and lower. She could almost feel the warm indentation of his navel dip beneath her fingers. The trousers rested low on his hips, a strip of white flesh bordering his belt.

Then came the long, hard legs; the buff trousers yielded to his soft moccasins.

When he came to stand before her, Rebecca felt suddenly shy, despite the fact that they had shared a child and a bed. She touched the rose to his chest, running the dewy petals across the black, springy hair.

He waited, his black eyes gleaming beneath thick brows.

Lifting the rose bloom upward, Rebecca traced the breadth of his muscled shoulders and neck. "Til stars do fall; and sun burns cold./Our kindling fire shall rise in flame . . ." she whispered, lifting her gaze to his.

Matthew's thickly lashed lids lowered, his mouth curving sensuously. "Have you come courting, Princess?"

For a moment, lost in the spell binding them, Rebecca swayed toward him. She smiled slowly, stepping nearer. When the tips of her breasts touched his bare chest, she watched his eyes darken with passion. "Courting? That I have, Mr. McKay."

The mist shimmered around her, the tiny drops shining like jewels in her flowing hair.

The tendons running beneath his tanned skin tightened, a muscle contracting in his lean cheek as he stood beneath her touch, waiting. There were bonds and pledges and sweet whispers to pass between them before . . .

"There are vows to be taken," he began slowly, black eyes locking with slanted green ones. "The year you promised your father will be gone."

"Aye. The forevermores." She gave the rose into his care, her fingers wrapping around his larger ones. Placing her smaller palm against his, she studied the strength and the dark skin blending with her smaller, softer hand.

Then, drawing his hand to her, Rebecca kissed the rose, meeting his hot gaze. His knuckles nestled in the warm, fragrant valley of her breasts, her hand pressed over his. "I pledge the forevermores, McKay. Until this time ends and another begins, I will love you with all my soul. And then I will love you more."

For a moment a blaze of passion washed over Matthew's dark face, then his hard mouth lifted slowly. His raspy voice, when it came, was ripe with emotion. "I do love you, lass."

She met his growing smile with her own, leaning to kiss the smooth expanse of his shoulder. Placing her splayed fingers upon his flat belly, she stood on tiptoe to whisper against his lips, "As I love you. But, McKay, until we can leave Sean safely to try out your round beds and champagne nights, until we have the new house completed and the countryside assured that I'm a proper wife to you, we'll have to make do."

His rough palm slid beneath her hair to curve around her neck. His thumb ran the length of her slender throat before his gentle tug drew her fully against him. For a long moment they savored the blend of hard and soft, man and woman, savored the past and the future. "Aye?"

She lifted her lips to his, trailing the tip of her tongue over the beloved contours. "I'm tired of you groaning like a restless old wolf in the night—running away at the very sight of my body.''

He caressed her round chin, tracing her smooth skin. Her teeth captured his finger, sucking it as her eyes darkened to moss green.

Matthew's breath caught somewhere in his lungs, and he had to summon it to whisper, ''I'm not a man to be tempted by silky skin when there is more at stake.''

His kiss at the corner of her mouth caused her to ache, the hungry trembling rising within her. ''I've been bound by honor.''

''Honor has its place.'' She felt his warm breath caress her face, his hardened body stirring against her hips. ''But Sean's birth was three long months ago, and—'' Her touch slid down his muscled arm and dropped to his lean stomach.

Her fingertip toyed in the furry circle of his navel, tempting. A flush rose up her throat to touch her cheeks. He fell into the golden specks of her green eyes, waiting—it appeared that when the Lady McKay came courting, he was as apt as an untried boy.

Rebecca leaned back against his hand, drawing his gaze to the new fullness of her breasts thrusting against the Mexican blouse. Matthew's throat dried at the sight. The fragrant, lush flesh had nestled against his back just this morning, her soft arms twining around him.

He trembled, and the raging passion rising within him barely cautioned. She was the mother of his child, still delicate from the birth.

His ragged breath escaped, his hot gaze enchanted by one rosy crest as the blouse dipped lower.

She caressed the flat plane of his stomach, feeling the muscles contract as her touch roamed lower. Her teeth nipped the curve of his chin gently, her fingers unbuttoning his clothing. When she had unknotted his cotton drawers, Rebecca's fingers slid to claim him.

''Ah, you're shanghaing me . . . despite my good intentions.'' He closed his lids, savoring the gentle possession.

Then, sliding his fingers within the loosely gathered bodice, he lowered the cloth to view his prize.

Fuller now since his son's birth, the mauve-tipped softness beckoned to him.

"I'm capable of kidnapping my own husband." Stepping back, Rebecca slowly undressed, her eyes dark and mysterious. Matthew's hot stare hungrily sought the curve of breast and waist and long legs, his lips pressed together tightly. He felt faint as a shapely buttock slid into view, the long line of her back ending in twin dimples in the pale, smooth flesh.

Then, her body shimmering in shades of creams and veiled in strands of black hair, she pressed herself against him, grinning. "Shy, Matthew?"

The dimple sank deep into his cheek, his teeth flashing in the growing light. He moved his hips against her softness, watched her soft mouth part. "I'm wondering how to keep your backside from the pine needles."

She winked, taking his hand to lead him to a blanket spread upon the ground. "I've come prepared to court you, as you did on our wedding night."

"I shall try not to faint beneath your care," he said teasingly, aching for her.

Sinking to her knees, Rebecca ran her hand up Matthew's thigh, testing the hair-roughened surface. Her hair slid down to her bare shoulders and breasts, flowing around her soft thighs as the birds chirped in the glade.

Taking his time, Matthew slid into her arms, closing his eyes as her silky body fitted against his. With the hardened tips of her breasts nestling against his chest, he savored the softness of her belly and long thighs.

Breathing hard, forcing himself to wait, Matthew caressed the long curve of her back and hips. His touch roamed to skim her soft belly, above the womb that had sheltered his son. A large thumb prowled the ridges of her hipbones, then slid lower to fondle that enticing mound.

Rebecca nuzzled his throat, teeth nipping his earlobe. Her breath fluttered against his hot cheek. "You're a tasty man, Matthew . . . Oh, I need you so!"

In a soft tangle of arms and legs and hungry kisses, Rebecca pulled herself astride him. Her hair fell like an ebony silk canopy around him as he allowed himself one small taste of her thrusting breasts.

The fullness throbbed within her, aching, demanding to be met as his mouth tugged gently upon her sensitive flesh. Matthew's warm hands caressed the pale mounds, kneading them gently, as his lips pressed a circlet of kisses.

With a small groan she rose to slowly envelop him.

For a breath or a lifetime they grew still, the mating of love and bodies final. Black eyes met darkened green ones as the strong current of love ran between them.

Smiling tenderly, Rebecca rested full-length upon him, taking care to preserve their joining as she would their marriage.

She moved her hips slightly, testing him with an impish grin. Matthew's cheeks flushed with his dark desire, her silken depths cherishing him. "Becky," he groaned unwillingly, running his dark hands down the sweep of her back. "You're pressing your luck. I'm not certain I can be gentle."

Rebecca smoothed back a damp curl from his brow, whispering huskily, "Love me, my love."

Matthew shuddered once, then swept her beneath him. Rebecca clung to him, her golden arms encircling the lean sweep of his waist as her legs locked to his. "I'll love you forever, Matthew," she murmured, taking him deeper.

His hungry kiss pledged his love, his hips moving into the velvety encasement of soft thighs. She rose to him, gathering him nearer, her softness flowing into his steely, demanding love.

When the tempo rose and crashed and left them straining with desire, Rebecca cried out her pleasure. The hot beat of passion circled them, the throbbing fulfillment straining for release.

As he flowed into her Matthew declared his love once more.

Resting upon him, her leg draped between his hard ones, Rebecca found the strength to kiss him.

His hand tightened leisurely upon her waist, drawing her once more to him.

The tender kiss wooed and grew honey sweet in soft, endless play as the birds chirped overhead.

Between the soft press of kisses, Matthew tenderly accused, "Wanton . . ."

"I'm daft over you, McKay," she whispered back, grazing his strong jaw with her parted mouth.

"Mmm. I've waited long enough. Any more icy creek baths and my manhood might be endangered."

Rebecca giggled, her hand sweeping down his body. "In another three months or so we'll try again . . . if you have the courage."

She squealed delighted as his hand lightly patted her bottom. "Woman, any longer and I would have wasted away!"

At ease, he stretched like a mountain cat resting on a high-country boulder.

His hand rose to trail across her ribs, then favor a full breast with a caress. "Sean?"

"Oh, you remembered our son!" Rebecca giggled, a low, musical sound that brought his gaze to her. "Now's a fine time to think of the poor child, after your own lusts have been satisfied. He's fed, sleeping with his bottom in the air."

She tugged the pelt of hair covering his chest. "He's as demanding as his father."

Matthew breathed the clean, fresh mountain air and the sweet, rosy scent of his wife. "Once we have our own bedroom, without half the valley sharing our home, I'll be happy."

She tugged his face down to hers. "Stop growling like an old bear. Emma and Jean are building their own home." She laughed, feeling cherished and loved. "Emma seems to like camping in the meadow. With the exception of taking a long bath once in a while, she never comes in the house. And Little Matt needs us until Wes can get a suitable housekeeper."

Matthew lifted the scarred eyebrow speculatively. "And Bruno?"

Rebecca thoughtfully trailed her fingertip down his damp chest. "He's leaving for Canada. When Stella walked into the Columbia, something snapped within him. He'll have to find his peace alone."

He wound her raven hair in his dark fingers, playing with the silky strands. "I can understand. If I were to lose you . . ." Using the strands to draw her near, Matthew sought the sweet curve of her lips. "My rose . . . my heart . . ."

For a lingering moment Rebecca gave her mouth to him, allowing his play. She watched his dark lashes close, his intent frown as he traced the sharp ridge of her teeth. When his black eyes opened, blazing down into hers, she whispered, "Pagan."

"You're finally mine then, Mrs. McKay," he said raspily, his large hand trembling as he stroked the gentle slope of her back.

She was silent, knowing that he, too, was thinking of Eric. "We have a son between us now, my love. Let the other go."

Matthew's gaze rose to the bright new day dawning beyond the shadowy pine boughs. "Your mother loved him too."

Smoothing the furry expanse of his chest with her palm, Rebecca laid her head upon his brawny shoulder. "He's at peace now, buried with his gold."

Matthew wound his fingers in her hair, drawing it across his chest thoughtfully. "I had Eric beneath my knife. I could have killed him."

"But Jean saved you both. You wouldn't want Eric's blood on your hands."

"For you . . ." His lashes closed, and he sighed tiredly. "Jean . . . it came back to me after Emma's twins were born. When we were children, Eric and I, there was a shy Indian boy playing at the skirts of an elegant lady. We played for hours, the three of us, until Eric found a knife."

Matthew took a deep breath that raised his wife's head. She placed her chin on her hand to study him. He stroked a curl back from her temple. "The three of us are blood brothers; we sliced our hands and mixed our blood that day, according to Eric's directions."

"Jean has found his home. So has Emma."

She kissed the tip of his nose, then feathered a row of kisses across his scarred eyebrow. "Forget Eric."

He smiled slowly, bathed by her intriguing caresses. "And what of witches with night-black hair who shanghai innocent husbands . . . ?"

"It's a practice I intend to keep."

Stroking the length of his jaw with her fingertip, Rebecca sighed wistfully. "The dreams are gone."

Matthew nodded, caressing the silky length of her thighs. "That's good. Then we can turn our thoughts to other things."

"Such as?" Rebecca's green eyes sparkled as she looked down at her husband.

As their lips met, the red rose petals fell to the pine needles, forgotten.

On the mountain a gentle breeze carried the lingering scents of lavender and roses through the mist-shrouded pines.

My midnight rose, my highland heart,
Wi' emerald eyes she calls me home.